Orphan #8

By Kim van Alkemade

Orphan #8

Orphan #8

Kim van Alkemade

wm

WILLIAM MORROW
An Imprint of HarperCollins*Publishers*

P.S.™ is a trademark of HarperCollins Publishers.

HarperCollins books may be purchased for educational, business, or sales promotional use. For information please e-mail the Special Markets Department at SPsales@harpercollins.com.

FIRST EDITION

Designed by Diahann Sturge

Library of Congress Cataloging-in-Publication Data has been applied for.

ISBN 978-0-06-233830-3

16 17 18 19 OV/RRD 10 9 8 7 6

To the memory of my grandfather Victor Berger,
"the ever-efficient boy of the Home"

Orphan #8

Chapter One

FROM HER BED OF BUNDLED NEWSPAPERS UNDER THE kitchen table, Rachel Rabinowitz watched her mother's bare feet shuffle to the sink. She heard water filling the kettle, then saw her mother's heels lift as she stretched up to drop a nickel in the gas meter. There was the sizzle of a struck match, the hiss of the burner, the whoosh of catching flame. As her mother passed the table Rachel reached out to catch the hem of her nightdress.

"Awake already, little monkey?" Visha peered down, her dark hair hanging in loose curls. Rachel nodded, open eyes eager. "You'll stay put until the boarders leave for work, yes? You know it makes me nervous when there's too many people crowding in the kitchen."

Rachel stuck out her bottom lip. Visha tensed, still afraid of sparking one of her daughter's tantrums, even though months had gone by since the last one. Then Rachel smiled. "Yes, Mama, I will."

Visha let out her breath. "That's a good girl." She stood and knocked on the front room door, two sharp raps. After hearing the boarders' muffled voices assure her they were awake, she crossed the kitchen and let herself out of the apartment. Going down the tenement's hallway to use the toilet, she allowed herself to think their trouble with Rachel was really over.

It had started with the colic, but she couldn't blame the baby for that, though Harry seemed to. For months, it wailed at all hours of the night. Only if she held it in her arms and paced the kitchen did the cries settle into sobs that at least the neighbors could sleep through. They hadn't been able to keep boarders then—who would pay to sleep next to that racket?—and Harry started working late to make up the income. To avoid the baby, he took to spending more nights at his Society meetings. Sundays, too, he'd managed to escape, taking Sam up to the Central Park or down to the piers to watch the ships. Visha might have gone crazy, boxed up in those three rooms with an infant who seemed to hate her. It was only Mrs. Giovanni coming by every day, for a visit so Visha could talk like a person, or to take the baby for an hour so she could rest, that got her through those long months.

Back in the kitchen, Visha poured boiling water into the teapot and also into a basin in the bottom of the sink before filling the kettle again and setting it back on the flame. She tempered the water in the basin with a splash of cold and set out a hard square of soap and a threadbare towel. She put the teapot, two cups, a jar of jelly, a spoon, and the slices of yesterday's bread on the table. In the front room, furniture scraped across the floor, then the door opened, and the boarders, Joe and Abe, emerged. The young men were bare chested, suspenders drooping from the waists of rumpled trousers, their untied laces slithering as they walked. Visha settled two damp shirts on the backs of the kitchen chairs. She'd washed them out late the night before, and at least they were clean if anyone complained. Abe went down the hall while Joe leaned over the sink to wash up. Visha edged past him into her bedroom and shut the door.

She lifted off her nightdress and hung it from a nail in the wall, then buttoned up a white shirtwaist over her shift and stepped into a long skirt. Her husband yawned when Visha sat on the bed to pull up her stockings. Harry's arm still stretched across her pillow from last night, when he'd stroked her shoulder and whispered in her ear: "Soon, my Visha, soon, when I'm a contractor with my own business, we'll move out of this tenement and up to Harlem, maybe even the Bronx. The children will have their own bedroom, we won't have to take in boarders, and you can sit all afternoon with your feet up like a queen, my queen." As he spoke, Visha pictured herself in the quiet bedroom of a new apartment building, windows open to the cool outside air. She imagined filling a tub in a tiled bathroom with hot water just waiting for her to turn the tap.

Visha had turned to Harry then, inviting. He moved over her quietly, the way she liked, not like Mr. Giovanni next door, whose grunts echoed in the stinking airshaft. She kept him inside her to the end, her heels pressed into the backs of his knees, the prospect of his success stirring her desire for another baby. Rachel was four years old already, the sleepless nights a long-ago memory, the tantrums apparently over. After Harry rolled off of her, Visha dreamed of the feathery weight of a newborn in her arms.

Rachel was getting restless as the boarders sat in the kitchen, stirring jelly into their tea and soaking their bread to soften it. From under the table, she reached out and tangled Joe's shoelaces.

"What is this now happening? Is there rats chewing on my boot strings?"

Rachel laughed. She nudged her brother beside her to wake up. "Tie them in knots, Sam, so he falls down," she whispered. "I can't tie knots yet."

Joe heard her. "What for you want me to fall over, to break my neck maybe? Be careful I don't pull you from under there and make trouble with your mother."

Sam wrapped his arms around his sister. "Don't start now, Rachel. Be good and quiet and I'll teach you what number comes after one hundred."

Rachel let go of the laces. "There's more numbers *after* one hundred?"

"Do you promise to be still until Mama says we can come out?"

Rachel nodded vigorously. Sam whispered in her ear.

"Say it again." He did. Rachel laughed like when she tasted something sweet.

"One hundred *and* one hundred *and* one hundred." Sam put his head down on the newspapers and listened, satisfied, to his sister's chanting.

Back in September when he started first grade, Rachel had gotten it into her head that she would be going to school with Sam. When he walked out the door without her, she had thrown a fit that was still going on when he came home for lunch. Rachel's screaming had driven even Mrs. Giovanni away and Visha was beside herself. "See what you can do with her!" she said to Sam, then shut herself up in the bedroom.

Sam had managed to calm his sister by teaching her the first five letters of the alphabet. Before he went back to school for the afternoon, his stomach rolling with hunger, he'd struck their bargain. For quiet and goodness, Sam paid Rachel with letters and numbers. It was April now, and already she knew as much as he'd been taught. That first day, Visha made up for his missed lunch by preparing for Sam his favorite dinner, pasta with tomato gravy just like Mrs. Giovanni's. "You saved my life today," she'd told her son, kissing the top of his head.

Visha, dressed, came in from the bedroom to make the boarders their lunches, wrapping cold baked potatoes and fat pickles in newspaper. Chair legs scraped and cups rattled as Joe and Abe got up from the table. Hoisting suspenders over damp shirts and grabbing jackets, they tucked the food into their pockets and stomped out the door.

"Come out from there now, you little monkeys," Visha said. The blanket flew back and Rachel scrambled up, followed by Sam. Visha gave them each a kiss on the head, then Sam grabbed his sister's hand and pulled her out of the kitchen and down the hall. While they took their turns at the toilet, Visha made a second pot of tea, refilled the kettle, rinsed the teacups, and put them back on the table.

When the children raced into the kitchen, Visha caught Rachel and lifted the girl onto her lap while Sam stood on his toes to reach the washbasin in the sink. He was tall already for a boy of six and seemed to Visha a small version of the man he'd one day become. His light brown hair was Harry's for sure, as were the pale gray eyes that made Visha's father doubt Harry was really a Jew. But where Harry was smooth and sweet-talking, Sam was sharp and quick, already getting in fights at school and tearing his pants playing stickball in the street.

Rachel put her hands on Visha's cheeks to get her mother's attention. Visha gazed at her reflection in her daughter's dark eyes, so brown they were nearly black. When Sam was finished, Visha dragged her chair to the sink so Rachel could stand on it to wash herself. After both children were at the table sipping tea and soaking bread, Visha dropped a whole egg into the kettle to boil and went in to wake her husband.

His breath still thick from sleep, Harry murmured in Visha's ear, "So, did we make a baby last night do you think?" Visha whispered back, "If we did, he'll need a papa who's a contractor, so get yourself out of bed already." Visha came into the kitchen with a shy smile on her face, Harry following her.

"Papa!" Rachel and Sam chorused. Their father dropped his hands onto their shoulders and pulled them close so he could kiss both of their cheeks at once.

"You give him a minute of peace," Visha clucked. She lifted the lid of the kettle to check on the bobbing egg while Harry went down the hall. It was a luxury this, every morning a whole egg just for Harry, but he said he needed his strength. If Visha had to get a bone with less meat for their soup or buy their bread already a day old to afford the eggs, well, it would all be better once Harry made good.

When he got back, Harry lifted Rachel onto his knee and took her seat. Visha put a cup of tea in front of him and some more bread, then fished out the egg with a fork and set it on Harry's plate to cool. She leaned against the sink, her hand absently resting on her belly, watching her husband with their children.

"So, Sammy, what did you learn from school yesterday?" Harry hadn't seen the children since breakfast the day before. He'd worked late, then gone directly to his Society meeting, coming home after even the boarders were asleep to whisper in Visha's ear. She used to resent these Societies of his, the dues so hard on their pockets, until Harry convinced her the Society would back him when he went into business for himself.

Sam squinted. "*B-R-E-D*," he said. "*T-E.*"

"And what's this?" Harry asked, looking at Visha with sparkling eyes.

"That spells *bread* and *tea*, Papa! We learned the whole alphabet already, and now every day we learn spelling for new words. C-*A*-T. That spells *cat*, Papa!"

"Already such a genius," Harry said, rolling his egg on the plate to shed it of its shell. Sometimes he saved a bite for Rachel, pushing the rounded egg white between her lips with his finger, but this morning he popped it whole into his mouth.

"What are you cutting today, Harry?" Visha asked. Rachel echoed her mother. "Yes, Papa, what are you cutting?"

"Well," he said, addressing himself to his daughter, "we got patterns for the new shirtwaists yesterday, and I had to figure how to lay them out. The contractor, he likes my cutting because I don't leave much scrap, but the material for the new waists has a little stitching running through the weave, and I had to lay out the pattern so the little stitch matched up at all the seams. It took me some time, that's why I missed supper last night." He glanced at Visha. "But I got it all figured out, so today I do the cutting."

"Can I be a cutter, too, when I grow up?" Rachel asked.

"What for you want to work in a factory? That's why I work so hard, so you don't have such a life. Besides, girls aren't cutters. The knives are too big for their little hands." Harry put Rachel's fingers in his mouth and pretended to chew on them until she laughed.

Harry turned to Sam. "You'd better get going now, little genius, or you'll be late for school."

Sam jumped up from his chair and dashed into the front room to dress. When he returned, Visha handed him his jacket. "And don't waste the whole lunch hour playing in the street, come straight home to eat!" she called as he banged out the door and clattered down the two flights of stairs.

Visha went into the front room to open the windows. The April morning was clear and fresh. Leaning out, she saw a policeman still wearing his influenza mask, but Visha felt they were safe, now the winter was over. She knocked on wood as the grateful thought passed through her mind. Then she saw Sam burst from the front of the tenement, dodging vendors' carts and motorcars and the milk truck's old horse. It amazed her that such a small boy could charge so headlong into the world.

Turning away from the window, she sighed. The boarders had left the room a mess, blankets tossed over couches, dirty clothes on the floor, their trunk gaping in the corner. She spent a few minutes setting the room to rights before coming into the kitchen. Harry had gone in to dress. Rachel was at the table, dropping pieces of stale bread into her cooling cup of tea and lifting them out with a fork. She pressed the dripping chunks of bread against the roof of her mouth with her tongue, squeezing out the tea and savoring the bread's softness.

Visha was wrapping Harry's lunch when he called to her from the bedroom. "Come in here a minute, would you?"

"You stay there now, Rachel," Visha said, leaving the wrapped potato and pickle on the drain board. "I'll be right back."

"Yes, Mama."

"Close the door, Visha," Harry said. She did. He caught her before she could fully turn around, his hands sliding down her hips.

"Harry, no, I'm already dressed." He grabbed a fistful of fabric in each hand and lifted her skirt to her waist. "You'll make yourself late." He steered her toward the bed, bending her over, pulling at her bloomers. "Rachel will hear!" Holding her down with one heavy hand, he guided himself into her with the other. It was Visha now who had to stifle a grunt. She turned her face into the mattress as Harry moved behind her. "You want another baby, don't you?" The mattress swallowed her answer of yes, yes.

In the kitchen, Rachel finished her cup of tea, but there was still a piece of bread on the table. The teapot was empty. There was the kettle on the stove, the chair still pulled up to the sink. She looked at the bedroom door, knowing she should wait for her mother, but she wanted the tea now. She took the teapot from the table and, standing on the chair, set it on the drain board, lifted its lid, and put in a pinch of tea from the tin. Then, with two hands, she picked up the kettle like she'd seen her mother do a thousand times.

The kettle was heavier than she expected. When she tilted it, the spout hit the teapot and knocked it over. Her two hands still clutching the kettle, Rachel watched, helpless, as the teapot fell and shattered. Dropping the kettle back onto the burner, the water spit and sizzled in the flame. Startled, Rachel lost her balance. The chair teetered over, toppling her to the floor. For a second she felt like she couldn't breathe. Then she gulped in some air and out came a scream like falling cats.

In the bedroom, Visha tensed at the sounds of breaking and

falling. She pushed up against the bed to stand, but Harry, not finished, held her down. Their daughter's high wail carried over the transom. "Harry, enough, she's hurt!" With a shudder, he pushed into her even deeper. When he finally pulled back, Visha stumbled to her feet, tugging her clothes into place over her slippery thighs.

Visha found Rachel on the floor, the chair on top of her. "Harry, come in here!"

Harry followed, buttoning his pants. He lifted up his screaming daughter and kicked aside the fallen chair. "What happened here? Is anything broken?"

Visha ran her hands over Rachel's legs, bending knees and ankles, then lifted each of her arms, checking elbows and wrists. Rachel kept up a constant scream that never wavered in pitch as Visha examined her joints. "I don't think so, Harry, she fell down is all." Visha saw the shards strewn across the floor. "And look at my teapot! What did I tell you, to stay in your chair!"

Harry stroked his daughter's hair, but now that she was in one of her fits nothing seemed to calm her. He handed her to Visha. "I got no time for this, already I'm gonna be late," he shouted over Rachel's screams.

"As if it's not your own fault!"

Harry scowled as he yanked his jacket from its nail and shoved his fedora on his head. Visha, sorry for the harsh words, lifted her cheek to be kissed, but he turned away and headed into the hall.

"When you coming home?" Visha called after him.

"You know I got to finish all the cutting." He paused in the doorway. "You just take care of this here. I'll be home when I'm home."

RACHEL WAS GROWING heavy in her mother's arms, her screams unnerving. Visha carried her daughter into the bedroom and sat her in the middle of the bed. "You calm yourself now." She looked around for something that might distract Rachel, thinking of how Sam managed to settle her. Visha reached for the money jar on the dresser.

"Rachel, can you count these out for Mama? Then you can come do the shopping with me. I'm not angry about the teapot, I promise. Please?"

Miraculously, Rachel seemed willing to calm down. Stifling her sobs, she took the jar and dumped it on the blanket. Rusted pennies, dull nickels, sleek dimes, even a few quarters. She began to make little piles, matching like to like.

Visha backed cautiously into the kitchen. She sat down and took a few minutes to settle her nerves. Mrs. Giovanni peeked her head in from the hallway, a flowered kerchief tied over her hair.

"Can I help you, Visha?" she offered.

"Thank you, no, she's quiet again." Visha looked mournfully at the broken teapot. "See what she's done."

"You need a teapot to borrow?"

Visha shook her head, gesturing to a high shelf over the sink. "I'll use the good one from my seder dishes."

"I'll come back to visit you later, yes?"

"See you later, Maria." Visha swept up the broken pieces of crockery and put them in the scrap bucket.

"Look, Mama!" Rachel called from the bedroom. "Can we get a rye bread today?"

Visha went in and glanced over the sorted coins, totaling their value. "Not today. Tomorrow when Papa brings home his pay we'll get a fresh rye and some fish. But today there's still the insurance man coming for his dimes, and a nickel for gas to make the soup, and another saved for tomorrow morning." Visha dropped coins in the jar as she recited the list of obligations, then looked at what was left on the bed. "There's enough for a yesterday's loaf, some carrots, a meat bone. I've got still an onion. And some nice pickles, isn't that right, Rachel?" On the first floor of their tenement was a shop where the pickle man tended barrels of brine and took in deliveries of cucumbers from a Long Island farmer; all the hallways of the building smelled of dill and garlic and vinegar.

Visha pocketed the coins and lifted Rachel down from the bed. "Come, let's get you dressed so we can do our shopping."

Passing through the kitchen, Rachel stopped and pointed at the wrapped bundle on the drain board. "Papa's lunch!"

"Ach, see what you made him forget with your crying! Now what's he gonna eat?" Instantly, Visha regretted the sharp words. Rachel's lip pouted and began to tremble. Soon the wailing would start up again. "I'm not angry, Rachel. Don't cry, please. Listen, how about we take it to him at the factory?"

Rachel clapped her mouth shut. She had never been to the factory. "Can I see where the buttons come from?" Most nights, Harry brought home an assortment of buttons twisted into a scrap of fabric, and it was Rachel's job during the day to sit on the floor of the front room and sort them into piles by color and size.

"Yes, and the sewing machines and everything. Now, can you dress yourself do you think?" Rachel skipped into the front room, yanked open a drawer in the dresser she and Sam shared, pulled stockings up her legs and a jumper over her head.

Visha smiled at her plan, then hesitated. Harry had told her he didn't want her coming to the factory. "A cutter is above the operators, Visha, you know that," he'd explained. "I got to keep my respect. I can't stop work just to show off my pretty wife." But after last night, and this morning in the bedroom, wouldn't he be happy to see her?

"So, Rachel," she said, buckling the girl's shoes, "you'll be good?"

"Yes, Mama, I promise."

"All right, then, we'll bring Papa his lunch, and we'll do our shopping on the way home." The factory was a good walk from their tenement—Harry took the streetcar in bad weather—but today was a fine morning that promised winter was over for good. Visha held tight to Rachel's hand as they pushed their way through the people crowding up to the pushcarts. They turned the corner and waited for the streetcar to pass, its hook sparking and snapping along the wire above. Crossing Broad Street, Visha lifted Rachel over a pile of horse droppings, then pulled her close as a delivery truck rumbled by, its big rubber tires taller than her little girl. Eventually Visha pointed to a brick building much bigger than their tenement. "There it is." They hurried across the street as the policeman at the intersection whistled for traffic along Broadway to stop.

In the building's lobby, Visha led Rachel to a wide door and stood still in front of it. "We have to take the elevator," she explained. The door opened, sliding sideways, revealing a young man inside. Made to haul freight and workers by the dozen, the elevator car was bigger than Visha's kitchen.

"What floor?" he asked as they stepped in.

"Goldman's Shirtwaist."

"Factory or offices?"

"Factory."

"They're on seven." The young man pulled the door closed and the elevator began to tremble and shake. Rachel let out a little cry.

"First time in an elevator?" he asked. Rachel looked at Visha, who nodded for her. "Well, you did good!" The car gave a last shudder. "Goldman's."

Visha led Rachel into the din of the factory. The open floor was punctuated by iron poles that reached up to the ceiling. Without walls to block the big windows, the space was bright, dust and threads floating through streaks of sunlight. Long tables stretched across the floor, one sewing machine yoked to the next, at each a woman hunched over her work. Runners were moving around the factory, delivering pieces of cloth to the operators and picking up the baskets of finished goods at their feet. In the corner, some little girls sat on the floor, the younger ones threading needles and the older ones, eleven or twelve, sewing buttons onto the gauzy blouses piled around them.

The machines clattered and buzzed so loudly Visha had to shout in Rachel's ear. "There's Papa!" He was standing at the cutting table, his back to them. Above his head, pattern pieces edged in metal hung from the ceiling like peeled skin pressed flat. Rachel leaned forward, ready to dash at him, but Visha kept hold of her hand. "He's cutting! The knives are sharp, we can't surprise him." Rachel shrank back; she'd already caused trouble once that morning. Together, they walked carefully past the sewing machines to the cutting table.

Harry looked around and saw them coming. His eyes darted over Visha's shoulder to one of the operators, a pretty girl with a lace collar buttoned up her neck. She met his gaze, hands frozen at the machine, her cheeks gone white. Seeing he'd put the knife down, Visha let go of Rachel's hand. She ran a few steps and jumped into her father's arms. He picked her up absently, watching the girl stand up from her machine. Moving as fast as she could down the crowded row, the girl ran across the factory floor and disappeared behind a door, the foreman chasing after her.

Visha was now standing in front of Harry, her mouth lifted for a kiss.

"What are you doing here?" he growled. She lowered her chin.

"We brought your lunch, Papa. You left it at home this morning."

"She was so upset you left it, I thought she'd have another fit. I told her if she was good we'd bring it to you." Visha offered the wrapped package.

"That's fine, Visha." Harry shoved the lunch into his pocket, grabbed his wife's elbow, and steered her toward the elevator, carrying Rachel. "But I told you I got a big order, I don't have time for this."

Rachel's lip began to tremble. "Aren't you happy to see us, Papa?"

"I'm always happy to see you, little monkey, don't get yourself upset. I just got a lot of work to do today. I'll see you at home later."

He set Rachel on her feet and left them to go back to the cutting table. When the elevator opened, it was crowded with crates full of wispy bits of cloth. "Maybe you could walk down?" the young man asked. "Scrap man's here."

Visha and Rachel went over to the stairwell and pulled the door in. On the landing of the stairs, a sewing machine operator was leaning against the wall, sobbing. She was merely a girl, Visha thought, seventeen at the most, and Italian from the look of her. Visha wondered what tragedy had brought on her tears. She placed a hand on the girl's shoulder but she threw it off with a shudder and ran back up the stairs. Visha shrugged and grabbed Rachel's hand, guiding her down. It was dozens of steps, with a turn between each floor; by the time they reached the lobby, Rachel's head was spinning.

Rachel's arm hung heavily from Visha's hand as they did their shopping: the butcher on Broad Street for the meat bone, the bakery on the corner for a yesterday's loaf. From a pushcart in front of their tenement, Visha haggled over a bunch of limp carrots and some potatoes with sprouting eyes. Only when they entered their building and stopped at Mr. Rosenblum's pickle shop did Rachel perk up.

"Look who's here for brightening my day." Mr. Rosenblum's smiling eyes crinkled his face. He spoke Yiddish with most of his customers, but with the children he practiced his English.

"Mr. Rosenblum, we went to the waist factory!"

"You did? Did you like the factory? You going someday to work there with your papa?"

"No, I don't want to work there. It's too noisy, it makes the operators cry."

"Ach, pickles never make for crying. Pick a pickle, Ruchelah." Mr. Rosenblum lifted the wooden lid from a barrel of brine, and Rachel chose a big, fat pickle.

"Taste it," he said. She took a bite, puckering her lips. "The more sour the pickle, the more better it's good for you."

"So good, Mr. Rosenblum, thank you."

"And for you, Mrs. Rabinowitz?" Visha asked for half a dozen pickles. Mr. Rosenblum gave her seven. "One for the boy," he said, winking at Rachel. "So he shouldn't be jealous of his sister."

In their apartment, Visha gave Rachel a slice of the newly purchased bread. "Look here, the middle's still soft. Take it in front and work on your buttons. I'm going to make the soup now."

In the quiet room, Rachel dragged the jar of buttons over by the window, where warm light stretched across the patterned linoleum. She reached into the jar and brought up a fistful of the little disks. She spread them out on the floor, then began sorting the buttons by color, dividing black from brown from white. Then she grouped them based on what they were made of: mother-of-pearl separated from ivory and bone, tortoiseshell from jet and horn. Last would be size, though Harry mostly brought home tiny shirt-waist buttons. Sometimes Rachel would find a burly coat button mixed in, so big she could spin it like a top. While she worked she recited the letters of the alphabet that Sam had taught her, all the way from *A* to *Z*.

Visha smiled at the sound of her daughter's chanting while she cut up the vegetables. Leaving the knife on the board, she dropped a nickel in the gas meter, struck a match, set the pot on the burner. In a smear of fat skimmed from the top of her last soup, she fried chopped onions, adding the sliced carrots and minced greens and a little salt. She put in the bone and let it heat through until she could almost smell meat, then wrapped her hands in towels to hold the pot under the tap while it filled with water. Setting it heavily back on the burner, she added the cut-up potatoes and put on the lid for the soup to simmer.

Not much of a meal, but it was almost payday. Tomorrow, after paying his Society dues, Harry would fill up the coin jar again.

Once he'd saved up enough to buy the fabrics and the patterns and hire a few piece workers, he'd get a contract for himself, deliver the finished goods for more than he'd spent on supplies and labor, reinvest the profits. He'd be a contactor of waists, and she'd be his wife, a new baby warm in her arms, its greedy mouth circling her nipple.

Sam came clattering up the stairs and into the kitchen, startling Visha from her daydreaming. "Home already," she said, getting his lunch. Rachel left the buttons in their little piles and climbed up on a chair beside her brother. While he ate his cold potato and pickle, Rachel told him all about going to the factory. When their mother stepped out to go down the hall, Sam said, "One of the boys, he got a real baseball. We're gonna get in a game before afternoon school and I'm the catcher." Sam was already on his feet when Visha came back. "Gotta go early, Mama, so I can practice my spelling." He winked at his sister then dashed out the door.

Rachel went back to her buttons. Soon after Sam left, it was the insurance man who came, a loose coat hanging down to his ankles despite the warm afternoon. Visha went into the bedroom and came back with the two dimes. He took a little book from his coat pocket and noted her payment.

"Still no insurance on the little ones?" he asked, peeking in at Rachel.

"God forbid anything should happen," Visha said, rapping her knuckles on the wooden table. "For now all we got money for is their Papa and me."

"God forbid," he agreed, shutting the little book and dropping the dimes into another pocket. They clinked against the coins he'd already collected on his trips up and down the stairs of tenements. Visha saw him out, then went back to her soup, thoughts of family stirring in her mind.

Rachel counted out ten mother-of-pearl buttons—one for each little fingertip. They were all the same size, round and flat with two tiny holes bored through the lavender-swirled shell. Whenever she had ten the same, she wrapped them together in a bit of cloth to give to Papa. On Saturdays when he got his pay, he'd give her a penny for sorting the buttons, and Sam a penny for going every day to school, and Sam would take his sister to the sweet seller's to spend their fortune. Rachel sorted buttons until she felt sleepy, then curled up on the couch for a nap. Visha came into the front room and sat in the light by the window to mend clothes. The afternoon would be quiet for a while now, the hush in the room made more special by the noise seeping in from the street below.

A HARD KNOCK on the kitchen door startled Visha and woke Rachel. Voices from the hallway penetrated the apartment even before she answered. A woman, fleshy and sweating, swept into the room, pushing Visha back against the table.

"Where is he, that bastard, that liar?"

"What are you talking about? Who are you?" Visha thought it must have something to do with the neighbors—the woman talked like Mrs. Giovanni, but louder, meaner. Visha wasn't upset. Not yet. Then she noticed, hanging back in the hallway, the pretty girl from the factory, the one who'd been crying in the stairwell. A sick feeling flowered in her belly.

"Hah-ree Rah-been-o-wits, that's what I'm talking about. You come out here, you lying bastard!" The woman took a look around the room, crossed the kitchen to the bedroom door, pulled it open, peered in, slammed it shut. "Where is he hiding?"

"He's at work, at the factory," Visha said.

"We already gone to the factory, what do you think? He got outta there quick, didn't he, Francesca?" The woman threw her question over her shoulder at the girl lurking in the hall. "So she comes running home to her mamma, telling me Harry's wife, his *wife*, she came to the factory, and with a child already. It's true? He has a wife?"

"I am his wife. My daughter's here, and our son is at school." Visha gathered her nerves, funneled them into a shout. "We have nothing to do with you, get out of my house!"

"*Your* house, *your* daughter, but what about *my* girl, hey?" All the noise brought Mrs. Giovanni into the hallway. She began talking in Italian with the girl, who started crying again, tears dripping from her cheeks onto her lace collar. Their words, a foreign catechism, circled in Visha's ears. Her cheeks lost their color. She asked the question to which she already knew the answer.

"What does she have to do with my Harry?"

"He promised to marry her, that's what he has to do with her! Twice a week he comes calling for her after work, takes her out to the dance hall. Such light eyes he has, I think he's some kind of American, not a dirty Yid coming to ruin my Francesca. Then he gets a baby in her, stupid girl, and says he'll marry her."

Mrs. Giovanni had been inching closer with every word, pulling the girl with her. Now all the women were in the kitchen,

Francesca so shaken that Mrs. Giovanni pulled out a chair and sat her down. She asked Francesca's mother a question in Italian, and the whole story was told again in the language of opera.

Visha backed into the doorway to the front room. Rachel crept closer, peeking from under her mother's skirt at the women gesturing and talking in the kitchen. Visha absently stroked Rachel's hair. It seemed to give her strength.

"Stop it, all of you!" she shouted. Mrs. Giovanni came to take one of her hands. Francesca's mother sat beside her sobbing daughter. "Harry married me, seven years ago. I have two children with him. It's a mistake, what you say." Visha drew in her breath, gathering the words to tell this woman Harry couldn't have taken her daughter dancing, he was busy with his Societies, saving money to be a contractor.

Then the truth clicked into place, like the tumblers of a lock. There were no Societies. There was no savings. He'd been out with this girl, spending his money on her, and Visha left at home to make soup out of bones. Her knees folded. Mrs. Giovanni caught her around the waist and guided her to a chair.

Visha buried her face in her hands. "Before he married me, he took me dancing, too."

"You know what happens to her if no one marries her?" Francesca's mother said. "She's damaged goods now. Ruined."

"I'm ruined." Visha said it so soft and sad, Rachel ran over and threw herself in her mother's lap.

Francesca's mother leaned across the table, pointing at Visha. "You tell Harry, that bastard, we need money to send Francesca upstate. There's a convent takes girls like this. She goes away for six months, to visit a cousin is what I say. Her bastard goes to the

Catholic orphanage. When she comes home, maybe people talk, but it's just talk, *si*?"

Mrs. Giovanna nodded her head. "She's so young and pretty, some man will still have her."

"It's her only chance. If Harry doesn't pay, you tell him next time it's not me who is coming here for him." The woman looked at Mrs. Giovanni. "You tell him what happens when Francesca's brothers start to see what Harry done to her. She has to get away before it shows. You tell him."

The woman got up, pulled her daughter into the hallway and down the stairs. Mrs. Giovanni tried to comfort her neighbor, but Visha brushed her away. "Leave me alone now, Maria, please." After extracting from Visha the promise to send for her if she was needed, Mrs. Giovanni left. The room seemed too quiet now. The soup bubbled on the stove. Rachel shifted on her mother's lap. "Go back to your buttons," Visha said, pushing the child off her. "Go on with you." Reluctantly, Rachel went into the front room. "And close that door."

In the kitchen, Visha fought to breathe, her chest tight around her swollen heart. She wanted to smash everything in sight, splinter the chair legs, shatter the good teapot, too, like the one that broke already that morning. Remembering the morning, she stood suddenly, grabbing a teacup. Turning on her heel, she hurled it into the sink, china shattering against cast iron. Then she leaned over the sink and vomited, sickened at the memory of Harry inside her, purging herself of the stupid excuses she'd made for her husband.

Rachel was trying to count buttons, but the sound of breaking startled her. Her lip pouted and trembled, but something kept her from letting out the upsetness inside her. Pillowing her head on her arm, she curled up on the floor and tucked her thumb in her mouth, piles of buttons surrounding her like cairns.

Visha collapsed onto a kitchen chair and stared at the wall, black eyes blank. She felt frozen now, her limbs numb. If Rachel had thrown a fit, if Mrs. Giovanni had come calling, Visha might have broken down like a crazy woman. Instead she sat still as a ghost, sounds from the hallway and stairwell and out in the street muffled by the surf in her ears.

Visha had no sense of how much time had passed before the apartment door creaked open and Harry slunk into the kitchen. Placing his warm palm on her cheek, he murmured, "Visha, my Visha, what's wrong?"

From the place where his hand touched her, a trembling started and spread over Visha's skin and through her muscles until her hands were quaking. As if released from a spell, Visha jumped out of the chair, backing away from her husband.

"What's wrong? You have the nerve to ask me what's wrong? I know everything! She was here, in my own kitchen, that Italian whore! All your promises, they were lies. All lies!" Behind her she felt the cold rim of the sink. She reached back and down, her hand closing on the knife, the blade slimed with vomit. Clutching the handle in her fist, she stepped closer to Harry. Her hand jutted forward. The knife caught his arm, splitting skin. A streak of red blossomed under his sleeve.

Harry grabbed her wrist, raising her arm and the knife away from him. "You crazy bitch!"

"You bastard, you liar!"

Rachel, hearing her parents scream and struggle, came running into the room. In her haste, she kicked a pile of buttons. The tiny disks skittered across the kitchen floor. She saw the blood on her father's arm, the knife in her mother's raised hand. Her lip trembled and a wail erupted from her throat. Now Mrs. Giovanni, drawn by the yelling, appeared in the doorway. She couldn't see the knife, knew only that Harry and Visha were fighting—and no wonder, after what that man had done. She came into the kitchen to grab Rachel's hand and pull her toward the hallway, thinking at least the little girl shouldn't see her parents like this. Suddenly, Sam burst into the crowded room, panting from playing in the street. He froze for a second, confused by the commotion. Harry twisted around to see what was happening. Sam saw the flash of a knife, his mother's distorted face. He lunged forward, hanging on his father's arm. Rachel twisted away from Mrs. Giovanni and ran to her mother, grabbing at her skirt. Visha lost her balance, pitched forward. Harry yanked his arm away from Sam.

The arm, relieved of Sam's weight, shot upward. The knife, clutched by both husband and wife, swung through the space between them. The blade nicked the side of Visha's neck under her ear. It seemed a scratch, nothing more. Then a fountain of blood pulsed against the kitchen wall. Harry, stunned, stepped back. The knife clattered to the floor. Visha sank to her knees, swallowing Rachel in her skirt. Sam beat his fists against his father's chest until Harry swatted him away, his grown man's strength landing the boy hard against a wall.

"Murder! Police!" Mrs. Giovanni screamed. She ran from the room, her words echoing down the stairwell.

Harry looked around wildly. He dashed into the bedroom, grabbed a box from under the bed and began shoving things into it. Sam crawled across the kitchen. Snatching the dishtowel, he pressed it to his mother's neck. It was soaked and dripping moments later when his father came back, the box under his arm.

"Papa!" Sam called. "Help us!"

Harry sized up his wife, his children, the pattern of blood on the wall. He wasted no scrap on sentiment. "Take care of your sister, Sam. You're the man here now."

Harry turned and flew down the stairs, running into the street and ducking into an alley before the policeman came from around the corner, whistle blowing.

Visha tilted over onto the kitchen floor, head turned to the side. The spreading pool of blood lifted the scattered buttons. They bobbed like tiny white boats.

Rachel swallowed her screams with gasping breaths. She put her hands on her mother's white cheeks. Their eyes met. Visha spoke, but the words were a burble. Rachel tried to read the shape of her mother's mouth. Then the mouth stopped moving and her face went still, the eyes black buttons on the far shore of a terrible sea.

Chapter Two

IT LOOKED LIKE THE RADIO WEATHERMAN GOT IT RIGHT FOR once—it was going to be another scorcher. Even at six-thirty in the morning, the humidity was as stifling as a wool coat out of season. I'd only walked three blocks from the subway and already sweat was beading up behind my ears and dripping down my neck. I dreaded to think how bad it would get as the day wore on.

Finally, the Old Hebrews Home rose up ahead of me. As I waited to cross the street to work, I contemplated the building, so out of place among the modern apartment blocks that had gone up all around it, as if some medieval European citadel had been dropped on Manhattan. I wondered, not for the first time, if it had shared an architect with my other Homes. Whose idea had it been to construct these castles for the keeping of orphaned and geriatric Jews? Perhaps they were showing off, those prosperous bankers and department store magnates who sat on the building committees and boards of directors. For them, the peaked roofs and rounded turrets must have seemed monuments to their magnanimous charity. Or maybe they were feeling besieged, the rich

Jews of New York, unwelcome at the yacht clubs and racetracks no matter how flush their pockets, their wives excluded from the society pages, their sons turned away from the Ivy League. I supposed they thought they were doing us a favor by surrounding us with fortress walls. Growing up, though, those walls felt designed to pen us in, not keep us safe.

The lobby of the Old Hebrews Home was cooler than outside, the high ceilings and marble floors holding back the heat. I waved to the receptionist behind her desk and to the switchboard operator in her cubicle. My shoes clicked past the piano, a gleaming baby grand donated by some famous conductor. I usually took the stairs, broad and curving like the stage set for a musical, but I was too tired today. I'd slept badly last night, tossing alone in the sheets, screams from riders on the Cyclone interrupting my dreams. I was about to press the button for the passenger elevator when the doors slid open. I didn't recognize any of the residents who exited. Without my uniform, they probably assumed I was a visitor, someone's dutiful daughter dropping by to check on her parents. They shuffled down the corridor to wait for the dining room to open at seven, the smell of coffee and eggs already in the air. Like me, they'd probably been awake since five, but while I'd spent the last hour nodding on the subway, they'd been sitting in their rooms, dressed and alert, watching the minutes tick past until they could come down for breakfast. I promised myself that when I eventually retired, I'd sleep late every morning, have my coffee brought to me in bed.

I rode up to the fifth floor and ducked into the nurses' lounge, eager to peel off my sticky street clothes. Early as I was for shift change, I thought I'd have the room to myself for a few minutes, but there was Flo by the open window, white cap teetering on her teased beehive.

"Look who's here," she said, extracting a Chesterfield from her pack and flicking at it with a gold lighter. Leaning her shoulders out of the window, she aimed her exhalation at the sky. "I love a smoke on a hot day, don't you, Rachel? Cools you off somehow."

"If you say so." I joined her at the window. We traded drags, her lipstick migrating to my mouth. No breeze came up on the rising heat, just the hiss of stopping buses and the occasional blast of a taxi horn. "I heard it's going to be a scorcher."

"Looks like it." She finished the cigarette, ground the butt on the sill, and tossed it out the window. "Mr. Mendelsohn died last night."

"Oh, Flo, I'm sorry to hear that. You'd gotten close to him, hadn't you?"

She shrugged. "Occupational hazard." She tried to sound tough, but I heard the catch in her voice.

Some of our patients fought tooth and nail against the end. Absorbed in their own suffering, they took their bitterness out on us: impatient, demanding, full of complaints. Not Mr. Mendelsohn. During the months he'd lingered on Fifth, he'd become a favorite of the nurses, thanking us for everything we did for him, grateful for our kindness. Though it had been nine years now since the war ended, he was my first patient with those numbers tattooed on his arm. I'd hesitated, when I bathed him, as my sponge passed over his inked skin. "Don't worry, Rachel, it doesn't hurt," he'd reassured me in his wheezy voice. Something about his accent made me feel very young. When I asked what I could do to make him more comfortable, he said all he wanted was to look at the sky.

I opened his window wider, shifted his bed so he could see the clouds. At night, Flo told me, he'd watch for the moon, naming its phases as it passed over the city.

"Heart stopped in his sleep," she said. "Best way to go. He deserved it, too, after everything he'd been through."

I nodded. "Is he still in there?"

She shook her head. "The on-call doctor signed off on his chart. They came for his body early this morning. I guess you'll be getting a new patient today."

"Gloria said they've been calling up from downstairs all week, wanting a bed."

"Speak of the devil," Flo whispered as the lounge door opened and Gloria Bloom came in. She always wore her uniform to work, stockings and all. I'd never seen her in anything but white from head to toe, her only adornments a thin wedding band, a sensible watch, and the rhinestones on her cat's-eye glasses.

"Good morning, Rachel. Clocked out already, Florence?"

"Just about to, Gloria." Flo crossed the room to the time cards. "Should I get yours, Rachel?"

"Sure, thanks." Flo clocked herself out and me in while Gloria retrieved her cap from her locker and pinned it over her gray bun.

"You'll be along soon, Rachel? We have to prepare Mr. Mendelsohn's room for a new patient."

"I'll be there as soon as I change, Gloria."

As the door closed behind her, Flo muttered, "No respect for the dead."

"You know that's not it. She's just doing her job."

I went to use the restroom. Flo, eager now to be headed home, had changed by the time I returned.

"Don't forget your cap," I said.

She laughed, lifted it off her hair, and stowed it in her locker. "I'd forget my own head if it wasn't screwed on. Oh listen, I've been meaning to tell you, my kids haven't stopped talking about that day with you at the beach. All I hear is, 'When can we visit Nurse Rachel?' Think you could stand to have us all over again sometime?"

"Sure, it was fun. Let me check the schedule." I went up to the calendar on the wall where Gloria wrote in our shifts, twelve hours on every other day, extra days off popping up as unpredictably as Jewish holidays.

Flo came to look over my shoulder. "How much longer is that roommate of yours going to be out of town?"

I flinched, keeping my face to the wall so Flo couldn't read my pained expression. It still took me by surprise, sometimes, to have my own lies parroted back to me. "A few more weeks," I said.

"Where'd she go off to again?"

"Miami, to visit her uncle. Look, I'm not seeing a good day. Anyway, with this heat, the beach will be too crowded. I'll let you know." I felt bad for the cold turn my tone had taken. I wondered if she'd noticed it, but she was shutting her locker and lighting another cigarette.

"Want me to leave you a few?" she asked, tapping at the pack.

"No, thanks, I don't want to get in the habit. You shouldn't smoke so much yourself. Didn't you read about that new study they did, with the mice? How cigarette tar gave them cancer?"

"Go on, they're good for me. Keep me slim. Calm me down. Pep me up. They're little miracles."

I had to smile. "Whatever you say, Flo."

Finally alone, I kicked off my shoes and hiked up my dress. My thighs above the stockings were pink and damp. What a relief to un- button the garters and roll them down my legs. I left them puddled at my feet as I pulled my dress carefully over my head. My slip was wet from perspiration. Irritated, I plucked the fabric away from my skin as I crossed the lounge, the soles of my feet sticking to the floor.

In the mirror above the sink, I saw that my penciled eyebrows were smeared from wiping sweat off my forehead. It annoyed me that Flo hadn't said anything. Without the weight of brows or the frame of lashes, my black-brown eyes loomed too large, making my face look blank as a child's doll. Shrugging off my irritation, I lifted my gaze to my hair. After all these years, I still couldn't believe it was mine—piles of deep red locks shot through with gold and garnet strands that crackled like embers. I couldn't count how many women had stopped me on the street over the years to comment on its color, how many men I'd heard mutter to no one in particular *Will ya look at that head of hair?* It was, without a doubt, the prettiest thing about me.

I turned on the cold tap, leaned forward, pressed my cheek against the porcelain basin. The water felt wonderful splashing over my face and down my neck. I breathed in short gulps, like the bowled goldfish children win at Coney Island. An electric fan on the table was swinging back and forth. I went to stand in front of it until the chill of evaporating water gave me goose pimples. After treating myself to a generous dusting of talcum powder, I put on my uniform, bleached and starched from the cleaning ser- vice. Buttoning it up the front, my hands paused to spread over my breasts. My touch must have reminded them of the pleasure they'd been missing; beneath my palms, the nipples puckered.

Sighing, I straightened the collar of my uniform. Just a few more weeks, I told myself. Rummaging in my pocketbook for the wax pencil and a hand mirror, I drew in my eyebrows, jaunty arches that gave my face an alert and compassionate expression. I pinned on the white cap, buttoned white stockings into dangling garters, laced white shoes. Arranging my things in the locker, I shut it with a clang.

Gloria looked up as I approached the nurses' station, those cat's-eye glasses balanced halfway down her nose. "Lucia, you can go now," she called over her shoulder to the other night nurse. "Rachel, would you get Mr. Mendelsohn's room ready for our new patient? When you're done, you can set up the cart for eight o'clock rounds."

I went down the long corridor of the fifth floor. The patients' doors were propped open to coax a cross breeze from the windows in each room, but the air moved sluggishly, weighed down with moisture. Mr. Mendelsohn's room was at the end, next to the old freight elevator. The night janitor had already done his job: the floors shone from a recent washing and the room smelled of disinfectant. Still, there was the mattress to turn, the bed to make, the nightstand to restock. The cards from Mr. Mendelsohn's children and grandchildren were still taped to the wall. I pulled them off one by one, thinking again how amazing it was that he'd had the foresight to send his children away before getting away had become impossible, the good fortune to have a relative in New York with the clout to sponsor them, the luck to get them papers despite the quota. Flo said it made her believe in miracles, but I didn't see it that way. For one person, one family, to have survived only reminded me of the thousands, the millions, who hadn't. I recalled the suffocating hush in the movie theater when they ran newsreels about the camps, those desperate eyes staring out of skeletal faces.

I pushed the bed back into place, put the visitor's chair against the wall, pulled the card bearing Mr. Mendelsohn's name from the holder by the door. I wondered how many times I had done this in the year since I'd been working on Fifth, but it wasn't a number I wanted to tally. I'd only transferred up here for the schedule. Downstairs, where each day was divided into eight-hour segments, I'd enjoyed rotating through the various shifts: morning, evening, night. But after moving out to Brooklyn, I figured the longer but fewer days on Fifth would save me hours I would have spent on the subway. This summer, though, rattling around the apartment by myself, I wondered what I needed them for.

I'd liked working downstairs. I could still picture it. In the dining room, breakfast plates would have been cleared by now, a few residents lingering over their cooling cups of coffee, newspapers folded open to the obituaries. In the bright solarium, gregarious men were shuffling cards for canasta while chattering women stacked mahjong tiles. I imagined them dealing past the empty seat where the new patient destined for Mr. Mendelsohn's room once sat, the absence explained with a glance at the ceiling and the familiar phrase "Gone up to Fifth." Later, there'd be a movie or a lecture, dance lessons or book club, the rabbi on Saturday, visits on Sunday, distractions to pull their thoughts away from the inevitable. Because, as pleasantly as their days downstairs rolled by, residents understood the companionable activities would last only as long as their health allowed. When they became senile, bedridden, terminal, they'd be wheeled into the freight elevator and brought up here. Unless some crisis required hospitalization, Fifth was where they'd die.

"The room is ready," I told Gloria, back at the nurses' station. "Should I start on the meds?"

"Yes, please. I'd like them finished before the doctors come up for morning rounds." She fished a jangling key ring from her pocket and opened the medication room. I rolled in the cart and began setting up—the little cups of pills in neat rows, syringes in parallel lines, charts following the order of patients' rooms up and down the corridor.

"Ready for the morphine?" Gloria asked. I nodded. With another, smaller, key she unlocked the controlled-substances cabinet and watched as I plunged syringes into carefully counted vials and drew up measured doses. She signed off and relocked the cabinet, following to the letter procedures designed to prevent the pilfering of opiates.

When my cart was ready, I pushed it down the corridor. Mr. Bogan's room would be first. He was propped up in bed, notes and papers scattered across the sheets. With a trembling hand, he tipped the pills I gave him into his mouth and accepted the cup of water I offered.

"How's the book coming along, Mr. Bogan?"

"Slow going, slow going. You can't rush a buh-buh-buh-book, though."

"Not a good one. And I'm sure yours is going to be great, Mr. Bogan."

"Thank you, Rachel. Aren't you a duh-duh-dear to say so."

I helped him straighten up his papers and settled the legal

pad on his bent knees. Wheeling the cart in and out of rooms, I stitched my way down the corridor. I returned to the nurses' station just as the doctors came banging up the stairwell, their deep voices oscillating the humid air. Gloria looked at me approvingly over her glasses.

IT WAS RIGHT after lunch—patients' trays stacked neatly in the tall cart they sent up from the kitchen, remains of their soft foods smeared across plates—when Gloria got the call from downstairs. "Finally," I heard her say. "We've had the room ready for hours." The other day nurse was on break, so Gloria sent me to wait by the freight elevator for an orderly to bring our latest patient up to Fifth. Through the elevator's metal gate, I heard piano music wafting up the shaft. I leaned closer, trying to discern the tune. I pictured a retired accompanist or an elderly music teacher seated at the baby grand in the lobby, liver-spotted hands searching out a familiar melody.

Sweat trickled down my neck. I fanned myself with my hand, as if that tiny gesture could beat back the heat. It had gotten worse as the day wore on, the sun baking the bricks on the east side of the building before rising to the slate roof. The tall ceilings, open windows, and swinging fans were no match against it. I checked my watch. I was supposed to be going on break in a few minutes myself. I pictured the staff cafeteria on the ground floor, how much cooler it would be down there, and wondered what was the holdup.

Finally, the gears whirred to life. The arrow above the elevator swept past numbers until its tip pointed to five. I pulled open the metal gate as the orderly lifted the door. It was Ken, the young veteran with the mechanical arm, a shiny hook where his hand had once been. I stepped into the elevator to help him maneuver the gurney.

"It's okay, Nurse Rabinowitz, I've got it." He grasped the rail of the gurney, his hook a pivot, and swung it around and into the hallway. "There you go."

"Thank you, Ken. And who do we have here?" The woman on the gurney looked ancient: gray hair lank and oily, face sinking away from her beak of a nose, the skin of her thin arms crinkled like wax paper. I leaned over to read the name on her chart. Mildred Solomon. I straightened up too fast and jostled the IV line going from her withered arm to the glass bottle hanging above the gurney. She moaned.

"I'm sorry about that, Mildred," I said.

"Doctor." Her voice was scratchy, insistent.

"The doctor will be making rounds again later this afternoon. I'll make sure he sees you, Mildred."

"Doctor!" Her eyelids pulled apart for a moment, watery slits.

"She doesn't want to see a doctor," Ken said. "She wants you to call her doctor. She used to be one. At least, that's what I heard."

"Oh." My stomach turned over. I should have eaten by now. "Is there anything else?"

He shrugged. "I guess not. She's due for her medication, I think. They couldn't decide if they wanted me to wait until after meds to bring her up, but then they said to go ahead, so here she is."

"I'll take her from here, then. Thanks again."

"Sure thing." He retreated to the elevator, using his good hand to pull the gate shut, then reaching up with his hook for the door. I looked away, down at my new patient.

"Come along then." What was the harm in humoring her, I thought? "Let's get you settled in, Doctor Solomon."

A tight smile stretched her thin lips. "That's a good girl."

It must have been the heat, because suddenly I became dizzy. My eyes played a trick on me, stretching the hallway like a funhouse mirror. I grabbed the gurney to steady myself, took deep breaths until the corridor regained its normal shape. Even so, as I pushed Mildred Solomon into Mr. Mendelsohn's old room, I had the strange sensation of going the wrong way on a moving escalator.

"Is everything all right?" Gloria peeked her head in. "You don't look so good."

"It's this heat. I'm a little light-headed, I'm afraid."

"Help me move her, then you go take your break. I'll settle her in." Gloria positioned the gurney beside the bed. I went around to the other side and leaned across. On the count of three, Gloria lifted and I pulled, shifting the old woman onto the mattress.

"You can go now, Rachel. Here, might as well take the gurney down with you." Gloria transferred the IV bottle to the stand by the bed, took the chart and examined it. "And who do we have here? Mildred, is it? Welcome to Fifth, Mildred."

I retreated, rolling the gurney out of the room and over to the elevator. Gloria's sharp voice carried into the hallway. "Doctor? The doctor will see you when he comes on his rounds."

I wasn't one to stretch out my breaks, but that day I lingered in the staff cafeteria, drinking glass after glass of iced tea until I gave myself a headache. Doctor Mildred Solomon. I rolled the name around in my mind, trying to find where it fit, like those pinball games you get in a box of Cracker Jacks. A memory sparked deep within my brain: a woman's face, tilting over me; me, standing in a crib, my eyes lifted to hers; my hands reaching up for the little tie around her neck; a voice, her voice, asking if I'd been a good girl. The face was nothing but a blur, but the name, Doctor Solomon, dropped into place.

If anyone had asked me that morning if I remembered the name of my doctor at the Infant Home—if I remembered much of anything before Mrs. Berger and Reception at the orphanage—I would have said no. Now, I was sure of it. But if the desiccated patient in Mr. Mendelsohn's bed was that same woman, or just had her name, I didn't know.

"Better?" Gloria asked when I returned.

"Yes, thank you," I lied, my eyes pinched from the headache I couldn't shake. "How's our new patient?"

"She's all settled in, but it looks like she missed lunch. I called down for a liquid meal, and it took this long for them to bring it up." Gloria handed me a tray with a bowl of broth. Beside it, a full syringe rolled across the folded napkin. "I noticed she was behind on her medication. I measured out the prescribed dose, but she must be in a tremendous amount of pain to need that much. See if you can get her to take some broth first; that morphine will knock her out. Oh, and listen to this. She told me I should call her Doctor Solomon. That's one I haven't heard before."

I took the tray, making an effort to hold my hands steady. "The orderly said she really was a doctor. At least, he thought she might have been."

Gloria lifted her eyebrows. "That hadn't occurred to me. I assumed she was confused. You know how they get."

I did. It wasn't unusual for patients to mistake us for their mothers or their maids, even their children. Maybe I was mistaken, too.

Chapter Three

MISS FERSTER LOOKED UP FROM HER DESK AT THE Jewish Children's Agency to see Miss Jones, a social worker from the court, enter the office with two young children, a boy and a girl. They were better kempt than the disheveled urchins she was used to seeing, their faces washed, clothes neatly mended, apparently well fed—at least their legs weren't bowed with rickets. Obviously not swept up off the streets or removed from some immigrant's hovel. Miss Ferster wondered what tragedy had brought them to her.

"The Rabinowitz children," Miss Jones announced, tugging off her gloves. Tucked under her arm was their file, still thin: a remand signed in night court, a carbon of the police report, an order naming the agency as temporary guardian. Miss Jones had added a few notes about their neighbor, Mrs. Giovanni, who'd dragged the children away from their mother's body, given them baths, dressed them, and kept them overnight. By the time Miss Jones arrived at the address on the court documents, the boarders had cleared out and the custodian was on her knees scrubbing the floor in the Rabinowitz apartment, pink bubbles frothing around the brush. Mrs. Giovanni had assembled the children's things:

some clothes, a hairbrush, an alphabet book, the photograph from their parents' wedding, a shoe box of official-looking papers. Miss Jones had picked a few documents out of the box but politely refused to take anything else, saying the agency would provide whatever they needed.

For Sam and Rachel, their first ride in a private car had passed in a blur of worry. Now, at the agency, they clutched hands and looked anxiously around the cramped office at desks stacked with paper, a couple of clattering typewriters, a big chalkboard on the wall.

Miss Ferster, her round face and even rounder glasses surrounded by curls, reached out a hand for the file. She read over the papers and clucked her tongue. "Poor lambs," she said, squinting at the children. "You'll be doing the initial follow-up, Miss Jones?"

"I'm on my way to interview the grandparents, but if the situation is unsuitable or the relatives refuse them, I'll take the case back to court for adjudication. The children will certainly be assigned to your agency—the census lists the parents as Yiddish—so there should be no disruption in care. At that point, the state's payment will start coming to you. Whether or not the father is apprehended will make no difference. Absconded or imprisoned, the children are as good as orphaned."

"Such a shame," Miss Ferster clucked. "Well, thank you, Miss Jones."

"Good luck to you, Samuel." Miss Jones offered to shake the boy's hand, but he turned away, upset over the words she'd used to talk about his father.

"And good luck to you, Rachel." She slid her fingers along the little girl's cheek. "You are very brave. It was my pleasure to meet you."

Watching Miss Jones leave the office, Rachel didn't feel brave, even if she looked it. Her parents' fight, her mother's death, the invasion of police—it all so shocked her, she forgot to have a screaming fit. Later, when she saw how Sam was so upset, she kept herself quiet for his sake. But below the stillness that was mistaken for bravery, her insides were as jumbled as a jar of buttons.

Miss Ferster came out from behind the desk to greet the children. "Have you eaten today?"

Rachel looked at Sam, who said, "Mrs. Giovanni gave us rolls and honey and coffee for breakfast. And butter."

"Mrs. Giovanni is your neighbor?" Miss Ferster glanced back at the file. "She sounds like a very nice lady. Now, Sam, you're six years old, in first grade, correct? And Rachel, you're four?"

Sam answered for her. "She'll be five in August."

"All right, why don't you two sit down over there and I'll see what I can do." Miss Ferster indicated a bench against the wall. On it, some other child had left a tied piece of string.

To distract herself, Rachel pulled the string taut between her fingers and held it up to her brother. "Cat's cradle with me, Sammy." Even though boys his age had long ago given up cat's cradle for marbles and stickball, Sam dipped his fingers into the string and pulled it from his sister's hands.

Miss Ferster sifted through the papers on her desk, then went over to the wall and picked up the receiver from the telephone that hung there. She talked into the mouthpiece for a long time. After replacing the receiver, she went to another woman's desk.

"No foster care available, Miriam, can you believe it? I'll have to assign him to one of the Homes."

Miriam looked up at the chalkboard. There was a column for each of New York City's Jewish orphanages. Below each heading, a list of children's names descended, kept carefully even across the bottom. "The last boy went to the Hebrew Orphan Asylum in Brooklyn," she said. "We'll have to send this one to the Orphaned Hebrews Home in Manhattan. For the girl, at her age the Infant Home's the only option."

"I wanted to put these two in foster care with the Sheltering Society." Miss Ferster took off her glasses and rubbed the bridge of her nose. "They've been through enough without separating them as well."

"You want them all to go into foster homes, that's your problem."

"These orphanages," she muttered. "They've become so packed this past year, what with the influenza, not to mention the Great War. How many are in the Orphaned Hebrews Home now? Over a thousand, isn't it? That's no kind of life for a child."

"It's better than the streets, or the State Home, you know that," Miriam reminded her. She was older than Miss Ferster, still remembered when the large institutional orphanages were being touted as the most efficient solution to the child care crisis. "Once the Cottage Houses are built, we can start sending children out to Westchester."

"I am looking forward to that. The group houses will be so much better for the children than those orphanage dormitories." Miss Ferster glanced at the children on the bench and sighed. "I suppose there's nothing else to be done for them, though. Can you cover the office, Miriam? I want to take the little girl myself. If you call Mr. Grossman he'll send a counselor for the boy."

Little rope burns were starting on their fingers by the time Miss Ferster came over to Sam and Rachel. She sat on the bench to explain their situation. "I haven't been able to find a foster home that can take both of you, not yet, but I am going to keep trying. So, just for now, Sam, you're going to stay at the Orphaned Hebrews Home, but that's only for children who are already six years old. That means you, Rachel, are going to the Hebrew Infant Home."

"Why can't we stay with Mrs. Giovanni until Papa comes back for us?" Sam said.

"That's not the way it works, I'm afraid."

Rachel's lip threatened to tremble. "I want to be with Sam."

"I know, dear, and I'm so sorry, but it's only going to be for a little while. I'll keep trying to find a foster family, someone nice like your Mrs. Giovanni. If you can be brave and good for a few more days, and do your best to get along without each other, I'll do my best to bring you back together. Can we do that for each other?"

Rachel's fingers were tangled with Sam's in the cat's cradle. She looked up to her brother with frightened eyes.

"But I'm supposed to take care of her. Papa said so."

"And you will. Just give me a few days to find a placement for you together. I'll take Rachel to the Infant Home, and when I come back I'll tell you all about it."

Miss Ferster pulled at the string to separate the children's hands. Rachel grabbed Sam's fingers and wouldn't let go. Miss Ferster picked her up and tried to pull her away from her brother. Rachel could no longer keep down the panic that rose from the bottom of her belly. It burst out of her throat in a wail that vibrated the air throughout the office.

"Now, now, Rachel, now, now." The distress in Miss Ferster's eyes made Sam want to help her.

"Rachel, listen. Soon we'll be together again, but only if you're good for the lady." Sam pried loose his sister's fingers. "By the time you can count to one hundred and one, that's when I'll see you again. Can you count for me, Rachel?"

Rachel tried. "One. Two." Every numbered utterance was swallowed by a sob. "Three." Miss Ferster lifted her up. "Four." Miss Ferster crossed the office, the struggling girl in her arms. "Five." The office door opened, and Rachel was carried out. "Six." The door shut behind them.

Inside, on the bench, waiting for the counselor who would take him to the orphanage, Sam counted under his breath, matching his numbers to his sister's. When he got to one hundred and one, he kept on going.

RACHEL LOST TRACK before she got to ten. She kept trying to start over, but it was too hard to concentrate. There was the taxi pulling up to the curb, then the drive through Central Park, Miss Ferster urging her to look at the horse-drawn carriages. After the park, the taxi crossed a bridge with stone towers, and through the window Rachel saw water and ships and white birds rising and diving in the air. They drove on until the houses were thinned by lawns and trees. Finally, the taxi pulled over.

"There it is," Miss Ferster said. A long line of black cars was parked along the curb in front of a building so tall Rachel could only see the roof by twisting her neck.

"Is it a factory?" she asked.

"No, dear, it isn't a factory. This is the Infant Home. This is where you'll live until I can find a foster family for you and your brother. Come along."

Miss Ferster took Rachel's hand and guided her up a wide walk that led to an arched doorway. Rachel thought of Sam's alphabet book: C is for *cat. Candy. Canary.* "Is it a *Castle?*"

"It does look like one," Miss Ferster acknowledged. "Let's go in and see." The lobby of the Infant Home was a soaring turret around which a winding staircase rose, floor by floor, until it reached a skylight in the ceiling far above them. Rachel made herself dizzy looking up at the clouds while Miss Ferster went to the receptionist's desk, positioned in an alcove. "I called from the agency. I have Rachel Rabinowitz for you."

The receptionist looked up, as if startled. "You're here too soon. The Ladies Committee just arrived. Mrs. Hess herself is here. You know who that is, don't you?" Miss Ferster shook her head. The receptionist whispered conspiratorially. "Her father was Mr. Straus, who founded Macy's. Her parents went down on the Titanic."

"Oh, the Straus family." Miss Ferster tried to look impressed, but she wasn't sure what any of this had to do with her little charge. "Well, here's her file. Shall I leave her with you?"

"No, not now, that's what I'm telling you. The ladies will want to spend time with the children in the playroom before their committee meeting. I couldn't possibly take a new child all the way to Isolation at this moment. Maybe you could bring her there? It's down this hallway and up the back stairs. All the new children start in Isolation." Again the receptionist whispered. "We've had a terrible problem trying to contain the spread of measles, you know." She looked at Rachel as if she might be infectious.

Miss Ferster thought of the taxi idling outside, its meter running. She had been anxious to return to the agency before Sam was taken to the orphanage, but there seemed no alternative. "I'll bring her then. Do you want her file?"

At that moment, a gaggle of women entered the lobby. Miss Ferster noticed the gleam in their mink stoles, the shine of their fine shoes, the iridescent feathers fixed to their hats. She smoothed her own cotton dress and wondered what it would be like to have all of Macy's at one's disposal.

"Bring the file with you, the Isolation nurse will take it." The receptionist stood and approached the women. "Good morning, ladies. Right this way."

"And who do we have here?" One of the women bent over Rachel, reaching out with a gloved hand for the girl's chin.

"Mrs. Hess, please don't. The child might be contagious." The woman straightened up and backed away. "She's being taken to Isolation now." The receptionist pointed at Miss Ferster, who grabbed Rachel's hand and hurried her down the hallway.

"What's *contagious*?" Rachel asked.

"It means catching," Miss Ferster said.

"Like catching a ball?"

"Don't worry yourself about it, dear."

Up the back stairs, Miss Ferster pushed open a door off the first landing, saying, "This must be it."

They entered a long room brightly lit by a bank of tall windows. Across from the windows was a series of glass-walled cubicles, each transparent room just big enough for a small table and a bassinet. Inside each bassinet lay a swaddled infant. Miss Ferster stopped, arrested by the strange sight, wondering if this was what the receptionist meant by Isolation.

"I want to see." Rachel raised her arms to be picked up. Miss Ferster lifted her off the floor, and together they gazed through the glass at one of the babies. It looked to Rachel like a toy, so listless and still. Then the baby kicked and yawned, startling her. "The doll moved!"

"They're not dolls, Rachel dear, they're babies." Miss Ferster could see clear through a dozen cubicles to the end of the large room, one baby after another, no adult in sight.

"Why are they all alone?" Rachel asked.

"I can't imagine."

From the far end of the room a nurse appeared. "You're not allowed to be here." She swept toward them, her white apron swaying from side to side, the white hat on her head fluttering like the birds over the river. "Please go before you disturb the babies." Some of the infants turned their faces toward the movement outside their glass compartments. One began to cry. "See what you've done?" The nurse stopped outside the crying baby's cubicle and began to wash her hands in a basin. "What are you doing here?"

"The receptionist directed me to bring this child to Isolation. I'm from the agency."

With a horrified look, the nurse said, "You mean she's from outside? Hasn't been in Isolation yet? Do you have any idea what diseases she might be carrying? Please, step back." She twisted her hands vigorously. "That's why Dr. Hess developed this method, to prevent the spread of infection. None of these babies has been sick a single day since they were placed here."

Miss Ferster looked through the glass at the crying infant. She guessed it to be eight or nine months old. Her own little niece had begun crawling at that age. She thought of visits to her sister's family, how they passed the baby from lap to lap, each family member fondling the little fingers and toes, the older children cooing at their tiny sister. "Are they always by themselves like that?"

The nurse was drying her hands. "Of course. It's how we guarantee their health."

"Can we play with one?" Rachel said, a silly question to which the nurse did not respond but which prompted Miss Ferster to ask, "How often do you handle them?"

"As infrequently as possible. Please, go back out to the stairwell. That door's supposed to be locked. The Isolation ward is on the next floor." The nurse waited until Rachel and Miss Ferster had retraced their steps before going into the baby's glass room.

Miss Ferster carried Rachel upstairs to the next closed door that confronted them. Cautious now, she knocked until a nurse came to open it. "I'm Miss Ferster, from the agency. This is Rachel Rabinowitz. I was asked to bring her to Isolation?"

"Yes, the receptionist just called to tell me a new child was on the way. I'm Nurse Shapiro. Come in here." She led them into a small room with metal furniture and tiled walls. "Put her down here so I can process her. I'll take her file."

Miss Ferster set Rachel on a steel table. "There you go, dear. This nice nurse will take care of you now."

Rachel studied Nurse Shapiro, who seemed anything but nice:

her face pinched, her eyebrows knit together, her large hands red and rough. "What's going to happen to me now?"

Miss Ferster looked to the nurse, who, with an impatient sigh, explained. "The process is the same for all new children. I'll cut off her hair so it and her clothes can be burned. Then I'll give her a bath and check her head for lice. When she's all clean, Dr. Hess will come in to examine her." She frowned at Rachel. "You look healthy enough to me, so I doubt he'll want you for one of his studies. I'll probably have you settled in the Isolation ward in time for lunch."

"And after Isolation?" Miss Ferster asked.

"That's a month, to make sure they aren't infectious. After that it's down to one of the children's wards in the Infant Home. There's a playroom for the toddlers. They even started a kindergarten for the older ones."

Miss Ferster seemed satisfied. "That sounds nice, doesn't it, Rachel? I'm still going to try to find a foster placement for you and Sam, so you be good for Nurse Shapiro until you see me again. Is there anything you want me to tell Sam when I get back to the agency?"

Rachel's face paled. The one person who connected her to her brother, and by extension to everything she had ever known, was about to leave her in this strange place. All she could think of to say, in a voice shrill with panic, was, "I forgot what comes after one hundred!"

"One hundred and one, dear." Knowing it was best to do these things quickly, Miss Ferster gave the girl a pinch on the cheek and was gone.

"ONE HUNDRED *AND* one hundred *and*," Rachel chanted as Nurse Shapiro stripped off her carefully mended clothes and tossed them into a bin like so much scrap. Then the nurse picked up a pair of shears. Rachel felt a series of tugs as her hair was cut off. She sifted her fingers through the dark strands gathering on her lap.

"Over here now." Nurse Shapiro dropped Rachel into a deep sink filled with warm water and scrubbed her with harsh soap and a bristle brush until her skin was almost as red as the nurse's rough hands. Wrapped in a scratchy towel, Rachel, shivering, was weighed and measured then perched back on the edge of the table.

Keeping one hand on Rachel, as if she might try to escape, Nurse Shapiro stretched to reach the door handle. "Ready for you, Dr. Hess," she called out. A man in a white coat came in. His smooth face and bald forehead made Rachel think of her papa's boiled eggs. He flashed a light into Rachel's eyes, depressed her tongue while peering down her throat, held a stethoscope to her chest, pressed his fingers along the sides of her neck and into her belly. While his strange hands walked across Rachel's body, he spoke words over his shoulder to Nurse Shapiro, who wrote them down on a clipboard.

"Lungs sound clear, no signs of pertussis or pneumonia. No conjunctivitis. No obvious signs of rickets or scurvy. No indication of measles. Get a diphtheria swab of the back of her throat, would you? I'll take a closer look in the lab." Dr. Hess folded his stethoscope. "We'll see where we stand after the isolation period."

When the doctor left, Nurse Shapiro pinched Rachel's chin, pulling down on her jaw. Rachel gagged as a swab was poked down her throat. "There now, all done." The nurse dropped a white gown over Rachel's head, pulled knit stockings up her legs, buckled soft shoes on her feet. Her rough hands squeezed Rachel's ribs as she lifted the child to the floor. "Come with me," she said, steering Rachel out of the tiled room and into Isolation.

The ward was as big as the shirtwaist factory, but instead of noisy machines it was filled with mewling children. White metal cribs lined all four walls; in the middle, children Rachel's size and smaller sat in tiny chairs at a low table. Every one of them, boys and girls, had shorn hair and wore a white gown. For a moment Rachel thought it must be school like Sam went to, but there was no teacher, only nurses putting down and picking up plates. Rachel was placed in a chair. Of the food in front of her, she managed to eat only the bread.

After lunch, the children were led into a small room with toilets along the wall. The other children her size lifted their gowns and sat down right in front of everyone. At home, Visha had taught Rachel to always close the door when she used the toilet. Alone in the stall, she'd watch Sam's shadow passing in front of the frosted glass while he waited for her, or she'd listen to Mr. Giovanni in the next stall, humming a song and rustling his newspaper.

"You shouldn't need help, a big girl like you," Nurse Shapiro said as she picked Rachel up and perched her on the cold porcelain, but Rachel was too shy to go. After the children washed their hands, they were herded back into the ward. Someone announced naptime. Rachel looked around for a couch where she could lie down, but instead one of the nurses dropped her into a crib. Standing, her eyes peered over the top of the bars. Rachel wanted to tell someone she wasn't a baby to be put in a crib—she could sort buttons and earn a penny and recite all the letters of the alphabet.

Rachel swiveled her head, looking around the ward. The other children had curled themselves up, thumbs tucked into mouths. Some of them were quiet, even limp; others whimpered until they fell asleep, snot smeared across their faces. Rachel wanted to go home, wanted Sam to come get her. She sat down in the crib and closed her eyes. She tried not to think about how much she needed to pee. Carefully, she counted to one hundred and one, making sure not to miss a single number. When she opened her eyes, she looked through the bars toward the door, expecting it to open.

The door stayed shut. Rachel could no longer avoid the terrifying idea that she'd been left there, forgotten. How would Sam ever find her? Her bottom lip pouted and trembled. Her belly tightened and churned. She tasted salty tears.

She screamed.

The child's wail was so high and sustained, Nurse Shapiro rushed over to examine her for some injury. Finding none, she took Rachel firmly by the shoulders. "There's nothing wrong with you, child. You best quiet down now."

Rachel managed to form five words, each one carried by a wail. "I. Want. To. Go. Home."

"This is your home now, and you'll find these hysterics do you no good here." She turned and walked away. "That one's going to try my nerves," she said to the other nurse on duty.

Panic squeezed Rachel's body. Her breath came out in gasping shrieks that hurt her own ears. Some of the other children, agitated by her cries, chorused their voices with hers. She wet herself, scrambling to a corner of the crib to escape the cooling puddle. Light-headed, she feared she'd never take a full breath again. The hiccupping sobs felt like drowning. The store of tears from which she drew seemed bottomless as a barrel of brine.

Finally, exhausted, the fit ebbed. The nurses took deep breaths and congratulated each other when the new child silently pulled the blanket over her head. "You see?" Nurse Shapiro said. "They all cry themselves to sleep eventually if you leave them alone long enough."

In the secret darkness under the blanket, Rachel intertwined her fingers and pretended she was holding her brother's hand. It seemed like only a second later that she was jolted awake by a dream of a baby doll come to life, black buttons sewn on with coarse thread where its eyes should have been.

THE NEXT MONTH, Miss Ferster was back at the Hebrew Infant Home, explaining to the receptionist that she'd come to reclaim Rachel Rabinowitz. She had promised herself not to forget about these two children, and when a foster placement finally became available, she'd been proud of her dedication. A Jewish couple in Harlem, honest working people who lived above their shoe repair shop, willing to take both the boy and the girl. Maybe Sam could pick up the trade—there was always good work in repairing shoes—and for that dear little girl there would be a kind woman's care. Miss Ferster couldn't wait to see the look on Rachel's face when she told her she'd be reunited with her brother. Impatiently she interrupted the receptionist, who was sifting through index cards. "I only brought her a few weeks ago, so I imagine she's still in Isolation. I can find my own way there if you prefer."

Climbing the back stairs, Miss Ferster hurried up past the door that led to the room of glassed-in babies. Entering Isolation, she recognized Nurse Shapiro and asked her to get the Rabinowitz child.

"I'm sorry, but you won't be able to take her. She was moved last week from Isolation to the hospital wing. She's in the Measles Ward."

"Oh, the poor thing." Miss Ferster recalled when her nephew caught measles last summer, the long nights her sister spent beside him, soothing the boy with damp towels and spooning cool pudding into his sore throat. "How long until she's recovered do you think?"

"Dr. Hess confirmed the diagnoses through a blood test last week. I imagine she's covered in rash by now. She'll be infectious until her skin is clear, but even after the rash subsides there could be other complications. Conjunctivitis is common, and we have to watch for pneumonia. I wouldn't expect her to be released until next month at the earliest, and then only if she doesn't contract anything else."

Miss Ferster's shoulders sagged. She'd been so excited about the foster placement that she'd asked Miriam to notify the Orphaned Hebrews Home to prepare Sam for transfer. She imagined his disappointment at having to wait another month, maybe more, before seeing his sister. "Could I visit her before I go? I wouldn't be susceptible, I had measles as a child."

"It's impossible for you to enter the Measles Ward. I shouldn't even let you into the hospital wing."

"Is there no way for me to at least see the child? I've come all this way."

Nurse Shapiro considered the request. It was nearly lunchtime in Isolation, with no new admissions to process. A walk to the hospital wing would be a welcome change in her routine. "If you insist, but only if I accompany you. There's a window in the door of the Measles Ward. I'll ask the nurse to wheel her crib over for you to have a peek."

"I'd be so grateful. I have a foster family waiting to take her, and I want to be able to tell them how she is."

To reach the hospital wing, Nurse Shapiro led Miss Ferster down the back staircase and across the lobby. They climbed toward the turret's skylight then turned down a wide corridor. They passed the various contagious disease wards: measles, pertussis, diphtheria, pneumonia. Knocking on the door to the Measles Ward, Nurse Shapiro explained their mission to the nurse, who went to find the Rabinowitz girl. While they waited, Miss Fertser looked around. Noticing the label on a nearby door, she asked Nurse Shapiro, "Isn't scurvy a nutritional deficiency? It's not contagious, is it?"

"No, but Dr. Hess is making a special study of scurvy. It helps his research to keep all the children together in one ward."

A knock drew their attention. "That'll be the child," Nurse Shapiro said, waving the ward nurse to step back. Would Rachel be able to hear her, Miss Ferster wondered, if she said a foster home was waiting as soon as she got well? The news would give the girl some hope. Her face close to the glass window, Miss Ferster looked into the crib that had been brought to the door.

The child in it was unrecognizable. Naked to avoid irritating the rash, her skin was the deep red of a bad burn, mottled and leathery. Her face was like a painted mask, the shorn hair plastered to her skull with sweat. Her hands were tied with strips of cloth to the bars of the crib, a necessary measure to prevent scratching and infection, Nurse Shapiro explained, but still piteous to see. When Rachel looked up, Miss Ferster took in a sharp breath. Conjunctivitis had reddened the whites of Rachel's eyes so they glowed with menace. Yellow pus stuck to the black lashes, giving the child a devilish look. Then the girl's eyes focused on Miss Ferster's face through the glass.

There she was, the agency lady, finally come to take her away from this place and back to Sam. The weeks since Rachel had been left here were an eternity of sadness and pain, but now it was over. She tried to reach out to the woman, but her tied hands were held back. She began to cry, great, gasping sobs of relief, a release of all the fear and hurt she'd kept bottled up since that first day at the Infant Home.

Miss Ferster looked at the hysterical child, so unlike the lovely, brave little girl she'd described to the foster parents—her terrible skin, those infected eyes, the gaping throat, that swollen, quavering tongue. She turned away from the sight, shaking her head. Nurse Shapiro waved the ward nurse to take the crib away. As the window receded, Rachel screamed desperately, further disfiguring her appearance. Choking on her tears, she coughed and retched. The ward nurse noted the potential development of pertussis on her chart. In her crib, Rachel thrashed and cried until, defeated, she crumpled to the mattress, tied hands sliding down the bars.

Miss Ferster followed Nurse Shapiro back to the receptionist's alcove in the lobby. "Thank you for bringing me to see the poor thing." She extended her hand, around which the nurse wrapped her own chapped fingers.

"It's better to face reality than to nurture false hope," Nurse

Shapiro said. "From the look of her, I expect the girl will be with us for some time."

"I expect so." Turning to the receptionist, Miss Ferster asked to use the telephone. First she'd let the Orphaned Hebrews Home know that Samuel Rabinowitz would not be leaving them, then she'd call Miriam back at the agency to ask if any other siblings had come in who needed a foster placement. There was no sense letting a perfectly good home sit empty for months on end, waiting for Rachel Rabinowitz to recover.

Chapter Four

I CARRIED THE TRAY OF BROTH AND THE SYRINGE OF MORPHINE to Mildred Solomon's room, set them on the nightstand, and cranked the bed. As her back lifted, the old woman squirmed with pain.

"It hurts."

"I know, I'm sorry. Let's have something to eat first, then I'll give you your medication." I spooned broth into her mouth, noting the effort it took for her to swallow. I studied her face, but it was so changed from what it would have been—thirty-four, thirty-five years ago?—that I recognized nothing. It seemed to me there was something familiar about her voice, her gestures, but I didn't trust that these impressions were real.

The broth revived her. When she was finished, she pushed the bowl away with more force than I would have thought she could muster and nodded at the syringe. "It's time for my morphine, isn't it? Not too much, but some, I need some. That doctor prescribes too much. I told him, just enough for the pain."

She certainly sounded like a doctor. I examined her chart again, searching for some indication of the medical degree she claimed, but there was none. I wondered if the nurses preparing her chart had thoughtlessly stripped her of her profession.

"He said I complain too much, can you believe that? I'm the doctor here, Mildred, he said. You're not the only one, I told him. He didn't like that. He said he'd send me up to Fifth if I didn't co-operate." She licked her lips and looked around the room. "Is that where I am, on Fifth?"

"Yes, you're on the fifth floor of the Old Hebrews Home. I'm your nurse, Rachel Rabinowitz." Would she remember my name? I peered into her eyes but saw no spark of recognition there. I reached for the IV line to inject the morphine, then stopped myself. All I had to do was ask. Ask now, before the morphine sent her into dreamland.

"Doctor Solomon?" I worked very hard at keeping my voice steady. "Do you remember if you ever worked at the Hebrew Infant Home?"

"Of course I remember. I'm not senile. It's just that damn morphine, he prescribes too much." Dr. Solomon closed her eyes against the pain in her bones. She seemed to be looking for some-thing behind the closed lids. Her mouth pulled into a smile.

"I did my residency in radiology at the Infant Home. I was re-sponsible for all of Dr. Hess's radiographs—for the scurvy experi-ments, his work on rickets, the digestion studies. He hadn't used barium X-rays for that before. Dr. Hess was still putting gastric tubes down children's throats. I conducted my own research, too."

So, she was my Doctor Solomon. An electric charge jolted through me, shaking loose fragments of memory. Images began popping into my head like camera flashes. The bars of the crib I was lifted into at night, like a baby, even though I was almost five. Holding someone's hand as I slept, though I couldn't imagine who that might have been. A number embroidered on the collar of my nightgown—I remembered tracing the raised threads with my fingertip. There was so much I wanted to ask, I didn't know where to begin.

She was looking at me now, eyes eager. "Have you read my article about the tonsil experiment I conducted? Is that how you know about the Infant Home?"

"No, nothing like that. I was there. When I was a child, I was in the Hebrew Infant Home. I think you were my doctor."

Mildred Solomon flinched. I assumed it was a jolt of pain. She obviously needed that morphine.

"What study were you in?" Her voice was tight in her throat.

"I don't know anything about a study. I know I had X-rays, but I don't know what was wrong with me."

She snorted, her head collapsing back against the pillow. "All the children got x-rayed, that was routine, doesn't mean a thing. The important work was our research. The article I wrote got me my position in radiology, ahead of a dozen men. After the Infant Home, I never had to work with children again." A twinge of pain pulled her mouth into a taut line. "Enough talking. I want my medication."

I checked the time: quarter to two. A full dose now would leave too much in her system when the next round of meds came at four. I knew Gloria wouldn't alter the next dose without a doctor signing off, but he didn't usually come around until after five. She could call him up, of course—if there was an emergency, she wouldn't hesitate to do so—but if he came early he'd want to get his rounds over with, and that would throw off the whole schedule. I knew what the schedule meant to Gloria.

I pushed the syringe into the valve in the IV line and depressed the plunger. I stopped halfway, just enough to keep her comfortable, and quiet, until four o'clock rounds. Mildred Solomon's face relaxed as her eyes fluttered shut, a drug addict savoring her fix. "That's a good girl," she whispered.

Withdrawing the syringe, I decided Gloria didn't have to know anything about it. At the nurses' station, I found an empty vial near the autoclave. I pierced its rubber cap and emptied the syringe of morphine, then dropped the vial in my pocket before calling Gloria over to initial Mildred Solomon's chart. I could see she was pleased. Fifth was on schedule, all opiates accounted for.

"It turns out she really was a doctor," I said. "Mildred Solomon. I knew her, once. She was one of my doctors at the Hebrew Infant Home."

"Infant Home?" Gloria peered at me over her glasses. "I never knew you were in an orphanage. When was that?"

"Back in 1919."

Gloria considered the date. "Did your parents die in the Spanish flu?" I made a sad sort of shrug, which she interpreted as a yes. "So, this Doctor Solomon, she took care of you?" Touching my hair, I nodded. "And now you can take care of her. That's fitting. I doubt she has anyone else. For a woman to be a doctor, in those days? She couldn't have been married. I guess you were all like her children."

"I suppose so." Something had come to me, an image so clear I wondered where it had been all these years. "When she came to get me for my treatments, Dr. Solomon had such a smile, you'd think it was only for you in all the world. She always told me how good I was, how brave."

"What were you being treated for?"

"I don't know."

"Of course not, you being so young. But you could find out, I suppose. Aren't there records?"

"She said she wrote an article."

"There you go then." Gloria pushed up her glasses, satisfied my problem had been resolved. "I'm sure they have those old journals at the Medical Academy library. You're off tomorrow, why not go find out?"

HEADING HOME, I practically collapsed into my seat on the sweltering subway. Once the train was above ground, across the river, the open windows helped ease the heat. I stretched my neck to catch what wind I could. We reached the end of the line at eight o'clock, the sky still light from the late summer sun. Avoiding the crowds, I walked the back streets to my apartment building, Gloria's question rattling in my mind.

Why hadn't I ever found out? I only knew I'd had X-ray treatments because Mrs. Berger always said it was a shame what they had done to me, but I didn't actually remember getting them. I blamed my ignorance on the way we were raised. At the orphanage, questions were usually answered with a slap from one of the monitors; even Mrs. Berger was evasive if I asked about my hair or where my father had gone. Doing as I was told hadn't come naturally to me as a child, but eventually I'd learned. Learned to stop asking questions. To eat everything on my plate. To open my mouth for the dentist. To stand with arms outstretched for punishment. To strip for the showers. To snap into silence.

I checked the mailbox in the entryway, my name and hers snugged together on that tiny label like any pair of roommates: widowed sisters, cohabitating spinsters, cost-conscious bachelorettes. I was hoping for one of her postcards scribbled with complaints about the Florida heat, but there was nothing. I imagined her lounging by the pool, too preoccupied to write. Disappointed, I rang for the elevator. As I pushed the button for my floor, I heard Molly Lippman's voice calling out to hold the door, but in my moment of hesitation—that woman can be so tedious—it shut, leaving me feeling a bit guilty. Upstairs I hustled to get into the apartment before Molly caught up to me. How many minutes of my life have I wasted with her while she went on and on about Sigmund Freud and that psychoanalysis club of hers? I might have been more abrupt if she didn't live right next door.

I went straight to the bathroom and started a cool shower. If Molly did knock, at least I'd have a good excuse for not answering. I shed everything head to toe in seconds, desperate to be naked, dying to feel the water on my limbs and scalp. I was clean in a minute, the Ivory slick against my skin, but I stayed under the cool spray until my toes began to wrinkle. Only when I pulled back the curtain did I realize I'd forgotten to take out a fresh towel. Reaching up to grab one from the linen closet, I felt that twinge again, a slight strain from lifting a patient out of bed a few months back. I'd thought it was better by now. No matter.

Dry and powdered, I went into my room, pulled clean pajamas from a drawer in my dresser. I noticed a layer of dust had settled on the collection of jade carvings arranged there. How had I gotten behind on housework, with nothing else to occupy my days off? I got a duster from under the kitchen sink and came back, flicking feathers at the stone animals until they shone. As long as I had the duster in my hand I wandered around the room, stroking the spines of my old medical texts, shooing away the particles that had settled into the clasps and hinges of the steamer trunk I kept at the foot of my bed. I dusted the framed pictures, too, a skimpy collection that substituted for missing images of family. Two girls at the beach, their legs dissolving in surf. A kindly old doctor with wire-rimmed glasses, stethoscope slung around his neck. The portrait of a young soldier, proud of his new uniform. Retying the black ribbon that slanted across the frame, I thought, as always, he'd been too young for war. Hadn't they all, though? The whole world had been too young for what the war unleashed.

Satisfied with my efforts, I went back to the kitchen. There wasn't much to eat in the apartment—I was so used to her doing all of the shopping, I kept forgetting to stop at the store—but I found a can of tuna and made a quick salad that I ate with crackers and ginger ale out on the balcony. The lights along the boardwalk began to flicker on as sunset drained the last light from the sky. I'd meant to call her as soon as I got in, never mind the long-distance charges to Miami. I'd wanted to tell her about Mildred Solomon, but it was getting late and I was too tired now. Better to talk tomorrow, after the library, when I actually had something to say.

I shouldn't have bothered cleaning. Dust rose up and churned in the air as soon as I turned on the fan. Sneezing, I got into bed, pulling up the thin sheet. Her room might have been cooler—she had a north-facing window—but it felt strange to sleep in her bed while she was gone. With the window wide and the fan blowing on me, I hoped I'd be comfortable enough to get a good night's sleep.

The dream began as it always did, its familiarity my first sensation, even though it had been a long time, maybe years, since I had had it last. I am a little girl, and Papa has brought me to the park to ride the carousel. Somehow I know it is a Sunday. I pick out the horse I like the best, one with fiery eyes and a black mane, and Papa lifts me into the saddle. Oh, that weightless feeling! He stands behind me, his hands on my waist to hold me steady. His thumbs meet in the small of my back, his fingertips touch across my belly. As the carousel starts to move, the horse bobs up and down, its cadence steady and reassuring.

It's not just a dream. It's a visitation. Here is Papa, strong and alive and mine all over again. I want to ride that carousel forever, stay a little girl and have him near me. But as I turn my head to show him my smile, he slides into the shadows.

The horse rises and falls more quickly now, like it's really galloping, leaping forward faster and faster, the pull of the carousel threatening to yank me from the saddle. The horse looks back at me, its eyes huge and wild, as if its pace is beyond its control. I wrap my hands tight around the bar, tighter, but I can feel it slipping through my fingers. I call out for Papa to make it stop. But somehow Papa is gone and Doctor Solomon is there.

In past dreams, I'd believed it was Mama who replaced him, but now I knew it had never been her, it had always been Mildred Solomon. She is young and healthy as she was back at the Infant Home. She is riding the horse with me, her arms reaching around for the bar. I feel her chest against my back, her chin against my ear as she tells me to be a brave, good girl. In her hands there is a huge needle threaded with yarn. *This is the only way to be sure you won't fly off*, she says. She begins to sew my hands together, stitching them around the pole. I feel nothing, but the sight of needle and yarn passing through my skin sickens me.

Then the carousel is gone, and the horse is a real horse, running free on the beach, and I am not a little girl anymore, but me as I am now. I am alone. No Mildred Solomon. No Papa. There is a shining moment of relief as I laugh and feel the ocean spray on my face. I urge the horse to gallop faster. In my dream I ride with confidence and abandon, though in reality I've only ever awkwardly balanced on a rented mare on the bridle path in Central Park. Looking down, I see my hands are tightly grasping the mane of the horse. I look more closely. Not grasping, no. They are held in place with horsehair, the mane threaded through the skin of my hands. Horrified, I try to pull my hands away, but the horse misinterprets my gesture and veers toward the sea. It gallops into the waves until the water is up to my waist, its flaring nostrils straining for air. The surf roars in my ears as the water covers the horse's head and rises to my chin.

I woke with a strangled scream, bolting up in bed, my heart thudding against my ribs. I rubbed my hands together, fingers sliding over the smooth, unbroken skin. With no one to distract or comfort me, I obsessed over the dream, unable to make sense of its horrible images. I glanced at the clock—it was nearly five. I knew I'd never be able to fall back to sleep, so I got out of bed, put up a pot of coffee, took a quick shower while it was perking.

Out on the balcony, the coffee uncomfortably hot in my hands, I watched the bright glow of the sun rising up over the ocean. I wished I was on the beach, my bare feet on the freshly raked sand, my view of the horizon unobstructed by apartment buildings and roller coaster tracks. As its rays lit up my skin, I felt the sun's heat. It was amazing to think of its energy traveling millions of miles to finally touch me. It made me think about that Japanese fisherman, the one who died from the radioactive fallout of the hydrogen bomb even though his boat was eighty miles from the test site. It had been upsetting to read about such a terrible weapon that could kill from so far away. The newspapers said not to worry, that Eisenhower would never let things escalate to the point of using the H-bomb, but I hadn't been able to shake the idea of a detonation powerful enough to wipe out all of Manhattan.

I supposed it was the bad dream that had turned my thoughts so morbid. Anyway, I was starting to sweat, so I retreated inside. Even after I'd gotten dressed and tended to my hair, I still had an hour to kill before I could leave for the Medical Academy. I didn't want to sit like an old lady watching the clock, so I gathered up my stale clothes from the hamper and headed to the laundry room. At least the basement would be cool.

I had just started the washing machine when Molly Lippman came in, lugging a wicker basket in her fleshy arms. "Oh, Rachel! I wondered who else was up at this hour." She was in her housedress, its garish flowers clashing with the pink curlers in her dyed hair. "I suppose once you're in the habit of waking up early for work, it's no good sleeping in." She loaded the other machine and got it started. I hoped she would leave—most us of went back to our apartments during the long wash cycles—but no, she settled down on a folding chair and fanned herself with a magazine someone left lying around. "It *is* your day off, isn't it?"

"Yes, but how do you—"

"I saw you coming in last night. I was too slow to catch the elevator, though."

"Oh, yes, I'm sorry about—"

"So, what are you doing today? Going to the beach with the rest of New York?"

"No, I have something to do in Manhattan. In fact, I should pop upstairs to—"

"Let me tell you, Rachel dear, I wouldn't have minded sleeping in myself this morning, but who can catch a wink in this heat? It gives me interesting dreams, though, or maybe sleeping badly just helps me remember them."

"That's funny, the same thing happened to me." As soon as I saw the eager expression on her face, I wished I could take back my words.

"Oh, why don't you tell me about it, dear? We can do a dream analysis. It'll be an interesting way to pass the time."

I hesitated but couldn't see how to back out of it. I wasn't in the habit of revealing much about myself, but I didn't see how anything in my dream could tip her off. Besides, it had been bothering me all morning. Maybe it would help to talk about it. So I told her, leaving Mildred Solomon out of it—that would have been too much to explain. It was the only time I can remember Molly not interrupting me.

"Fascinating, Rachel. Simply fascinating."

"So, Molly, what does it mean?"

"Oh, that's not for me to say. Dreams are the vehicle through which our subconscious mind speaks to us. That's why the analysis can only come from a deep exploration of our experiences and feelings, our fears and desires."

Did she imagine I was about to share my deepest feelings with her, here, in the laundry room? Perhaps she sensed my hesitation because she said, her tone softening, "I can offer some observations, if you like."

"Sure, go ahead." I suspected anything she said would be as meaningless as the fortunes you get for a nickel from that mechanical Gypsy on the boardwalk.

"Well, the part about your father taking you to ride the carousel, that could be simple wish fulfillment. You grew up in an orphanage, didn't you?" Surprised, I nodded; I didn't realize Molly knew about the Home. "So, in your dream, you live out your wish. That's one way to think about it."

That made some sense, actually. "But what about my hands? I certainly don't want anyone to sew my hands together."

"Of course not. Like I said, a dream is the subconscious speaking to us. Sometimes dreams use wordplay or images that seem strange but are fairly obvious if you think about it." She paused, eyebrows raised, but I couldn't guess what she wanted me to say. "Well, your hands are literally tied. Maybe you feel helpless about something, unable to do something, constrained by some outside force. You have to figure out what that could be for you, what your subconscious is telling you."

"I'll have to think about that, Molly." The washing machine had stopped agitating and gone into the spin cycle. If I skipped the dryer, I could be out of there in a few more minutes.

"Professor Freud teaches us that dreams about horseback riding typically indicate a desire for the phallus." She raised an eyebrow at me, but I just shrugged. "The rising water, though, that's very interesting. More Jungian than Freudian perhaps. At the meetings of the Coney Island Amateur Psychoanalytic Society, we often discuss dream analysis. One of the young men—he's a homosexual, poor boy—he has a similar image in his dreams. His interpretation is that rising water represents repressed emotions because it's not a solid thing you can get a grip on, the way it slips through your fingers, yet it's capable of overwhelming you, of swallowing you up."

The machine shuddered to a stop. I flipped up the lid and pulled out my wet clothes. "You've given me a lot to think about, Molly, thanks, but I have to get going now."

"Aren't you going to dry your things?"

"Oh, I'll just hang them on the balcony. Seems silly to pay a dime to dry something on such a hot day."

In the elevator I exhaled, relieved at having escaped. I did puzzle over her comment about the boy in their group. They knew he was gay, but he was still in their Society. Maybe Freud's obsession with sex had made them more accepting than I thought. Accepting, but pitying.

It had been a mistake to humor her. After hanging out the laundry, I put on my sandals, picked up my pocketbook, and headed out to the Medical Academy. If I got there a few minutes before they opened, so be it; I could always sit in the park across the street. Never mind about cryptic symbols and the subconscious. I was going to get real answers.

Chapter Five

FROM HER CRIB IN THE PERTUSSIS WARD, RACHEL STARED at the cart of picture books parked near the door. She had already looked at every illustration and every letter of every word in the book in her crib a hundred times. "One hundred and one," she whispered. What she wanted was a different book, and she could see them, there on the cart, but Rachel knew better, now, than to ask the nurse to get her one. She'd had a fit, once, when the book she was given turned out to be the same one she'd had the week before. "You'll have no book at all until you control yourself," the ward nurse had said, exasperated. Without anything in her crib to look at, Rachel had nothing to do but watch the shadows on the ceiling shift with the passing hours of the day. At last the nurse had relented and brought her the book about the animals getting on a boat, warning, "You must be a good girl from now on or I'll take it away again." Rachel had promised, and she had been, for weeks and weeks now, but today, more than anything, she wanted a new book.

The nurse, Helen Berman, was sorting through the paperwork covering her desk. Every now and again she scanned the ward through the window in the wall that separated the nurses' station from the children. A cramped room built into a corner of the ward, the station served as office, break room, and, when the cot stored under the desk was set up for the night, bedroom. Helen had taken the job at the Hebrew Infant Home last summer when she was just nineteen, fresh out of nursing school and glad to get the position. A year later, though, she felt the walls of the Pertussis Ward closing in. She reminded herself that whooping cough was better than diphtheria or measles—only rickets would have been easier, and the Scurvy Ward was too disturbing—but still the paperwork was overwhelming. Every child's chart had to be meticulously noted: each meal, every cough, daily temperature, changes in disposition, weekly measurements of height and weight. Nursing school hadn't prepared her for the precise record keeping required of medical research.

Glancing up, she noticed one of the girls climbing out of her crib. Probably needing to use the toilet, Helen thought. The bathroom was connected to the ward, so there was no danger of a child wandering off. She used to yell at them to stay in their cribs until she realized this put her at their beck and call at all hours of the day and night. It strained her back, lifting their heavy bodies half a dozen times a day—or, worse, changing their sheets when they wet the bed, which they managed to do anyway, the boys in particular. The little ones she kept in diapers, but the bigger ones, well, it was best to let them take care of themselves.

Except for trips to the toilet and a weekly bath, the children in the Pertussis Ward were confined to their cribs; even meals were delivered to them there. When Rachel had been brought here at the end of May after recovering from the measles, she was so exhausted all she could do was lie limp, her eyes, still sore from conjunctivitis, half-closed. Occasionally the coughing would start up, so violent she could hardly catch her breath, until finally she retched and collapsed in relief. All that long summer, as flies buzzed through the open windows of the ward, the whooping cough had come and gone. Eventually, though, as the nights became cooler, the paroxysms came less frequently until finally they had ceased.

As Helen Berman updated Rachel's chart, she saw that the Rabinowitz girl had turned five last month. Counting back from today's September date, Helen noted there hadn't been an episode of whooping cough for weeks. As she finished notating the chart, she decided this one could finally be transferred into the Infant Home itself, where she would join the other girls in kindergarten. Five months in the hospital wing was more than enough for any child.

Rachel hoisted herself over the iron bars of the crib and landed on her bare feet. She crept past the other children who were napping or staring into space or muttering to themselves until she reached the book cart. She wanted to pick a book she'd never seen before, but to do that she had to look at each one, carefully turning the pages. As soon as she recognized a picture, she dropped that book on the pile accumulating in her lap and reached for another. She was absorbed in her task when the ward door opened. Rachel was surprised to see the big nurse with red hands, the one who had taken her clothes and cut her hair back on that first day. Rachel tugged at her hair, long enough now to cover her ears, and hoped she wouldn't be seen behind the cart.

"There you are!" Nurse Shapiro dashed into the nurses' station, startling Helen. "Dr. Hess is on his way here. He's giving the new resident doctor a tour of all the wards. I wanted to warn you that . . . wait, where is that child?" Nurse Shapiro pulled Helen into the ward and pointed to the empty crib. Turning frantically, she spotted Rachel crouched behind the book cart.

"Are you in the habit of letting them run loose?" Nurse Shapiro's chapped hand closed on Rachel's arm, hoisting her up, but the books in her lap tipped her forward and she fell, hard, on her knee. "Oh, for goodness sakes," Nurse Shapiro muttered, picking Rachel up and carrying her over to the crib.

"Believe me, I never let them out unattended," Helen stammered. "This one is very sneaky." She shook Rachel's shoulder. "What have I said about climbing out of your crib?" What she had said was not to bother her just to use the toilet, but Rachel was too confused to answer.

"Listen," Nurse Shapiro said. "I came to tell you—" The ward door opened again. She and Helen turned as Dr. Hess stepped into the room, guiding a young woman whose dark hair was pulled back in a severe bun. A member of the Ladies Committee, Helen assumed, though the woman's jacket and skirt were exceptionally plain, nor was she wearing a hat.

"Ah, Nurse Berman," Dr. Hess said. "I'd like you to meet Doctor Solomon, our new resident in radiology."

Helen blinked, puzzled, and looked over Dr. Hess's shoulder for this new resident. Beside him, the young woman cleared her throat and extended her hand. The nurse was grasping the woman's fingers before she put it together. "Oh, *you're* Doctor Solomon." She offered a friendly smile that was met with a withering stare. Helen instantly formed the opinion that this woman doctor was unattractive, though there was nothing particularly offensive about her features—except, perhaps, her beaked nose. As the doctors brushed past them Nurse Shapiro whispered, "I tried to warn you," before slipping out of the ward.

Ignoring the nurses, Dr. Hess continued his conversation with Mildred Solomon. "Now, as I was saying, I've been skeptical of these new pertussis vaccines. As you well know, the whooping cough comes and goes over the course of months. What may seem like a cure one week could simply prove to be a temporary cessation of the symptoms. Only by comparing a number of subjects over the entire course of the disease can we begin to develop reliable results. What was needed was a controlled experiment. So, for the past hundred days that's precisely what we've done." Dr. Hess waved his arm across the room, taking in the cribs and the children in them. "I enrolled nine of the children as material for the study. Three were vaccinated before being introduced to the ward, three were vaccinated at the first evidence of whooping cough, and three were never vaccinated at all. I've just completed my assessment, and as I suspected, the current vaccination is ineffective."

"Dr. Hess, I cannot tell you how impressed I am by the opportunities for research the institutional setting affords." Doctor Solomon's voice, though pleasant in pitch, was not melodious. She made an effort to keep her tone flat, countering the natural tendency of her voice to rise at the end of each statement.

"I've always maintained," Dr. Hess said, "that the questions being asked in modern pediatric medicine cannot be answered by experiments on animals but must be decided by clinical observations on infants. The ability we have here to control conditions is unparalleled. Nutrition, sunlight, activity, exposure to disease—everything can be controlled and measured. This has proven invaluable for my work on the causes and cures of scurvy. In my study of rickets, however, some unanswered questions remain. For instance, I had hoped to establish whether, if Negro infants were deprived entirely of sunlight, they would develop rickets to the same degree as white infants placed in similar conditions. Without the cooperation of my counterpart at the Negro orphanage, however, such an experiment has proven to be impractical."

"Still, Dr. Hess, your use of X-rays in the diagnosis of rickets was a tremendous innovation." When it came to conversing with distinguished physicians, one lesson from medical school Mildred Solomon had taken to heart was the strategic deployment of flattery.

"That's true, yes. We routinely x-ray every child coming into the institution, as soon as they are cleared of disease, of course."

Dr. Solomon nodded. "The radiography facilities here at the Infant Home are renowned." She might have added they were the reason she'd applied for the residency, but she knew people preferred to believe it was some feminine affinity for the care of children.

"There I must credit our donors for their generosity in building and equipping this hospital wing." Dr. Hess tilted his head in a studied gesture of humility, assuming his connection to the Straus fortune was common knowledge. "Not only do we have a modern X-ray room, but our laboratory is also fully equipped for microscopic tests, throat cultures, and blood work."

"I am eager to see the X-ray room," Dr. Solomon said, turning slightly to indicate her readiness to continue their tour.

"Excuse me, Dr. Hess." Helen had been standing beside them, unnoticed, a chart in her hands. "I was wondering if you would sign off on this child? Since your study has concluded, and she appears to be fully recovered, I thought perhaps she could be released from the Pertussis Ward?" Helen wouldn't usually display such pluck, but after Nurse Shapiro's disapproval, she was anxious to rid herself of the troublesome girl.

Dr. Hess took the chart, frowning at the interruption, his pen poised over the paper. His experienced eye took note of a decline in the child's weight. "Which one is this?"

"Right here," Helen said, leading them to Rachel's crib. Dr. Hess glanced down and was struck by the girl's pallor. Rachel, recognizing his egg-shaped face from her first terrifying day at the Home, cringed. "As long as we're here, Dr. Solomon," he said, handing the chart back to the nurse, "would you allow me to demonstrate my method for diagnosis of latent scurvy?"

Mildred Solomon offered a look of professional interest, masking her impatience. "Of course, Dr. Hess."

"If a child presents with the acute symptoms—loss of teeth, bleeding in the mouth, redness of the gums—there is no question as to the diagnosis. Just last week at the city hospital where I conduct a clinic, a child was admitted with scurvy that had advanced to necrosis of the gum tissue. I can tell you, the odor was extremely unpleasant. In such cases the only course of action is immediate treatment with the established cure of orange juice by mouth. With the latent cases, however, there is opportunity for experimentation, knowing that at any time the progression of the disease can be reversed. Recently, for example, I've been attempting intravenous injections of citrated blood."

"That sounds promising," Dr. Solomon offered, though it seemed to her a ridiculous idea.

"The results so far are not encouraging." Dr. Hess looked thoughtfully at Rachel. "See here, Dr. Solomon, the pale skin, the peculiarly alert and worried expression? I have found these to be symptomatic." He reached for Rachel, who scampered away from the sudden movement with a cry. "Sometimes in cases of latent scurvy, I find as we approach a child's bed, it whimpers or cries out in terror. Typically, though, it lies quietly on its back with one thigh everted and flexed on the abdomen. Nurse?"

"Yes?" Helen stepped forward.

"Have you noticed this one in such a posture?"

Unsure of what she was being asked, she answered, "I suppose so, at times?"

Dr. Hess harrumphed. "Further examination will show if one or even both thighs are swollen and exquisitely tender, or if there is merely tenderness." Dr. Hess squeezed Rachel's leg, pressing the spot where she had fallen on her knee. She cried out. "Ah, you see? Finally, we palpate the ribs for beading." His fingers dug into her sides, squeezing the breath from her lungs. "This is where the X-ray has proven most valuable, for the beading, which is apparent in the radiograph, is not always discernible through palpation."

Rachel, released from his grip, retreated to a corner of her crib, panting.

"You can perform your first X-ray on this one, Dr. Solomon. If, in the radiograph, you see beading on the ribs or the characteristic separation of the shoulder, I'll enroll it in my scurvy study."

Dr. Solomon leaned over the crib, her elbows balanced on the metal bar. Her thoughtful gaze landed on Rachel, though she was thinking not of the little girl but of her own ambitions. Still, the steadiness of her eyes gave Rachel a feeling she hadn't known in months: the sensation of being noticed. Rachel thought the lady looking at her was very pretty. She liked how her dark hair and brown eyes brought out the pink in her cheeks. The loose bow tied around her neck swung over the crib; Rachel reached up and tugged at it. Dr. Solomon, excited at the prospect of finally getting her hands on the Home's excellent X-ray equipment, allowed herself to be amused by the girl's antics. After all the discouragement, the competition, the sniping from the other medical students, she, Mildred Solomon, had gotten the coveted residency in radiology, and here, tugging at her necktie, was her first subject. A smile swept across her face, too swift to be stopped. The little girl smiled back. It seemed a good omen. Dr. Solomon straightened up, composed her features, and made her pitch.

"Dr. Hess, knowing of your interest in childhood nutrition and digestion, I wonder if you've considered supplementing your use of gastric tubes with barium X-rays?" Dr. Solomon lifted Rachel's chin with her hand, stretching out the throat. "I recently saw a demonstration of the barium swallow using a fluoroscope—the images were stunning—but wouldn't it be interesting to chart the entire digestive tract? With a group of subjects of similar size and weight, we would soon develop a basic understanding of normal rates of digestion that could be useful for comparison in cases of blockage or other complaints."

Dr. Hess considered the idea. "Does the barium remain reflective throughout the entire tract?"

"For the lower intestines, an enema is called for, but yes."

"It's a very interesting idea, Dr. Solomon, one well worth pursuing. If the X-ray is negative for scurvy, why not use this one for your first barium series? Either way, let's transfer her to the Scurvy Ward."

Dr. Hess nodded to Helen Berman, who made a note on Rachel's chart. She was sorry the child wouldn't be joining the others in kindergarten but glad the troublesome girl would, at least, be out of her ward.

RADIOGRAPH SHOWS NO *evidence of scurvy*. Mildred Solomon made the note on Rachel's chart with a sense of satisfaction. Now the girl would be hers for the initial series of barium X-rays. If she could impress Dr. Hess with this study, Dr. Solomon hoped she'd get approval for an experiment of her own design, though she hadn't decided yet what she would propose. Eager to get started, she gave the nurse in charge of the Scurvy Ward instructions that the Rabinowitz girl was to have no food whatsoever for the next twenty-four hours.

"Not even a little milk? She's sure to cry."

"No, only water, nothing else. It's very important for the quality of the radiograph."

"Yes, ma'am," the nurse said, then corrected herself. "Yes, Doctor."

Mildred Solomon made no effort to hide her irritation at the subtle insubordination. The nurses never questioned Dr. Hess's orders the way they did hers. Simply because they were all women was no reason for the nurses to assume they were on the same level. Perhaps once they saw her taking charge of a study, they would begin to show her the deference a doctor deserved.

The next day, Dr. Solomon alerted the technician to ready the X-ray room while she prepared the barium drink, mixing the powder thoroughly in cold water. Entering the Scurvy Ward, she approached Rachel's crib, a large metal cup in her hand. "You must be very hungry," she said.

Rachel looked up at the pretty doctor. All of the nurses had been so mean to her, leaving her in the crib while the other children ate, ignoring her crying as her stomach cramped and growled. "I'm so hungry. Did I do something bad? Is that why they won't give me any food?"

"No, you haven't been bad. In fact, you're doing something very important for science." The girl looked at her quizzically. "Very important for *me*," she said, and saw Rachel's face soften. Dr. Solomon hoped the nurses could hear how kindly she talked to the child. She demanded their respect, yes, but she wouldn't mind if they liked her—she had endured enough hostility in medical school. "I brought you this milk shake. I want you to drink the whole cup, and then we'll go to the X-ray room again, like we did a few days ago. That didn't hurt a bit, did it?"

The X-ray room, with its maze of pipes and pulleys, the hum and sizzle of its generator, had unsettled Rachel, but she didn't remember anything bad happening to her there. Thinking back, she found she could remember only entering the strange room, not leaving it; her next memory was of waking up from a nap in her crib. "No, it didn't hurt."

"Good then, now drink up."

Rachel, starving, grabbed for the cup, but after a few swallows she pushed it away. "I don't like it. It tastes like chalk."

"It is very important for you to drink it all, and quickly. You are a good girl, aren't you? That's what the nurses told me. That's why I chose you, of all the children, to help me in my work."

Rachel wasn't used to being told she was good, and it had been a long time since she had been helpful. She thought of how pleased Papa had been when she matched buttons for him, how Mama had depended on her to sort their coins. The wall of grief that separated her from the warmth of those memories turned her away from the past, forcing her attention on the woman in front of her. Rachel wanted desperately to please the lady doctor. She started to drink but gagged at the chalky taste. Dr. Solomon tipped up the bottom of the cup, filling Rachel's mouth, leaving her no choice but to swallow. Soon the cup was empty and Rachel was left with a scratchy feeling in her throat.

"I'm very proud of you, Rachel. Now, let me take you to the X-ray room." Lifting the girl out of her crib, Dr. Solomon strained at the weight. Grudgingly, she wondered how the nurses managed it day in and day out. She'd have to get one of them to bring the girl to her next time.

She took Rachel's hand and led her out of the Scurvy Ward and down the hallway. As they walked, Rachel felt the milk shake sloshing in her belly. "Was I very good?"

Mildred Solomon looked down at the child. Again, excitement at the prospect of conducting her own research lit her face with a smile that spilled over onto Rachel. "You are a very good girl." They turned a corner and went into the X-ray room.

The technician assured Dr. Solomon that the generator was working perfectly and that the Coolidge tube was in place and ready for its electric charge. She hadn't expected to have such expert support—most radiologists had to manage all the equipment themselves, risking shocks and burns. This technician had gotten his training in X-rays during the Great War, hauling the equipment around France in a van and setting it up outside field hospitals spitting distance from the trenches.

"Thank you, Glen. I can manage from here if you want to take your lunch break, but I'll need you back in an hour. I'm screening the new infants for rickets this afternoon."

"Yes, Doctor," he said, nearly saluting her. Something about Mildred Solomon brought out his military manners.

Dr. Solomon turned her attention to Rachel. "Let's arrange you on the table." Stepping on a small stool, Rachel climbed up. "Careful!" Dr. Solomon pushed down on the crown of Rachel's head, which had nearly collided with the Coolidge tube. Rachel ducked, then stretched out on the table. As Dr. Solomon leaned over her, Rachel reached for the necktie and gave it a tug, pulling it loose.

"No playing now," Dr. Solomon said, catching the girl's hand. "You have to lie very, very still when I make the X-ray." She placed Rachel's arms down along her sides and secured them with straps that buckled over her wrists and elbows. Her legs, too, were strapped down, and finally a strap was wrapped around her forehead.

"Now, I want you to breathe in slowly and deeply." Dr. Solomon placed a stiff mask over Rachel's mouth and nose that made it hard for her to breathe at all. The chalky taste was rising into the back of her throat as Dr. Solomon dripped chloroform onto the mask. Though she was lying quite still, Rachel began to feel dizzy. "Breathe in, that's right. That's a good girl." As the room started to spin, the doctor's voice sounded farther and farther away.

Once the child was unconscious, Mildred Solomon turned the crank on the table, tilting it to forty-five degrees. She loosened the strap around the girl's forehead to turn the head to the side, then rebuckled it. She clipped the plate in place under the table, positioned the Coolidge tube, set the generator, and stepped behind the lead screen. Wanting the exposure to be perfect, she counted out thirty seconds on the watch she wore pinned to her jacket before switching off the flow of electricity to the tube. Allowing five minutes for the barium liquid to further its journey down the child's esophagus and into her stomach, she repositioned the Coolidge tube and replaced the plate, then made another exposure. Five minutes later, another exposure, the X-ray focused on the duodenum, then a fourth, aimed at the ileum. Dr. Solomon wasn't sure if the intervals were optimal—she'd discover that when she reviewed the radiographs. Based on her findings, she would adjust the timing of the next series of X-rays accordingly.

Strapped to the table, Rachel began to stir and whimper. Enough for today, Dr. Solomon decided. She unstrapped the child and sat her on the table. "Can you stand up?" she asked, but Rachel's woozy stare suggested not. As if she were a bridegroom, Dr. Solomon carried the girl out of the X-ray room and back to her crib in the Scurvy Ward.

"Nurse, come here, please. When she is alert again, begin with some milk, then soft foods for the rest of the day. Tomorrow she can eat normally. There's a potential for constipation, so if she hasn't had a stool by tomorrow evening, you can use a suppository. I'll wait until her digestion has normalized before ordering another fast." Dr. Solomon gazed down at Rachel, conscious of the nurse peering over her shoulder. "You were a brave little girl today," she said, offering Rachel a smile. Then she turned to the nurse. "Next time, I'll have you administer the barium drink and deliver the child to the X-ray room."

"Yes, Doctor."

"I DON'T WANT to drink it!" Once again, Rachel had spent an entire day without food, her stomach growling with hunger, but now she refused to take the cup the nurse offered her.

"Please, Rachel, it's the same as last time. Like a milk shake, remember? Be a good girl and drink it all up." The nurse pushed the cup at the child who had previously been so cooperative, but Rachel clenched her teeth tight, pressing her lips into a hard line.

"Oh, for heaven's sake, I give up." Walking away with the cup, the nurse left the ward and returned with Dr. Solomon. "I'm sorry to involve you, but she won't take the drink, and I wasn't sure what you wanted me to do. Perhaps this one has participated enough? I could begin one of the other children on a fast."

"No, I need to complete this series today; the next one will be the last, and that's the enema for the lower tract. Rachel, listen to me." Dr. Solomon fixed the girl with a stern look. "This is the last time you have to drink the milk shake, I promise. Now be a good girl and drink it down." The barium would only taste worse, she knew, the longer it sat in the cup, settling in the warming water.

Rachel's throat had closed up. Shame and anger trembled her lip. "I can't do it," she yelled, swatting at the cup in Dr. Solomon's hand.

"You leave me no choice," Dr. Solomon said. "Nurse, go get a gastric tube and a funnel." When the nurse returned and handed the items to Dr. Solomon, Rachel began to realize she'd made a terrible mistake. She had seen Dr. Hess threading that tube into the open mouths of other children, watched them choke and cry as he instructed them to swallow it down. She tried to say she'd drink the milk shake, but it was too late. The nurse held Rachel's head back while Dr. Solomon poked the rubber tube down her throat. Panicking, she retched.

"Don't make this harder than it needs to be," Dr. Solomon said. Tears leaked from Rachel's eyes and pooled in her ears as she gagged on the tube. When it was finally down, Dr. Solomon held the funnel up above Rachel's head while the nurse poured in the barium drink. Rachel, helpless, felt her stomach swell. Dr. Solomon pulled the tube out slowly so the girl wouldn't throw up and ruin everything.

Rachel's throat burned as if she had gulped a scalding cup of tea. The nurse carried her down the hallway, following Dr. Solomon to the X-ray room.

"Thank you for your help," Dr. Solomon said as the nurse placed Rachel on the table. "I can manage from here." As she secured Rachel's limbs Dr. Solomon leaned over and frowned. "I'm very disappointed in you," she said, cinching the straps. Rachel was desolate at having angered the one person who was kind to her. For once, she welcomed the chloroform.

Early the next morning, Rachel's belly cramped as the barium clotted in her intestines. The ward nurse inserted a laxative suppository, then sat her on a toilet. Rachel stared past her swinging feet at the tiles on the floor, black and white hexagons swimming in and out of focus. Afterward, relieved of her discomfort and now ravenous, Rachel looked around for the nurse to ask for her breakfast. She wasn't in the room, or behind the desk at her station. The door to the Scurvy Ward stood slightly open; she must have gone into the hallway. Rachel peeked out, hoping the nurse would be nearby.

No one was in sight. Rachel wobbled down the empty hallway, passing the Pertussis Ward, the Measles Ward, the Diphtheria Ward. She had just passed the X-ray room when she heard a door slam somewhere. Startled, she ducked into the nearest opening.

Rachel found herself in a small room with no windows. Light from the hallway illuminated a chair and a table. The top of the table slanted up and seemed to be made of glass. Rachel, curious to know if she could see through it, crawled underneath, but from below all she saw was a flat wooden surface. Footsteps approached and Rachel crouched down, waiting for the person to pass. But they didn't pass. Whoever it was came in, shutting the door and snuffing the room into darkness. A thin line of light outlined the door, then Rachel heard the sound of a curtain being pulled and even that little bit of light was extinguished. It was so dark Rachel couldn't tell the difference between her eyes being open or shut.

In the radiograph room, Dr. Solomon welcomed the darkness, settling into her chair with a sigh. She felt along the tabletop until her hand encountered the timer. By feel, she turned the dial to fifteen minutes, the quick ticking loud in the quiet room. She held her eyes open, seeing nothing, imagining her retinal cones relaxing as the darkness coaxed her eyes into maximum sensitivity. There was nothing to do now but wait and think.

The digestion study was nearly complete. Dr. Hess assured her the barium X-rays had given him great insight into the normal rates at which food moves through a child's digestive tract. It would aid him immeasurably as he continued his nutrition studies.

Her name might be added as a coauthor on his next article—at the very least, her assistance would be acknowledged in his credits. He had begun to hint that she might take over next year as attending physician to the Infant Home, while he focused on his research. But Mildred Solomon's ambitions would not be satisfied doctoring orphans. She needed to write an article under her own name, make her own reputation, if she was ever to get out from under Dr. Hess and away from all of these children, but she had yet to initiate her own experiment.

A rustle on the floor caused her to pull her legs up with a gasp. How silly, she thought, to be scared of a mouse after all of the rodents she'd handled in the laboratory. Yet it was a perfectly natural reaction when startled in the dark. Holding her knees to her chest, she listened for the mouse's rustle. Instead, she heard a shallow panting. She pictured a lost dog, though that was impossible.

"What's there?"

A small voice under the table said, "It's me, Dr. Solomon. It's Rachel."

She waved her hand under the desk, brushing against Rachel's sleeve. Her fingers curled around the little elbow and guided the girl out from under the desk. Dr. Solomon's voice sounded close to Rachel's ear. "What are you doing in here?"

"I got lost, I'm sorry." Rachel tensed, waiting for Dr. Solomon to switch on the light, but nothing happened. "Why is it so dark?"

"I'm letting my eyes adjust before I read the radiographs." Dr. Solomon didn't have time for this; if she turned on the light now, if she so much as cracked open the door, she'd have to start all over again. "You'll have to stay with me. Come up here, so I know where you are." She pulled the child onto her lap and wrapped her arms around the small body. "You're not afraid of the dark, are you?"

"I'm a little afraid. It's so, *so* dark."

"You just sit here with me and you won't have anything to be afraid of."

"Am I in trouble?"

"Not if you stay quiet and still. Can you do that for me?"

"I'll try."

"Good girl. Hush, now."

The ticking of the timer infiltrated every crevice of the room. Mildred Solomon aligned her breathing to the timer, five seconds in and five seconds out. Unnoticed, her heartbeat, too, began to slow. The heaviness of the lady doctor's arm around her waist, the softness of her breathing, made Rachel feel safe and calm. She began rocking slightly as she relaxed against the doctor's chest, cheek on collarbone.

A bell went off, startling them both. "Time's up," Dr. Solomon said. Rachel expected they would get up now and leave the little room, but instead she felt Dr. Solomon reach out, heard a switch flipped. A faint green light came on, but in the darkness, their eyes fully dilated, it was enough to illuminate the room. "Stay here," Dr. Solomon said, getting up and walking carefully around the table. She lifted some brittle radiographs from a drawer and mounted them on the light board. Resuming her seat, she settled the girl on her lap and wrapped a rubber cape around them both. Rachel's head peeked out, just below Dr. Solomon's chin. "Keep your hands under the cape. I have to put gloves on now." She did, the thick rubber exaggerating her fingers. "Ready?"

"For what?" Rachel asked, and then she saw.

Mildred Solomon flipped another switch, and the light table buzzed and flickered. The white light was intense, and over it were the radiographs, dark and mysterious images through which emerged white streaks and swirls and clouds.

"What are they?"

"These are the pictures we make with the X-ray machine." The chair moved—Rachel realized it was on wheels—and together they rolled closer to the images. "The X-rays pass right through you, through your skin and your muscles, to reach the bones and organs. The X-ray makes the radiograph. Then, when the light shines through the radiograph, it shows all of the shapes and shadows. Because I know how to read them and I understand the anatomy, the radiograph lets me see what's inside you."

The doctor's words sparked a memory in Rachel's brain. She was in the tub in Mrs. Giovanni's kitchen, warm water up to her chin, being scrubbed with a rough, red cloth. "It's all my fault," Rachel whimpered, thinking of the broken teapot, of Papa's left-behind lunch, of the operator from the factory, of her mother's black eyes. "You listen to me now," Mrs. Giovanni said, taking the little face in her soapy hands so she could look into the girl's eyes. "Nothing is your fault. Never think that again. God can see inside you, right into your soul, and He knows you did nothing wrong. Remember that, Rachel, if you ever feel alone or afraid." Looking at the X-ray images, Rachel imagined this was what God saw when he looked at her. Where on the radiograph, she wondered, did it show right from wrong?

"See this bright squiggle?" Dr. Solomon's gloved hand pointed. "That's why you drink the milk shake, so I can see what's inside your intestines. And look here, these are your ribs." Dr. Solomon slipped off one rubber glove and reached under the cape. As she pointed to the white shapes on the radiograph with her gloved hand, the other touched Rachel's ribs. "And there is your spine." Rachel felt a finger slide up the middle of her back. "See your shoulders there, and your hip bones, here? These big clouds are your lungs. And on this one, with your head turned to the side, see your jaws, and all your baby teeth, with the grown-up teeth behind them, ready to take their place? And see that little swirl, there? That's your tonsils."

Mildred Solomon leaned forward, lost in thought as she contemplated the radiographs. She remembered learning about Béclère's experimental X-ray treatment of a tumor on a young woman's pituitary gland. The tumor had shrunk after exposure to the rays, but how had Béclère solved the problem of burning the skin? Oh yes, he varied the angle of the rays, focusing on the tumor from different points of entry. If he could use X-rays to shrink a tumor, Mildred Solomon wondered if the tonsils, too, could be eliminated through X-rays. It was the most common procedure in pediatric medicine, performed on thousands and thousands of children a year. Those surgeons, so superior, regarded radiology as little more than a mapping service to guide them in the real work of cutting people open. With X-rays, though, surgical tonsillectomy might become a thing of the past. At the Infant Home, it was standard practice to excise the tonsils and adenoids of every five-year-old. If she could develop a technique using X-rays, it might replace the tonsillectomy, sparing countless children the risks of surgery.

Mildred Solomon quivered with excitement. This would be her experiment: the X-ray tonsillectomy. After a series of X-rays, testing varying lengths of exposure, the results could be confirmed through surgical excision. She would need a number of subjects as her material. She thought it through in her mind. Eight orphans should do.

In the glow of the light table, Rachel tilted her head to look up at Dr. Solomon's face. On the warm lap with the heavy cape around them both, Rachel had a surge of affection for this woman whom she wanted so desperately to please. She twisted to wrap her arms around Dr. Solomon's neck.

Mildred Solomon would have normally been irritated by the child clinging to her like that, but she was flush with the thrill of her brilliant idea. In an unusual show of feeling, she stroked the girl's head. Her hand came away covered with strands of brown hair. It was a predictable side effect of the X-rays; really, she should have expected it. Taken by surprise like this, though, she couldn't help but shudder.

"What's the matter?" Rachel asked, then followed Dr. Solomon's gaze to the hair in her hand. For a horrible moment, Rachel thought it had grown there.

"That's enough for today," Dr. Solomon pronounced, removing the cape and setting Rachel on her feet. She brushed her hand against the side of her skirt to wipe away the girl's hair. "Let's get you back to the ward. I have an idea for a new experiment you can help me with."

Chapter Six

I EXPECTED TO BE EARLY TO THE MEDICAL ACADEMY, BUT there was a delay transferring to the Lexington line, so by the time I got there it had just opened. I'd always thought of it as an exclusive club for physicians and had forgotten about the library until Gloria reminded me. Wandering around, I was impressed by its gilt chandeliers and carved ceiling beams, the stunning views of Central Park through Palladian windows. I lost count of the marble busts and portraits in oil. I thought of my share of the rent for that old walk-up in the Village—that entire place could have fit three times over in this one reception hall. I knew there were magnificent spaces like this all over New York, but I forgot, sometimes, that a brick facade was as likely to encompass unused ballrooms as cramped apartments.

I found the library on the third floor. The card catalog stretched the length of an entire wall. Dozens of drawers high, its little brass card holders were multiplied as in a kaleidoscope. It was amazingly easy to find what I was looking for—the librarians had cataloged not only authors but also coauthors and citations. I walked my fingers over the cards, their edges softened by years of inquiry, until I came to Solomon, M., M.D. I felt a little thrill on discovering this tangible proof of the old woman's claims. I thought of how pleased she would be to hear I had actually looked her up until I realized that, at her prescribed dose of morphine, she was unlikely to be lucid enough to understand me. I'd have to be content with finally learning what I had suffered from that necessitated all those X-rays.

Mildred Solomon was sole author of an article published in 1921, "Radiography of the Tonsils: Efficacy of a Nonsurgical Approach." She was coauthor, along with Hess, A., M.D., of a study on childhood digestion, and she was cited in Hess's book *Scurvy: Past and Present*. There was also a citation in a recent article about breast cancer by a Dr. Feldman, but that one, I imagined, must be a different M. Solomon. I copied down call numbers from all of these cards, then walked down the catalog and pulled the drawer for Hess as well. Besides his work on scurvy, there were a number of articles on rickets—a quaint affliction one never heard of in Manhattan anymore and of no interest to me. I did notice the Hebrew Infant Home listed as a subject heading for an article on pertussis; I decided to jot down that call number, too, even though it didn't cite Dr. Solomon.

I went to hand in my numbers, but the librarian was nowhere to be seen. I rang the bell on the counter and soon she appeared, a tall woman with a pixie haircut wearing trousers that reminded me of Katharine Hepburn. She looked over my list of call numbers as I peered at the name tag pinned to her tight knit top: DEBORAH. "It may take me a while to pull these. There's a coffee shop on the ground floor that should be open by now, if you'd rather wait there?"

"No, I'm fine, but could you tell me where's the restroom?"

"The only public ladies' room is on the first floor, off the reception hall. Here, why don't you follow me?" She lifted a section of the counter and tilted her head. Together, we went through to the stacks, metal shelves from floor to ceiling as far as I could see. "The staff use this one over here." She showed me to a simple bathroom with a frosted window high in the wall. "The lock's a bit tricky if you're not used to it, but you won't be disturbed. The other librarian doesn't come in until noon."

After I freshened up, I found my way to the reading room and settled down to wait. I had the quiet space to myself. Not quite as grand as the rest of the Academy, the reading room was stuffy and hushed, the shelves lining its walls packed with dusty leather-bound books, the huge oak table gouged and scratched by decades of note-taking doctors. I went over to the window and sat in the deep sill, looking across Fifth Avenue to the park. I would have lifted the sash for some fresh air but wasn't sure if it was allowed, so I contented myself with the view as I searched my mind for more memories from the Infant Home. It was frustrating. I knew they were in my brain somewhere, but I couldn't make them materialize.

My sources must have been deep in the stacks; it was twenty minutes before Deborah returned, balancing the volumes in her arms. As she bent to put them on the table, I couldn't help but notice how her breasts fell forward, straining her top.

"Let me know if you need anything else," she said. I blushed, hoping she hadn't caught me looking. Thanking her, I turned to the task at hand, excited at the prospect of pulling the past into the present. I wanted to save Dr. Solomon's article for last, so I started with Hess's pertussis study. I took the heavy volume of bound journals from the pile and cracked its spine.

If I expected to find some Dickensian description of the Hebrew Infant Home in those pages, I quickly saw I'd be disappointed. The sentences read like dry kindling—clinical descriptions of experimental designs, dispassionate recommendations based on results. Dr. Alfred Hess used the word *material* for the children in his study, as if we were guinea pigs or rats. The article pointed out that orphans made particularly good material for medical research, and not just because there were no parents from whom to wrangle consent.

> It is probably also an advantage, from the standpoint
> of comparison, that these institutional children
> belong to the same stratum of society, that they have
> for the most part been reared for a considerable
> period within the same walls, having the same daily
> routine, including similar food and an equal amount
> of outdoor life. These are some of the conditions
> which are insisted on in considering the course of
> experimental infection among laboratory animals,
> but which can rarely be controlled in a study of man.

I remembered how upset I was at being kept in a crib; it seemed now I should have been grateful they didn't keep us in cages. Still, as I continued reading, I saw his pertussis study consisted of little more than extended observation. One hundred days of it, to be exact. The charts in his appendix struck me as cold, the way children were numbered and plotted instead of named, but wasn't that how medical articles were always written? Other than enduring months of boredom, I couldn't see how the children he'd studied were any worse off. Yet his choice of words rankled: "these institutional children," as if we were a different breed or race. I doubted he'd compare his own children to laboratory animals. It made me glad to think that Mildred Solomon had been there to mitigate Dr. Hess's dispassion with a woman's touch.

I was eager now to dispense with Dr. Hess. I flipped hastily through *Scurvy: Past and Present* on my way to the index, planning to turn to the pages where Dr. Solomon was mentioned. Halfway through, my hands froze, the book opened to a black-and-white photograph. It was cropped to show a child's mouth. Just that, not his or her face, only the mouth stretched wide, the camera's lens focused on a bloody sore. Transfixed, I stared at the photograph. It was as if that picture had been pulled from a shoe box of memories that now fell from a high shelf in my mind and spilled open on the table before me.

My fingers trembled. I forgot to breathe. I remembered.

I wasn't one of them, the children in the scurvy study, but from my own crib I watched as they wasted away, joints swelling, sores migrating from lips to arms to legs. One of the nurses charged with supervising their meals began crying one day, spooning some kind of mush into the mouth of a bruised boy too weak to stand, while in the next crib a child was being urged to finish her orange juice.

"It's almost over," another nurse encouraged her. "They'll all be back on orange juice in a few days, you'll see how fast the sores disappear."

"Why make them suffer? Dr. Hess can see already what happens when the children don't get any citrus. Why is it still going on?"

"That's what they're trying to learn from all this—how much is necessary, how much is too much. It's for the good of all children."

"Not this one, " the nurse said, stroking the sunken cheek of the boy she was feeding.

I blinked hard to dissolve the scene from my mind's eye. For pertussis, he'd simply confined the children and observed how the disease progressed—it wasn't as if there was a cure being withheld. But with scurvy? Could it be true that he actually brought on the condition just to test different treatments? I leafed through the book again, catching some passages describing experimental treatments he'd tried: feeding infants dried thyroid glands; infusing blood somehow with citrus and injecting it back into the child. When I was placed in the Infant Home, did anyone know what was going on there? Of course they did. They must have. Here was the book to prove it.

Realizing I would be there all day if I settled in to read, I turned to the index, anxious to discover the extent to which Dr. Solomon had been involved in this. I was relieved to see she was credited with the X-rays, nothing more. I looked at some of the radiographs reproduced in the book, eerie images of children's bodies cut off at the neck and waist, the captions noting the "characteristic beading of the ribs," a characteristic I failed to see, that I began to doubt even existed. Dr. Solomon had said all the children were x-rayed, that it was routine. It wasn't as if it was her experiment. I thought of what Gloria had said, that it must have been hard for her to be a doctor in those days; even today virtually all of the doctors were men. I supposed Mildred Solomon had to do as she was asked. She was only a resident anyway, wasn't that what she'd said? She couldn't have interfered with Dr. Hess's experiments no matter how much she might have wanted to.

I shut the scurvy book and pushed it to the side. I didn't want to believe Mildred Solomon had been part of the work Dr. Hess was doing, but there was the article they wrote together, "Rates of Digestion in Children: A Radiographic Survey." It described the study's objective—the use of barium to X-ray the digestive tract—along with hand-drawn charts and graphs plotting the various settings and exposures. The conclusions seemed simple enough: how much time, in minutes and hours, it took for the barium drink to pass through a child's intestines. I wasn't sure why this information was necessary, but again it seemed Dr. Solomon's role was confined to the radiology. Dr. Hess was the one obsessed with childhood nutrition.

Then I turned the page and saw a picture of one of the radiographs. I felt like I was tipping back in my chair; I actually grabbed at the edge of the table. I had seen this before. A child's body from shoulder to hip, the barium a bright squiggle through the intestines. But how could I have seen it? On the next page it showed a head turned to the side, the radiograph glowing white where the substance coated the tongue and esophagus.

I knew how it tasted before I realized how I knew. Whether or not the image was of me—that seemed too fantastical—I remembered drinking the milk shakes, the chalk gritty in my mouth. I remembered the time I refused to drink it, that tube shoved down my throat. But who had done these things to me? The impressions and sensations were so vague I hesitated to call them memories. There had been a nurse with big hands, chapped and red. She must have been the one who force-fed me that day. Not Dr. Solomon. Mildred Solomon had only done the X-rays, but those I couldn't remember. Reading through the article, I realized why.

Chloroform was administered to render material motionless for the duration of the exposure. No wonder the treatments were obscured in my memory like taillights in the fog. I'd seen chloroform used in the Infirmary at the orphanage—Nurse Dreyer kept some in case she had to give a wriggling child stitches. I could imagine Dr. Solomon hovering over my mask with the dropper. Strapped to the table, I would have been unconscious while she positioned the Coolidge tube and made the exposure.

Weren't the straps enough? I could recall them now, those buckles up and down my arms and legs. I couldn't understand why Dr. Solomon wanted us chloroformed as well. Did it make it easier for her to think of us as material if we couldn't move or talk? Maybe it was just our struggling that she didn't want to see. I thought of the cancer mice, how they must squeak and squirm when the doctors shave their fur to smear cigarette tar on the raw pink skin.

Still, it hadn't been her idea. She was only the coauthor. These experiments were Dr. Hess's work. It was Mildred Solomon who took care of me. Hers was the article I cared about, the article I hoped would tell me what I had been treated for. Perhaps I'd had tonsillitis—it seemed likely that's what had been wrong with me. It wasn't unusual for children who'd had measles or whooping cough to develop tonsillitis. Had I had measles? Most children did in those days. In the confusing rush of images in my mind, a few details stood out as solid and true: Dr. Solomon's smile; how she'd say I was good and brave; the way she looked at me, as if she could see right into my soul. I thought about everything Mildred Solomon had given up to be a doctor. Maybe we did substitute for the children she never had—why else would she have sought a residency in an orphanage? God knows we were all starving for mothers.

With a steadying breath, I opened the article authored solely by Mildred Solomon. The opening paragraphs described the context for her study. She wrote that surgical tonsillectomies, though common, carried risks of infection. Some children reacted negatively to the anesthesia, while others were distressed if the procedure was done with a local anesthetic. She referred to famous cases where X-rays had been used to shrink tumors. She made it sound like a reasonable idea to attempt to treat tonsillitis with X-rays. She couldn't have known at the time what it would do to us. I was sure, now, that's what happened: when I developed tonsillitis, Dr. Solomon attempted to cure me with this innovative, noninvasive technique.

Except, as I continued to read, I learned that wasn't it at all.

Material was chosen expressly for the health and vigor of existing tonsils to exclude the possibility of infection compromising results. For each subject enrolled in the study, the angle of the rays and the number of filters was kept the same in order to isolate results from this initial experiment on the optimal length of exposure. Of the eight subjects enrolled, each was given a calculated increase in exposure (see chart in appendix). The forthcoming paragraphs will describe in detail these calculations and will be of interest primarily to radiologists, as will the illustrations (see figures 1 through 3) of the positioning of the material and the angle of the Coolidge tube. Surgical excision of the tonsils at the conclusion of the study yielded promising results and point unequivocally to the continued need for further experimentation. Summarily, my conclusions were thus: of those subjects receiving the least amount of exposure, the tonsils reflected deterioration inadequate to replace surgery. Of those subjects at the mean, it was the opinion of the surgeon that the tonsils were deteriorated sufficiently to make surgical excision redundant. Of the subject at the extreme, however, burns associated with the penetration of the rays caused irritation and the potential for scarring at the points of entry. While all material developed alopecia as a result of their exposure, it is my opinion that the condition will resolve itself for most of the subjects. In future iterations of this experiment, I would strongly suggest starting with younger children so that a more sustained follow-up period can be accomplished within the controlled conditions of the institution. Unfortunately, these subjects were transferred from the Hebrew Infant Home at the conclusion of the experiment, and thus were unavailable for further observation.

I pushed my chair back. The pulse in my neck throbbed and the corner of my eye twitched. The walls of the reading room closed in on me, dusty and suffocating. I had to get away. On unsteady legs, I went downstairs to the coffee shop. The bitter liquid filled my mouth as the caffeine focused my thoughts.

Mildred Solomon was no better than Dr. Hess. She had used us like lab rats, for no reason other than medical curiosity. But it was more than that, wasn't it? Hadn't she told me this article secured her position in radiology, that she never had to work with children again? Not only wasn't she trying to cure us—she was using us to make her reputation. I felt like one of those girls you read about sometimes in trashy magazines, the ones who are drugged at parties and wake up, minds blank and bodies defiled.

My coffee had turned cold. I went back to the reading room to find the librarian gathering up my sources. "I'm not done with those yet," I said, reclaiming the volumes.

"I'm sorry. You disappeared, so I just assumed." Deborah leaned over to place them back on the table. I'll admit, this time I did stare. I guess I needed some distraction—I even imagined she stared back—not that it worked. As soon as I was alone with Dr. Solomon's article, I read it again, more angry and indignant with every line. This time, though, I examined the chart in the appendix. It showed the cumulative X-ray exposures for each child in the experiment. We weren't named, of course—we were just orphans, "institutional children," expendable, disposable, numbers on a graph. Suddenly it made sense to me, the embroidered number stitched on my collar. What was it? I remembered the endless circles I would trace with my fingertip, following the stitches around and back, over and around again. Tracing the chart with my finger, I found #8 and followed its line.

There I was, the most exposure of them all.

IT FELT AS though I'd been cooped up in that reading room for months. Looking through the window, I saw green treetops and a cloudless sky. I was desperate to be outside, sweltering though the midday heat would be, but there was one more article I'd had the librarian find for me. I pulled the volume closer, figuring I might as well finish what I'd started. I'd certainly never be coming back here again. It was that recent study, published just a couple of years ago. I checked the bibliography—it was Mildred Solomon's tonsil article he cited, but why this Dr. Feldman would have referenced it I couldn't imagine. With a slack hand I lifted the cover. Newly sewn into the binding, the pages of *Modern Oncology* resisted. I had to stand and bring weight into my arms to hold open the pages. I skimmed the article until my eyes caught a sentence. *For women who were exposed to excessive radiation as children, malignancy rates are markedly increased, with tumors becoming evident as these women reach their forties.*

My thoughts flew to the other side of the world, to that Japanese fisherman on the *Lucky Dragon*. I pictured the radioactive ash sifting down on him from miles and miles away, how he brushed the mysterious flakes from his sleeves and went on hauling up his nets. It was only later, safely ashore, that the dying began. With a deep sense of foreboding, I started Dr. Feldman's article from the beginning.

By the time I finished, I was a wreck. I needed to collect myself before leaving the Medical Academy. Deborah wasn't around, so I lifted the counter and went through the stacks, letting myself into the restroom. Staring into the mirror over the sink, I lifted my chin to expose the underside of my jaw. I'd always assumed they were birthmarks, those two shiny patches of skin, round as dimes. Now I recognized them as the faded remnants of an X-ray burn. I kept seeing that chart, as if it were a slide projected over my vision, the line for #8 rising steeply.

I shrugged my shoulder where the armpit had been feeling sore. A wave of anxiety swept over me as I began to put two and two together. I had to check immediately, to reassure myself I was imagining things. Right there, in the staff restroom of the Medical Academy library, I began to unbutton my blouse. I had just reached back to unhook my bra when there was a light knock on the door.

"Are you okay in there?" Deborah asked. "Do you need anything?"

I managed to say I was fine. Worried the lock would give way and she'd see me with my shirt open, I fumbled to close the buttons. I splashed cold water on my cheeks, dried them with a paper towel, checked to see if my features were composed. My eyebrows, at least, hadn't smudged. I opened the door to find her standing there. She didn't step back but held her ground, blocking me in the doorway.

"Have you been crying?" She touched my face, a tender gesture, her fingers cupping my jaw. She gazed at me with such frank, steady eyes I knew she had caught me looking earlier, knew now she'd known all along what it meant. I was so used to pretending to be something I wasn't, it shocked me to be seen for what I was. In that vulnerable moment, that shock of recognition drew me to her. I hardly knew what I was doing as the slight distance between us closed.

I wasn't the one to get things started, but as soon as Deborah bent back my head I leaned into her, sliding my leg between her knees, filling my hand with the weight of her breast. Her lips were softer than I expected, her kiss tentative at first, then deeper as I opened my mouth to her. I didn't know who I was in that moment.

Someone more reckless and daring had taken my place. I could tell she liked this person, liked her very much.

The sound of that stupid bell on her counter brought with it the reality of an impatient medical student lurking on the other side of the wall. She stepped back abruptly, her mouth shiny with my spit. "I'll just go see what he wants." Checking her watch, she said, "The other librarian will be here any minute." Deborah trailed her hand down my arm, reluctant to leave. "Wait here, I'll give you my number. For later."

I did wait, for a minute, trying to convince myself there'd be no harm in it. Then I pictured her, in Miami, asleep in the sun on a lounge chair, a paperback open on her thigh. She was the one I wanted to be with, not some butch librarian. I was so lonely with her away. I hated sleeping by myself, waking up alone, coming home to an empty apartment. I missed those times she'd push aside the coffee table and sway me in her arms to the sound of the radio. The way she'd brush the back of her hand against mine, as if by accident, as we walked down the street. How she'd take my hand in the dark movie theater, our fingers interlaced under the sweaters on our laps.

It worried me to think how far I might have gone, caught up in the moment, if that bell hadn't rung. I couldn't risk waiting, not even to explain why I had to go. I found another way out of the stacks, took a back stair down to the ground floor, located an exit to the street. Outside, I was clobbered by the heat. Short of breath and dripping with sweat, I rushed to the subway, worried Deborah would come running up behind me, pulling at my sleeve, expecting me to be someone I wasn't.

Chapter Seven

EIGHT CHILDREN CROWDED INTO THE TAXICAB: FIVE IN back, two more up front between the driver and a nurse from the Hebrew Infant Home, and Rachel, the smallest, perched on the nurse's lap.

"Does Dr. Solomon know we're leaving?" Rachel asked as the taxi pulled away from the curb.

Looking down at her, the nurse said, "Dr. Solomon's experiment is over. You're almost six years old now—a few of the others already turned six—so you're all being transferred together."

Rachel had been surprised, that morning, to be dressed in street clothes. When she and the other children were taken from the Scurvy Ward, Rachel had looked back at the receding hospital wing, expecting Dr. Solomon to come say good-bye. "Are you sure she doesn't need me anymore?"

"I told you, she's done with you. Done with the lot of you."

Crossing the bridge with its little stone towers, Rachel squinted against the brightness of the sun. She hadn't been outside for months, none of them had. Exposure to sunlight was a variable Dr. Solomon liked to control.

Eventually the taxi turned off Amsterdam Avenue. A brick

building big as a castle seemed to turn the corner with them, its south wing extending halfway down the block, window after window after window. The wrought-iron fence rose in height as the street sank toward Broadway. By the time they pulled over, the stone foundations of the fence were level with the taxi's roof, and Rachel had to tilt her head to see the pointy tops of the iron bars.

"Wait for me here," the nurse told the driver. "I won't be long." She stood Rachel on the curb, pulled out the other two, then opened the back door and herded those children out as well. "Come along, now, and stay together." The nurse led them up some stone steps to an iron gate. It swung open on hinges that made a lonely sound.

They emerged into a vast empty space. No grass or trees. No swings or balls or scattered bats. Just gravel and sun and, on the far side, the fence again with a matching gate onto the next street. Rachel's legs wanted to run across the open space, to see how long it would take to reach that far fence.

"Come along to Reception." Rachel turned toward the big building, then felt a hand on her shoulder. "No, this way." The nurse pointed to a squat structure nearby. As they entered, Rachel heard ringing coming from across the gravel yard, loud as a fire alarm. She turned to see, but the door swung shut, smothering the sound.

The children huddled together in a small lobby. The nurse talked to a woman who said, "I'll go get Mrs. Berger, wait here."

Rachel tugged on the nurse's skirt. "Where are we?"

"This is the Reception House. You'll have to live here for a while before going into the Orphaned Hebrews Home."

Orphaned Hebrews Home. The words resonated in Rachel's memory. They reminded her of the dream in which she had a brother with brown hair and light eyes who taught her the alphabet. But if she was awake and this place was real, maybe the dream was real, too. Rachel was suddenly certain she really did have a brother. Maybe this was his home. She looked for someone to ask when another woman waddled into the lobby.

"Oh, the darlings!"

"Mrs. Berger? I'm from the Hebrew Infant Home."

"Yes, of course, Mr. Grossman told me to expect you." Fannie Berger seemed made of ovals, the circles of her chest and the roundness of her hips separated by a thin belt around the waist of her dress. A couple of years ago, widowed and impoverished, she'd come to the Orphaned Hebrews Home to give up her son. By a miracle, Mr. Grossman, the superintendent, was, that very day, interviewing candidates for a position. Even as she signed away her son to the Home, Mr. Grossman hired Fannie Berger as Reception House counselor. Though they shared the same address, her boy lived in the Castle while she was confined to Reception, their time together limited to stolen minutes after school and Sunday afternoon visits. Fannie Berger was left to lavish the affections of a frustrated mother on all of her charges.

Mrs. Berger knelt down and opened her arms, the flesh hanging like a soft hammock from armpit to elbow. "Come here, children, and welcome." She gathered them all, somehow, into the circle of her embrace. When she stood, each of the eight still held some piece of her, her fingers distributed among four of them, a fifth pinching her wrist, the rest with fists full of her skirt. "I'll take them from here."

"And their records?"

"You can leave them with Mable, thank you very much." Fannie surveyed the children clinging to her. "All completely bald?" Rachel looked up. Like the others, she'd been given a knit cap to wear, even though the day was warm. She reached up and pulled it off. A chill passed over her scalp, a little damp with sweat, and Rachel shivered. Fannie stared at her face. "Even the eyebrows?"

"That's what the X-rays did to them, yes. But Dr. Solomon thinks the hair might grow back. For some of them, at least."

"Poor things," Fannie said, shaking her head. "Well, my kittens, at least I don't have to shave your heads, now do I?" It was the task that bothered her most. And these eight, coming from the Infant Home, would be easier in every other respect as well—apparently, they wouldn't even need their tonsils removed. Transfers often went directly up to the Castle, but quarantine in Reception was being required for this group to see which, if any, would recover from their alopecia. Mr. Grossman had already decided to foster out the children whose hair didn't start to grow. All new admissions to the Home were made fun of for their baldy haircuts, but a perpetually bald child would be mercilessly teased.

Fannie Berger brought the children to the second floor of the Reception House. "This is where the girls will sleep," she said, stopping in front of a cozy dormitory. Rachel saw a dozen metal-framed beds and a wall of washstands in a room that was bright from open windows and comfortable from the breeze passing between them. "The boys are just across the hall. The bathroom is here. And this way . . ." Fannie walked awkwardly with the eight children clutching her, but still she didn't shake them off. "This way is our dining room. Come, sit, it's almost lunchtime. Anyone need the bathroom first?" Some of the children did, so she left the rest of them seated on a bench at a long table. Rachel, at the end, was nearest the window. It faced the open gravel space, which was now full of children, the sound of their voices rising up on the dusty air. Rachel watched them running, skipping, shouting. There seemed to be hundreds of them. One hundred *and* one hundred *and* one.

Maybe one of the boys was her brother.

When Fannie returned, Rachel asked, "Mrs. Berger, does Sam live here?"

"There's a lot of boys named Sam here. Sit down," Fannie said, intent on getting lunch ready and served. Mable was now in the kitchen, filling pitchers with water, dumping stewed prunes into bowls, making sandwiches from what was left of last night's dinner.

"My brother, Sam. When I went to the Infant Home, he went someplace else. Is he here?"

"What's your name again, dear?"

"Rachel. Rachel Rabinowitz."

"Sam Rabinowitz?" Fannie stopped and stared at her. She could see no trace of the boy she knew by that name. "How old is your brother, kitten?"

Rachel didn't know how to answer. The last time she'd said her age, she was still four, her brother six. "Nobody told me if I had a birthday. When is my birthday?"

"Never mind, dear, I'll find out. Now eat." The new children were joined for lunch by those already in Reception. Rachel compared those who had come with her to the other boys and girls crowded around the table. Their heads had recently been shaved for lice, so all were bald to some degree, from smooth scalps to transparent stubble to thicker growth that begged for the touch of a palm. It made her feel at home.

Fannie made sure each child got an equal serving from the plates and platters on the table. Mable had poured half-glasses of water, which Fannie topped off and even refilled. She didn't believe in the Home's policy of restricting water. Intended to prevent bed-wetting, she knew it didn't work. Anxiety, loneliness, fear—these were the reasons children woke in wet blankets.

After lunch, the new children were supposed to join the others downstairs in the schoolroom, but Fannie knew that transfer day was exhausting, especially for such little ones. She took them to the dormitories, assigned them beds, and told them to rest. When she looked in on them after her own lunch, eaten with Mable in the Reception House kitchen, they were all asleep.

Fannie got their files and opened Rabinowitz, Rachel. She read a summary of the police report and shook her head. "Poor dear," she muttered. "Such a thing to see." She read the litany of infections at the Infant Home: measles, conjunctivitis, pertussis. There wasn't much detail about the X-rays, just *Enrolled as material in medical research by Dr. Solomon.* Then Fannie saw what she was looking for: *Brother, Samuel Rabinowitz, assigned to Orphaned Hebrews Home.*

"So, it is Vic's friend, Sam." Like every other child, Sam had come through Reception. Fannie wouldn't have remembered him so clearly except he'd become fast friends with her own son. Once Sam finished his quarantine, he'd joined Vic and all the other six- and seven-year-old boys in the M1 dorm. Vic had brought Sam into his circle of friends, sparing him much of the hazing other new admissions suffered. In turn, Sam was quick to raise his fists in Vic's defense.

Fannie shook her head, thinking of Sam and his temper. It was one thing to stand up for yourself—she knew the boys, especially, had to show they were strong—but Sam still hadn't learned to accept the authority of the monitors. Fannie saw how often his cheeks were streaked red from their slaps. "At least now he'll have some family of his own," Fannie said aloud, closing the file and hoping his sister's presence would calm the boy.

Fannie woke the new children from their naps and sent them downstairs with Mable to be seen by the dentist, but Rachel she held back. "Your brother, Sam, he does live here. He comes over after school with my boy, Victor." Fannie lifted her watch from where it was pinned to her chest. "They'll be here after three. That's in one more hour. When you come back from the dentist, your brother, Sam, will be here to meet you."

It was like being told she'd have a circus as a birthday present: impossible to believe but gorgeous to imagine. Memories exploded in Rachel's mind, like the time a photographer took pictures of the children in the Scurvy Ward—pop and flash and the smell of burning. A kitchen table. Cups of tea and a jar of jelly. Piles of buttons. A stripe of sunlight across patterned linoleum. A man's stubbled chin against her cheek. Rachel shuffled through the images for a picture of her brother, but she couldn't remember his face. This worried her more than the scraping of the dentist's tool and the taste of blood in her mouth.

While Rachel waited for the other children to finish with the dentist, she looked around the examination room. There was a chart on the wall made of letters from the alphabet. She got closer to see the tiny letters at the bottom. Beside the chart was a mirror. At first she thought it was someone else's picture, but the image moved with her. She stared for a long time before accepting that the pale, smooth thing reflected there was herself. Rachel knew she was like the other children who'd gotten X-rays, had felt her hairless scalp with her own hand, but it hadn't changed the picture of herself she carried in her mind's eye. From looking in the little mirror that hung above the sink for Papa to shave in, she remembered herself with long hair framing dark eyes. Rachel had been worried she couldn't remember what Sam looked like; now she worried he wouldn't recognize her.

After the dentist, Mable led Rachel upstairs to the dining room. With a hand on Rachel's shoulder, she pushed the child through the doorway. "Here she is, Fannie."

Two boys sat beside each other on the long bench. Fannie was standing, having just set cups of milk and a sandwich in front of each of them. Both boys looked at her, one with bright blue eyes, the other with gray eyes fierce as storm clouds. The storm-cloud eyes swept over Rachel, lingering on her scalp, then slid away. The bright blue eyes looked right at her, lifting at the corners with a smile. Rachel slunk along the wall, gradually drawing closer, trying to decide which boy was her brother.

"Hello, Rachel," said the bright blue boy. She shivered at the sound of his voice. She ran and circled her arms around him, squeezing him tight.

"Oh, Sam, she's a strong one!" the blue-eyed boy said. Rachel looked up at Mrs. Berger, confused.

Her hand on the other boy's shoulder, Fannie said, "This is your brother, Sam." Two years in the orphanage had hardened his eyes from the lightness Rachel remembered. Sam held his little sister's gaze now, his jaw tight, as if it hurt him to look at her. Vic unwrapped Rachel's arms and handed her over to her brother. She slid down the bench and pressed against Sam.

"Come, Vic," Fannie said. Her son followed her into the kitchen. The door swung out after them, then back in, out, in.

Sam lifted his hand to stroke the girl curled up against him, but he couldn't bear to touch her naked scalp. Mrs. Berger had explained how his sister lost her hair from the X-ray treatments, but the sight of her so bald and pale, like a hatchling fallen to the sidewalk, rebuked him. Unlike Rachel, he remembered perfectly the last day they were together. He'd known as he made it that his promise to come for her was an empty one. As weeks, then months, disappeared without anyone reuniting them, he worried for her, knowing no one could calm her the way he could. Even as he learned to negotiate the rules and regulations of the Home, his nights were disturbed by dreams of his mother, his days consumed by anger at his father. The thread connecting him to his sister chafed until he came to resent its persistent burn.

It took all his courage for Sam to put his arms around Rachel and draw her onto his lap. He braced himself for her crying, but it never came, only the scratching of her nails as she clutched at his arms.

"It's okay now, Rachel. I'll watch out for you from now on." He didn't want it to be another empty promise. He frowned, puzzling out how to protect her when she'd be on the girls' side of the Home, in a different class at school, at another table in the dining hall. He imagined her in the play yard, at the mercy of a thousand children who, Sam knew, sniffed out weakness like sharks scenting blood. As orphanage kids rose in rank from inmate to monitor to counselor, each promotion intensified their bullying as they gained the authority to subject others to what they had once endured. His fists clenched at the thought of his sister in their midst.

Sam kissed Rachel's head, ashamed at the way his lip curled back from her clammy scalp. He pushed her off his lap, held her at arm's length, looked her in the eye. "I'll make sure no one ever hurts you again." It was a promise that left no room for softness.

Rachel nodded, but something in his tone scared her. "Who's going to hurt me?" she asked, lower lip trembling.

"No one, Rachel, don't start that now. Here, eat Vic's sandwich." Rachel bit into the soft bread spread with mashed potato. "Listen, Mrs. Berger's the nicest lady in this whole place. And me and Vic, we come by every day on the way back from school. We can't stay long, just one bell. By Study Bell we gotta be back in the Castle or the monitor'll give us standing lessons." Sam finished his milk. "I'll come by after school tomorrow, okay?"

"You're leaving?" Rachel whispered.

"I have to go, but listen, in school they taught us already how to read and write. Me and Vic, we'll teach you everything we learned from second grade so far. School year's almost over, so that's a lot!" He was gratified to see his sister smile.

Vic was in the doorway. They didn't need Fannie to look at her watch for them to know it was time to leave. Like all the children in the Orphaned Hebrews Home, their bodies counted the intervals between bells in heartbeats. Rising Bell. Dressing Bell. Breakfast Bell. School Bell. Lunch Bell. School Bell again, then Yard Bell. Study Bell. Dinner Bell. Club Bell. Washing Bell. Last Bell.

"Bye, Rachel. See ya tomorrow, Ma," Vic said, accepting a quick kiss from his mother.

The boys ran out. As they disappeared, Rachel dashed to the window, crawling onto the sill. She looked out over the yard, nearly empty now. Sam and Vic appeared below her, running across the gravel toward the back of the Castle, where fire escapes zigzagged across the building like shoelaces. They got there just as Rachel heard the sound of a bell. An older boy stood at the door, arms crossed over his chest. As Vic and Sam reached for the handle, the boy's arm flew out. He slapped them each across the face. Vic covered his cheek with his hand and, head low, entered the building. Sam kept his chin up, stared at the boy, then followed his friend. Even though the sound of the slaps didn't carry to the window, Rachel covered her ears with her hands.

That night, Rachel whimpered in her bed. Mrs. Berger came into the dorm, her braid unpinned and swishing down the back of her nightgown. She sat on the edge of Rachel's bed, the little girl curled around the warmth of her body.

"Hush now, kitten," Fannie Berger murmured, stroking Rachel's back until she fell asleep.

LIFE IN THE Reception House fell into a comforting rhythm. Meals were taken in the dining room, Fannie Berger clucking over the meager portions sent from the Castle's huge kitchens. Mable took the Reception children outside to play, but only when the Home children were at school and the yard was empty. In the afternoons, a counselor who was taking college classes came to give the older children lessons so they didn't fall behind their grade. In the schoolroom, Rachel crept close as they read out loud or recited multiplication tables, attracted to the sound of learning. Most days, Sam and Vic stopped in after school. Rachel sat by Sam while he ate whatever Mrs. Berger had managed to set aside for the boys. Between them they practiced the alphabet and counting until Rachel could write the letters from *A* to *Z* and numbers up to a thousand.

Sundays, during visiting hours, Vic and Sam spent the whole afternoon in Reception. The boys took books from the schoolroom shelves and showed Rachel how the letters combined to form words. Vic always had a smile for Rachel, and she liked it when his bright blue eyes were on her. With Sam, she wanted to be pressed up against him, but the way he looked at her made her feel a little afraid, so she settled for the hug that ended each visit.

After a month, there was no evidence that any of the children from Dr. Solomon's experiment were recovering from the alopecia. One by one, they disappeared from Reception, placed in foster homes. But Rachel had just been reunited with her brother, and Fannie was against separating them. Finding a foster home for both children, however—one of them a willful eight-year-old boy—would be next to impossible. Fannie knew there was a lot Sam hated about the Home, but he was like a brother to Vic now, and she didn't want to see him go.

"Let her stay," Mrs. Berger suggested to the superintendent. "She can spend the rest of the summer in Reception and go into the Home after Labor Day. If her hair doesn't grow back by then, maybe the board could buy her a wig." Mr. Grossman wasn't a man to make exceptions, but it was difficult to find counselors willing to work for the wages the orphanage paid. To keep Fannie Berger happy, he agreed.

Summer settled over Manhattan. With school out and windows open, the children's voices rose from the gravel yard on shimmers of heat. If they weren't practicing with the marching band or deeply involved in a game of baseball, Sam and Vic spent long stretches of the day at Reception. Sam became easier around Rachel. He smiled when she showed how she could read words for herself, and when she held out her hands twisted with string, he cat's cradled with her—as long as no boys were looking. One Sunday afternoon late in July, Mrs. Berger took the two boys and Rachel for a picnic in Riverside Park. When Rachel imitated Vic in calling her Ma, Fannie didn't correct the girl.

Sam and Vic were having their turn at summer camp when a new girl was admitted to Reception. Rachel, who followed Mrs. Berger like a gosling, saw her brought in. "This is Amelia," the agency lady said, her hand on the girl's shoulder. "She just lost both of her parents in that ferry accident in the East River. All of her relatives are somewhere in Austria." The lady's hand moved from Amelia's shoulder to her hair. "What a shame it will be to lose this, won't it? I hardly think it's ever been cut." The girl's hair cascaded down her back in thick swirls, little eddies around her temples. It was deeply red; where the light touched it, Rachel could see the strands sparkle with gold and garnet.

"Such a beauty," Fannie said, lifting the girl's delicate chin. Amelia's face was a fine oval, her amber eyes rimmed with fluttering lashes. Rachel's eyes followed the hand from Amelia's chin up to Mrs. Berger's face, which was soft with feeling. Rachel sensed the flow of Fannie's affection shift to this new girl with her pretty face and beautiful hair. Mrs. Berger had never called Rachel a beauty—she was always "my poor kitten." Rachel realized it was pity, not love, Mrs. Berger felt for her. Suddenly she understood why Sam's eyes slid sideways when he looked at her. Compared to this new girl, Rachel was ugly, damaged, unlovable.

Rachel's lungs tightened so she couldn't breathe. Her lower lip trembled. She watched, helpless, as her hand, controlled by an impulse of its own, reached for Amelia's hair. Grabbing, the hand pulled, hard. Amelia cried out.

"Rachel, I'm ashamed of you!" Mrs. Berger slapped Rachel's fingers. "Go to the playroom, now."

Rachel slunk away. In the playroom she sulked, rubbing the back of her hand. It didn't matter, though. By dinner, Amelia's beautiful hair would have been swept up from the floor, her scalp showing pale after the shave Mrs. Berger was giving her right now. The thought of a broom pushing that red hair across the floor made Rachel smile. She took her favorite puzzle from a shelf. By the time the children were called in for dinner, she'd solved it twice.

At dinner, Amelia was dressed in the same institutional clothes as the rest of the children. She'd been stripped and scrubbed, her teeth examined and a tonsillectomy scheduled. But, among the children whose heads had been recently shaved, Amelia's hair remained, excessive and resplendent.

"I just couldn't do it," Fannie explained to Mable. "Such beautiful hair! I called up to the office and I told Mr. Grossman, I said I can't cut off this girl's hair. I promised I checked her head for lice, I didn't see one nit. So I asked him please, don't make me do it. Both parents dead in that terrible accident, and from a good family, but no relatives in America to take her. Enough already, I said, not her hair, too."

Mable shook her head. "What you get away with, Fannie."

Fannie looked at Amelia spooning soup into her mouth across the table. "Sometimes you gotta be a person, Mable."

"Sometimes *you* do," Mable muttered.

That night in the girl's dorm, Rachel heard Amelia crying and the sound made her glad. Then Mrs. Berger came into the room and settled her weight on the edge of Amelia's bed.

"It's all right, my beautiful girl, don't cry." Amelia circled her arms around the woman's waist and sobbed. Fannie ran her hands over the girl's hair until she was calm and breathing quietly. Rachel watched, resentful. Even the blue moonlight sought out the ruby threads in Amelia's hair. Rachel covered her scalp with the thin summer blanket and squeezed her hands together, pretending she wasn't alone.

ON THE MORNING of Labor Day, Fannie Berger was exasperated. Mr. Grossman had decided that every child in Reception who'd had at least two weeks of quarantine and a doctor's clearance would go over to the Castle that day to be ready for the start of school tomorrow. Fannie was run off her feet getting them all packed and prepared.

"Where's your wig gotten to now, Rachel?" Fannie had been so pleased to present it to the girl, but Rachel refused to wear the thing. She hated how the coarse brown hair sprouted from the scratchy cap, how it made her scalp itch and sweat drip behind her ears. She kept taking it off and hiding it behind playroom shelves or in kitchen cabinets. Fannie finally found it under a radiator, dusty and tangled.

"I'm tired of putting this back on your head." Fannie slapped the wig against her thigh to shake off the dust. "You want to go to the Home looking like a boiled egg? Fine. But wait until you're out of Reception to lose it again." She shoved the matted thing into Rachel's hand. Amelia, on line behind her, snickered.

"Now, children, are we ready? Your cases are all labeled?" Fannie surveyed the line, four girls and half a dozen boys, a small cardboard suitcase containing a change of clothes beside each one. "I'm taking you out at playtime and giving the girls to Miss Stember, since you're all going into F1. Boys, after I leave the girls in the yard, I'll take you to your counselors. Your cases will be under your beds when you go up to your dormitories."

"How will they get there?" Rachel asked.

"Enough with the questions. Just do as the monitors tell you. Now, are we ready? Follow me, children." Rachel held back, stuffing the wig into the case on which were stenciled the letters of the alphabet that spelled her name. She caught up to the end of the line. Even without the wig, Rachel didn't stand out so much from the rest of the group with their recently shaved heads. Compared to Amelia, though, Rachel couldn't shake the idea that she did, indeed, look like a boiled egg. She kept as far from the luxuriant hair as possible.

The children trailed Fannie down the stairs and through the door to the gravel yard where they had previously played only when no one else was out. Now, the entire expanse was crawling with children and the air was thick with the dust they kicked up. The Orphaned Hebrews Home was at capacity, and it seemed that every one of its thousand inmates was playing outside.

Fannie led the children across the yard to the only adult woman in sight. Miss Stember was leaning against a brick wall in the striped shade of a fire escape, scuffed and dusty shoes peeking out from under the hem of her creased linen dress. To the youngest children she was known as "Ma," though Fannie knew Millie Stember was just twenty-two.

"Are these the new girls for F1, then?" Miss Stember squinted as she stepped away from the wall and into the sunlight.

"Amelia, Sarah, Tess, and that one is Rachel." Fannie gestured to each in turn.

"My, aren't you a lovely girl." Miss Stember lifted a hank of Amelia's hair and looked questioningly at Fannie. "No baldy for her?"

"I got Mr. Grossman's permission to leave it. I just couldn't cut off such a beautiful head of hair."

"And is that one of the X-ray children? I thought they were all fostered out." Millie Stember gazed down at the top of Rachel's head.

"The rest of them were, but this one has a brother here, my boy Vic's friend, Sam. You remember him from last year?"

"Of course! I can't believe they're moving up to M2 already. I'll take the girls over to their monitor. They can play until Lunch Bell."

"Thank you, Millie, I have to find three different counselors for the boys. You'll be good girls, won't you, kittens? Now, boys, follow me." Mrs. Berger turned and crossed the yard.

"Come along, girls," Miss Stember said. They made their way across the graveled expanse, occasionally bumped by children chasing each other. They approached a girl with a wild tangle of black curls cut blunt across her neck.

"Naomi, you're the new F1 monitor, aren't you?"

"You bet, since the day I moved up to F2," the girl said. Naomi was only eight years old, but she was tall for her age. Her blouse and skirt were the same as any other uniform in the yard, but little things made her unique: a turned-up collar, an open button at the neck, a belt buckled over the untucked blouse.

"These are some new girls from Reception for F1. Can you see they come in at Lunch Bell and find their places?"

"Sure, Ma, you can leave 'em with me." Naomi looked over the group while Miss Stember retreated to her slice of shade. Rachel waited for the cooing over Amelia's hair that seemed to follow every introduction. Instead, Naomi said, "Which one of you is Sam's sister?"

"I am," Rachel said.

"All right, girls, go on and get a run in." Amelia took the hands of Tess and Sarah and skipped off across the gravel. "You stick with me, Rachel." Naomi dropped a hand onto the girl's shoulder. It felt heavy and warm. "Sam and Vic came by, asked me to keep an eye on you. Are you a troublemaker or something?" Naomi turned down her mouth, acting stern, but her smiling eyes told Rachel she was joking.

"I won't make any trouble."

"Well, I hope you make some, or I won't believe you're Sam's sister." Naomi lifted her hand to Rachel's scalp in the same gesture she'd have used to muss a kid's hair. Rachel shrank down, then eased back up as she sensed Naomi's intention. "Here, have a catch." Naomi pulled a kind of ball from her pocket, made of crushed newspaper wrapped around a stone and tied with string. She tossed it to Rachel, who stumbled back to catch it. Back and forth it went, arcing through the space between them.

Across the play yard, a counselor's voice, high and penetrating, called out two long syllables, the vowels stretched to breaking: "A-a-a-a-l Sti-i-i-i-l." As the sound carried, the cry of All Still was taken up and repeated by the monitors. As the drawn-out words curled into eardrums, they seemed to have a magical effect on each listener, freezing the muscles. Naomi pushed the makeshift ball into her pocket and kept her hands there. Moving only her eyes and lips, she whispered urgently, "Don't move." Rachel did as she was told.

No one told Amelia what to do when she heard the cry of All Still. Over the din of the playing children, she'd barely distinguished the words. She was still skipping, the sound of gravel scuffed beneath her shoes suddenly audible, when an older girl stepped up and slapped her across the face. Amelia's eyes spilled tears as a red mark bloomed on her cheek. Just then, a bell rang, breaking the spell. All the children turned, moving like a school of fish toward the Castle and funneling through its doors.

Rachel stayed close to Naomi, keeping her in sight as she was carried along by the flow of children down a staircase and into the dining hall. It was a vast space, the ceiling held up by metal columns dotted with rivets. Sun filtered in through small windows high on the walls. A maze of long tables and benches somehow accommodated all the children who'd been crowded in the play yard. Rachel followed Naomi to a table and clambered onto the bench. Meals were supposed to be eaten in silence, but the collective whoosh of whispers gave the room a seaside sound. Monitors grabbed food from the platters first then passed them around their tables. Most children quickly devoured whatever was apportioned to their plates, hoping for seconds.

Rachel ate slowly. She was entranced by the rye bread, soft inside with a chewy crust, and she let the vegetable pie and stewed peaches languish. The girl to Rachel's left dove in with her fork, stuffing the peaches into her mouth until Naomi noticed, reached across the table, and gave her a hard pinch on the arm. Rachel pushed the rest of the bread into her cheek and quickly ate what was left on her plate.

A thousand children were seated and served, fed and finished, in half an hour. Still silent except for the hiss of whispers, the tables emptied two at a time in a pattern everyone seemed to have always known. Groups of boys and girls, led by their monitors, filed out of the dining hall. Rachel saw they would be going past Sam, who was sitting with Vic at the M2 table. Ahead of her, Rachel saw Sam drop his slice of rye bread into Naomi's pocket. Rachel hadn't seen Sam since he'd returned from camp and she wanted say hello. She reached out for him but he drew back and turned away, leaving her fingers to brush across his shoulders.

Rachel followed her group up two flights of stairs, down a wide corridor, and into the F1 dormitory. Huge windows were open on both sides, drawing in as much of the warm September air as possible. Most of the girls lined up for the sinks and the toilets, but Naomi pulled Rachel, Amelia, and the two other new girls aside.

"I'll show you your beds," she said, her words muffled by the bread in her mouth. One hundred iron bed frames stretched along the sides and down the middle of the dormitory. Each was made up identically, cotton blanket carefully tucked, pillow centered, towel over the footboard. Under each bed was a cardboard case. Walking along the rows, they stopped at a bed without a towel.

"Looks like this is yours," Naomi said to Tess. "There's your case. Take a new towel when you go to the lavatory, then come back here to hang it up. You'll use it for a week, then they all go in the laundry and you get a new one. Underwear goes in the laundry every day, blouses twice a week, skirts once. Let me know when things start to get too small, I'll tell the counselor you need a new size. Same goes for shoes. In the winter you'll each get a coat and stockings. You all hear this?" Naomi turned to the three girls waiting behind her. They nodded. "Okay, you sit here a minute."

Tess was left sitting alone while Naomi led Amelia, then Sarah, and finally Rachel to their places. Rachel sat for a minute on the bed Naomi said was hers.

"If you don't wet the bed at night, you'll get to keep the mattress," Naomi told her, sitting beside Rachel and swinging her legs. "If you pee, though, they'll take it away and just fold some blankets over the wires. You don't wet your bed, do you?" Rachel shook her head no. "Good. One less thing to get you picked on. Say, don't you have a wig?"

"I do but I hate it. I put it in my case."

"Sure you don't wanna wear it?" Naomi kicked at the cardboard under the bed with her heel.

"It itches and it's ugly. Mrs. Berger says I look like a boiled egg without it, but I can't stand it."

"A boiled egg?" Naomi laughed, then looked thoughtfully at Rachel's scalp. "They're bound to call you something. You could do a lot worse. Listen, if anyone bothers you more'n just calling you names, you come to me. Sam told me to watch out for you special." Rachel thought of the slice of bread in Naomi's pocket.

A bell rang. Naomi jumped up. "Come on, you still gotta wash up."

Rachel stood, then looked around. "How can I tell which bed is mine?"

"You'll get to know soon enough. For now, look, you're in the middle row, facing west, see how the sun's coming in? So just count." They hurried down the row toward the lavatory, Naomi gesturing for the other new girls to follow her. Rachel tapped the corner of each bed they passed. Nineteen. She repeated it to herself as she stood at one of the sinks, above which was a long shelf of cups, each labeled with a name and containing a toothbrush.

Rachel heard a flush and turned around. There was a row of toilets out in the open, some with girls perched on them, others with the seat up. A girl finished; as she stood, underwear disappearing under her skirt, the seat flipped up and the toilet flushed automatically. The next girl pulled the seat down, then sat. Rachel took her turn, and when she finished, she found if she didn't stand fast enough the spring-hinged seat nearly pushed her off. She took a towel from the laundry cart, washed up, then ran back into the dorm, counting to nineteen, to hang it over her bed. Racing to catch up with the last of the girls, she followed Naomi out of the dormitory.

"You'll have to be faster than that once school starts tomorrow," Naomi whispered. "You've only got an hour to come in for lunch, get cleaned up in the dorm, and get back to your classroom. But today's a holiday, so now you're gonna sit out on the fire escapes and watch the marching band practice."

"You're not staying?"

"I'm in the color guard! Gotta go." Naomi rushed down the crowded corridor. Then she turned and shouted back, "See ya later, Egg!"

Rachel was stunned by the betrayal. She saw Amelia, the red mark fading from her cheek, smirk and whisper to the girls near her. When Rachel got closer, Amelia said, "Don't fall off the fire escape and crack your head, I mean, your egg!" She led the girls in a chorus of giggles. Rachel vowed to always hate her.

The afternoon was long and hot. The marching band moved in rows across the dusty yard. Then Study Bell rang, and the girls of F1 shuffled back into the dormitory for a quiet hour. Rachel dozed on her bed, head heavy from the sun and heat. The Dinner Bell jarred her from sleep. Rachel's stomach growled as platters of thinly sliced beef and bowls of carrots and loaves of bread landed on the table. This time, she shoved everything from her plate into her mouth as fast as she could, swallowing almost before the meat was chewed. For dessert there were stewed prunes. Rachel curled her arm around her bowl so she could spoon them slowly into her mouth, savoring their sweetness.

After all the dinners had been eaten, the children dispersed, older ones going to the library or to a club meeting, the youngest back to their dormitories. For Rachel's group, the bell after dinner meant getting ready for bed, even though the sun was still high. Rachel, having washed her hands and face and brushed her teeth and changed into her nightgown, lined up for inspection. The monitors, though only eight or nine years old themselves, prowled the rows of younger girls like drill sergeants, inspecting outstretched hands for clean nails. Naomi stopped in front of Rachel.

"Show me your teeth!" she demanded, and Rachel bared her teeth in an exaggerated smile.

"Now stand on one foot!" Rachel did as she was told, swaying slightly.

"Okay, put your foot down, Egg." Naomi gave her a wink. Rachel remembered what Naomi had said, that they were bound to call her something. Egg wasn't so bad. Even though the girls down the row giggled, Rachel lifted her chin and winked back at Naomi. A bell rang. "Lights out, better hurry!" The girls, released from their inspection, scurried to find their beds. After the quiet routine of the Reception House, her first day in the Castle had been stimulating to the point of exhaustion. Despite the snuffles and whispers and coughs of a hundred girls, Rachel soon fell asleep.

The next day, Rachel found herself awake even before the Rising Bell, her head swirling with thoughts of school. Jostled and jostling, she washed and dressed and bolted breakfast. The elementary school was turned to face Broadway, but its back was to the Castle. While children from the Harlem neighborhood held parents' hands to negotiate sidewalks and cross streets, Rachel and the others from the Home simply crossed the yard, an orphan army five hundred strong. Rachel was so excited to finally go to school herself, she skipped across the gravel.

No one had reminded Rachel to wear her wig. In the classroom, she realized her mistake and was afraid of being teased. But the rivalries and alliances so crucial in the orphanage were forgotten when the children went out into the world—even that portion of the world only a stone's throw away. Mutual defense was the sworn duty of every Home child. The first time a neighborhood boy laughed at Rachel's bald head, he found himself pinched, hard, by every Home child he passed in the hall, including Amelia. Teachers, too, favored the Home children, knowing they could be relied on to finish their homework and show respect. Their report cards were all sent to Mr. Grossman, who took it on himself to mete out any needed discipline.

Sam had already taught Rachel everything first grade had to offer, but she wasn't bored learning the lessons over again. Looking around the room, there was always something to interest her eye, and her hands loved the materials of school. Scratched wooden desks. Worn pages of books. Chalk and slate for learning to write that was replaced in later grades with paper, ink, and fountain pen.

For the next six years, Rachel would hardly ever leave the two city blocks that encompassed both the elementary school and the Home. Even the transition to junior high would be circumscribed, Rachel one among a herd of Home children filing down Amsterdam Avenue to the nearest school. Only in high school did they begin to disperse, fare for the streetcar dispensed by the Home as orphaned adolescents fanned out across the city to pursue various courses: secretarial, industrial, college preparatory, nursing. Rachel would stay in the F1 dorm until she turned eight, then move up to F2, F3, F4, F5, each dormitory identical, different counselors but the same monitors, bossy girls perpetually two years older.

Day to day, week to week, season to season, the routine of the Orphaned Hebrews Home followed the strict rhythm ringing through the building. Rising Bell. Dressing Bell. Breakfast Bell. School Bell. Lunch Bell. School Bell again, then Yard Bell. Study Bell. Dinner Bell. Club Bell. Washing Bell. Last Bell. On Saturdays there was synagogue led by Mr. Grossman, then marching band or baseball. On Sundays they had visiting hours, which Rachel spent in Reception with Sam and Vic. In summer, each child had a much anticipated turn at camp while those in the city crowded onto fire escapes to watch outdoor movies projected against the side of the Castle. Each autumn brought the start of a new school year. In winter, the occasional blizzard snowed them in. In spring, there was Passover dinner and a dance to celebrate Purim.

Thus years could lapse, and did.

Chapter Eight

I HURRIED AWAY FROM THE MEDICAL LIBRARY, MY MEMORY still fragmented by the articles I'd read, my heart still racing from kissing that librarian. Scurrying down to the subway, I hesitated. The last place I wanted to go was our empty apartment. I wasn't prepared, now, to confront the suspicious soreness in my chest, yet I needed to distract my mind from running wild with fatalistic scenarios. I decided to stay on the Lexington line until Grand Central, where I transferred to the Broadway, drawn back to the place I hadn't called home in decades.

Climbing up from the subway, the heat rose with every step I took. Starting up the steep block, I lifted my head and looked around. The apartment buildings across the street seemed unfamiliar. How many years had it been, I wondered, since I'd last come to the Orphaned Hebrews Home?

The stone wall rose above my head. There was a break in it where steps led up to the yard. I reached for the gate, hoping it would swing open, but my hand groped at nothing. The gate had been removed. Only the iron hinges were still there, embedded in limestone, a relic of times past when they'd locked us in at night.

They gave me a strange feeling, those hinges, like I'd seen them someplace else.

I looked across the gravel yard. Hot and empty, it seemed too small to have once held the hundreds of us who stirred up dust with our running feet. I gazed up at the Castle. From the back it looked as solid and intimidating as ever. Instead of children's voices, though, construction noise drifted down from the building. I tried to get closer, to see what the commotion was, but a fence had been unrolled between the yard and the rest of the property. Turning to the Reception House, I saw that it was gone, dismantled, its foundation a stockpile for bricks and pipes and salvage.

Examining the Castle more carefully, I noticed the iron ornaments were missing from its roofline, gutters swung loose from the building, fire escapes had been torn off. I realized with a shock that it was being torn down. I knew the Home had been emptied before the war, the remaining orphans transferred to other institutions or siphoned off through the agency to foster homes. I'd always thought the Castle, though, would stand forever.

I went back through the gap in the wall to the sidewalk and made my way up to Amsterdam Avenue. Rounding the corner, I was brought up short by what I saw. The mansard roof had been knocked in, leaving a yawning hollow where the clock tower used to loom. Windows were broken, glass shards reflecting sunlight at crazy angles. The double oak doors had been wrenched away. Just the brick facade stood, like a bombed-out building. The noise I'd heard came from men swarming over the structure, dropping pieces of steel, tossing bricks, stepping on broken glass. I stood by the missing front gate, mesmerized by the destruction until a worker noticed me standing there. He came toward me,

hair caked in dust, taking advantage of the break to light a cigarette on his way.

"Hey, lady, you can't be hanging around here, we're gonna start
up the ball again soon as we clear some salvage outta the way." He
pointed up at a wrecking ball hanging silent from a crane. I didn't
move.

He exhaled a deep drag, apparently in no particular hurry to
get back to his crew. The man cast a curious eye over me. "Everything all right, ma'am?"

"When did this happen?"

"This job? We been at this about a year now. It's built like
a fortress, this thing. Tearing it down to make a park, but who
knows how much longer it's gonna take. They're hauling most of
the rubble down to the Battery for fill, but there's some valuable
salvage in there, you know? Copper's not what it was during the
war, but it's still worth pulling the gutters and plumbing for scrap.
And me, well, I can't resist some of the flourishes. There's these
balustrades in white marble, beautiful stone. They're a bitch—
excuse me, ma'am—to haul, and I can only keep what I can get
out before they start up the ball again. So." He took a last drag and
stepped on the smoldering butt. "I gotta get back to it, and you
better step back."

"Can't I watch?" My eyes were on the sky where the clock face
used to be. "I lived here, back in the twenties. This used to be my
home."

"You don't say. When I started on the job the place was empty,
just some old guy rattling around there all alone. Tried to chase
us out when we first scouted the building to place our bid. And I
knew the army'd used it as a barracks for a while. But yeah, once

we got in there, saw all those toilets, I mean, I never seen so many toilets in my life, and the rows of sinks, and those kitchens? The old guy, he told us all about it, said he'd been caretaker since it was an orphanage." The man stared at me. "So, you an orphan, then?"

The question sounded strange in the present tense. I used to think that *orphaned* was something I'd been as a child and since outgrown. It occurred to me, though, that was exactly how I'd been feeling all summer.

"I guess anyone alone in the world's an orphan," I said.

A whistle blew. "They're starting up the ball. Better cross the street if you want to watch it." He hurried away.

I crossed Amsterdam to the Avenue. The sun was beating down; I hid from it under a ginkgo tree that shaded a bench facing the Castle. There was a low rumble and a belch of smoke as the crane came to life. The smell of diesel fuel wafted across the street. The ball began to swing like a hypnotist's watch, knocking at the building as if asking to be let in. Each knock brought a cascade of brick and dust, exposing steel and splintering wood. The ball swung away, but the Castle hardly seemed to get smaller. I sat in the shade as the wind brought specks of the orphanage into my lungs. I felt as if I were living in two time periods simultaneously, images from the past projected onto my view of the present. There was the Castle, coming down brick by brick. And there I was, my first day in Reception, clinging to Mrs. Berger's skirt. Or there, in the dorm, counting down the rows to find my bed. Or there, in the yard, having a catch.

As I watched the Castle give up its bricks to the wrecking ball, it occurred to me where I'd seen those hinges before. At least, what they reminded me of. It was at some small gallery in the Village, an exhibit of photographs taken in Europe before the war. I couldn't recall the photographer's name, but I remembered standing, fascinated, in front of that one picture. Black and white, large format, close-up. Huge hinges in stone walls, the print shining silver where sunlight touched metal. The card beside the frame read: JEWISH GHETTO, VENICE, ITALY. The iron gates that once creaked shut each night had been gone since Napoleon, but the hinges were embedded too deep to extract. The hinges were all the photographer needed to evoke the plight of the Venetian Jews, locked in from sunset to sunrise. Just like we were in the Home.

Wasn't it Pieter Stuyvesant who said that first boatload of Jews could stay in New Amsterdam only as long as they took care of their own and asked for nothing? So take care of ourselves we did. They always told us how lucky we were to grow up in the Orphaned Hebrews Home, schooling us in its illustrious history. Didn't we weather the blizzard of 1888, kept warm by our own stockpile of coal, fed from the ovens of our own bakery? And while children all over the city succumbed to cholera at the turn of the century, didn't we emerge unscathed, the city's water filtered before it reached our lips? After the Great War, people fell to influenza by the tens of thousands, but in the Home not a single child died. No matter how impressive, though, our Home was a kind of ghetto, the scrape of metal as the gates swung shut the same sound in Manhattan as in Venice.

I went once, during nursing school, to help vaccinate children in a state orphanage. The conditions were so bleak they made me ill. I hadn't realized, before, what advantages our wealthy donors had bought us: our teeth straightened, our health tended, our clothes washed, our educations secured, our stomachs filled. But did that mean they had the right to experiment on us, as Dr. Solomon had on me? I supposed it seemed fair—the use of our bodies in exchange for the keeping of them. All my life, I thought the poison of those X-rays was the price I'd paid to be cured of some disease. Now that I knew the truth, it seemed the cost of my childhood had been borrowed from usurers, interest compounding over the decades, the final tally perhaps too dear to pay.

The shade was retreating with the shifting sun. I couldn't sit on that bench forever. With a heavy sigh, I resigned myself to going home. I crossed Amsterdam, returned the foreman's salute, turned the corner. As I followed the sloping street down to the Broadway line, I made a last survey of the Castle. Missing doors, broken glass, dangling gutters. Sky where there should have been a clock. The empty yard. The gateless hinges.

I MANAGED, ON the long train ride home, to talk myself out of the inevitability of dropping dead from radiation cancer. Dr. Feldman's article had sent my imagination leaping to conclusions. I was a nurse, for heaven's sake. What I needed was a medical opinion, not the fevered suppositions of an addled brain. I'd seen in the author's note that Dr. Feldman practiced in Manhattan, so the first thing I did, after grabbing the mail and letting myself into the apartment, was look up Dr. Feldman's number in the city directory.

"Let me see what I have for you." The woman's tone over the telephone—reminiscent of Gloria's terse superiority—led me to assume she was Dr. Feldman's nurse and not just his receptionist. I heard the rustle of turning pages. "His first openings are in September."

My casual attitude crumbled. "I couldn't possibly wait until next month."

"I can give you the names of some other oncologists who might be able to see you sooner."

"It has to be Doctor Feldman. I was just reading his article, about the long-term effects of childhood X-rays?" I needed this nurse to realize I wasn't an ordinary patient.

"Yes, I'm familiar with his work." She wasn't prepared to give; I had to offer something more personal.

"In the article, he cited an experimental study that was done at the Hebrew Infant Home by Dr. Solomon." I paused for dramatic effect—if this didn't sway her, I was afraid I'd never get the appointment. "I was one of the orphans in that study. I thought Dr. Feldman would be interested in evaluating me as soon as possible. For his work."

The silence on the line lasted long enough for the imperious nurse to decide her employer's interest would, indeed, be piqued by my case. "He's in surgery tomorrow morning and booked for the rest of the day, but there's been a cancellation day after tomorrow. Can you be here at ten o'clock?"

"I'm off that day, so that's fine. I'll be there."

"We'll see you then." The receiver clicked as Dr. Feldman's nurse hung up. I kept the phone in my hand, ready to place a call to Florida. I was desperate to hear her voice, never mind the charges, but I needed to compose myself first. I wanted to tell her about Mildred Solomon, but that would lead to the Infant Home and the experiments, the medical library and Dr. Feldman's article. I hesitated, adding up all the minutes it would take to tell her the whole story. Maybe I could cut it short, stop at Dr. Solomon arriving on Fifth?

I hadn't realized the line was still open until the operator spoke up, asking if I wanted to make another call. I wouldn't say anything about anything, I decided, just be comforted by her voice in my ear. I asked for long-distance, gave the number in Miami, and listened to it ring. No one answered. Out by the pool again, or maybe at the beach? I pictured her gathering seashells on the sand, oblivious to my needing her. I'm not sure how long I stood there before I gave up and put down the receiver.

It was just as well. I didn't want to worry her with my wild speculations—better to wait until after my appointment, when I'd have something definitive to say. I grabbed some leftover tuna salad, reminding myself to stop at the grocer's. Sitting at the kitchen table, I sorted through the mail: a bill from New York Telephone, a statement from her bank, a flyer from the furniture store down the block, and an invitation addressed to me from Mr. and Mrs. Berger of Teaneck, New Jersey. Tearing open the envelope, I saw Vic's son, Larry, was having his bar mitzvah. After three girls, no wonder they were making it a big occasion. They must be inviting everyone they'd ever known to have gotten to my name in their address book—since Vic's mother died, we'd exchanged cards at Rosh Hashanah, but nothing more.

I was stuffing the invitation back into its envelope when I saw Vic had scribbled something on the RSVP. *Hope you can come, too bad Sam couldn't be there.* Nothing about her. If I'd been married, of course my husband would have been included. Vic knew who I lived with, even if he had no idea what it really meant. It was the same at work. The other nurses pitied me for being alone, a spinster, an old maid. It rankled that I couldn't correct them. The lounge echoed with their ceaseless talk about husbands or boyfriends while I swallowed my words, unable to say *I know how you feel, we had a fight last night, too,* or *I'm so excited to get home, it's our anniversary.* They yammered and complained while I feigned interest and shared nothing. When I saw them meet their men on the street, lips turned up for a kiss in front of all the world, I hated them all a little. I might have come to hate myself, too, if I didn't have someone of my own to come home to.

Or maybe Vic did know, or at least suspect, his exclusion an intentional rebuke. The thought made me bitter. I'd send a check with my regrets—that's all they were really after. I'd spare myself suffering through that celebration, the single friend seated with married couples and their boisterous children, odd one out at the round table.

I set up a fan facing the couch and turned on the television, hoping a soap opera would help me pass the time. The program was irritating, all scheming wives and cheating husbands. I began nodding off. I was so tired—tired from remembering, from feeling betrayed, from being afraid. From the heat. From loneliness. No wonder I acted like a character in a paperback and kissed that librarian. I was a drowning woman flailing for anything to keep my head above water. For as long as Deborah's mouth was on mine, I could forget about Dr. Solomon and what she'd done to me. Now it invaded every thought. I imagined myself in the X-ray room, my little body strapped to that table, the radiation penetrating my cells.

It was ridiculously early for bed, but I just wanted this day to be over. I went in to take a shower before putting on my pajamas. Standing naked in front of the bathroom mirror, there was no more avoiding it. I raised my arm above my head and felt that twinge. I'd been skirting it all summer, favoring my other arm or keeping the elbow low when I sprayed on my deodorant. With shaking fingers, I followed the line of muscle down from my armpit and across my chest.

Only a willful act of ignorance could have prevented a nurse from diagnosing a condition so evident. How could I have been so blind? It must have been growing secretly for months, even years. But never having felt it before—the tumor, pinched between my fingers, was big as an acorn—it seemed to me it had manifested overnight, conjured into existence by Dr. Solomon's arrival on Fifth.

I took a sleeping pill to kill the hours until morning. Getting into bed, I tried not to obsess over it, tucked my hands beneath my hips to keep from groping myself. Women had lumps all the time—benign tumors, fluid-filled cysts. I had my appointment; best to put it out of my mind until Dr. Feldman could render his verdict.

There was too much light in the room. I pulled a sleeping mask from my nightstand and settled it over my eyes. Better. Hopefully, the next thing I knew it would be morning and I could set my course for the Old Hebrews Home. I pictured my patients, how helpless they were, how they counted on me to keep them clean and safe, to take away their pain. How would one of them feel— how would Mildred Solomon feel—if I treated her like a labora- tory animal instead of a person? She had a lot to answer for. What would she say, I wondered, when I confronted her with what her experiments had done to me? She'd have to be apologetic; sorry, at least, for not knowing then the harm X-rays could do. They thought radium would be a cure for cancer, not the cause of it. But once she saw how she had damaged me, what choice would she have but contrition?

I was imagining our conversation until I remembered that, at her prescribed dose of morphine, she'd be too incoherent to understand, let alone speak. I still had that vial in my pocketbook from the morphine I'd held back. I would have to hold back more if I wanted to prod her into consciousness. I'd never gone against a prescription before yesterday—even when I knew a doctor was wrong, I always followed orders. The idea of toying with Mildred Solomon's dose gave me a secret sense of power. Instead of counting sheep, I fell asleep figuring out how to adjust her dose to get what I wanted from her. It would be my own little experiment.

Chapter Nine

THE NIGHT BEFORE THE PURIM DANCE, THE GIRLS IN F5 all washed their hair—except, of course, for Rachel. No matter they'd have to sit up late in the under-heated dormitory while it dried, or sleep with pin curls pricking their heads. It was thirty minutes before Last Bell and the monitors hurried them along. Naked under the steaming showers, the prospect of dancing with boys led the adolescent girls to assess one another with a competitive eye. These hundred girls had been showering together and using the toilets in front of each other as far back as any of them could remember. They saw each other change, felt themselves changing. They knew when one's monthlies started, saw when another sprouted hair between her legs, envied those who filled out early, at fourteen or fifteen already with the figures of women.

Rachel, however, seemed barely to have matured: nipples still inverted, hips slim, skin smooth as wax. Unlike Amelia, whose beauty had deepened from oval-faced childhood to round-breasted adolescence. She had become a queen among the F5 girls, casually accepting the tributes of her coterie—messages delivered from boys, extra portions of dessert, homework answers, hair ribbons.

Now legendary in length, Amelia made her hair more alluring by wearing it braided and pinned in a romantic swirl. Most of the girls had their hair bobbed short, the Home's barber encouraging the simple style with magazine pages cellophaned to his wall. But Amelia refused the barber, instead visiting Mrs. Berger every few months for the slightest trim.

Rachel, with her bald scalp and looming eyes, was in a category by herself. Not that she had no friends; there was a companionship of sorts among the misfits, loose alliances that splintered into small subsets of girls in corners of the play yard. Various slurs had been flung at her over the years—mummy, Martian—but only Egg had stuck, repeated so often it had long ago lost its sting. Because Rachel didn't try for any prizes, no one was jealous of her excellent grades. While other girls learned to sew or took up the violin, Rachel spent Club Bell in the Home's library, losing herself in the pages of a book. Her favorites were biographies of courageous explorers; she had no patience for fiction.

Rachel's connection to Sam and Vic, two of the most popular boys in the Home, afforded her some dignity. Vic, clever and outgoing, was involved in every activity and backed by his mother's access to the superintendent. Sam had grown handsome and tall, his storm-cloud eyes threatening to boys and irresistible to girls, lauded star of the baseball team, ready to raise a fist at the slightest challenge.

Naomi had remained an ally. Though Rachel could never be her equal—a monitor's authority depended on her prestige among her peers—Naomi kept a protective eye on Rachel, stepping in with a smack if someone shoved her on the stairs or tossed a handful of gravel at her in the yard. Rachel understood Naomi's protection was funded by Sam's tributes, slices of bread replaced over the years by pilfered coins and stolen magazines, but by demanding nothing from Rachel herself, Naomi seemed more confederate than mercenary.

In the Home, everyone did a thing or no one did, so Rachel also showered the night before the Purim Dance. Near her was a novelty—a girl new to F5, just come over from Reception that morning, the loss of her parents a fresh wound. The girl's baldy haircut and pockmarked cheeks were already drawing insults. At first, she'd thought Rachel was also new and lined up next to her for the showers. Close up, the smooth sheen of Rachel's scalp showed that her hair hadn't simply been shorn. When Rachel hung her towel and stepped under a showerhead, the new girl realized with a thrill she'd spotted something more valuable than an equal: someone worse off than herself.

"Are you some kind of fish? What do you have, scales instead of skin?" She glanced around the shower to gauge the others' reactions. A few were giggling; it had been a long time since their attention had been drawn to Rachel's body. Still, they hesitated to join in.

It was Amelia who picked up the thread. "She's not a fish, she's an Egg, like a lizard's egg. When it hatches, she'll come slithering out from under a rock." The giggles turned into laughter. Amelia approached Rachel, wet hair flowing down her elegant back. "I hope you're not counting on getting asked to dance tomorrow. No boy's going to be interested in you. "

Rachel couldn't hide the blush that colored her neck and cheeks. The new girl, wanting to be accepted by Amelia, joined in. "No boy would want to dance with a hairless freak!"

The monitor watching the showers called Naomi over. She ignored the new girl and grabbed Amelia by the arm, pulling her out from under the shower. "Go dry off."

"I'm not done yet," Amelia said.

Naomi slapped her face. Amelia's friends bowed their heads at her misfortune. The new girl slunk away before she, too, could be struck. "You're done when I say you're done." Naomi shoved a towel at Amelia and pushed her away. Her friends hurried after her, wrapping her in comforting arms. Rachel kept her back to the commotion, grateful and embarrassed.

"Finish up now, girls!" the shower monitor yelled. "One more minute!" They hastily rinsed the soap from their hair. The monitor turned the tap, and the sizzle of a score of showers became a forlorn drip. The girls grabbed their towels and filed back into the dorm, the monitor following.

Rachel, wrapped in a towel, left last. Naomi, too, hung back. Placing a hand on Rachel's shoulder, Naomi said quietly, "Don't listen to that bitch. I think you're real pretty. Always have." Rachel dropped her eyes as a different kind of blush crept up her face. She waited for Naomi to lift her hand before walking away.

At her bed, Rachel dried off quickly and pulled on her nightgown. The shower monitor was pushing the laundry cart through the dormitory. As Rachel held out her towel, the monitor leaned in and whispered, "I'd watch out for Naomi, if I were you. She's not a normal girl. You know what I mean? She's not natural." Rachel looked confused. "Just don't say no one warned you." The monitor grabbed the towel, threw it in the cart, and continued down the row.

Rachel curled up on her mattress and pulled the blanket over her head. She'd heard the accusation leveled before but wasn't sure what it meant. She'd heard it said about girls whose close friendships were intense and dramatic, but Rachel wasn't even sure if Naomi was her friend or just her protector. The way Naomi never seemed afraid of anyone wasn't normal, not at the orphanage. How nice she was to Rachel might seem unnatural to anyone who didn't know Sam paid her for it. But he didn't pay Naomi to tell Rachel she was pretty, did he?

When Naomi made her rounds before Last Bell, telling girls to quiet down, she paused near Rachel's bed. "Night, Egg," she whispered. Rachel, pretending to be asleep, didn't answer.

THE NEXT DAY was infused with excitement for the Purim Dance. The children too young to attend were animated by jealousy; those twelve and up fidgeted through the school day, their minds on the coming evening. Dinner was eaten in fewer minutes than usual and everyone hustled out of the dining hall so preparations could be made for the dance: tables moved, benches stacked, decorations hung.

In their dormitory, the F5 girls spent the hour brushing their hair, trading ribbons, sharing tubes of contraband lipstick, and doing what they could to make their clothes special. Rachel changed into a clean dress and stockings, then pulled her cardboard case from under the bed and studied the wig.

"Why don't you put it on?" It was Tess, whom Rachel numbered among her friends.

"It itches my head, and besides, it hasn't been brushed out in forever."

"Try it on, let me see you."

Rachel reluctantly pulled the wig on her head. It was snug—because she hardly ever wore it, she hadn't been given a new one since F3.

"You look wonderful, Rachel," Tess said. "Here, let me brush it for you." She sat on the bed behind Rachel and began running her brush through the wig's hair, but she tugged too hard and it shifted. "Sorry! You better hold it." Rachel pinched her fingers at the temples and held the wig in place. Tess brushed it until the dark hair shone.

"Doesn't she look swell?" Tess asked Sophie, whose bed was next to Rachel's.

"Let me have a turn," Sophie said. Tess surrendered the brush. "Here, tie this around it." A ribbon appeared and was looped around Rachel's head, a bow knotted at her crown. The girls appraised their work.

"Too bad you don't have eyebrows," Tess said.

"It won't matter with the masks," Sophie said. "No one will know you, Rachel."

When the girls of F5 entered the dining hall later that evening, it was transformed. The space, cleared of tables and benches, seemed to stretch on forever. Strings of colored electric lights were twisted around the poles and swagged between the beams. Platters were piled with buttery hamantaschen; fruit juice mixed with seltzer fizzed in punch bowls.

At the door, members of the Dance Committee handed out masks—sashes of colored fabric decorated with feathers and sequins, oblong holes cut out for eyes. Girls and boys accepted the masks, wrapping them around their faces and tying them behind their heads. With everyone's hair cut by the same barber, virtually all of them brunette and in similar clothes, the simple masks were amazingly effective at blurring identities. Even friends didn't recognize each other until they were up close. They enjoyed the thrill of anonymity, the opportunity to imagine themselves for the night as something other than orphans.

At the front of the room, a stage was set up for the members of the band who had rehearsed dance tunes. When the superintendent mounted the stage, the band director cued the trumpet player, who gave a flourish to catch everyone's attention.

"Welcome to the annual Purim Dance," Mr. Grossman said. "I invite the committee to come forward to make a few announcements."

Five boys made their way onto the stage, Vic stepping up to speak for them. His mask hung untied over his shoulder, and all the girls knew who he was. Widely considered to be the most handsome sixteen-year-old in M6, his romantic attachment to one of the F6 girls had been chronicled in the gossip column of the last Home newsletter—but that didn't stop every other girl from hoping for a dance with him. Sam had helped set up, but since he wasn't on the committee, he stayed on the floor, his back against a wall.

"On behalf of the Dance Committee, welcome!" Vic waited for the round of applause to dissipate. "We're going to have a great time tonight. How do you like the decorations?" More applause and a few whistles. "Our kitchen staff is working late to keep us supplied with punch and pastries, so let's show our appreciation." Another round of applause. "And special thanks to the members of the band who have been rehearsing a great set of songs, and yes, there will be a Charleston!" Claps, whistles, and foot stomping.

"Now, there are a few rules, and if we all follow them, we'll have lots of fun and make all the work our committee has done worth it. No one leaves the dining hall, except to use the facilities. Counselors will be attending both the girls' and boys' bathrooms, so no funny business." A wave of nervous laughter. "All other corridors are off limits. The dance will continue until Last Bell. When you hear it, F4 and M4 will exit first, followed by F5, M5, and F6. And remember, the younger kids are sleeping, so be quiet! M6 boys will stay to help take down the decorations and put all the tables and benches back in place for breakfast."

"Thank you, Victor," Mr. Grossman said. "And thank you, members of the Dance Committee, for all of your hard work in planning this affair." A final wave of applause as the boys stepped down from the stage. The band director lifted his hand, counted a quick four-four time, and the dance began.

With her wig on and the mask around her face, Rachel felt transformed. She milled around with her friends for a while, then thought she recognized Sam from his tight jaw and the set of his shoulders. As she got closer, his gray eyes showed through the holes in his mask.

"Aren't you going to dance with me?" she asked. As he heard his sister's voice, his scowl softened.

"Rachel, is that really you? Vic, here's Rachel. Can you believe it?"

"If someone told me you could look prettier than usual, I wouldn't have believed it if I didn't see it for myself," Vic said. "You better come back and dance with me, Rachel."

Sam took Rachel out just as the band started a fast waltz. Neither of them knew how to dance to it, so they just held hands and twirled and laughed. Rachel enjoyed seeing Sam's smile up close—usually, he was only this happy when the Home's baseball team won a game. By the time the dance ended, Rachel was breathing fast. As the band started a tango, Vic came up and put his hand on Sam's shoulder.

"May I cut in?" he asked, mimicking a movie star.

"Why, of course." Sam gave Rachel's hand to Vic and bowed.

"Madame, may I have this dance?"

"Certainly, sir." Rachel curtsied. Vic lifted her hand up to his shoulder and placed his other hand at her waist, his fingertips pressing into the small of her back. The members of the Dance Committee had asked Millie Stember to give them lessons, and Vic led Rachel across the floor in measured steps. When he spun her in a twirl, she looked around to see who was watching. Amelia, her hair undisguisable, had her eyes on them. Vic kept turning Rachel so she caught only passing flashes of Amelia whispering to a tall boy and pointing in her direction. She knew the other girls must be watching her, too. Rachel smiled, imagining their jealousy. When the dance ended, Rachel's face was flushed, her dark eyes shining through the mask.

"You're a fine dancer, Rachel," Vic said. Bending, he planted a kiss on her cheek. Suddenly awkward, Rachel stumbled a little and let go of his hand.

"See ya later!" Vic headed off toward the refreshment table. Rachel was at a loss for a moment until Tess and Sophie surrounded her.

"He kissed you, we saw it!" Rachel was about to say it was just because Vic was Sam's friend, that he was like a brother to her, but she swallowed the words. She let them think Vic liked her, enjoying, for the first time, their admiration and envy.

Finally, the band started up a Charleston. "Let's dance!" the girls shrieked. Forming a line, they kicked and wobbled their way around the dining hall. The faster they moved, the harder their hearts beat in their chests. Rachel's smile lifted her cheeks until she could feel the fabric of the mask tighten around her face. Afterwards, the girls mobbed the refreshment table, gulping punch and brushing crumbs from their chins.

When the band took a break, many of the girls, Rachel's little group included, went to the bathroom. The din of their talking and laughing echoed from the tiled walls. Jostling in front of the mirror, they removed their masks to splash cool water on their faces. "Here, Rachel!" Tess touched a lipstick to Rachel's mouth, brushing the red cream with her finger. "Take a look!" It was a moment before she found her reflection in the mirror. So this is what it feels like to be pretty, Rachel thought.

Eager for another dance, she urged her friends to hurry up. She wanted to see her brother's smile, hoped Vic would dance with her again. Impatient, she tied the mask around her face and left the girls behind. She took quick steps in the direction of the dining hall.

"There you are." A voice from the side corridor that led to the bakery startled her.

"Me?" she asked. A tall boy stepped out of the shadows. He wasn't wearing a mask. Rachel recognized Marc Grossman, the superintendent's son. He reached for her arm, closing his hand over Rachel's elbow.

"Come with me." He pulled her down the corridor.

Rachel was so used to accepting the authority of teenagers barely older than herself, so trained to line up or be still or move faster, that her body followed pliantly even as her brain sparked with questions. She wanted to ask what was the matter, if she'd done something wrong, if maybe Sam needed her, but she'd been slapped often enough for talking out of turn that she swallowed her words. Past the bakery, an exterior door was tucked into a dark alcove. Rachel pulled back, afraid now that Marc was planning to take her outside. There was no worse trouble a Home child could get into than going out on their own. But he didn't try to open the door. Instead, he shoved her against it so hard and sudden Rachel was stunned.

Marc brought his face close to Rachel's. She saw how his eyebrows met in a fan over the bridge of his nose. "Back at the dance, some of the boys were saying that couldn't be Egg, not with all that pretty hair, but one of the girls told me it was you, so I made a bet with the boys to prove it."

So this was who Amelia had been whispering to. Rachel thought of Naomi's warm hand on her shoulder when she told her, *I think you're real pretty*. Rachel knew now it must have been a lie. She squeezed her eyes shut and lowered her head. She expected Marc to pull off her wig and laugh at her. Instead he pressed his forearm across her collarbone and slid his free hand down Rachel's ribs to her hip. Her bones recoiled from his touch. "To win the bet, I can't take off your wig or your mask." He pushed his knee between her thighs. A tingling sensation spread over Rachel. It made her feel sick. "But I heard your head's not the only place you're bald, isn't that right, Egg? Aren't you bald everywhere?" Marc's hand reached under her dress, snaked under the garters of her stockings and tugged at her bloomers. Rachel gagged on the saliva that filled her mouth.

She tried to push him away now, but he simply leaned in, his height and weight defeating her. Marc's fingers stroked and probed until Rachel felt a pain that so shocked her she screamed.

"Hey, no funny business!" Millie Stember's voice echoed along the corridor.

Marc backed away and shoved his hands into his pockets. Rachel's trembling knees folded.

"No funny business here," Marc said, sauntering into the light and past the counselor.

Millie ran up and pulled the mask down around the girl's neck, knocking the wig askew. "Rachel, not you!" The surprise in Millie's voice made Rachel wonder if she wasn't pretty enough even for this. "Come on, sweetheart, I'll take you up to see the nurse. Can you walk?"

She put her arm around Rachel's waist and lifted her up. It seemed to Rachel she could still feel Marc's hand between her legs. A few girls had gathered at the bright end of the corridor. Seeing who it was emerging from the darkness, one of them ran to get Naomi.

Rachel clung to her old counselor. "Did he get to you?" Millie whispered. Rachel nodded, though she had the feeling she was being asked something more than she knew.

Naomi appeared. "What happened? Did she faint or something?"

"Marc Grossman," Millie began, then remembered herself. "Never mind, Naomi, Rachel will be fine, just go back to the dance. Maybe let her brother know she'll be in the Infirmary."

Millie Stember guided Rachel up three flights of stairs and along a silent hallway. Rachel couldn't seem to catch her breath; by the time they reached the Infirmary, she was pale and faint. Millie called out for the Home's resident nurse, Gladys Dreyer. She came in from her adjoining apartment, hair in curlers, wiping cold cream from her face.

"What's happened?"

"Marc Grossman got to her."

"How bad?"

"I don't know, but she's so shaken up, I assumed the worst."

Nurse Dreyer led Rachel to a bed and sat beside her, close. Her sweet perfume, such an unusual extravagance in the Home, twitched Rachel's nostrils. The nurse took both of Rachel's hands. "Listen to me, dear," Gladys said. "It's very important that you tell me exactly what he did. Do you understand?"

Rachel started shaking, tremors dissipating through her fingertips. Trembling, she faced the nurse. As if listening to someone else's words, she said, "He pushed me against the wall. He put his hand under my dress. He . . . touched me."

"That's all?"

Rachel blinked. "It hurt. I screamed, and Miss Stember heard."

"And you're sure it was just his hand under your dress? He didn't open his pants?"

It occurred to Rachel now what she was being asked, what worse thing could have happened. She felt nauseated. "I'm sure."

"Well, thank goodness for that." Gladys Dreyer addressed herself to Millie. "I'll take care of her from here, you can go on. It sounds like she'll be all right."

Millie stood to leave. "Have you tested him for syphilis yet?"

"Mr. Grossman won't let us, even though I've sent three girls to the hospital for Salvarsan treatment who say it was him."

Millie Stember shook her head. "It's fortunate I came along when I did, Rachel. Promise me you'll stay out of dark corridors from now on."

Rachel tried to say she hadn't wanted to go down that corridor, but Millie was gone. The nurse took Rachel into the adjoining bathroom and started a tub of hot water. From a high cabinet, she took a tin of sweet-smelling bath salts and sprinkled them into the rising steam. "Soak as long as you want, Rachel. I'll have you sleep up here tonight." Leaving a nightgown folded on a stool, she closed the door.

Rachel untied the tear-stained mask from around her neck. Looking at it, she felt foolish for ever believing she was beautiful. Her clothes and the hated wig discarded on the floor, she lowered herself into the tub. At first she felt a sting where Marc had touched her, but it soon went away. Rachel closed her eyes and sank down until water filled her ears, trying to forget. She didn't hear the commotion when Art Bernstein, the M6 counselor, burst into the Infirmary. "Nurse Dreyer, you're wanted in the superintendent's apartment. Marc Grossman has been beaten pretty badly. I think his nose is broken."

"About time." Gladys tied a kerchief over her curlers before grabbing her bag. "All right, let's go."

When Rachel emerged from her bath, the Infirmary was quiet. She found an empty bed and curled up under the blanket. Clasping her hands together, she surrendered herself to sleep.

NAOMI APPEARED EARLY the next morning with a change of clothes. Draping an arm over Rachel's shoulders, Naomi asked how she was feeling.

Rachel shrugged her off. "Okay, I guess. He just. . . ." She hesitated, searching for words. She felt strangely disconnected from what had happened in the corridor. "It wasn't so bad as it could have been. What did you tell Sam?"

"I told him Marc Grossman got to you and you were going up to the Infirmary. He disappeared from the dance right after that. I figured he was coming to see you."

Nurse Dreyer put a tray on Rachel's lap and insisted she eat the buttered rye and drink some tea before leaving. Rachel managed the tea but the bread felt thick and dry in her mouth. She pushed the plate toward Naomi, who ate it as a favor. Gladys, seeing the crumbs, nodded with satisfaction. "I think you'll be just fine, Rachel. Go on now."

Naomi led Rachel to the synagogue for the Saturday morning service. Going down the stairs, Rachel felt light-headed. She held Naomi's hand until they reached the ground floor. There, they joined the lines of children coming up from breakfast and through the synagogue doors. Rachel slid into a pew alongside other girls from F5. She spotted Amelia at the far end of the row and looked away. Naomi went up front with F6. Sam and Vic were also up front on the boys' side; Rachel could see the backs of their heads. She wished she could tell Sam she was all right. That he didn't have to defend her. That he hadn't failed her.

There were some opening words, a hymn, announcements. Then Mr. Grossman mounted the stage. His predecessors having been rabbis, it was tradition in the Home for the superintendent to deliver the sermon. But Lionel Grossman was trained in social work, not religious studies. He used these occasions to make rambling speeches about the virtues of hard work and the importance of following rules. The children settled in, their eyes drifting to the ceiling.

"I'm going to talk to you today about violence." There was an unusual quiver in his voice. "Violence cannot be tolerated in our Home. Here, we live like brothers and sisters. Here, we live in an institution dedicated to your health, your education, your future as productive American citizens. We cannot have this marred with violence. When violence breaks out among us, it must be met in no uncertain terms. An example needs to be made of those who tarnish our Home." Rachel thought he was talking about what Marc had done to her, or the worse things he'd done to other girls. She wondered if the superintendent was going to sacrifice his own son, like Abraham in the Old Testament.

"Samuel Rabinowitz and Victor Berger, come forward." All sound was swallowed up as a thousand children took in and held the same breath. Sam and Vic stepped into the aisle. "Come up here, boys."

Rachel started trembling as they mounted the stage. She could see Sam's knuckles were raw, like he'd caught a ground ball on gravel. Vic looked back over his shoulder to their counselor, Bernstein, who nodded encouragement. Sam faced the audience, his back rigid.

"These boys have brought violence into our Home," Mr. Grossman pronounced, his voice shrill. "They assaulted my son." The grown man faced the teenaged boys. He stiffened his open hand. Swiftly, he slapped each cheek so hard their heads swiveled. A thousand children gasped.

Mr. Grossman pointed to a spot at the end of the front row. Rachel couldn't see Marc seated there. She imagined him with black eyes and a bandaged nose. "Apologize to him."

Vic's eyes followed the line of Mr. Grossman's trembling arm. "I'm sorry," he said. His voice was clear, but Rachel saw his lip curl.

All eyes turned to Sam. He stood silent, his cheek blazing. He stared back at Mr. Grossman, mouth shut.

The outstretched arm reached back and swung forward. This slap knocked Sam from his defiant stance. He stumbled, then righted himself. A whisper began to rise among the congregated children as a line of blood seeped from Sam's nose.

"Apologize!"

Vic stood beside his friend. Rachel knew his thoughts were the same as hers. *Just say the words. They don't mean anything. Save yourself.* But Sam wouldn't speak. Rachel's guilt and shame mounted. She imagined running onto the stage and throwing herself in front of brother. Her muscles tensed but her body didn't budge.

Mr. Grossman's face burned as red as Sam's. He reached back a third time, this time his fingers curled into a fist. Bernstein jumped up from his seat. In two strides, he was beside the superintendent, the fist caught in the middle of its arc.

"Not here, Mr. Grossman." Bernstein's low voice barely carried back to Rachel's row. "Not in front of the young ones." He gestured toward the back of the synagogue. Mr. Grossman followed the counselor's gaze to the six- and seven-year-olds in the farthest rows. Even from this distance, he could see the fear in their eyes.

Mr. Grossman lowered his arm. "I'll deal with you later," he growled to Sam, then stepped back. "Take them, then." Bernstein led Vic and Sam from the stage. All eyes followed the boys as they made their way down the long aisle. Mr. Grossman cleared his throat. "Let me speak now of brotherhood," he began.

Rachel would have jumped up and followed her brother out of the synagogue were it not for the look Naomi shot back at her. More trouble, that's all she would cause. She closed her eyes and made her mind go blank, stuffing her ears against the words spilling from the stage. Every passing minute felt like an hour.

Finally Rachel sensed the children around her rising from the pews. Led by their monitors, their shuffling feet the only sound, they filed out of the synagogue. Once in the hallway, their voices, unleashed, echoed up the marble stairs as they recounted what they had seen. A counselor called out, "All Still." For the first time in the history of the Home the words were ignored, no monitor willing to enforce the order with a slap.

Naomi caught up with Rachel. "Bernstein will have taken Sam up to Nurse Dreyer for sure. Come on."

They retraced their morning's steps. They found Sam in the Infirmary balancing an ice pack on the bridge of his nose. Bernstein was still there, and Vic, too, in a chair beside the bed. Rachel sat at her brother's feet and laid her head on his knees.

"Oh, Sammy, you shouldn't have gone after Marc, not on account of me."

Sam lifted the ice pack and glared down at her, dried blood crusted on his mouth. "Do you even know what a brother's supposed to do for his sister?" Nurse Dreyer pushed him back against the pillow and settled the ice. With his eyes closed, Sam said, "I only stick around here for you, but what's the point? I can't protect you. Naomi does a better job of that than me. I might as well run away."

Rachel sat up. "No, Sam, you wouldn't really leave me here alone, would you?"

"Look around you, Rachel. You're not alone. Besides, what difference does it make if I'm here or not? I don't think I can take much more of this."

Rachel remembered the slap she'd seen all those years ago from the window in Reception. She wondered how many Sam had endured between that day and this.

"Come on, all of you," Gladys Dreyer said, her perfume wafting over their heads. "It's too crowded up here. Bernstein, you stay. Mrs. Berger's coming over to talk to you and Sam. Everyone else, go on now. Sam'll be fine."

Vic dropped an encouraging hand on his friend's shoulder. "You'll be good as new, Sam. Don't let them get you down. Tell my ma I'm all right, will ya?"

Sam nodded, then looked at his sister. "Go on then. You heard Nurse Dreyer, I'll be fine." Rachel saw a distance in her brother's eyes that made her shiver, like he was staring at her through a scrim of ice. She leaned in to hug him, but he held her off. "Don't," he said. Rachel started tearing up again. "Don't worry, I mean. I'll see you tomorrow, at Reception, when we visit Mrs. Berger. Okay?"

Rachel nodded. "Okay, Sam." She followed Naomi and Vic out of the Infirmary. Bernstein lagged behind, conspiring with Nurse Dreyer.

If she hadn't been so worried about her brother, Rachel might have minded the whispers and pointed fingers that followed her through that long Saturday. Just before Last Bell, Naomi took Rachel aside in the F5 dorm and told her she'd heard from Millie Stember that Marc Grossman was being sent away to a military school up in Albany. Rachel was glad to hear it, even though the only consequence of what happened in the dark corridor that mattered to her now was Sam. She could hardly sleep, her anxiety alternating from his threat to run away to what else Mr. Grossman might do to him.

The next afternoon, when Rachel went to Reception, Mrs. Berger and Vic were there, but not her brother. Fannie Berger wrapped Rachel in her fleshy arms. "He's gone, kitten. Even with Marc away at school, it wasn't safe for him here anymore." Rachel barely listened as Mrs. Berger explained how she and Bernstein had pooled their money to stuff Sam's pockets with crumpled bills before he slipped through an unlocked door and scrambled over the wall.

Rachel broke away from Mrs. Berger. "But what will happen to him? Where will he go? Won't the police bring him back if they catch him?"

"He's practically a grown man, he can take care of himself," Fannie said. "He's left the city, that's all I know, but wherever he's gone, I'm sure he's fine." Vic looked at his mother, a question raising his eyebrows, but she shook her head.

"He'll be all right out on the road, a tough kid like Sam," Vic said. "He wanted me to tell you how much he loves you." He gave Rachel a kiss on the forehead. She turned away, ashamed of the blush that colored her cheeks.

Rachel remembered when the agency lady took her away from Sam, how he promised to come for her. She knew it wasn't his fault he broke that promise. He was as young as the M1 boys, some so small she could rest a bent elbow on top of their heads. Sam couldn't help it then, but he was sixteen now, not six, and this time he had left her behind on purpose. She felt as abandoned as on that first day at the Infant Home. Of the thousand children in the Castle, the millions of people in the city, none now belonged to her.

In the distance, a bell rang. Across the yard, doors were flung open and children flooded out. Rachel felt their shouts smack against the glass like unwitting birds. She said her good-byes and left Reception. Wading through the crowded yard, dust gathered in her eyes. She had no lashes to blink it away.

Chapter Ten

THE SLEEPING PILLS DID THEIR JOB. THE NEXT THING I knew, the alarm was kicking me out of bed. It took a pot of strong coffee (I had to drink it black, I was out of milk) to clear the fog from my head. I was so eager to confront Dr. Solomon that I got to the Old Hebrews Home even earlier than usual. I had it all figured out in my head—dose Mildred Solomon first, but lightly, at eight o'clock rounds, then get to her last at noon. By that time she would be coming out of her morphine haze. I needed her coherent. She had so much to answer for.

I had changed and was about to clock in when I noticed the calendar. Damn it. Gloria had me scheduled for tomorrow. When had that happened? We always had one or two days off between our long shifts. Speak of the devil, as Flo would say. Or think of her, anyway.

"Good morning, Rachel. Bright and early as usual."

"Gloria, I don't understand the schedule. I should be off tomorrow." The potential delay of my appointment with Dr. Feldman threw me into a panic. It was taking all I had to hold my fears in check; the false calm wouldn't last another day.

"We talked about that a week ago. The other head nurse asked if I could switch with her, and I asked if you'd change, too, so I'd have someone I could depend on with me that day. Don't you remember?"

It rang a bell. Last week, I had no reason not to agree to changing shifts; this summer, one day was as long and lonely as the next.

Gloria's eyebrows drew together over her cat's-eye glasses. "I was waiting for her to confirm her plans, so I didn't write it on the calendar until I was leaving the other day. I'm sorry, Rachel, but I can't see how to change it now. I've already switched everyone else around. And look, you'll have three days off in a row afterward. You could spend some time on the beach, soak up the sun."

"But I made an appointment for tomorrow. . . ." I turned away from Gloria, afraid I was about to cry. I felt her hand on my shoulder.

"Is something wrong, Rachel? Do you want to tell me anything?"

"I'm fine, Gloria. I'll reschedule my appointment, is all."

"Glad to hear it. You know how I rely on you." Her locker clanged as she took out her cap and pinned it over her bun. "I'll send Flo in as long as you're here."

Flo. I'd ask her, plead if necessary. Instead of following Gloria out, I lingered in the nurses' lounge until Flo came in.

"They say the early bird catches the worm, but really, Rachel, you're making the rest of us look bad."

"You could never look bad, Flo." I trailed her to the window. "I'll have one, if you're offering." She looked surprised but knocked a Chesterfield out of the pack and handed it over, even lit it for me. The smoke did feel good, the warmth in my throat balancing the hot summer air. After a few drags I felt more steady. "Flo, I hate to ask, but Gloria changed my shifts around after I made an appointment for tomorrow. I was wondering, is there any chance you could switch with me? Come in tomorrow morning, then I'll cover you that night?" I tensed. How much sympathy would I have to garner for her to agree? Nothing could be more pitiable than the truth. I braced myself to reveal it.

"Sure, I could do that. I'll be dead on my feet, but I'll take any excuse to be out of the house." She blew a smoke ring—I didn't know she could do that. "My mother-in-law is visiting. She thinks I'm lazy, sleeping all day, even though I work nights. Bangs pots around in the kitchen making my kids what she calls a 'real dinner.' I would've asked you, but who wants to trade day for night?" She ground out the butt, tossed it out the window. "What kind of appointment?"

"Oh, it's to do with my hair." It was a stupid thing to say, but I hadn't thought that far ahead. "Sounds silly, I know, but I had to wait ages to get in."

"Like I said, any excuse to be out of the house while she's here. Be thankful you don't have to put up with a mother-in-law." She grabbed my hand. "Oh, Rachel, I'm sorry. I'm an idiot, don't listen to me."

I supposed she was remembering I'd grown up with no mother at all. Or was it that she felt bad for rubbing it in, me not being married? Whatever it was, I shrugged it off. "Don't worry about it, Flo. I can't tell you how much I appreciate it."

I clocked her out and myself in, then went to tell Gloria about the change. "Flo? The night nurse?" She scowled. "There's a reason I wanted you, Rachel. I won't pretend I'm not disappointed."

I'd never let Gloria down before; it was surprising how much her disapproval stung. I scurried off to prepare the cart for morning rounds.

"Do you think you could get Mildred Solomon to take some broth again?" Gloria was checking off lunch trays, portioning them out to me and the other shift nurse. "She hasn't eaten since you last fed her. I left a note in her chart for the doctor, asking if her dose might be lessened so she'd be able to take some food. See what he wrote back." Gloria showed me the chart. The attending had replied to Gloria's meticulously penned request in a barely decipherable scrawl. *Start her on a feeding tube if she can't swallow.* We snorted in unison, the universal sound of nurses who know better than the doctors whose orders we follow. "See what you can do." Gloria handed me the tray with Mildred Solomon's broth and her next syringe of morphine. She would have never directly suggested I ease off her dose, but the possibility was implied.

If only Gloria had known. The vial I carried in my pocket already held over half of Dr. Solomon's eight o'clock dose. It was a risk, holding back so much, but when I saw her in bed it broke over me like a wave, everything she'd done to me. I wanted to shake her, smother her, smack her sunken cheek. Withholding some morphine seemed a restrained alternative. She'd be in pain, I knew, but the righteous thought that it served her right took hold of me. When I left her room after morning rounds, I'd closed her door to muffle any moans that might escape her parched throat as the morphine began to wear off.

Entering with the tray, I saw Mildred Solomon's arms and legs twitching beneath the sheets, like a child playing at snow angels.

Bone cancer brings pain to the deepest parts of the body; no position of her limbs would ease their pinch and burn. She looked up
as I entered the room, eyes bleary but expression sharp. "You're
late with my medication! Give me my dose, quickly." Her voice
scratched at my memories, like nails on a chalkboard. She rested
against the pillow, anticipating the relief to come. "Be a good girl
and hurry up, would you?"

"I want you to eat something first. Can you do that for me?"

"What do I care about eating? Can't you see I'm suffering?"

I sat in the visitor's chair, the tray on my knees. "The doctor has
ordered a feeding tube if you won't take any nourishment." I knew
that would rile her.

"Arrogant bastard," she said, trying to raise herself up in bed.
I cranked the handle to lift the mattress—as her hips bent, she
moaned. "Let's get this over with then." She opened her mouth,
an echo of that photograph of the child in the scurvy study. I
spooned the broth between her shriveled lips. She gagged with
each labored swallow. Determined, though, to outwit the doctor,
she consumed all the broth I offered until she dropped her head
back, exhausted.

"There, I ate it all. Tell that to the doctor. Feeding tube, indeed.
Do you know how uncomfortable those things are? Inhumane."

"I do know." It was she, wasn't it, who had shoved that tube
down my throat? Not some anonymous nurse but Dr. Solomon
herself. I remembered now, her necktie swinging over my face as
she held up the funnel.

Her breath was coming in shallow gasps. She gestured at the
syringe. "It's time. Not too much, but some, I need some. I need
some now."

Instead of reaching for the syringe, I said, "In a minute. I want you to do something first."

She squinted suspiciously. "What now?"

I didn't answer. My eyes locked on hers as I unbuttoned my uniform to the waist, shrugging my arms out of the stiff, white fabric. Reaching behind, I unclasped my bra and pulled it away from my body. I looked down at my breasts, pale and tipped in pink, the nipples still small as a girl's. I lifted Dr. Solomon's hand, the fingers like a bird's claw, and placed the tips under my right breast, pushing up. "I want you to feel this."

She didn't have the strength to pull away. "Then I'll get my medication?"

"Soon, soon you'll get your dose." I pressed her fingers deeper. "Now, feel."

At first, the fingers were stiff, remote. Then the hand that had been trained as a diagnostic tool began to move of its own volition. It searched my breast, as if looking for a coin lost deep in a pocket. I winced at the pressure, the tissue tender. In a pucker of flesh, her fingers found a shape, circled it, judged its size and weight. Her pain seemed to be forgotten as Dr. Solomon exercised her profession.

"There it is!" Excited as a squirrel, she pinched the buried acorn. Then the pain asserted itself and her smile twisted into a grimace. As her elbow sank toward the mattress, I leaned farther over the bed. Finally, she dropped her hand.

"I don't understand. Why did you want me to find your tumor?"

"Because," I said, our faces close. "Because you put it there." I expected her to balk at the accusation, wrack her mind for what she might have done to deserve it, recoil as she confronted the consequences of her actions.

"Don't be ridiculous. What do you mean, I put your tumor there?" Dr. Solomon's voice was tight with pain. "You said I'd get my medication. You promised."

With shaking hands, I hooked my bra and buttoned the uniform, adjusted my collar and cap. She didn't understand, not yet. I'd have to prod her memory, pose the questions her medical articles had left unanswered. When she put it together, I was sure she'd be ashamed of the way she'd treated us, repentant for how she'd used me. I wondered if she'd ask me to forgive her. Would I be able to?

"Do you remember the experiment you did at the Hebrew Infant Home, aiming X-rays at children's tonsils?"

"Of course I do, I'm not senile. It's just that damn morphine, I can't think straight, he prescribes so much." Dr. Solomon closed her eyes. She seemed to be looking for something. Was she finally remembering me?

"Put me on the map, that study. No one had used X-rays on tonsils before." She looked at me eagerly. "I met Marie Curie because of it, when she toured New York. Did you know that? Shook her hand, that very hand whose burns gave her the idea radium could be used in medicine. She congratulated me. Me! Thanked me, too, for my small donation to her radium fund. It was infuriating that the woman who discovered radium couldn't afford any for her own research." She stared at the ceiling, her suffering pushed back by the pleasure of remembering.

"I almost didn't get that residency at the Infant Home. Sure, they were starting to let women into medical schools, just enough of us to close down places like the Female Physicians College, but we weren't exactly wanted, I can tell you that. Made me live in the dean's house, where his wife could keep an eye on me. It was that, or room with the nursing students." She spoke fast now, as if the words were outrunning the pain. "The Hebrew Infant Home had one of the best X-ray rooms in the city, all the radiologists wanted that residency. Dr. Hess only ranked me second because the dean's wife made her husband put pressure on him. She championed me in her own stupid way, thought second place would satisfy my vanity, but why would I want second place when I deserved first? Then the idiot who'd been ranked ahead of me dropped a vial of radium. Can you believe the incompetence? We were in the laboratory at the medical college, passing it around—tiny thing, a tenth of a gram, but still worth thousands—until he bobbled it and let it fall into the sink. I remember his stupid face as he watched it disappear down the drain. Had to get a plumber in to melt the lead joints in the pipes to recover it. Once Dr. Hess heard about that, he nixed the idiot's application. Well, everyone else had already accepted their residencies. My only prospect was a position in an outdated X-ray clinic in the middle of nowhere— Nebraska, I think it was, or maybe Wyoming—which I was putting off as long as I could. I was the best in my class, I should have had my choice of residencies. That's what it was like for me, killing myself to be first just so I'd be in a position to capitalize on the stupidity of others."

I was surprised how long she spoke; she must not have had an attentive audience for quite a while. I was confused, though, by her story. Was she angling for my sympathy? I knew what it was like to be excluded, kept at the margins, denied recognition everyone else enjoyed, no matter how undeserving. But I wasn't like her, I reminded myself. She'd exploited me when she should have cared for me. What difference did it make that she had to struggle? Over us, she'd had all the power, and I knew now how she'd used it.

A twinge of pain tugged at Mildred Solomon's mouth. "Why do you want to know about my tonsil study?"

"Because," I said, watching for her reaction, "I was your material."

Dr. Solomon blinked, confused. She stared at me, as if trying to focus on print too small to read. "You were one of my subjects?"

I nodded, imagining for a moment that Dr. Solomon recognized me: her brave, good girl. She lifted her hand to my face. I tilted my head toward her curved palm. I hadn't realized how much I craved this tender gesture until it was happening. It hadn't been her fault after all. She'd wanted to be kind to us, treat us like her own children, but she had to prove herself. The world was so unfair, she wasn't allowed to show affection. Not then. Not until now. I rested my cheek in her hand.

But no, it wasn't a caress. Dr. Solomon bent my head back to expose the underside of my chin. Her thumbnail circled the scars there, tracing the dimes of shiny skin. Then she placed her fingers against my drawn eyebrows and wiped away the pencil. Finally, she reached up to my hairline and pushed along the brow. My wig shifted. She pulled her hand back in surprise. It wasn't tenderness I saw in her face, not even regret. Fear, maybe? No, not even that.

"So the alopecia was never resolved? I was curious about that, always meant to follow up. What number were you?"

I adjusted my wig. "Eight," I said. I expected it to happen any second now—Dr. Solomon would ask to be forgiven. For everything she had done to me, for the repercussions of a lifetime, Mildred Solomon was about to atone. My eyes were on the old woman's face, greedy for the words I wanted to hear.

Dr. Solomon squinted, as if seeing into the past. "Number Eight. I do remember you." She closed her eyes, the lids stretched tight. "You were such a clingy little thing."

The words stung like a slap. She collapsed back against the pillows, her breath fast and shallow. The pain was getting worse, I could see. Good, I thought. The bitch deserved it.

I thought she'd lost her train of thought until she said, "How is it my fault, exactly, your tumor?"

"Because of the X-rays you gave me. All those X-rays, for no good reason." I wanted to spit the words out, sharp as nails, but I sounded like a bleating lamb.

"I had my reasons. Good ones, too. Didn't you read my article?"

"Yes, I did. I read how you thought you were saving us from surgery. But you used us, you used me. We didn't even have tonsillitis. We were perfectly healthy. Maybe you did have your reasons, but aren't you at least sorry for how it turned out, those X-ray experiments? For what they did to us, to me? First my hair, and now this." I clutched my breast. "What's going to be left of me after this?"

"It's too bad for you, Number Eight, sure, but if researchers gave up their experiments because they were worried about the consequences, we'd still be dying of smallpox."

"Why are you calling me Number Eight? My name is Rachel, Rachel Rabinowitz. You never even knew that, did you?"

Over a grimace of pain, Dr. Solomon's face flushed with anger. "Dr. Hess told me never to use your names. Just numbers, he said, they're just numbers. How else can a researcher maintain objectivity, especially working with children? You don't think it was hard to keep my composure, with those damn nurses bursting into tears every time I turned around? It was all I could do to get them to respect me. They were always questioning my methods, as if we were equals." She snorted derisively. "Nurses. I'd like to see them dissect a corpse."

She was panting, almost hyperventilating—soon she'd begin to tremor from withdrawal. I picked up the syringe, eager now to shut her up. I eased the needle into the IV, depressing the plunger until her breath, still shallow, steadied. I didn't want to speak to her again, not today. Still, I withdrew the syringe at just half the prescribed dose, squirted the remainder into the vial in my pocket. She'd be in pain again soon, but so what? It would be gratifying, at four o'clock rounds, to see Mildred Solomon suffering. I'd give her a full dose then, leave her quiet for the night nurse.

Gloria noted the empty bowl of broth, the empty syringe of morphine. "Good job, Rachel. You see why I wanted you on shift with me. Go ahead and take your lunch break."

On my way to the staff cafeteria, I realized what luck it was I'd switched with Flo. There was only one other nurse on the night shift, and no supervisor. Tomorrow night, I'd have Dr. Solomon to myself. She would be the one at my mercy.

Chapter Eleven

THE DAY AFTER SAM RAN AWAY, RACHEL COULDN'T GET herself out of bed at Rising Bell. Naomi came to jostle her just as Breakfast Bell rang. "You better get up now, and hurry. The other monitor will give the whole dorm standing lessons if you make us late."

Rachel sat up, her knees, neck, and back aching. Tears spilled over as she whispered, "I just can't do it."

"All right then." Naomi hustled off, then quickly returned. "I sent the rest of them down, I'm taking you to the Infirmary."

Gladys Dreyer didn't seem surprised to see Rachel back so soon. "Delayed reaction most likely. You had a very upsetting experience. I'll keep you here for a couple of days so you can rest up. We'll say its mononucleosis if anyone asks." Grateful, Rachel fell into the bed Nurse Dreyer offered. Naomi dashed out and soon ran back in with a book from the library. "I thought this was one you'd like," she panted, holding out a volume about Scott's expedition to the South Pole. Rachel had read it before but accepted gratefully, knowing Naomi had made herself late for school on her account. She expected it would be Naomi's last kindness, now that Sam and his bribes were gone.

It was a luxury unheard of in the Orphaned Hebrews Home: an entire day spent reading in bed. Nurse Dreyer even brought lunch on a tray. It occurred to Rachel this was how children with families lived. Children with quiet bedrooms in apartments where time was told by the soft ticking of a clock instead of the screech of bells. Children with fathers who came home from work to ask what they had learned in school that day. Children whose mothers kept them home when they were feeling too fragile to face the world.

After school, Naomi was back, this time with Rachel's homework. "Your teacher says to get better quick, and so do I." Naomi squeezed Rachel's hand before hurrying off. Rachel looked at the notebook and math text on her lap, pleased but puzzled by Naomi's continuing attentions.

The doctor from Mount Sinai who attended the orphanage noted Rachel's fatigue but doubted it was mononucleosis because she had no sore throat or fever. Gladys Dreyer persuaded him. "She could be infectious, even without those symptoms," she argued. "She'll only be allowed to stay with your diagnosis. I wanted to give her a few days, after what she's been through. . . . " She took the doctor aside and spoke with him in a voice too quiet for Rachel to hear. He listened, nodded, cleared his throat.

"Better to keep her away from the other children, just in case," he concurred.

So Rachel spent the week lazing in bed, reading the books and doing the homework Naomi brought her and getting used to the idea that Sam was gone for good. With Marc Grossman sent upstate, it was mostly Sam's abandonment that weighed her down. She wondered if the idea of his running away depressed her more than the fact of his absence. Other than Sunday afternoons in Reception, she'd spent so little time with her brother over the past nine years. They were in separate dorms and different grades, never in the same clubs after school or the same table for meals, on opposite sides of the lake during summer camp. Her life in the Home would hardly be changed without Sam there. She'd no longer look for him across the dining hall or in the yard, was all; no longer search him out when the baseball team was playing; no longer try to catch his eye as they passed each other, silently, in the wide corridors of the Castle.

"When are you coming back to the dorm, Rachel?" Naomi asked on Friday when she dropped off Rachel's homework. "It's no fun there without you."

Rachel smiled, daring to believe Naomi might have been a true friend this whole time. "Nurse Dreyer thinks I've rested up long enough, she says I should go back on Sunday."

"Good! Then you won't miss the brisket." Naomi settled herself on the edge of Rachel's narrow bed. "You ever wondered why Sunday dinner is the best meal of the week? I mean, it really ought to be Friday night if you think about it, right? But it's Sunday because that's when the board of trustees has their meeting. You know, those men in suits who look in on us while we eat? They like to see where their money's going." Naomi left with a wink that made Rachel smile for the first time since the Purim Dance.

Saturday night, though, one of the boys in the Infirmary who'd been running a fever had a crisis. Rachel woke from an unnerving dream to find Gladys Dreyer examining the boy with a panicked expression. "Can you lift your leg for me, Benny? Just lift it up.

No? Then how about your foot, can you move your foot? Are you really trying?" The boy's fevered face scrunched with effort, but the leg remained inanimate.

Gladys went to her desk and dialed the in-house extension for the superintendent's apartment. "Mr. Grossman, we'll need the doctor from Mount Sinai here first thing in the morning." Her voice dropped to a whisper, as if the louder she spoke the word the more likely it was to be true. "I think it's polio. Yes, of course, isolation procedures immediately."

On her way back to attend to the boy, Gladys saw Rachel sitting up in bed, taking advantage of the uncharacteristic light to read her book. "I'm afraid you might be with us for a while longer, Rachel. I'll confide in you because I know I can count on you not to frighten the younger ones. We may be dealing with a case of polio. We're going into isolation—no one in or out of the Infirmary until we can be sure none of us is contagious."

When the doctor examined Benny the next day, he wasn't as convinced as Nurse Dreyer had been. There was too much hysteria over polio, he thought, and most of the cases he saw were in infants. Still, he ordered that the boy be moved to the Infirmary's private room while he sent a sample to the Rockefeller Institute for analysis. He agreed that isolation procedures should be followed until the results came back. At their meeting that afternoon, the trustees were informed of the situation by Mr. Grossman, who assured them isolation would be complete: doors at either end of the Infirmary hallway were locked to prevent errant contact, and a dumb waiter would be used to deliver food and supplies. The abundance of caution let the trustees go home to their own families, congratulating themselves once again that the Orphaned Hebrews Home was the best child care institution in the country—if not the world.

Benny's fever broke, though his leg remained terribly weak. Results came back positive for poliomyelitis, which meant the Infirmary stayed in isolation for the full six weeks—the rest of March, all of April, and into May. And so Rachel was trapped, along with a despondent Gladys Dreyer and the dozen children who happened to be in the Infirmary at the time.

A few of them were in serious condition: a girl in danger of developing pneumonia, a boy with bronchitis, a stitched knee that risked infection, a broken arm requiring elevation. Most, however, soon recovered from the sprains, cuts, scrapes, coughs, aches, and bumps that had sent them to the Infirmary in the first place. Rachel was the oldest and she wasn't even sick, so Nurse Dreyer enlisted her as a nurse's aide. She taught Rachel how to clean the pus from infected stitches, how to prepare a mustard plaster for bronchitis, how to check for fever and take a pulse.

Only Nurse Dreyer attended to Benny, assiduously following the disinfection protocols set out by the attending doctor. Between visits to the boy, however, Gladys leafed through the pages of *Look* magazine and sipped tea in her apartment while Rachel circulated among the children. During the night, if one of them called out, Gladys stayed in bed, listening for Rachel to get up in her place.

"I don't know how I'd survive isolation without you, Rachel," she said one day over lunch in her cozy kitchenette. "You've taken a real interest in the Infirmary. Have you thought about becoming a nurse? You could start a course in the fall. I'd be glad to put in a word for you with the Scholarship Committee." Rachel hadn't thought about what came after the Home, but she liked the idea. Nurse Dreyer lent her an old copy of Emerson's *Essentials of Medicine*, which she read eagerly. Even if she didn't completely understand it, she enjoyed the pages dense with anatomical terms and diagnostic descriptions, illustrated by simple drawings of various systems and organs. She worked through the glossary letter by letter, *abscess* to *xanthin*. In bed at night, she'd run her finger down a column in the index and choose a disease to read about: bilious fever, creeping pneumonia, hookworm, mumps, palsy, typhoid. Bacillus tuberculosis, at twenty-six pages, put her to sleep for a week.

In addition to daily supplies and meals and piles of library books to keep the children occupied, the dumb waiter delivered a substantial package of schoolwork for Rachel, including all her texts and lessons. Tucked into the pages of Tennyson's poems, Rachel found a note from Naomi.

> *Hi Rachel, Sorry you're stuck in isolation! I got worried they'd nab me, too, for visiting you in the Infirmary. It could have been fun, though, if we were both there together! I hear you're practically running the place. Did you know Nurse Dreyer had a boyfriend? He actually showed up asking about her, but when he heard the word polio you better believe he hightailed it out of here. Doubt she'll ever see that one again. Amelia even says to say hi, but I think she's just rubbing it in that you're stuck up there. Everyone hopes you don't catch it, though, that's for sure. I'm still waiting to hear if I'll get a counselor position, then I can live here while I go to Teachers College at Columbia. That's what Bernstein's doing. Not Teachers College, of*

course, he's going to City to be a lawyer. I wish the Schol-
arship Committee would back girls for that. I'd be good at
arguing cases, don't you think? But teaching's better than
secretarial school, that's for sure, and anyway, only boys
can go to City. All the F6 girls are trying to catch Bern-
stein's eye, I can tell you. Amelia practically trips over
herself every time he walks by, but she's not his type. He'd
make a good catch, though, don't you think? I'll write more
later, take care of yourself! Your friend, Naomi

Rachel had never had a confidante before, and the connection
warmed her. Naomi addressed her as an equal in a way she never
could have in the F5 dorm. That night, she read the note again.
Naomi wrote about Bernstein with such admiration, Rachel wondered if she was among those girls trying to catch his eye. The idea
of Bernstein and Naomi seemed so natural, she wondered why it
made her jealous.

THE ISOLATION PERIOD ended in May. Benny was left with a slight
limp—enough to keep him off the baseball team but not so severe
as to attract attention. Thanks to Nurse Dreyer's precautions, tests
confirmed that none of the other children had contracted polio.
But Gladys had come to depend on Rachel so much, she asked
Mr. Grossman to let her stay on as an assistant until the end of
the summer. They'd count it as an apprenticeship, she argued, to
strengthen her case for the Scholarship Committee. Mr. Grossman
agreed, provided Rachel completed her schoolwork and passed her
exams. Rachel had gotten used to the autonomy of the Infirmary
and welcomed the idea of staying through the summer instead of

going to camp. The habit of visiting Mrs. Berger and Vic had fallen away with Sam's leaving, replaced, now that isolation was over, by Sunday afternoons with Naomi in Nurse Dreyer's apartment. Rachel had come to believe their friendship had nothing to do with Sam's bribes.

On Rachel's fifteenth birthday in August, Gladys had slices of pound cake and stewed peaches brought up to the Infirmary for the occasion, and Naomi presented Rachel with a card made from folded construction paper decorated with pictures cut out of a magazine. Naomi could hardly wait to finish singing happy birthday before she burst out with the good news. "You're looking at the new counselor for F1. Ma Stember's finally leaving, to get married, can you believe it? I'm even moving into the counselor's room."

"Congratulations, Naomi."

"Listen, I'm going to Coney Island to visit my aunt and uncle next Sunday, to tell them all about getting the counselor job. Why don't you come with me?"

"What a nice idea," Gladys said. "Get some color back in your cheeks." Rachel raised a hesitant hand to her scalp. "I'll lend you my cloche hat, it'll cover you right up." Gladys got up and lifted the hat, a new and prized possession, out of its round box and placed it on Rachel's head. The bell-shaped felt covered her scalp, curving prettily from her brow to the nape of her neck. Stylish women were wearing their hair so short, such hats revealed little more than a fringe above a bare neck. On Rachel, the look was perfect.

"You're like from a magazine," Naomi said. "Come see." They gathered around a mirror. Rachel hardly recognized herself. Her transformation was so stunning, Naomi and Gladys were both at a loss for words.

"You're sure you don't mind?" Rachel asked, meeting Nurse Dreyer's eyes in the mirror.

"Of course not, dear. I know you'll take care of it."

"And everyone wears bathing caps on the beach," Naomi said.

"All right, then, I'll go with you." Rachel's smile made her even prettier. The image startled her, and she turned away from the mirror.

The subway ride to Coney Island was the longest Rachel had ever taken. On the way, Naomi told Rachel about her Uncle Jacob. He was her father's older brother; the two of them had taken passage together from Kraków to New York. Naomi's father was Jacob's apprentice, but Jacob was too busy establishing their woodworking business to find himself a wife, so the younger brother married first. They all lived together in an apartment above the workshop. "I used to sweep up the shavings. I remember I had a collection of the nicest ones."

"Do you remember your mother?" Rachel asked.

Naomi shrugged. "I remember how I felt when I was with her, and I know what she looked like, but I don't know if that's from my memory or from the pictures at my uncle's house. I was only six when they died of influenza." Naomi finished her story, telling Rachel that she was left with no one but her uncle. "Uncle Jacob was a single man back then, and my father died just when he took on a big order for the carousel. He didn't have much choice except to take me to the Home. He told me I'd have more fun, with so many children to play with." Naomi and Rachel sat beside each other in silence. Neither had to say that any child would choose a family of their own, no matter how shattered, over the rigors and routines of the Home.

At the Stillwell Avenue station, families and couples surged toward the boardwalk. Naomi took Rachel's elbow and steered her down Mermaid Avenue, the hot sidewalks emptying as they left behind the beaches and amusements.

"There it is." Naomi pointed to a brick building that looked like a stable. Rachel didn't understand how this could be anyone's home, but Naomi led the way up an exterior staircase to a second-story door painted glossy blue.

A bearded man with gnarled hands opened it to her knock. "Naomi, dear, come in." They embraced and kissed.

"Uncle Jacob, this is my friend Rachel, from the Home."

Rachel, too, was kissed, Jacob's whiskers tickling her cheek. "Welcome. Estelle, they're here!" he called over his shoulder. He stepped back to usher Rachel into the sitting room of a tidy apartment. She could see through to a small kitchen from which Estelle emerged to join them.

"Naomi, darling, how are you?" Estelle, whose hair was piled up in braids on top of her head, shared Jacob's Polish accent. To Rachel they seemed to be from another century. The apartment's furnishings—table, chairs, chifforobe—were all ornately carved and brightly painted. Instead of radiators, there was a woodstove with a black chimney pipe. The walls were decorated with framed pictures of temples and castles. Rachel thought they were drawn to look like lace, but as she stepped closer to the pictures, she saw the images were made of paper cut out to show every detail of crenulated rooflines and leaded windows.

"You like that?" Estelle asked, coming to stand next to Rachel.

"That one I did, but over here is one Jacob made." She pulled Rachel toward a larger picture. Within the boundaries of the frame a whole city unfolded: cut paper trees and a cobblestone street, paper horses drawing a wagon, small houses with paper smoke rising from chimneys, and on a hill above the town a domed paper temple.

"I've never seen anything like this," Rachel said.

"This one he made back in the Empire, before America. Now he doesn't have time for the paper cutting, only the horses, always the horses. I don't cut paper anymore, either. Now I am painting the horses. We will show you after we eat. Come now, Naomi, Jacob, come and sit."

They pulled chairs up to the table, already set for lunch with decorated plates, to eat their brown bread and pickled onions and slices of smoked tongue. Naomi's news about the counselor position elicited warm congratulations from her uncle and his wife. Jacob was much older than Estelle, but Rachel could see their fondness for each other, and for Naomi. It made Rachel think of those Sunday afternoons in Reception, when she and Vic and Sam would gather in the kitchen with Mrs. Berger. A deeper memory stirred, an image of a table set with cups and a jelly jar and a woman with eyes like black buttons pouring tea. Then came the image Rachel tried to avoid by never attempting to remember a time before the Home: a spreading red pool and rising white buttons. She shuddered.

"Someone walking on your grave?" Jacob asked.

Rachel paled. It was like he was reading her soul. Naomi saw her expression.

"He always says that when anyone shivers like you just did. It's an old superstition. Don't say such things, Uncle Jacob," Naomi admonished him with a flick of her napkin.

"So, Naomi, we have some news for you," Estelle said, smiling at Jacob.

Naomi brightened. "Are you going to make me an aunt finally?"

A troubled look passed between them and Naomi blushed, apologizing. Jacob took Estelle's hand. He said, sadly, "That is a blessing maybe not for us. When Estelle came off the boat we were thinking the house would be crowded already with babies. Otherwise, we would have taken you out from the Home to live with us. I waited too long, I think, to send for my beautiful Estelle."

"Don't draw an evil eye to our troubles, Jacob," Estelle whispered. She turned to Naomi. "Our news is we have for you something." Estelle got up from the table, opened a small drawer in the chifforobe and pulled out an envelope. "For your high school graduation, and to help with the college."

Naomi opened the envelope. There were five- and ten-dollar bills, worn soft but clean and ironed flat.

"Fifty dollars? Uncle Jacob, Aunt Estelle, it's too much!" But they insisted, and Rachel could see this gift was both an investment in their niece's future and an apology for her past. Naomi finally accepted, grateful. Even with room and board included with her position as a counselor, it would be a strain for her to pay tuition from her paltry earnings. She'd been about to go in front of the Scholarship Committee to beg her case. "Now I can walk into the bursar's office after Labor Day and pay for all the classes in cash like a Rockefeller," she said. This pleased her aunt and uncle, and they finished their lunch amid happy chatter. As Estelle cleared away the dishes, Jacob showed Naomi how to hide the money under the insole of her shoe.

"You want to see the workshop before you go down to the beach?" Jacob asked. Rachel thought they'd go back outside, but instead he led them through the bedroom and out another door onto an interior balcony that overlooked a cavernous space. The smell of pine and turpentine rose to the rafters. Down below, Rachel saw the blocks of wood, the workbenches covered in tools, the jars of paint lining the walls on shelves, and everywhere the carousel horses. Horses with flaring nostrils, eyes rolled back and hooves beating the air. Docile horses with soft lips and broad backs. Fancy horses with braided manes and gleaming teeth.

"Since the carousel at Coney Island, horses is all I get orders for," Jacob explained. "Not that I'm complaining!"

On the far wall above the big workshop doors was something different: a carved lion with a majestic mane and the uncanny eyes of a guardian spirit. Jacob saw Rachel staring at it.

"Ah, that was my test, to show I was finished being an apprentice. You should have heard Naomi's father complaining! First we haul it on a cart to the train station. Then we sit with it in the baggage car all the way to Bremen. When we are hauling it up the gangplank to the ship, my brother wails, 'What for do we have to carry a temple lion all the way to America?' 'When you finish your apprenticeship, you'll understand,' I told him." Jacob paused to sigh. They'd gotten so busy so quickly in America, he never took the time to subject his brother to the same grueling training he had endured. He shook the regret from his head.

"That is not my first one! No, that lion is the third I carved.

The first one my master in Kraków he rejects. Such a lion is not worthy to guard the Torah, he says. My second one also is not good enough. So I carve until the blood from my fingers soaks into the wood. Then, with this one, my master says in Yiddish, *dos iz gute.* I mount it on the wall over our workshop, so we don't forget where we come from."

Rachel was entranced by the story. She had no idea where her people were from. Europe, she supposed, but what empire or country or village? If her parents had been born in New York, she and Sam would surely have been claimed by grandparents— unless they were dead, too. She envied Naomi her connection with family. Most children at the Home had some relative who visited them on a Sunday afternoon, bringing candy or coins. Many, like Vic, even had a living parent, and Mrs. Berger wasn't the only widowed mother working at the orphanage. Sometimes it seemed to Rachel that the Home was like a big library, with children being checked in by relatives unable to care for them, then checked out when fortunes changed. She had decided long ago her father must have died, or he would have found a way to get her and Sam back, too.

Naomi kept a bathing suit at her aunt and uncle's, and Estelle lent hers to Rachel, saying Naomi could return it on her next visit. It was afternoon by the time the girls went down to the board-walk. Ahead, the Wonder Wheel turned slowly and the Cyclone slunk up and over its tracks. They went past the amusements and toward the water. Sharing a rented changing booth, they stuffed their shoes and summer dresses into the straw bag Naomi carried and put on the knit suits, a bit old-fashioned but still exposing arms and legs. Naomi helped fit a bathing cap over Rachel's head.

Pulling open the curtains of the booth, the sun blinded Rachel as she stepped onto the warm sand. She liked the way it shifted beneath her bare feet. The girls spent some time basking before going into the water. In the roiling ocean, they stayed near shore, jumping over incoming waves and tasting sea salt on their tongues.

The afternoon took on a dreamlike quality. With the summer sun suspended overhead, time ceased passing. The trips from sand to sea and back were timed not by the hands of a clock but by the evaporation of water from their swimsuits. The regimented ringing of bells was replaced in Rachel's inner ear by the sound of surf bubbling onto the beach and the whoosh and plummet of the roller coaster.

They stayed until the slanted light told a story of evening. In the close darkness of the changing booth, hips bumped as they bent to roll the damp suits from their salty limbs. Standing, their eyes met. For the first time in ages—maybe in forever—Rachel felt lifted by joy. In gratitude for the day, she kissed her friend on the lips. Naomi became so still and serious, Rachel wondered if she'd done something wrong. Then Naomi put a hand on Rachel's waist and kissed her back, pursed lips pressed together. The moment stretched beyond friendship into an unmapped territory Rachel could not name. The sounds of surf and children on the beach faded as Rachel's awareness exaggerated each tremor of lips, every shift in pressure. The tip of Naomi's tongue touched her own, sparking an electric shock. Without meaning to, she pulled away, lips still tingling.

A giddy joy bubbled up between them, filling the gloomy booth with their laughter and dispersing the tension. They finished dressing, Rachel covering her head with the cloche hat. Naomi made sure the money was still secure in her shoe. They stopped for Italian ice on their way to the station, turning their tongues red. On the long ride back to the Home, they sat with linked arms and dozed. When Rachel licked her lips, she tasted sea salt and cherry syrup.

Manhattan felt crowded and dirty after the openness of the beach. Under the shadow of the clock tower, they pulled open the heavy oak doors of the Home. Naomi turned to say something to Rachel, but a bell rang. Both girls were stunned to realize they didn't know which it was. Then they saw the children coming up from the dining hall. "Club Bell already! I'm late. Gotta go." Naomi dashed off to her duties while Rachel went up to the Infirmary.

"I almost didn't recognize you, Rachel. You're cheeks are positively glowing. And that hat makes you look so normal." Gladys caught herself. "I mean to say, it looks so natural on you."

Reluctantly, Rachel handed the hat to Nurse Dreyer, exposing her bare scalp. The monitor's warning about Naomi came back to her. *She's not a normal girl . . . she's not natural.* Rachel shivered, as if someone had walked on her grave.

As the summer came to an end, Nurse Dreyer finally had to let Rachel go. The Saturday before Labor Day, Rachel prepared herself to rejoin the girls in the F5 dorm, though it hadn't quite been settled if she'd move that night or the next. Tuesday she'd start her nursing course, thanks to the support of the Scholarship Committee.

"I don't know what I'll do without you, Rachel," Gladys told her. She was lingering over her magazines as Rachel collected the lunch trays. "You've been such a help." A bell rang, spurring Gladys up from the table. "I don't suppose you'd mind going down to the office for me one last time? I've still got curlers in my hair."

"Of course not," Rachel said. She took the back staircase from the Infirmary to the ground floor and followed the long hallway past the synagogue, the library, the band room. The club room door was propped open. Rachel saw Vic inside. Naomi had told her he'd started a new club, the Blue Serpent Society. Rachel had heard they were planning a party for next Rosh Hashanah. Vic saw her passing and dashed into the corridor.

"Rachel, I haven't seen you in months! How are you? You look like you've gotten some sun. Were you at camp?"

"No, I've been here all summer, helping in the Infirmary. But Naomi took me to Coney Island last Sunday." Rachel felt her cheeks redden. "I got burned, I'm afraid."

"No, you look lovely." Vic smiled, and Rachel noticed again how blue his eyes were.

They stretched the conversation. It was between bells and the corridor was quiet. Rachel told him about going back to the dorm and starting a nursing course. Vic had graduated, but he was staying on, too. He was going to be a counselor himself, in M2, and a freshman at City College.

"What do you hear from Sam?" Vic asked.

Rachel looked at the floor. "Nothing. I don't know where he is or even if he's all right."

Vic seemed confused for a moment. He opened his mouth as if to speak, then shut it, then opened it again.

"What is it?"

"No, nothing, it's just . . . I'm sure he's safe, Rachel, I'm sure he's okay. Sam knows how to take care of himself." A bell rang. The door of the club room opened and the members of the Blue Serpent Society came into the hall, jostling them.

"Well, I gotta go. Why don't you come to Reception tomorrow, visit my mother with me? She hasn't seen you in so long, she asks about you all the time."

"Sure, tomorrow, I'll meet you there. At Study Bell?"

"Study Bell, yeah. Okay, see you then, Rachel." Vic lifted his arms to make some kind of gesture, then seemed unsure what to do. He ended up placing his hands on Rachel's shoulders and drawing her toward him. He kissed her cheek. "Take care of yourself," he whispered.

Rachel made her way through the corridor, now crowded with children. The place on her cheek where Vic had kissed her felt warm, and she put her fingertips there to hold on to the feeling. She smiled to herself, thinking it was the most natural thing in the world.

Entering the office, she greeted Mr. Grossman's secretary, who thought nothing of handing over the Infirmary's small pile of mail to Rachel. On her way back, she sorted through the letters in her hands. One, addressed to Nurse Dreyer, had its stamp canceled in Colorado. Curious, Rachel turned over the envelope to see who had sent it. On the back no return address was written, but the envelope was printed with the name of a business, ink pressed into the rag paper. *Rabinowitz Dry Goods, Leadville, Colorado.*

A coldness swept over Rachel, like a drift of snow. It couldn't be a coincidence, she thought. The letter must have something to do with her. She hurried her steps, eager to ask Nurse Dreyer about it—but no. She stopped. No matter whose name was written on the front, if it was about her she had a right to open it. She could think of only one place where she could be alone to read it.

Rachel climbed three flights of stairs, then slipped behind the small, secret door of the clock tower. The darkness blinded her at first, but as her eyes adjusted, she could make out the steep metal stairs, like a fire escape, leading up to a landing. Beyond that, a wooden ladder stretched up to a dusty platform. She climbed up and settled herself in the dim light that filtered through the clock face.

Again she examined the envelope, questions bouncing through her mind. *Rabinowitz Dry Goods.* Hadn't her father been in the garment trade? Was that the same as dry goods? *Leadville, Colorado.* Could her papa still be alive? Maybe he'd gone to Colorado after the accident that killed their mother. Rachel had always believed it was their neighbor's shrill voice screaming murder that drove her father to flee. Was it possible he was sending for her, now, after all these years? Or maybe Sam had tracked him down. Rachel's heart beat very fast. The letter must be from Sam. It was addressed to Nurse Dreyer because Sam found out somehow that she was staying in the Infirmary. Maybe that's why Vic seemed so confused when Rachel said she hadn't heard from him. Maybe Sam had written to them both but Vic had gotten his letter already.

The coldness that had washed over Rachel when she first saw the envelope melted away in this new understanding. She smiled, imagining seeing Vic on Sunday and being able to tell him that Sam had written to her, too, that she'd gotten the letter that very day they talked. She put her fingers to her cheek again, then tore the envelope and drew out the letter. Inside were two pieces of paper, one folded inside the other.

Dear Nurse Dreyer, Please give the other letter in this envelope to Rachel. I heard from Vic she's been staying in the Infirmary. Thanks again for all of your help after what happened with Mr. Grossman. I know I shouldn't have gone after Marc like that but you know what he did was wrong and he had it coming. Sincerely, Sam Rabinowitz

In her lap was the second letter, still unfolded. She was certain now it would be an invitation from her brother to join him in Colorado. To join him and Papa. With trembling fingers, she unfolded her letter.

Dear Rachel, Vic says you've been staying in the Infirmary learning to be a nurse. You'll be good at that. I'm writing to let you know I'm safe and you shouldn't worry about me. I can't tell you where I am cause I don't want Grossman to find me, but just know I'm fine and take care of yourself and do good in school. Love, Sam

Rachel read it over and over again, searching for more meaning between the lines. Finally she had to acknowledge the truth. Sam didn't want her, didn't even want her to know where he was. He'd been corresponding with Vic before ever writing to her. A flash of anger shook her hands. She tore both letters into tiny squares and tossed them down the shaft of the clock tower. They twirled like snowflakes and settled onto the dusty floor. There was nothing left for Rachel to do but let the tears come. The shadow of the clock's hands moved slowly across Rachel's face until, inevitably, a distant bell rang.

Rachel was wiping her eyes when a thought flowered in her mind, a thought so bright and supple it pushed back the sadness and dried her tears. Sam was always doing what he thought was best for her, from paying for Naomi's protection to beating up Marc Grossman. It was like the time he promised to come for her if she'd be good for the agency lady, just so she wouldn't cry. Maybe his letter, too, was an effort to do what he thought was best—stop her from worrying, let her finish school, allow the Home to care for her.

But Sam was wrong. He'd been wrong about Marc Grossman; Sam's running away hurt Rachel more than what Marc had done to her. He'd been wrong about Naomi, too; she'd have stood up for Rachel, been her friend, even without Sam's bribes. And he was wrong now. The Home, the nursing course, what did any of that matter when she could be with her brother and, maybe, their father as well?

Sam didn't know what was best for her. Only she did. All these years she'd been doing as she was told. Maybe that's all she knew, but it wasn't what she wanted, not anymore. Her lower lip jutted forward as something stirred in her, born of the same stubborn impulse that once sent her into tantrums.

She still had the envelope. Sliding a fingertip over the words *Rabinowitz Dry Goods* she made her decision. She would go to Leadville, join her brother, reunite with their father. Somehow she would make her own way, show Sam she could take care of herself, that he didn't have to protect her anymore. It was far, and the train ticket would be expensive. She wasn't sure how much money it would take, but with an awful clarity, she knew where she could get it.

THE SHADOW HAND made a full circle around the clock face before Rachel climbed down the wooden ladder and the metal stairs and closed the secret door behind her. The corridor was crowded with children streaming down to dinner. She made her way against the tide to deliver the rest of the mail to Nurse Dreyer. The clatter of the children's voices disturbed her thoughts. For the first time since she'd been at the Home, Rachel filled her lungs and shouted, "All Still!"

Instantly the din ceased. With a long exhalation, she looked up over the heads of the frozen children. Naomi, their new counselor, was at the back of the Fl group, twice the height of her charges. She looked at Rachel, confused and concerned. Rachel lowered her head and hurried along to the Infirmary. After she passed, she heard Naomi call out, "Okay, girls, go ahead." The children sprang to life, like a stalled heart shocked back to beating.

At the Infirmary, the doctor had been summoned to set a boy's broken arm, so Rachel's lateness was not noticed. When the boy was resting, wrist in a damp cast, Gladys Dreyer put away the gauze and plaster. "I wanted to go watch the movie," she said, "but he'll need some looking after. The Warner brothers sent over a new Rin Tin Tin."

"Go ahead, Nurse Dreyer, I'll stay with him until I go down to the dorm to sleep."

"So you've decided to go back to the dorm tonight? That's good,

Rachel. Get back in the routine before school starts up. Thanks so much for staying."

"What's one more evening?" Rachel hesitated. "Can I ask you something?"

"Of course, dear."

"Do we all have accounts?" She knew that whenever a child won some prize—a dollar for best essay, fifty cents for an outstanding speech—they were never given the money but told it would be added to their account.

"Most of you do, yes."

"Is there any way to know how much is in it? And, how do we get it?"

"Mr. Grossman's secretary keeps the books. I think all the money is on deposit at the bank. They don't keep it in cash, I can tell you that. Whenever you're old enough to leave the Home, they'll close your account and give you what's in it. But you'd have to ask at the office to find out how much there is." Gladys looked at Rachel, curious and skeptical. "Have you won many prizes?"

Disappointed, Rachel shook her head, wanting to change the subject. "No, I was just wondering, that's all." She hadn't expected any other answer but felt she owed it to Naomi to at least ask.

After the nurse left, Rachel read to the broken-armed boy until he fell asleep. Closing the book, she quietly dragged her cardboard suitcase from under the bed she'd come to think of as her own. She packed up the few things that had gathered around her in the Infirmary since she'd taken up residence there: change of clothes, nightgown, toothbrush, her birthday card, a jacket. From the desk drawer she added a big pair of scissors, black handles tapering to shining points. She picked up and put down *Essentials of Medicine* when her eyes fell on Nurse Dreyer's cloche hat on a hook near the door. Knowing that, by tomorrow, this small theft would be overshadowed, she took the hat and placed it in her case.

The movie was still running as Rachel made her way through the empty corridors. The flickering light played against the windows as she passed. She paused to watch as Rin Tin Tin, his projection huge on the outside wall of the Castle, ran across the crest of a distant hill. Waves of clapping erupted as the credits started to roll and children began stirring from their places on the fire escapes. Rachel hurried along to the F1 counselor's room. She entered and turned on the light. She was worried Naomi might be wearing the pair of shoes she was looking for, but no, there they were, under the little dresser.

Rachel set down her case and knelt on the floor. Reaching for the shoe, she drew it out and peeled back the insole. Fifty dollars. Hopefully it would be enough. She told herself that Naomi could still manage her tuition from what she earned if the Scholarship Committee pitched in. And if it turned out to be more than Rachel needed, she could send back the rest. She pulled out the bills and stuffed them into her case. She was about to leave when the door handle turned. Rachel froze.

Naomi came into the tiny room. "Rachel, what are you doing here?"

Caught, Rachel should have panicked. Instead, she felt strangely calm. Maybe she was already beyond the reach of the Home. "I'm moving back to F5 tonight," she lied. She studied Naomi to see if she would be believed, but all she noticed was how beautiful her friend was. The visit to Coney Island had brought out the freckles on Naomi's nose and cheeks. She had always worn her hair cropped, but now that it was fashionable her bob made her look modern. Rachel regretted, for the thousandth time, the nakedness of her own scalp.

"I figured as much, but I mean, why are you here, in my room?"

Rachel found herself unable to spin the elaborate story she'd rehearsed in her head. Something about the way Naomi looked at her gave Rachel a new idea. On an impulse, she dropped her case and stepped forward, slyly kicking the shoe, its insole curled out like a snake's tongue, back under the dresser. Reaching, she took Naomi's face in both her hands and drew the girl's mouth close until their lips pressed together.

The room was very quiet, the sound of hundreds of feet moving along the corridor muffled by the closed door. As the kiss extended, their lips softened, then opened. Tongues touched, again sending a shock through Rachel. Their knees beginning to bend, Naomi pulled Rachel toward her narrow bed.

Rachel had thought one kiss would be enough to distract Naomi from her theft, like the kiss in the changing booth. Now, another agenda imposed itself. Haste drained away as they stretched out side by side. Arms around each other, mouths together, there seemed no end to the ways two girls could kiss. Tiny kisses tiptoeing over nose and chin. A tongue-tip tracing open lips. Soft kisses skipping down a neck. Humid breath kissed into an ear. Lips pressed together, mouths open, inhaling each other's exhalation until they drained their lungs of oxygen.

It should have been enough, more than enough. Naomi pulled away, thinking of Rising Bell and the day to come. But Rachel was uninhibited by thoughts of morning, her secret knowledge making her bold. She asked, "What else is there?"

"There's this," Naomi whispered, undoing Rachel's dress.

"Show me."

"Are you sure?"

"Show me."

Naomi exposed Rachel's pink-tipped breast. Cupping the other, still clothed, in her hand, Naomi took the nipple in her mouth. Rachel felt something inside her come to life, like a hard seed ripening. She arched her back and wrapped her hand around Naomi's neck. Naomi pushed Rachel's dress off of her shoulders, licked the other breast. The seed started to split, roots shooting down. Rachel lifted her hips and Naomi shifted. Fabric stretched taut as she pressed her thigh between Rachel's legs. The seed opened. A light began to glow inside Rachel's closed eyes. If she looked at it, it slipped away, but if she let her eyes gaze past the light, it grew brighter, purple and gold. The seedling reached for the light, striving, growing. They were close, the bright new leaves of the seedling and the sparkling light. They were near.

They met. Rachel gasped and trembled. Naomi pressed against her, urgent, then buried her mouth in Rachel's neck and muffled a moan. Together they were quiet, Naomi's cheek resting on Rachel's collarbone. Her hand still on Naomi's neck, Rachel floated away with the receding light into a welcoming darkness.

Rachel couldn't tell how long she lingered in that darkness before the glowing lamp on Naomi's desk brought her back. "I have to get to the dorm." She sat up, pushing Naomi aside, and fixed her dress.

Naomi whispered in Rachel's ear, "I've always thought you were so beautiful, just like you are, so smooth and beautiful."

Rachel almost let herself believe it. Then she thought of the

money and the scissors in her case. She shrugged Naomi off and
stood, more abruptly than she intended.

"I have to go."

Naomi sat up in the bed. "It's all right, Rachel. Everything's all
right."

"I know," Rachel said. On the desk she saw Naomi's watch; it
was after two. "It's just so late. Maybe I better go back to the Infirmary after all."

Naomi reached out, but Rachel, knowing she didn't deserve
it, turned away from the offered hand. She grabbed her case and
stepped into the dark corridor, the slice of brightness across the
floor narrowing as she shut the door behind her.

Rachel moved silently through the sleeping orphanage until
she found the entrance to her old dormitory. Setting the cardboard case down and taking off her shoes, she drew out the scissors before slipping inside. The rows of beds stretched away, pale
mounds in the blue moonlight. Rachel was suddenly uncertain.
After all these months, she didn't remember where everyone slept.
She took a slow breath. She'd simply have to creep down every
row until she spotted the girl she was after. Gripping the scissors,
she padded through the dorm. In the summer warmth, girls slept
openly with light blankets swept off their shoulders. They didn't
stir; years of sleeping together had inured them to the night noises
of girls dreaming or snoring or shuffling to the toilet.

It was in the next row of beds that Rachel found Amelia sleeping on her side, braided hair snaking across the pillow. Amelia,
who was always so beautiful. Amelia, who ruined everything.
Rachel cringed at the memory of Marc Grossman's hand. She
clutched the scissors. Leaning over, she placed the red braid be-

tween the bright blades. It was amazing how this thing that grew from Amelia was so dead it could be cut an inch from her scalp without her waking. The braid dropped into Rachel's hand. She closed her fingers around it, dragging it on the floor as she walked out of the dormitory.

In the corridor, Rachel put her shoes back on and opened the case. In it, she placed the scissors and Amelia's braid. She'd planned to leave it on the floor to mock the girl, but for some reason her hand had been unwilling to let it go. From the case, she withdrew the cloche hat and put it on before descending to the basement. Past the dining hall, Rachel steeled herself to walk to the end of that dark corridor. She hid in the shadows near the door the baker would unlock when he came in to start the day's loaves of rye. By Rising Bell, she'd be gone.

Chapter Twelve

AT FOUR O'CLOCK ROUNDS, WHEN I FOUND DR. SOLOmon in terrible pain, I enjoyed seeing her writhe and squirm. I resented the morphine for bringing her peace, then regretted there wasn't enough in the syringe to snuff her out. The vengeful feelings terrified me. Who was I, what was I becoming? First that librarian, and now this. Already wobbly from spending the hot summer on my own, I'd been knocked off my axis by Mildred Solomon's arrival. All day I'd been suppressing my anxiety over tomorrow's appointment with Dr. Feldman. I kept telling myself to keep it together until I got out of work, that I could fall apart once I got her on the phone in Florida, knowing her words could put me back together.

I hurried home, desperate to get behind the closed door of our apartment, to hear her voice, to know I wasn't alone. I let the phone ring and ring but still no answer. It was eight o'clock at night, where could she be? I began to panic, anxiety capitalizing on my old fears of being abandoned. It was as if she'd dropped off the end of the earth and left me behind, the same way Sam left me behind, again and again.

It seemed the refrain of my life: when had I last seen my

brother? At least I had something to remember him by. I went into my room, grabbed the leather handle on the side of the steamer trunk at the foot of my bed, and tipped it up on end. Undoing the clasps, I opened it like a book on its spine. Behind the curtain where dresses once hung, I now stored folded quilts layered with mothballs. On the other side, each drawer that once held gloves or stockings was now dedicated to a different person's correspondence. From Dr. and Mrs. Abrams there were letters of encouragement while I was in nursing school, annual holiday cards, his obituary clipped from the *Denver Post*. From Simon I'd saved the childish notes that matured over the years until, at last, his heartbroken mother had mailed me his military portrait along with the carvings I'd sent each year on his birthday, saying in her letter that he'd wanted me to have them. There was Mary's drawer, which I preserved like a museum. In another, my collection of movie ticket stubs, torn reminders of nights out together over the years. Craving the memories, I sifted through the tickets, reading a few of the movie titles I'd scrawled on the back of the stubs—*Adam's Rib*, *Notorious*, *Jezebel*, *Stage Fright*—but each flash of memory only made me lonelier. I shut that drawer.

Kneeling before the open trunk, I pulled out Sam's drawer, spread its contents across the floor. I shuffled through the couple dozen postcards Sam had sent from out west, color-tinted pictures of canyons or mountains, a different postmark on every one. Counting them out, they averaged two a year. He'd never been much for writing. Then the last card, from that apple farm in Washington State. He hadn't signed his name to it, just scrawled *Arriving New York Penn Station Friday*. That and the date: *December 8, 1941*. I dwelled for a while in the memory.

Whenever December seventh rolls around and people remember that infamous day, all I can think of is hearing my brother's voice for the first time in a dozen years. I was just coming off shift at the hospital where I used to work. All day, radios had been tuned to breaking news about the attacks. Nurses understood that a declaration of war would affect us, too. They'd be needing us, and for a lot of girls I worked with, the Army Nurse Corps became the opportunity, and challenge, of a lifetime. During the war years, I kept in touch with some of them. I envied their adventures, their trials, their purpose—some even got commissions and benefits—and there were times I regretted not volunteering. It seemed selfish and petty to have let my worries about how I'd manage with a wig in a field hospital stop me, but they did, and not just that. I worried what I might do, who I might turn to, if I was away from her for too long.

A group of us were nearly out the hospital door when the switchboard operator shouted across the lobby. "Nurse Rabinowitz, there's a long-distance call for you. From a man," she added, prompting the nurses around me to squeal, their speculations finally answered. Telephone lines were hopelessly clogged that day, but somehow Sam had charmed a Bell operator into putting through his call. I hadn't heard his voice, let alone seen him, since Leadville. And now Sam was calling to tell me he was coming to New York to enlist. "Lots of Home boys are already in the military," he said, his voice delayed by the distance. "You can be damn sure the rest of them will be lining up to volunteer." He was right about that; the war was well timed for orphans. The army was somewhere else for the boys to go where they'd be fed and clothed and told what to do. But Sam was too old for all that, wasn't he?

"I'm not thirty yet, and anyway, I figure I'll have a better chance of seeing action if I join up with a unit from New York." I could hear from the excitement in his voice that he was ready for a fight.

The other nurses had milled in the lobby, waiting to hear my news. Disappointed that it was only my brother, they strutted off, anxious to get ready for dates with young men who would soon be soldiers. I walked home quickly across Washington Square, so excited Sam was coming back I barely noticed the cold.

A few days later, I was in the train shed of Penn Station, flakes on the glass roof making me feel like I was inside a snow globe, watching the board for the arrival of Sam's train. For a moment I panicked, wondering if I'd recognize him in the frantic crowd. I stood on a bench, not caring how desperate I looked to anyone else, scanning the sea of faces. When I spotted him, I wondered how I could have ever doubted I'd know him. Seventeen or twenty-nine, his face still fit the contours of my memory. He told me later he was confused, looking up, to see a pretty young woman with red hair calling to him in his sister's voice. Then our eyes met, and what we saw in each other reached back to those mornings under the kitchen table, waking hand in hand.

I set aside the postcards and took out his military letters. Sam had gone to enlist right away, but the army was taking too long to get new units organized, so he joined the National Guard upstate, figuring once they deployed, his age wouldn't hold him back. He wrote from basic training to tell me how easy it was. Not that the exercises and the drills weren't hard—they had one sergeant who made them run until they vomited. It was just that it all came back to him: the rules, the orders, the discipline. Everyone sleeping and showering and eating together. *It's like the Home was basic*

for the military, he scrawled. He knew all the training was important and he excelled at it, but he chafed at being garrisoned. It was
the summer of 1943 before their unit finally mustered up for the
ground war in Europe. *We better not win this thing before I get my
chance to fight.*

He needn't have worried. The conflict dragged on in a way no
one had expected. Soldiers were coming home, not in victory but
on stretchers. Wounded veterans began showing up in my hospital. It was like the Infirmary all over again except the boys were
bigger, their bloody noses and scraped knees now shrapnel wounds
or severed limbs. And those were the lucky ones. I tried not to
think about the men left behind, killed on some battlefield or too
wounded to survive the voyage home. Once he was overseas, Sam
wrote when he could, each stained page containing the fewest sentences necessary to assure me he was safe, there being no words
for what he was really seeing. Despite his reassurances, every long
stretch between letters tempted me to imagine him among the
dead.

After victory in Europe, I worried Sam might be sent to the
Pacific, but there was enough of a mess to mop up in Germany and
Austria to keep him out of that until it was all over. When Sam's division shipped home in '46, he got assigned to an army barracks up
on Amsterdam Avenue, where they were housing soldiers in a big
old building that looked like a castle. I thought, after the war, that
Sam would settle down in New York, give us a chance to become
reacquainted. It turned out, though, he had more leaving to do.

It had been awhile since one of Sam's letters had arrived from
Israel. I kept them all in order. The very earliest ones, bearing the
stamp of Palestine, had been delivered promptly. Then there was

the heart-stopping gap, months and months in 1948 when nothing arrived and all the news was terrible—fighting, bombings, sieges. That first envelope with a stamp all in Hebrew dropped me to my knees in relief. Even after the post became reliable, Sam's correspondence was spotty. On the rare occasions that a blue airmail envelope arrived, I drew out the time until I opened it, running my fingers over paper that felt dry as the desert. Cutting open the edges, I inhaled the captured scent, imagining orange groves and palm trees. The paper folded flat felt gritty; sometimes I'd find grains of sand in the creases. Sam now had so much to say that he filled every available space with his scrawl. I struggled to follow his talk of the fighting and of politics, but I savored his descriptions of the country: the sparse beauty of the dry hills, the night sky over the desert, the sparkling expanse of the Galilee. When he recounted his struggle to learn Hebrew, I wrote back, teasing, that he should have paid better attention at the Home studying for his bar mitzvah. *It's not about religion*, he replied. *It's so we speak our own language, the only language that's even been ours alone.*

After the Armistice Agreements, he left the permanent army and joined a kibbutz, became one of its leaders from the way he talked about it, though he claimed no one person was in charge. Instead of skirmishes and negotiations, his letters became devoted to irrigation schemes and housing plans. Then came a letter that took me by surprise, though I should have expected it eventually. Sam was getting married. He'd met his wife, Judith, on the kibbutz. She was a young refugee who'd spent the war hiding in a cellar only to emerge into a Europe purged of our people. I wrote back with congratulations, sent as a gift for the newlyweds a box full of seed packets, varieties of tomato and cucumber that thrive in heat.

A year later, instead of a blue airmail letter, a small cardboard box arrived. In it, a roll of film was carefully sealed into its canister with electrician's tape. I had it developed at the camera shop. Apparently the roll had been in the camera for a long time—the pictures told the story of an entire year. I opened the envelope of photographs again that night and dealt them out on the floor in front of the open trunk, fingering their scalloped edges.

There was Sam, smiling broadly, his gray eyes squinting against the sun. The beautiful woman with a wash of freckles across her nose must have been Judith. In one image they were beside blue water in what seemed to be their underwear, though I supposed it must be bathing suits. In the next, they had scarves around their necks and shovels in their hands, pointing proudly to a row of saplings. In one picture, Judith wore a printed dress and held some wildflowers while Sam, in uniform, faced her. Their wedding picture. Every time I looked at it, my eyes stung. Why hadn't I been there? That I didn't have money or time for the journey seemed a meager excuse, even if they had thought to invite me.

I shuffled through unpeopled pictures of gardens and fences and cinder block dwellings, their prominence in each frame telling of Sam's pride. Then the picture of Judith turned to the side to show her pregnancy. He hadn't written they were expecting—that photograph had been my first inkling. The last pictures on the roll were of an infant. I couldn't tell if I had a niece or a nephew until I saw the baby crying in Sam's arms, the rabbi hovering over him for the bris.

I stuffed the pictures back into the envelope and abandoned

myself to a good cry, stretched out on the rug, my head pillowed on my folded arms. God knows I needed to let the tears out, and that picture of my nephew brought them on every time. What good did it do me to finally have a family if they were half a world away? Sometimes I thought Sam was being deliberately cruel, dangling from a distance the only child in the world who could have filled that place in my heart. I'd assumed the baby was named after our father, imagined my nephew as Harold or Hershel or Hillel, until a letter, dated before the film was sent, arrived a few days after. *He's a true sabra*, Sam wrote, *born a Jew in a Jewish state. We named him Ayal.* I had been surprised until Sam's words rang in my memory. "Our father left us, Rachel. We don't owe him a thing." Not even, apparently, the memory of a name.

Wrung out, I put everything back in the drawer, slid the drawer into its place, closed the trunk. Needing some air, I stepped out onto the balcony. The sky was as dark as it gets while the board-walk and the rides were still lit up. The hot air carried notes of carnival music from the carousel. Who knows what was happening on the beach or in those shadowy places under the boardwalk. Men who met each other secretly, women who gave themselves up to their lovers, boys like that awful Marc Grossman looking to ruin some poor girl. Entire trajectories of lives were being set in motion, like balls across a billiards table.

I used to think it was the terrible accident that felled my mother and drove my father away that had set my life along its course. Now, though, I saw it was Dr. Solomon who'd made the break-ing shot. If she hadn't used me for her experiment, I would have arrived at the Orphaned Hebrews Home whole and undamaged, pretty enough that Sam wouldn't have felt ashamed to look at me. If I'd been a normal girl, Marc Grossman wouldn't have been goaded into hurting me, Sam wouldn't have had to come to my defense, and Mr. Grossman wouldn't have given him the beating that forced him to run away. Without all that anger he carried, Sam might not have even gone to war, and if not, then neither would he have felt compelled to fight for Israel. He would have met some other girl, had different children. I'd have had nieces and nephews who grew up here where I could know them, build sand castles with them at the beach, cat's cradle with them when I babysat, shower them with the love I would have given my own children.

I could see now that it was hopeless. My mind would never stop running along these crazy tracks. I took a sleeping pill and surrendered myself to my empty bed. I felt again for the acorn in my breast, hoping against hope that Dr. Feldman would test it and find the cells benign, reassure me it was only a cyst. Now that I understood how my fate depended on Mildred Solomon, it seemed not only my life that hung in the balance, but hers as well.

Chapter Thirteen

RACHEL WATCHED THE SKY LIGHTEN THROUGH THE soaring windows of Pennsylvania Station. She thought she'd be nervous, scared even, to be out on her own. But during her solitary wait for the subway, the enormity of what she was doing overwhelmed her anxiety. As she passed between the limestone columns of the station and emerged into the vaulted waiting hall, she felt she was leaving behind her identity as an orphan of the Home. She wrote herself a new history in which she was a nursing student going out to Colorado to join her family in Leadville. For practice, she told this story to the ticket agent when he rolled up his window.

"Colorado?" He looked her over, adding up the bell-shaped hat, the plain dress, the cardboard case. Definitely not first class. He snorted. "Well, Pennsylvania Rail'll get you as far as Chicago, but from there you'll have to buy a ticket to Denver from another carrier. Try Burlington and Quincy, they're out of Union Station. Once you get to Denver, you'll ask about Leadville, they'll at least have a mail train out there. The Broadway Limited and the Pennsylvania Limited, they're both first-class trains, get you to Chicago in less than twenty-four hours. You got the money for that?"

"I've got fifty dollars for the whole trip." She'd thought it was a fortune, but the ticket agent frowned.

"I can't get you past Chicago on a Limited for that." A practiced observer of strangers, he tried to figure the girl's age, but something about her face threw him off. He looked over her shoulder—no one else on line yet. His thermos of coffee, still hot, put him in a generous mood. "Let me see what I got." He checked the fare tables and the timetables and the passenger lists.

"Okay, I can put you on the Western Express. It's a local, all coach, departs at noon and gets into Chicago tomorrow night. Should leave you enough for the Burlington ticket. Now, you ever ride a train before?" Rachel shook her head no. Eyebrows, he realized. She didn't have any, or lashes either. What could account for that? He leaned through the ticket window. "Here's what you do. There's no dining car or nothing on this train. On a lot of the platforms somebody'll be selling sandwiches, but they'll gouge you for sure. You go out this morning and get some food to take on with you, enough for the whole trip. There's drinking water on board, so don't worry about that. Then when you get on, you tell the conductor I said to put you by a nice family. I wouldn't want no sister of mine next to some strange man all night."

By the time the agent got her ticket together, a couple of people were waiting behind Rachel. She thanked him quickly. "You watch yourself," he said, then lifted his head. "Next!"

Rachel went down Eighth Avenue until she found a grocer's. She bought rolls, pears, a wedge of cheese, peanuts in a paper bag, some peppermints. On her way back to the station she got a pretzel from the newsstand for her breakfast. She wasn't worried about anyone from the Home noticing she was gone. Vic and Mrs.

Berger might wonder what she was up to when she didn't turn up in Reception at visiting hour, but since it was against the rules for Home children to mix with new admissions during quarantine, what could they say? And tomorrow would be Labor Day; even if someone did miss her, with all the commotion of the marching band playing in the parade this year and the counselors run off their feet herding the children down Broadway to watch, there'd be no time to report a runaway. It would probably be Tuesday before her absence was finally noticed. Until then, Nurse Dreyer would think Rachel was in the F5 dorm, and Naomi would assume she'd gone back to the Infirmary.

A tingle shot through Rachel's body at the memory of what she had done with Naomi. It hadn't felt strange or wrong. It had felt like the most natural thing in the world. Then the shame of having stolen from her friend turned the tingle into nausea. Whatever it was they had done, it didn't follow the pattern of anything Rachel had been taught in school or read in a book. She thought of the girls crowding around her at the Purim Dance after Vic had kissed her, their excited congratulations. That's what girls were supposed to want: to marry boys, to become mothers. Not to kiss each other. Rachel shook the memory of Naomi from her mind.

In the station's lobby, Rachel checked the board and the clock, noting the time until the Western Express was due to depart. Settling herself on one of the oak benches, she yawned. She tucked the case under her feet, wedged herself into a corner of the bench, and looked across at the ticket agent. He caught her eye over the shoulder of the customer he was serving and gave her a wink. Content she'd be watched over, Rachel dozed, lulled by the rising din of the station.

It turned out she didn't need to say anything to the conductor. When he saw she was alone, he placed her in a compartment with a group of women, teachers returning at the last possible moment to Fort Wayne after spending the summer on Long Island. The train clicked and rocked out of Manhattan, under the Hudson, across New Jersey, through Pennsylvania. Towns and meadows and woods and pastures and farms and streams washed across the window like a motion picture, except in color. The teachers invited Rachel to join their game of cards, but she said no, thank you, preferring the scenery. In the long evening light of summer, Rachel watched the window picture show until darkness dimmed the screen. Confronted with her reflection in the dark glass, Rachel relished the notion that no one in the world knew where she was. The freedom was intoxicating, like living inside a secret.

Made sleepy by the swaying train, the women finally stretched their legs across the space between the facing seats, fitting their feet between each other's hips. The next day, the Western Express made its halting way across Ohio and Indiana until the teachers tumbled out at Fort Wayne. By the time the train pulled into Chicago's Union Station, Rachel had stopped measuring the passing hours by which bell would be ringing back at the Home. The conductor told her there was a coach car on the Overland Express to Denver, and she climbed the stairs from platform to mezzanine, anxious to get a ticket.

Rachel had barely taken in the barrel ceiling and stone columns when two boys came chasing each other through the station. The smaller one was running full out to stay ahead, skidding across the marble floor and careening around a statue. The older boy caught at his jacket, and the little one, twisting to get away, ran into a column right in front of Rachel, his head bouncing back from the force. Blood started to drain from the boy's nose. He let out a howl that sent the older one scurrying. Rachel scooped him onto her lap and settled on a bench, tilting his head up in the crook of her arm. She pinched the bridge of his nose with one hand while fishing out her handkerchief with the other.

"Now, now, it's not so bad as all that," she murmured as the boy coughed and cried. "Was that your brother chasing you?"

The boy looked up at her and nodded, tears mixing with the blood that drizzled across his face to puddle in his ear. Rachel wiped his cheek, then held the handkerchief under his nose. "Just breathe through your mouth, it'll stop in a minute. Relax, now, relax. It's all right," she said, mimicking Nurse Dreyer's soothing tone.

"My brother's always chasing me. I hate him," the boy whimpered. His breath smelled of iron.

"Can you imagine if you had a hundred brothers, how many bloody noses that would add up to?"

He frowned. "No one has a hundred brothers."

Rachel lifted the handkerchief. The bleeding had stopped, but she kept up the pressure on the bridge of his nose. "I had a thousand brothers and sisters."

His eyebrows lifted. "Really?"

Rachel checked to see if the blood was still flowing. It wasn't.

"How about you, is that your only brother?"

He was draped across her lap, his head heavy on her arm. "No, I have a baby brother, too, and a sister. But I'll never chase my baby brother like Henry chases me."

"Of course you won't. What's your name?"

"Simon. What's yours?"

"Rachel."

Henry was being dragged toward them by an imposing man in a top hat and evening jacket.

"Father, Henry chased me!" Simon tried to sit up, but Rachel held him.

"You have to keep your head back for a while longer or your nose'll start bleeding again."

"Yes, Simon, do as the lady says." The man's eyes swept over the young woman cradling his son. "Are you a nurse, miss?"

Rachel nodded, the lie she'd told the ticket agent and the teachers sounding truer with each retelling. "A nursing student. I was doing my apprenticeship at an orphanage in New York. Now I'm going to Colorado to care for my father. He went out west last year for the cure, but my mother wrote that he's taken a turn for the worse and she needs me there."

"You've certainly taken good care of Simon. What do you have to say to your brother, Henry?"

"I'm sorry, Simon."

"Now go back to your mother." The boy walked away, breaking into a run as soon as his father wasn't looking. The man sat on the bench beside Rachel and placed his hand on Simon's forehead. "All better, son? Ready to try sitting up?"

"Oh, not yet, it's best not to rush these things," she said.

"Rachel has a thousand brothers and sisters, Father!"

"Is that so, miss?"

"At the orphanage, they liked the children to think of each other as siblings. I got in the habit of seeing them all as my younger brothers and sisters." She smiled, liking the way that sounded.

"And you're going to Denver?"

"Leadville, actually, but Denver first. I was hoping to make the Overland Express." She looked around, anxious. "Do you know when it leaves?"

"It was scheduled for eight o'clock. You would have missed it, but there's been a delay, some problem loading the horses. I was supposed to see my family off before attending a function this evening, but I couldn't very well leave my wife to watch these ruffians by herself. Would you allow me to introduce you to Mrs. Cohen?"

"I'm afraid I should arrange my ticket." Rachel sat Simon up gently.

"I'll take him," his father said, picking up the boy.

"I'm not a baby, I can walk, Father!"

"Very well." He set Simon on his feet and extended a hand to Rachel. She stood.

"I'll talk to the ticket agent to be sure there's a place for you. I know my wife will want to thank you personally."

They found Simon's mother on a bench surrounded by luggage, a baby in one arm and a little girl sprawled, sleeping, across her lap. A purple satin jacket strained to contain the roll of fat around her waist. The feathered hat perched on her head looked like a seagull bobbing on flotsam.

"Oh, Simon! Just look at your collar. See what you've done, Henry!" Henry, beside her, hung his head.

"Althea, this is Miss . . . ?" The man looked at her.

"Rabinowitz, Rachel Rabinowitz. Pleased to meet you, Mrs. Cohen."

"My pleasure, dear," Althea said, distractedly offering a limp hand. "David, when can we board? I need to settle them into the car before they drive me to distraction."

"Rachel is a nursing student, dear. She took care of Simon's bloody nose just now. She's going to Denver, to see her parents." Althea looked at her husband and lifted an eyebrow, as if an idea had been communicated between them.

"Really? Do you have your ticket yet?"

"No, I need to arrange it."

"Listen, dear, I know this is abrupt, but would you consider traveling with me? The children's au pair was taken ill and Dr. Cohen won't allow her to travel, but I don't see how I can possibly manage on my own."

"Oh, come with us, Rachel! We'll have such fun on the train," Simon pleaded.

"Thank you, I'd be happy to travel with you, Mrs. Cohen, if I can be of help." Simon applauded; Rachel interrupted him. "But, are you in coach as well?"

Althea let out a laugh. "Oh, dear, no, we're in the Pullman, but you'll join us, please. You can use the au pair's ticket. I can't express to you what a comfort it will be to have someone with me." As if everything had been settled, Althea handed the baby to Rachel then shifted the sleeping girl off her lap. She stood and smoothed her skirt with gloved hands. "Just look at these creases," she muttered to herself.

Their train was announced. The doctor escorted his family and Rachel down to the platform and into their compartment, where they said their good-byes. Soon after the train pulled out of Chicago, a porter arrived at their compartment to deliver their luggage and introduce himself. "Mrs. Cohen, my name is Ralph Morrison."

His voice was deep, with a hint of bayou in the vowels. "I am here to make your journey as pleasant as possible. The dining car has been holding dinner, and I'll be making up the beds while you enjoy yourselves a late supper. If you need anything at all, just call for me." He cleared his throat. "Now, you are welcome to call me porter, or Ralph, but as I am lately a grandfather, I'm afraid I'm just a little too old to answer to 'boy.'"

Ralph Morrison paused to gauge their reaction to his speech, which he delivered with a calibrated smile to every passenger, as if inviting them to be amused by the novelty of treating a person of color with respect. Althea was too distracted by the children to have paid much attention, but Rachel couldn't see why anyone would call the tall man with a sprinkling of white in his close-cropped hair a boy.

Dinner was remarkable, thick steaks on china plates, silverware gleaming against the linen tablecloth. Rachel cut the meat for the little girl, but Simon insisted on struggling with the steak knife himself. Returning from the dining car, Rachel thought Ralph Morrison must be a magician to have transformed the plush compartment, with its upholstered couches and curtained window, into a bedroom, the four beds made up with stiff sheets and soft pillows. They took it in turns to undress in the tiny restroom, complete with washstand and toilet. Despite the polished faucet and beveled mirror, Rachel saw when she pulled the chain that their waste emptied onto the tracks rushing beneath them, just as it had in the coach car from New York.

It was the best night Rachel could remember. Never mind that the train stopped twice to take on cargo, the coupling of cars lurching her out of sleep. The spells of wakefulness allowed her to savor the night. The boys had the top bunks; Mrs. Cohen had taken the baby into her bed, leaving the little girl, Mae, to sleep in Rachel's arms, the small head resting lightly on her elbow. Rachel wrapped her arms around the girl's breathing warmth and let the swaying train rock them to sleep as Illinois and Iowa rolled away beneath them.

IN THE EARLY morning, while the train was stopped in the yard at Omaha, Althea rang for the porter to bring coffee and rolls. Rachel feared Mrs. Cohen would remark on her bald scalp before she could settle the cloche hat over her head, but Althea was either too tactful to say anything or too distracted to notice.

"Just look at that sky," Althea murmured. "That's what I miss most, is that big western sky." While they enjoyed breakfast in the quiet of sleeping children, Althea whispered her family's history: how her father, Dr. Abrams, had come out to Colorado to start the Hospital for Consumptive Hebrews, and met her mother, the daughter of pioneers who'd been in Colorado since gold rush days. Althea met her own husband when he came out from Chicago to intern at the hospital; they'd been married in Temple Emanuel before Dr. Cohen moved them back to Chicago to establish his own practice. Rachel listened contentedly while she finished her coffee, wondering what it would be like to know so much about her own past. Althea rang for more rolls and cold milk as the children stirred awake.

"Do you know what happened with the horses last night, Mr. Porter?" Henry asked, sitting on his mother's bed and popping a roll into his mouth.

"It's Mr. Morrison, Henry," Rachel corrected. Ralph Morrison glanced at her, then back at the boy.

"How's about you call me Ralph and I'll call you Henry, all right? And I sure do know what happened with those horses. My good friend saw the whole thing with his own eyes." He took a knee in the open doorway of the compartment. Henry and Simon both came closer. "A whistle blew in the train yard, and one of Mr. Guggenheim's prize stallions spooked going up the ramp into the horse car. When he reared up, his back hooves slipped off the ramp and he tumbled down on the tracks. Just then, the caboose got coupled on the back of the train and bumped the horse car. That stallion got caught under the carriage."

Ralph glanced at Mrs. Cohen, seeking approval to continue the gruesome story. His tip—indeed, his career as a Pullman porter—depended on never giving offense. But anything that entertained her boys was fine with Althea. "Go on," she said.

"Well, that horse was whinnying to shatter glass, and all the horses on the car started bucking and neighing. It was pan-de-mo-ni-um. Mr. Guggenheim's trainer was raising heck with the conductor. The engineer moved the train back off the horse, and the poor creature had to be put down. Not only that, but then the horse had to be chained up and dragged off the tracks."

"I wish I could've seen it," Henry said.

"What was the horse's name?" Simon asked.

"Now, that's a very good question, young man, but I don't know the answer." Ralph Morrison took the pot to refresh their coffee. "Lunch will be served between twelve-thirty and two. Would you like the first or second seating, Mrs. Cohen?"

"First seating, please, the children will be hungry again."

As the train rocked across Nebraska, Rachel took the boys down to the observation car. She waved away cigar smoke as they pressed against the window, the prairie sweeping past under a huge blue sky, the boys searching in vain for buffalo. After lunch, Althea tried to wear the boys out by letting them race along the corridor, to the unspoken dismay of the porters, while Rachel stayed in the compartment with Mae and the baby, both napping. Sitting by the window, she watched the sagging telegraph wires rise and fall like waves between the pine poles. She wondered what messages were pulsing through those wires, dash dot dash.

It was nearly ten o'clock that night when the Western Express pulled into Denver's Union Station. Rachel had her cardboard case ready. She expected to say her good-byes to Mrs. Cohen and the children in their compartment, but Simon had fallen asleep and needed to be prodded to his feet, Henry was cranky, and Althea asked Rachel to take Mae while she carried the baby. Ralph Morrison, handing Mrs. Cohen down to the platform, looked satisfied, though not impressed, with the tip she pressed into his hand. He tucked the money into his pocket, adding it to the generous amount he'd gotten, with a knowing wink, from a banker traveling with his mistress.

Rachel followed the family off the train and up the ramp to the station, Mae's sweaty little fingers in one hand and her case in the other. Henry ran ahead, Simon followed, and Mrs. Cohen hurried after them, the feathers on her hat bobbing above the crowd. In the station, Mrs. Cohen embraced a man Rachel assumed was her father, Dr. Abrams; the boys were bouncing around him while he cooed at the baby. Before Rachel could get near enough to hand

Mae to her mother, the group had moved toward the arched doors. Rachel looked over her shoulder at the ticket window—a few men were gathered there, as well as porters emerging from the tracks with carts of luggage—but before she could stop Mrs. Cohen, the family was outside. Rachel hurried to catch up, pulling Mae along, only to see them piling into a black sedan. As she reached the car door, Althea, settled up front with the baby on her lap, called back to the boys to make room for Rachel and Mae. Henry reached out and grabbed her case. Hoisting Mae onto her lap, Rachel rode the tide into the car.

They disgorged at Althea's parents' house, an impressive Queen Anne with steep gables. Its shingled turret looked like a doll's house to Rachel compared to the clock tower of the Castle. The children ran to their grandmother—even little Mae toddled up the brick walk—but Rachel hung back. Dr. Abrams came up behind her, carrying one of Althea's bags and the cardboard case. "Would you take these?" he said. "I'm going back for the rest of the luggage now."

"Excuse me, sir, but I need to go on to Leadville. Perhaps you could bring me back to the station with you?"

"The Mail to Leadville doesn't leave until the morning. I'm afraid there aren't any more trains tonight."

Dr. Abrams called his wife down from the porch. After a hurried consultation, he got back in the sedan and motored away. Mrs. Abrams spoke to Rachel. "It's been settled. You'll stay with us tonight. Now come on in, dear."

Rachel sat with the boys while Althea and her mother went upstairs to settle Mae and the baby. By the time they came back down, Simon and Henry were nodding in their chairs. "I'll take them, Althea, if you want to wait up for your father," Mrs. Abrams said.

"I'm too exhausted for conversation, Mother. I'll drop the boys off in the nursery and get into my old bed. I'll see you at breakfast."

As Althea and the boys climbed the stairs, the front door opened and Dr. Abrams came in with the luggage. It took him two trips to carry it all in from the car and up the stairs. When he was finished, he dropped into a chair and removed his round wire-rimmed glasses to wipe his forehead with a napkin. Mrs. Abrams poured him a glass of iced tea, her strong arms managing the heavy glass pitcher as if it were weightless.

"I checked on the Mail to Leadville. It leaves at nine, but you won't arrive until the afternoon, it makes absolutely every stop along the way. Perhaps I could arrange for someone to drive you?"

"I could do it, Charles. A day trip to Leadville would make a nice diversion for the children."

"No, thank you, Dr. Abrams, Mrs. Abrams, I won't mind the time on the train." They didn't seem to believe her. "I've been so busy helping Mrs. Cohen with the children I haven't had any time to prepare myself. My father, you see, is very ill."

"As you wish. The scenery will be spectacular at least, especially around Breckenridge," Dr. Abrams said. "I'll say good night now."

"I'll be right in, Charles, I'm putting Rachel in the Ivy Room."

Mrs. Abrams took Rachel upstairs, past the bedrooms where Althea and the children slept, to a narrow staircase. Rachel followed her up to a cozy room in the attic, where she found a freshly made bed, a small dresser, and a sink with hot and cold taps. The electric light brought green vines and goldfinches out of the wallpaper.

"I meant to have the au pair in here. I hope you don't mind, Rachel."

Rachel didn't mind in the least. Tucked into the circular turret, its view of Colfax Avenue fractured by the small panes of a leaded window, the Ivy Room made her feel like a princess in a tower. Pulling shut the curtain, she took off her hat and clothes and washed herself from head to toe with a warm, soapy cloth. She opened the case to pull out her nightdress. Rachel had forgotten about the braid. Catching the light, Amelia's hair smoldered accusingly.

DOCTOR ABRAMS DROPPED Rachel at Union Station the next morning. Buying her ticket for the Mail train, she was grateful to have traveled from Chicago with the Cohens—what she had left of Naomi's money might not have covered the whole trip. But on the slow train that took most of the day, Rachel didn't worry about what she'd do if Sam wasn't in Leadville after all. Instead she pictured his face spreading into a smile as she appeared. He'd be impressed that she'd done this all on her own, relieved to know it wasn't his job to worry about her anymore.

And this Rabinowitz who owned the dry goods store? The more Rachel thought about it, the more she convinced herself he must be their father. She thought of Simon in the house on Colfax Avenue, securely circled by his mother, his brothers and sister, his grandparents. And back in Chicago his father and another set of grandparents, and cousins, maybe, and aunts and uncles. Even Naomi had her Uncle Jacob and Aunt Estelle, and Vic had his mother, too. Didn't she at least deserve to have a father?

The engine chugged over ravines and along creek beds high in the Rockies, stopping often to drop off mailbags and take on passengers. Finally, the conductor called Leadville. Rachel stepped off the train onto a wooden platform. The evening sky, still bright, was overbearingly blue. The few rough men who'd gotten off the train with her quickly scattered. She asked the man picking up the mail if he knew where she could find Rabinowitz Dry Goods.

"Sure, it's next to the Tabor. Just go up Harrison Street, it'll be on the left, can't miss it."

Rachel made her way along the raised sidewalk, stepping up and down at each street crossing, mud caking to her shoes from the unpaved roads. Her breath quickened and her heart thudded after only a couple of blocks. She worried she was getting ill until she remembered what Dr. Abrams had told her about the altitude. She rested a moment, looking around at Leadville. Only a few people were out—men in work clothes, women in plain dresses— and traffic was a car motoring past a horse cart. The entire town consisted of the one road and the few muddy lanes that crossed it. Beyond was nothing: no bridges or rooflines or streetlamps. Althea Cohen had spoken of the Rockies as expansive and open, but to Rachel, Leadville seemed a lonely island overshadowed by snowy peaks. Its isolation was as oppressive as the closeness of the sky. She wondered how her father had ended up here, how Sam had found him. Taking as deep a breath as she could, she lifted the cardboard case and continued.

She nearly passed it before noticing the letters T-A-B-O-R affixed to the facade of a large building. She hadn't expected "the Tabor" to be an opera house. Rachel looked around, her eyes scanning above doorways. There it was, Rabinowitz Dry Goods, painted on brick, faded and peeling. She peered through the shop window, stuffed with dusty goods, and saw a long counter stretching the length of the store. A row of enameled ovens marched down the center aisle, which was blocked by barrels of nails and stacked wheelbarrows. The walls were obscured by shelves piled with cooking pots and hatchets and pie pans and bolts of cloth.

Rachel tugged at the door. A bell jangled as it opened. "Be right out!" a man's voice called. Through the maze of goods, she saw a figure emerging from the back of the store. White hair circled his head, dipped down his cheeks, and crossed his upper lip. Beneath his jutting eyebrows, he squinted through round glasses. He was older, of course he was, but there was something deeply familiar about the shape of his chin, the reach of his nose, the slope of his shoulders. As he neared, Rachel flew back in time. She was four years old and a man with this nose, this chin, was lifting her to those shoulders, kissing her cheek, calling her a little monkey. She dropped her case. In two running steps she met him, her arms around his neck.

"Papa!" All the anxiety of her long journey was released in a rush of child's tears.

Chapter Fourteen

DR. FELDMAN'S NURSE WAS NAMED BETTY—I READ IT on the nametag she wore pinned to her uniform. From her stern voice on the telephone, I'd expected someone Gloria's age, but she was younger than she sounded and more fashionable, too, with manicured nails and hair sprayed into place. Still, the brisk way she took my information left no doubt who was in charge. Once she'd started my chart, she led me into an examination room and told me to get undressed. "Right down to your panties, then put this on." After I'd changed, she tied the cotton gown for me behind my back, tugging each little bow securely in place. She'd be a reassuring woman to have as a mother, I thought. Polished and dependable, if a little intimidating. Flo was nice as could be, but it pained me to see how her kids ran her ragged.

When I returned from providing a urine sample, Betty had me perch on the examination table while she took my pressure and pulse. I was surprised to see her ready a draw kit without being given an order. "He always wants blood drawn from new patients," she said, answering my unasked question. As she wrapped the rubber tube around my upper arm and patted the inside of my elbow to raise a vein, I wondered what she got paid. It would be nice to work in a doctor's office: steady hours, a good salary, no changing shifts or heavy lifting of patients. Why hadn't I ever applied for a job like this?

"Oh, I hear Dr. Feldman coming now," Betty said. The door from the adjoining office opened abruptly.

"And who do we have here?" I opened my mouth to introduce myself when I realized Dr. Feldman hadn't asked me, wasn't even looking at me, but instead was reaching for the chart Betty held out to him. He settled thick glasses on a nose so biblical I couldn't help but think of him as a rabbi.

"Call if you need me," Betty said to him, turning to leave. The look they exchanged was so intimate, as if they knew everything about each other, it reminded me why I preferred the more impersonal environment of a hospital or the Old Hebrews Home.

"So, what brings you here today, Miss Rabinowitz?"

Facing him, I found myself tongue-tied. I'd had no trouble telling it all to Betty: the Infant Home, the X-ray experiment, Dr. Feldman's article in the library. Wasn't it all in my chart already, or had he only pretended to read it? Mute, I touched my breast.

"Yes, well, my nurse tells me you've found a lump. Let's start there, shall we?" Dr. Feldman positioned himself beside the table, facing my back, and tugged open the gown. I moved to lie down, but he stopped me. "Just place your hand on top of your head." I did, feeling like a child playing Simon Says, while his fat fingers, yellowed by nicotine, searched my breast. I was embarrassed to see my nipple harden—from the air-conditioned cold as much as his prods and pinches—but he seemed to take no notice. After bruising his way up and down one side of my chest and armpit, he had me switch hands, forgetting to pull the gown back up over my shoulder, leaving me naked to the waist. He accompanied his examination with rumbling sounds in the back of his throat.

"Very good. You can get dressed now." He called for Betty on his way out, lighting a cigarette before the door was even closed. When I was presentable, she ushered me into his office. It reeked of smoke. Next to the overflowing glass ashtray on his desk was a pretentious blue pack of French cigarettes. The air conditioner rumbling in the closed window seemed only to recirculate the sickly smell.

"Miss Rabinowitz," he said from behind the fortress of his desk. "I'll need to see the results of your blood work, but my examination of your breast, coupled with the X-ray treatments my nurse tells me you received as a child—"

"They weren't treatments," I interrupted, surprising both of us with my vehemence. "It was an experiment. I was experimented on, not treated."

"Be that as it may, I have been noticing a statistically significant correlation between excessive childhood exposure to radiation and cancers later in life. Now, forgive me for asking, but have you ever given birth to a child or nursed a baby?"

"No, of course not." I sounded so prudish, I said again, simply, "No, I haven't."

"Have you experienced normal menses? Are you postmenopausal?"

"I didn't start until I was sixteen, and I've never been exactly regular."

"I see. Is there any chance of pregnancy?"

"None."

"Well, we'll see what the urine test tells us. As I was saying, based on my examination, I'd say you're quite lucky. The tumor is distinct with discernible edges. Though it may be fast growing, we have caught it in time to qualify you for surgery. If it was too advanced, you see, it wouldn't be advisable to cut across the cancer field."

He walked across the room and flicked a switch. A spotlight turned on, illuminating a laminated poster of a woman on his wall. He took a crayon from his pocket and began drawing on it. I could see smudges from past demonstrations. "I begin with an excision of the tumor, which is examined for cancer cells. If the results are negative, I finish the procedure and do what I can to repair the remaining breast tissue. If the results are positive, as I expect they will be, I proceed directly to a mastectomy of the entire breast and related lymph nodes. Unlike some of my colleagues, I don't find it advisable to remove the pectoral muscle, but as a prophylactic measure, I'd recommend taking the other breast as well. For a woman with your history who's never had a pregnancy or nursed an infant, it would be the wise choice."

His dashed lines crisscrossed the woman's chest as if he were planning a military maneuver on undulating terrain. I wanted to cover my breasts with my hands, to reassure and comfort them. Instead I gripped the arms of my chair. I hated how he kept mentioning babies, as if this wouldn't have happened if I'd been a normal woman.

"And, of course, I'll perform the castration." His crayon dipped below her waist, dabbing the lower abdomen where her ovaries were hidden. His back to me, he didn't see the blood drain from my face.

"Oophorectomy is standard procedure for all breast cancers, though I usually prefer to accomplish castration with radiation. Obviously, that wouldn't be recommended in your case. Neither would X-ray treatments following surgery, another reason to be aggressive while I have you on the table. Take them both and be done with it." He paused and considered his two-dimensional patient. Speaking more to her than to me, he said, "The operation is disfiguring, but at least in your case there's no husband to consider."

He switched off the light and took his seat behind the desk. He reached for the pack of cigarettes, lit one for himself, then tilted them in my direction. I was tempted but declined; I didn't want him to see how badly my hands were shaking.

"This isn't a cure, you understand. In my experience with this disease, even the most complete mastectomy merely delays a recurrence. But that delay can be significant. Two years, five. I have one patient who has survived eight years since her operation. The sudden onset of menopause due to the castration may be unpleasant, but we'll cross that bridge when we come to it, shall we?"

I couldn't muster a response. My reticence annoyed Dr. Feldman.

"Is there anyone you want me to speak to?" he asked when I hesitated to agree with his surgical plans. I lifted the tip of my tongue to the roof of my mouth to pronounce her name, but it stuck there, unsaid. "No one, then?"

It galled me for him to think I was an old maid. "I don't live alone," I said, defensively. Dr. Feldman looked confused. "I have a friend, my roommate."

"I was talking about relatives," he said. "I usually discuss these matters with the husband."

If only I could have told him how I sometimes called her husband—but only when she got that teacherly tone and instructed me on how something ought to be done. She was usually too emotional to be the husband, and though I never claimed that role, I wasn't much of a wife, either. She did the shopping and cooked dinner, but only because I was hopeless in the kitchen and had no patience for the grocer's. I balanced our checkbooks, but she was the one who could use a wrench to fix a leaking faucet. In the bedroom, it's true, she took the lead, but it was what we did in there that disqualified us from these categories in the first place. For some of our friends it was obvious who was butch and who was femme, but if we could have married, I wondered, which one of us would have been which? Right now, I know what I would have chosen—me dissolved in wifely tears, her the strong and reassuring husband.

It seemed my interview with Dr. Feldman was coming to a close. "Let me call my nurse," he said, pressing a buzzer on his desk. "Betty will get you on my surgical calendar and schedule a preoperative appointment. I'd like to move quickly." With that, he stood and extended his hand.

I got to my feet and mirrored his gesture. His yellowed fingers closed loosely over mine. From his examination, I'd expected a firmer grip. In a daze, I followed Betty out of the room.

"You're a nurse yourself, aren't you?"

"Yes, I am."

"That'll make things so much easier. Some of these women, they really don't understand what's happening, and of course it falls on me to hold their hands. They say doctors make the worst patients, but they should say nurses make the best." She sat at her desk, flipping through the pages of Dr. Feldman's appointment book, then wrote some dates and times on a card she handed to me. "I'll have you come back into the office the day before the surgery to review our procedures, and I'll get your vitals again."

I looked at the card in my hand. "Next week?"

"Dr. Feldman had an opening on his surgical calendar, and he did say it was important to move quickly. Where cancer is concerned, the sooner the better." Betty must have seen the anxiety rising in me. "Is there anyone you can bring with you?"

"My roommate. She's away, but I can call her to come back." She would come back, wouldn't she? All I had to do was tell her what was happening, if I could ever get her on the phone. I imagined the timetable in my mind: the overnight train left Miami every morning, getting her into New York the next day. If I called tonight, she could be here the day after tomorrow.

"I meant a relative, dear. They only allow immediate family in the hospital."

"I don't have any family." I panicked at the idea that they might confine her to a waiting room, prevent her from being by my side. I blurted out, "I'm an orphan, remember? It's not my fault I don't have anyone else."

Betty placed her hand on my forearm, a steady pressure. *Steadfast*, that's the word she brought to mind. "How about I put down that she's your sister. That way she'll be able to visit you, all right? Bring her with you next week, why don't you."

Next week. I still didn't understand why it all had to happen so soon. It was only three days since Mildred Solomon had arrived on Fifth. How had she managed to ruin my life so completely in such a short time?

Betty walked me out. "Dr. Feldman's the best, Miss Rabino-witz. You're lucky he could fit you in."

The last thing in the world I felt was lucky, and I knew who was to blame. I could picture her, withered and twitching, unre-pentant. I had planned to go home, get some rest before facing the night shift, but the notion of a nap was ridiculous when all I could think about was confronting Mildred Solomon. She'd have to be sorry when I told her what Dr. Feldman had in store for me, and all because of her. And if she wasn't? Well then, I had the rest of the day and all night to make her sorry.

BACK OUT ON the heat-shimmered sidewalk, the cold of Dr. Feld-man's air-conditioned office clung to my skin. The subway was so awkward from there, I decided to walk through Central Park. A meandering diagonal along its shaded paths would bring me, eventually, to the Old Hebrews Home. Gloria would be glad to see me, and Flo, I was sure, wouldn't mind going home in the middle of the day. I passed a phone booth and resisted the urge to dial long-distance right there on the street. I'd call tomorrow morning, I decided, when I got home from the night shift. She'd still have time to get here before Dr. Feldman took his knife to everything she loved about me.

As I walked, the August sun burned off my chill, replacing it with a caul of sweat. The park was cooler, but not by much. People were tucked up in shaded places, avoiding the lawns and walks. I listened for squirrels chattering in trees or pigeons cooing for bread crumbs, but all I could hear was the metronome of my heels on the asphalt path. There was a stretch, around the Harlem Meer, where I seemed to be the only person moving under that indifferent sky.

If it wasn't for the appointment card in my pocketbook, I'd think I dreamed the whole thing. Three days ago I was fine— lonely, sure, but that would have been over by the end of August. I'd insisted we wait to celebrate my birthday until she was back, dinner at our favorite restaurant in the Village with a few of our old friends. How I wished now we'd never moved. Who would visit me, the long days I'd be recuperating? Molly Lippman? The idea made me shudder, as if someone had walked on my grave.

Where would we put my grave? What cemetery would sell us side-by-side plots, and what could we carve on my headstone? Everything I was—everything we were—would be forgotten, no chiseled *beloved* or *loving* to bear witness that I'd been more than a spinster. I wasn't named on her pension; she wasn't in my will. She'd have to masquerade as my sibling just to visit me in the hospital. Built on the insubstantial foundation of our feelings, the life we had created together seemed a figment of our imaginations that dissolved into fairy dust in the face of something real, and deadly, like cancer.

By the time I got to the Old Hebrews Home, I was racked with anxiety and dread. I took the stairs to steady myself, anticipating the sanctuary of the nurses' lounge.

Flo was there. "What are you doing here already? I was just on my way down to the cafeteria for lunch."

"I got done sooner than I expected."

She peered at me. "I don't see the difference." For a second I feared she could read the cancer in my face until I remembered I'd told her I had a hair appointment.

"Oh, well, I don't like much of a change. Listen, Flo, thanks again for switching with me, but as long as I'm here, why don't you sign out early and head home, let me cover the rest of the day? I'm here until morning either way."

"Sure, if that's what you want. Day shift's got me tired already. You'll see, nights you can sit quiet, think your own thoughts." She sat on the windowsill and lit a cigarette. "Have one with me. Might as well get paid for my lunch break. I'll eat when I get home. My mother-in-law's baking a noodle kugel, if you can you believe it, in this heat?"

I took the cigarette she offered and sat beside her. "What do you think of our new patient?"

"No trouble at all, not with all the morphine she's on. I barely managed to get a bowl of broth into her."

"Did she say anything?" I asked, worried what Dr. Solomon might have revealed about me.

"Just that I should tell them she wanted to eat some chocolate pudding. It was funny how she said it: tell ate I want chocolate pudding. Made me wonder if she'd had a stroke."

Dr. Solomon hadn't had a stroke, I knew. She was referring to me by number. By morning, I swore, she'd know my name.

"Anyway," Flo said, "I doubt she'll last much longer. Probably be someone else in Mr. Mendelsohn's bed next time I'm on." She exhaled contemplatively. "I used to sit up with him. He never seemed to sleep. We'd talk all night sometimes. A couple of weeks ago, he was telling me about his grandson visiting, showed me the card he'd gotten, thanking him for helping the boy study for his bar mitzvah. I said something along the lines of that being the reason God spared him from the camp. Mr. Mendelsohn got so quiet, all you could hear was the wheezing from his lungs. I was wondering—I hardly knew I said it out loud, but I finally asked—

how *did* he survive? It was the middle of the night. Lucia was out at the nurses' station, sound asleep probably, the whole floor so dark and quiet. He said, 'Are you sure you want to hear about that, Fegelah?' He always called me by my Jewish name. Anyway, I said yes, and then he told me the strangest story."

"What was it?" I was curious, too; I'd always taken an interest in survival. "Tell me."

"He said all his life, he had a condition where colors and emotions were connected. Like the first time he saw his wife, she was wearing a dress the color of daffodils, so golden and bright, he said he fell in love with her before he even knew her name. So, he explained, yellow was love, green was a peaceful, calm feeling, and brown was sad, like when his little dog died. He said gray was anxious, so before an exam at school everything seemed blanketed in a dreary fog. Black and white meant nothing special to him, but blue—he said blue was full of hope, so if he looked up into a blue sky on his way to school, he'd become optimistic that he'd pass his exams. His whole life he suffered from this, he said, as if parts of him that should have been separate were linked."

"I read about that once," I said. "Or something like it. The Greeks had a name for it, didn't they, when people mix up sounds and colors?"

"Synesthesia. I looked it up." Flo stared at the sky, seeming far away. "I guess it was something like that, or maybe it was all in his mind. Mr. Mendelsohn thought it was real, though, but I didn't know why he was telling me about it when I'd asked how he survived the camp. I was afraid he was going to tell me they pulled him aside to study him, but instead he said, 'My wife died in 1936, that's why I sent the children away. I should have gone with them, but I had a business to run, profits to protect. When they herded us into the ghettos, I had plenty of money for bribes and the black market, so I fared better than others. Later, on the train, we were packed in so tight a person could hardly breath, but my face was against the side of the car and there was a gap in the boards, so I had fresh air the whole way. Some of us fainted just from the stench and the standing. Only when we unloaded at the camp did I realize the man standing next to me for the last two days had been dead the whole time.' Can you imagine, Rachel?"

I shook my head. It was too awful to contemplate.

"He said by the time they were unloaded, they were all exhausted, starved, and filthy. He said, 'Without thinking, we went where they pointed, left or right, like rats in a maze. They must have thought they could wring some work out of me because I was sent to the labor barracks. Everything was gray or brown, and that was as it should be. Grief, anxiety, despair—if the mud wasn't already brown it would have turned that color in my eyes. Weeks went by, then months, and every day I managed not to die. I pushed others aside to put in my mouth whatever food there was. I kept my head to the ground and did my work. I expected every hour to keel over, but somehow I stayed on my feet. They called us out every morning to line up and be counted. Even the dead had to be counted. On days the mortuary wagon didn't come, we had to drag the body back and forth to take its place in line.'" Flo's cigarette had burned down to her fingertips. She shook the ashes from her hand.

"One day, he said, he finally did collapse, out in a field digging something, potatoes maybe. He said he tried to fall facedown, to bury himself in the dread and the despair, but accidentally he fell on his back. He squeezed his eyes shut, glad it was finally over. His children were safe in America and his wife hadn't lived to see the horror, so already he felt more blessed than most. It was enough. He said, 'I was done. But then a fly landed on my face and without thinking I blinked it away. In that second my eyes were open, in came the brightest blue I'd ever seen. Above the camp and the guards and the ovens there was the sky, not a cloud, the sun far enough west that I didn't squint. The blue filled my vision, blocking out everything else. I tried to close my eyes because it was a perversion to have such a feeling in that place. But there was nothing I could do. I was on my back in that godforsaken field, my body shrunk to nothing, wishing for death to take mercy on me, and yet my heart was full of hope. It wouldn't let me die, that blue. Two weeks later, the camp was liberated. You want to know how I survived, Fegelah? That's how. There was no God in that place, no reason, no mercy. Only the sky.'"

We sat side by side, Flo dabbing at her eyes with a handkerchief. "Have you ever heard such a story in your life, Rachel?" I hadn't, no. Silently, we had another cigarette, each of us trying not to think what the smoke reminded us of.

"See those clouds?" she said after a while, tossing the smoldering butt out the window. "Towering cumulous. Storm's coming."

"I hope it breaks this heat wave, it's got me completely wrung out."

We got up. Flo caught both of my hands in her own, pulling me close. She smelled of tobacco and soap and rubbing alcohol. "Everything all right with you, honey? I've been meaning to ask."

I imagined, for a moment, what it would be like not to keep everything bottled up, but if I started letting it all out—Mildred

Solomon, the X-rays, my tumor—how could I stop before blurting out how lonely I was, and why? I avoided Flo's eyes. "I'm not sleeping well, that's all."

"Are you sure?" She wouldn't let go of me.

"I'm fine, really. Just tired of the heat. You go on home."

"Well, you don't have to ask me twice." She went to her locker. It only took a minute to toss her soiled uniform in the laundry cart and shimmy into her dress. "Zip me up?"

I did. Lifting her pocketbook from its hook, she shut the metal locker. "Clock me out, will you? And have a good night."

"I'll try." I got into my uniform and went to wash up. The mirror above the sink showed me a middle-aged face in an old-fashioned hairstyle. How had forty years come and gone already? On my last birthday it had depressed me to think how old I was getting, but now those years seemed far too few. How pathetic if my coming birthday turned out to be my last. I splashed water on my face to chase back the thought.

Dipping my hand into my pocketbook, I felt for the glass vial. The morphine in it sloshed as I wrapped it in a handkerchief and tucked it into the pocket of my uniform. It was remarkable, how such a little thing held such sway over pain. Everything around me was falling apart, but it gave me purpose to know that over this— over Mildred Solomon's pain—I was the one in control.

Gloria lifted an eyebrow as I approached the nurses' station. "I told Flo I'd cover the rest of the day," I said. "I was done with what I had to do earlier than I expected, and I didn't see the point in going all the way home just to turn right around and come back again."

"That makes it a long night for you, but I can't say I'm sorry to see that Florence go. Always sneaking off to the lounge. And her charts are sloppy."

I thought of Flo and smiled. "I'll go ahead and prep the meds?"

"That's not necessary. I just finished noon rounds. I didn't trust Florence to get it done on time. You can do four o'clock."

I'd missed my chance with Dr. Solomon; I'd have to wait all afternoon before I could begin to wean her off the morphine. She wouldn't be coherent until the beginning of night shift. I told myself to be patient. There would be plenty of time to wring my apology from her.

Chapter Fifteen

T
HERE NOW, THERE NOW," THE MAN SAID, STROKING RA-
chel's back. He drew out a handkerchief and pressed
it into her hand. Rachel stepped back and blew her
nose. The handkerchief smelled of dust but was stiff
and new, as if it had just been pulled from inventory.

"You wouldn't by any chance be Rachel, would you?"

"Papa, you remember me!" Rachel felt she was in a reunion
scene from a movie, ecstatic actors with exaggerated smiles.

"Not so fast. I'm not your papa. Your papa, Harry, he's my
brother. I'm your uncle. And I wouldn't have known you, except
your brother showed up here out of nowhere in the spring, and
he's talked about his sister, so's I figured that's who you must be."

Rachel blinked. Like film caught in a projector, the magic of the
moment melted away. "My uncle?"

"That's right, Uncle Max. Your brother's up at the Silver Queen
with Saul—that's my son, your cousin." Max pulled a watch from
his pocket and opened it. "They'll be back anytime now. I was just
putting their supper on the table. Come on back." He picked up
her case and receded down the aisle.

The rapid shift in emotions left Rachel dazed. For a moment

she'd thought she was in her father's arms. Now it turned out she had an uncle and a cousin—family she'd never heard of before. As if wading through an undertow, she followed Max through the store to a doorway hung with a curtain. Beyond, there was a small kitchen—sink, icebox, Hoosier cabinet. In the corner, a stew pot simmered on an old cast-iron stove. Three plates were set out on the table, with a loaf of bread and a pitcher of iced tea in the center.

"Sit yourself down." Max pulled out a chair for Rachel, then sat across from her. "Are you hungry?"

Rachel shook her head. Though it had been a long time since breakfast with the Cohens, she was in no mood to eat. Her mind was a jumble of questions; she asked the first one that surfaced. "What's a Silver Queen?"

Max laughed. "*The* Silver Queen. It's a mine, most famous one in Leadville. When Sam showed up, Saul was already working at the Silver Queen, so he got your brother a job there, too. Been talk in town of them shutting down operations for the winter. Not that they can't mine any season of the year. Once you're down there the weather don't matter. Silver market's gone bust is what it is."

Rachel was relieved when Max stopped talking to pour himself some tea. It was all so much to take in. He gestured with the pitcher. "Thirsty?"

"Yes, please."

"Here you go." Max filled a glass and pushed it toward her. "Better?"

"Yes, thank you, Uncle Max," she said, trying out the phrase.

Max waved away her thanks. "Why'd you think I was Harry back there?"

"Sam wrote me from here, to let me know he was safe. He didn't tell me about you or Saul. But when I saw Rabinowitz Dry Goods on the envelope, I thought maybe it was our father." Rachel dropped her head. "All the days on the train, I hoped it was."

Max was incredulous. "You hoped your father was here? After what he done to you kids?" Before Rachel could respond, Max had another question that bothered him more. "Where'd you get money for the train from New York? Did Sam send it to you?"

Rachel's eyes drifted upward. Overhead, an electric bulb dangled from a cord in the ceiling. She'd thought about the question, expecting Sam to ask. She couldn't admit to her theft, but now that she knew how much a ticket cost, he'd never believe she came by that much money honestly. She'd planned to say she had met the Cohens in New York and come to Denver with them, but it was a story she hadn't yet rehearsed. She was so long answering, Max took her silence for assent. "I thought as much." He polished his glasses on his shirttail then settled them back on his nose, magnifying his watery eyes. "Well then, let me get a look at you. Take off your hat."

Rachel froze. She'd had the cloche hat on her head every waking minute since she'd run away from the Home.

"Now, don't be shy. Sam told me about your hair and all. From some medical condition, isn't it? Never mind about that. I just want to see my only niece."

Rachel took off the hat and placed it on her lap. Max appraised her like a piece of inventory he was trying to price. "Not so bad. I heard Hasidic women shave their heads when they get married, to make themselves ugly to anyone but their husbands."

Rachel lowered her face and hunched her shoulders. *Ugly.* The word rang in her ears, blotting out the jingle of the bell.

"That'll be the boys now," Max said. "Lock it up behind ya'all!"

"Already did!"

Rachel recognized Sam's voice. She stood so quickly the hat rolled to the floor. She reached for it, then heard footfalls closing in. She straightened, not wanting to be doubled over when Sam first saw her. The curtain was swept back. Her brother stopped in the doorway so suddenly his cousin ran into him from behind, pushing him into the table and jostling the pitcher.

"Rachel? What the hell are you doing here?"

Sam looked taller, older, though it was only six months since he'd run away. Thinking of the last time she saw him, all the events of the Purim Dance rushed into Rachel's mind. Sourness gagged her mouth and her bottom lip quivered. A sound like a bad trumpet note escaped her throat as she felt her knees weaken. Sam stepped forward and wrapped his arms around her. Rachel felt the grit of silver dust on his skin.

"Don't now, Rachel, don't."

"She arrived sooner than you expected, is that it?" Max said. Sam looked at him, as baffled by his uncle's words as by the anger in his voice. "Come on, son. Let's take a walk around the block, leave these two to their reunion."

After the door's jingle assured them they were alone, Sam settled Rachel in a chair. He leaned over for the hat and set it on her head. "Better now?" he asked. She nodded. He pulled a chair close to hers so their knees touched.

"How did you get out here? How did you even know where I was?"

Rachel explained about the envelope, then told the story she hadn't managed to spin for her uncle. "I didn't have a plan when

I ran away, I just went to Penn Station to find out what the train would cost when I met this nice family," she began, ending with, "Mrs. Cohen even bought me the ticket for the Mail to Leadville. But Max thinks you sent me the money. I didn't say you did, but I didn't have a chance to tell him you didn't."

Sam sat back, taking in his sister's story. Finally he said, "Well, I'm glad you got out here safe. It is good to see you." He smiled and squeezed her hand. His kindness drew out the question Rachel had been suppressing ever since he ran away.

"How could you leave me like that?" She cringed at the petulance in her own voice. Why was everything about this day the opposite of what she had imagined it would be?

"God damn it, Rachel, I didn't want to leave you, I had to leave that place. I had to get out."

"But why not take me with you?"

"I couldn't take a girl along. Mrs. Berger, she looked in our file for me, saw there was a note from an uncle in Colorado asking whatever happened to us, but it was from years ago. I didn't know if he'd still be out here, but I didn't have anyplace else better to aim for. They put a few dollars in my pocket, sure, but it wasn't near enough for a train ticket. I hopped a freight for Chicago, saved my cash. Didn't know how long I'd need it to last. Turns out, it didn't last longer than two days."

Sam pulled a pouch of tobacco from his shirt pocket and rolled a cigarette. His hands were blistered, his nails black crescents. At the Home, Rachel thought, he'd have gotten a standing lesson for hands that filthy. He struck a match on the bottom of his boot. Smoke curled around the hanging lightbulb.

"I got rolled on the freight car before it reached Illinois, robbed of everything. I had to fight to keep my shoes. By the time I got to Leadville, it was a week since I had a decent meal. I was in rough shape, I'll tell you that." Sam drew deeply on the cigarette. Rachel remembered the luxury of the Pullman and felt nearly as guilty as she did about stealing from Naomi.

"So, Max thinks I sent you the money to come out here? Let's let him keep on believing that. It'll get him off my back for a while if he thinks I'm too broke to make a move."

"What kind of move?"

"I'm saving every cent I earn to get out of this place before winter hits."

"But where else would we go? Shouldn't we stay here, with our family?" On the back of her tongue, Rachel tasted jam stirred into a cup of tea. "Maybe we should try to find Papa."

Sam snorted. "Why the hell would you want to find him?"

Rachel was beginning to think everyone else knew something about her father that she didn't. She wanted to ask Sam what it was, but he had started talking again.

"Max has been decent enough, and Saul's a good fella, but there's nothing for me here. Max says business has been real bad since the last crash. All his money's tied up in inventory and nothing's moving. Once the Silver Queen lets the summer workers go, I'll just be dead weight around here. And now I gotta carry you, too."

The door jingled. Max and Saul clomped through the shop, intentionally heavy footed, and came into the kitchen. Saul took his place at the table and Max brought over the stew pot. The boys could no longer hold off their hunger after a day's work in the mine. While Sam and Saul shoveled in stew, Max prevailed on

Rachel to take a few bites. The lumps of meat looked unappealing, but she found that she, too, was starving.

In between bites, Saul filled the room with talk about Sadie, the girl he was engaged to. He didn't look much like her brother, Rachel observed, but when he spoke, his mouth and ears moved in just the same way. It made her like him. "Sadie moved out to Colorado Springs with her folks last spring, but they're all coming back in November for the wedding." He looked at his father, who busied himself with some dishes in the sink. "Sadie's father started up a factory, he's got a job lined up for me and everything. I told my dad a million times he oughta sell this place, come out to Colorado Springs, too, but he's too stubborn to budge. Can't tell you how glad I was when Sam showed up, and now with you here, too, Rachel, I know my dad'll have all the help he needs. You can work in the shop and Sam can make the deliveries."

"You got it all figured out, don't you, son?" Max said over his shoulder.

It sounded perfect to Rachel, but her brother scowled, muttering under his breath, "What deliveries?"

After dinner, they made an occasion of Rachel's arrival with a few hands of cards while they listened to the radio. There were only two bedrooms on the second floor—the rest of the space was unfinished storage—so Max suggested Rachel sleep in the kitchen, where she could have some privacy washing up at the sink after all the men had gone upstairs. "Which is where I'm heading right now," Max announced. "Come on, son." He opened a door that Rachel had assumed was a pantry, revealing a steep back staircase. "Your brother'll get whatever you need. Good night, niece."

"Good night, uncle. Good night, cousin." The familial words felt novel in Rachel's mouth.

Sam rummaged around in the store and came back carrying a bedroll and a cot, which he set up for her. "You'll need this," he said, shaking the dust off a camping blanket. "As high up as we are, it gets cold at night, even in summer." Rachel curled up under the itchy wool, realizing how exhausted she was.

"Good night, Sam." She reached out and squeezed his hand.

"Good night, Rachel." Sam switched off the swinging bulb, plunging the room into darkness.

AFTER BREAKFAST, SAM and Saul left for the Silver Queen, their packed lunches in a pail. Rachel cleaned up after them, then wandered into the shop and asked her uncle what else she could do.

"I need an inventory," he said. "I haven't had to order much lately, just replacing the things I sell: soaps and thread and whatnot. It's been a while since I had a clear idea of what all's in here. Think you can do that for me, Rachel?"

She scanned the crowded aisles, the sagging shelves. "I can do that, Uncle Max. Do you have a ledger started?"

"Somewhere around here." Max went to find it. Rachel decided to work from top to bottom, so at least the dust would sift down to the floor and she could sweep it up at the end of each day. She climbed up a stepladder to start with the jumbled pile of goods on the highest shelf. Max hurried over to steady her, his hand lingering on her hip. "Here you go," he said, handing up the dusty ledger. While she took inventory, her uncle hovered nearby, his hands quick to close around her waist whenever she had to climb up or down.

Max could have done the inventory himself in as much time as he spent talking to her, but Rachel didn't mind. She liked handling the stock, dusting off items, comparing her count to the numbers scrawled in Max's book. She'd never seen most of the things he carried in the store, didn't know what half of them were for. Cooking, building, camping, hunting, fishing, mining—all were pursuits strange to her. No matter how foreign the items in her hand, it satisfied her to sort, stack, and put them in order.

"I came out west when I was about your age, Rachel. How old are you again?" She told him she'd just turned fifteen. "Fifteen, that's right. Back in my day, you were a man already by fifteen, and plenty of girls were mothers, too. Harry, your father, he was still in knee pants when I took my chances and came out here. Spent every cent I'd managed to save on an order of coats and dragged them as far west as I could get. Sold them for five times what I paid. For years I went back and forth until I set up shop here permanent. Married Saul's mother, may she rest in peace." He polished his glasses on his shirttail. "Back in the 1890s, I tell you, Leadville was the place to be."

When Max said it was time to put a stew on, Rachel followed him into the kitchen, but she was of no help at the stove. In the Home, she had been served thousands of meals but had never so much as seen an egg cracked. "Oh well, cooking isn't everything in a woman," Max said, stroking her hand. "I've learned to fend for myself since Saul's mother passed. There's other things you can do for us, isn't that right, Rachel?"

The boys came home with the fading light, dusty from the mine, starving for supper. After the meal, Rachel cleaned up while the men smoked and listened to the radio, too tired for cards. Then it was night, and the cot, and the sound of her brother's footsteps on the floorboards above her head.

The next day was Saturday, and though the boys had to work, Max took Rachel to meet the rabbi. On the walk to the synagogue and back, he showed her the town. It wasn't much to take in. Every family or business worth a brick building was on Harrison. Cross streets petered out within a block or two, wood-frame houses giving way to shacks, rutted roads devolving into dirt tracks that narrowed to mule trails into the mountains. Sunday brought Mr. Lesser, Max's Denver supplier, in his hiccupping delivery truck. After taking a few minutes to unload the truck, the two men sat for an hour around the kitchen table, sharing news and sandwiches and lazy cigars. From what Rachel could see, the visit was more nostalgia than commerce, the small order for Rabinowitz Dry Goods hardly worth a weekly drive.

IN THE COMING weeks, women patronized the store more frequently now that this new young woman could quickly hand them those knitting needles or that spool of Carlisle ribbon that Max was never able to find. One day Rachel was surprised to see Max tear September from the calendar on the wall. The month had gone by so easily, the routine of shop and family absorbing her as if she'd always had a part to play.

Before she knew it, Saul's wedding was around the corner. "I'll be leaving with Sadie and her parents after," Saul said one night at dinner, glanced over at his father by the stove, then smiled warmly at Rachel. "I'm so glad you've come. Dad's happy for your company. Aren't you, Dad?"

"Aren't I what?" Max asked.

"Glad to have someone who'll listen to your stories all day long?"

"That I am, son, that I am." Max's look at Rachel was so penetrating she blushed.

Sam, embarrassed for his sister, cleared his throat. "Talk's starting to go around town of a big project, an Ice Palace to attract tourists out from Denver. They claim it'll put Leadville back on the map." The men took up the topic, Max optimistic about the jobs it would bring after the mine shut down for the season. It sounded exciting to Rachel, but her brother was unconvinced. "Who the hell's gonna come out here in the dead of winter to see a house made of ice?"

Sadie and her parents were expected a couple of days before the wedding. Max enlisted Rachel's help in cleaning out the upstairs rooms and rearranging the beds. "They're only having the wedding out here because it's cheaper," Max complained. "If they had it in Colorado Springs, Nathan, that's Sadie's father, he'd have to invite the whole synagogue. He always was a penny-pincher. Won't even stay in the hotel while they're in town. So, we'll put Nathan in here with me and Saul. Sadie and her mother, Goldie, they can share the other room. Sam'll have to bunk down in the kitchen with you. You won't mind, will you, Rachel?"

Rachel smiled. "I won't mind at all, Uncle."

The wedding party arrived on the last day of October, and Rachel was swept up into the preparations. That evening, everyone gathered around the kitchen table for a simple supper of cold cuts and smuggled bottles of wine set aside before Prohibition. The men debated the consequences of Tuesday's stock market crash in New York while the women talked of veils and flowers.

Nathan called for a toast, and Rachel joined in, seeing rainbows in her wineglass where it caught the light. By the time everyone else went upstairs, Rachel's head ached and her stomach gurgled from the unaccustomed alcohol. She lay down gingerly while Sam unfolded a second cot for himself alongside hers. In the darkness, he lit a cigarette and smoked it dreamily. The wine had made him nostalgic.

"Do you remember how we used to sleep in the kitchen, under the table?"

Rachel searched her mind. There was the dark underside of a table, the scrape of a chair, someone's untied shoelaces. "I remember, Sam."

He pinched out the cigarette and dropped it to the floor. He reached across the space between their cots and found his sister's hand. Their fingers intertwined. Soon Sam started snoring. Rachel stayed awake as long as she could, savoring the beating of her heart.

RACHEL WOKE TO find her brother's cot empty. She supposed he'd gone to work earlier than usual. The shop was busy that day with old friends dropping by to visit with Nathan and Goldie. In the afternoon, Sadie and Saul had to go to the synagogue. "The rabbi wants to give us the marriage talk," Sadie whispered to Rachel. Max announced that he would go along with them. Goldie took the opportunity to go upstairs for a nap. Nathan went out for a walk. Rachel, alone in the store, wandered the aisles, handling the familiar goods, imagining her life here with her brother and uncle after their cousin was married and gone.

Sam came home dusted with silver. "Good thing for Saul he

quit yesterday, cause they would've fired him today anyway," he said while he washed up at the kitchen sink. "Bunch of us got canned. They're closing the shaft early, cause of that business with the stock market."

"It'll be all right, Sam, we'll just work for Uncle Max. Or maybe you can work on that Ice Palace."

"You think I want to stay in this dump? Look around you! Rabinowitz Dry Goods is a joke. If Max didn't own the building, he'd be out on the street, broke. There's no future for me here."

"But, Sam, he's family. He's Papa's brother. He wants to take care of us."

Sam snorted. "You, maybe. He's taken a shine to you. But me? If I'm not earning a living, I'm just dead weight around here. Only reason he's been off my back about money is cause he thinks I sent all my savings out to you. Just see what happens when I tell him I'm out of a job."

"He's not like that. And anyway, where else would we go?" She added, softly, "If only we knew where Papa was."

Sam's face twisted like he'd eaten something spoiled. "Why do you keep bringing that up?"

Since she'd mistaken Max for her father, Rachel hadn't been able to shake the idea of finding him. She wanted to ask Sam, now, why he got so angry whenever she mentioned Papa. Sure, she'd say, it was terrible how he left them, but it wasn't his fault, was it? He hadn't wanted to, Rachel was sure of that. He was afraid of the police was all, that they would never believe it was an accident.

Before Rachel could say anything, the store's bell sounded a succession of returns: Saul and Sadie, followed by Max, and a few minutes later, Nathan. The noise brought Goldie down as well. In the rush of talk, there were no more private words between Rachel and Sam.

"We're headed out to the Golden Nugget," Max announced later. "Going to send my son off in style. You haven't forgotten about the back room at the Nugget, have you, Nate?"

"I haven't forgotten how much you hate to stand for a round, Max."

"Don't get yourselves arrested for drinking," Goldie warned. "We've got a wedding tomorrow."

"Leadville's sheriff has never been persuaded that enforcing Prohibition's exactly his job," Max assured her. "Better worry about the groom being able to stand up straight at the ceremony."

Rachel watched her brother hustle out of the store, so much unsettled between them.

"Mom, what do you say we take in the show at the Tabor?" Sadie said. "Everything's ready for tomorrow."

Goldie looked wistful. "It's been a long time since I looked down on that stage. And it's a variety tonight, not one of those foreign operas Baby Jane used to bring in to impress the Guggenheims. Sure, let's us girls go to the opera house. Rachel, that means you, too. It'll be my present."

Outside, frost dusted the sidewalks. Despite the cold, the women didn't put coats over their dresses, the theater being just next door. The show had already begun, but there were plenty of seats available. Goldie, wanting to avoid the raucous miners on the main floor, led Sadie and Rachel up to the third tier and through a curtained doorway. Space sank away in front of them. Rachel reached for the railing to steady herself. Goldie guided her along the front row, settling Rachel into a seat so oblique to the stage she could see into the wings.

The Tabor boasted of being the finest opera house west of the Mississippi; Rachel had certainly never been anywhere so grand. That this elegance was on the same block as her uncle's dusty shop astonished her. Gas jets flickered around the tiers and lit the stage, on which a magician was combining and separating solid brass hoops. Each flourish and clink of the hoops sent the violins in the pit scurrying. Rachel wanted to ask how such a thing was possible, but Goldie was busy whispering that she'd known old Horace Tabor personally, back before the silver crash devastated his fortune. Sadie whispered back that Saul had once delivered goods from the store to his widow, Baby Jane, who lived like a hermit up at Tabor's spent mine, getting battier with each long winter.

Rachel tilted her head to see who was waiting to take the stage next. Half hidden in darkness stood a regal woman in purple velvet whose neckline glittered in the gaslight. A final flourish, a flutter of doves, and a round of applause marked the end of the magician's act. Dramatically wrapping himself in his cape, he stalked off-stage. The hot spotlight swung over to the opposite wing, pushing back the darkness. The regal woman stepped out as the master of ceremonies announced, "From the greatest stages of Europe where she has performed for royalty, Madame Hildebrand!"

The orchestra struck up an aria as Madame Hildebrand proceeded to play her part as the culture of the program. The emotion of her brows and lips exaggerated by stage makeup, she flung soprano notes over the heads of her audience. Rachel's gaze followed the woman as she strutted across the boards, but she wasn't listening to the song. It was the woman's hair that her eyes devoured. It was the same smoldering garnet as the braid hidden in the bottom of Rachel's cardboard case.

She had almost forgotten about it. But there it was, Amelia's hair on this woman's head. Perhaps she was Amelia's true mother, not dead but run away, like Rachel's father. The possibility spun in her mind until the aria ended and applause cleared the notes from the air. The soprano bowed and backed into the wing from which she had come, the spot following her. Rachel leaned over to watch her exit. Hidden from the orchestra seats by a side curtain, the soprano paused, her shoulders rounding. She reached for something in her hair—a pin or ornament? But no, she crooked her finger under the brow of her hair and lifted it off her head. The spot shifted across the boards to pick up the next performer just as the soprano removed her wig.

Rachel was jittering with excitement. "Excuse me, please, I'm feeling dizzy." Sadie and Goldie stood to let her pass. "I just need some fresh air."

Rachel ran down the stairs to the lobby of the opera house, then looked around for some way backstage. There wasn't one. She went out front and around the corner. In back, a truck was pulled up to the open stage door, ready to be loaded after the performance. Rachel ducked past the dozing driver. Inside, she could hear the muffled laughter of the audience as she negotiated the backstage maze. A woman pushing a rack of costumes pointed when Rachel asked where she might find Madame Hildebrand. She peered through a partly opened door. There was the soprano in a dressing gown, seated before a mirror and touching up her greasepaint. Thin brown hair streaked with gray was plastered to her skull. Next to her on a wig form was the hair so like Amelia's.

Rachel's eyes met Madame's in the mirror. "Don't just stand there, child. Come in." Rachel slunk into the dressing room. "What do you want? An autograph?"

"The wig you were wearing. . . ." The words dried up in her mouth.

"What about it?"

Rachel pulled the cloche hat from her head, letting the bald scalp speak her desire.

Madame turned to look kindly at Rachel, her heavy jewelry peeking out from the dressing gown. "Come here." Rachel took a step closer. "Which one do you want to try on?"

Rachel realized then that the red wig was not alone. Beside the one she'd seen onstage were two more: one with a cascading mass of black curls, another with golden braids so long they circled the neck like a noose. None was rough and dead-looking like the wig they'd given her at the Home.

"This one would match your coloring," Madame said, gesturing to the dark hair. "I wear that when I sing *Carmen*."

But Rachel stepped closer to the red wig, reaching out to stroke a crackling curl. "May I try this one?"

Madame smiled. "Yes, this one is special. Somehow it always puts me in the mood for Mozart. Come, sit." She rose and offered Rachel her seat before the mirror. It reflected the naked oval of her face.

"Here." Madame settled the wig gently on Rachel's head, tugging under the ears until it settled in place. "It's loose on you. Your head is smaller than mine. Mrs. Hong makes every wig custom for a perfect fit. There. What do you think?"

Rachel was overwhelmed by the sight of so much hair falling around her face. It was as if Amelia's ghost had come to swallow her up. Then she remembered Amelia whispering to Marc Grossman, and she tasted bile. If anyone deserved to have the hair, it was Rachel.

"How does it feel?"

The wig was a bit loose, and the hair was heavy, but against her scalp it was soft, soothing, strangely alive. "It's lovely. It doesn't itch at all. The one they gave me when I was a girl, it itched so much I couldn't wear it."

"Wool lining, probably, and sometimes they use hair from horses' tails. Mrs. Hong's girls crochet the lining from silk, and of course she uses only human hair."

Without taking her eyes off of her reflection, Rachel asked, "Who is Mrs. Hong?"

"Only the best wig maker I've ever known. I get all of my wigs from Mrs. Hong's House of Hair in Denver."

Rachel's eyes lingered on the image in the mirror. She ran her hand over her head, wrapping the hair around her neck. "What does it cost?"

"Oh, child, it's nothing you could dream of, I'm afraid. Even I can only afford one a year." Madame Hildebrand reached out for the wig. Rachel hunched her shoulders, edging away.

"What if I already had the hair?" she asked. When she had cut Amelia's hair, her only motivation was revenge. She'd never known why her fist had closed around the braid, why she'd dragged it halfway across a continent. Now Rachel understood. The brown wig she'd worn to the Purim Dance had betrayed her with false promises of beauty, but a wig made from Amelia's hair would do more than mask her ugliness. Such a wig would elevate Rachel to match its splendor.

Madame Hildebrand looked at Rachel's greedy eyes in the mirror and pitied her. She thought this strange girl must have some hair wrapped in tissue paper, the strands thin and oily from whatever illness had left her bald. Scarlet fever could do that sometimes, she'd heard. "I'm sorry, dear. I can't imagine what it would cost. I don't even know where Mrs. Hong has her shop. She always comes to my dressing room at the Municipal Auditorium when I'm in Denver."

The woman with the rack of costumes appeared at the door. "Ten minutes, Madame. I have your gypsy costume."

"Excuse me, dear, I need to prepare for my next aria."

Madame lifted the wig from Rachel's head and settled it back on the form. Rachel's scalp felt bereft. Resentfully, she put on the cloche hat, mumbled her thanks, and retraced her steps to the stage door. She stood in the cold as long as she could stand it, her breath misting the air.

Goldie and Sadie were in the lobby looking for Rachel when she entered. Sadie was too nervous about the next day to sit through another act, so they returned to the shop. They were upstairs arranging the wedding dress when they heard the men stumble in below. Going down to the kitchen, Rachel hoped for a chance to talk with her brother, but Sam flopped down on the cot and began snoring without even taking off his boots. Rachel undid the laces, pulled the boots from his feet, and covered him with a blanket.

Before crawling under her own covers, Rachel opened the cardboard case and brought out Amelia's hair. She remembered the first time she had seen it, so abundant and beautiful it made Mrs. Berger love the girl it belonged to. The braid belonged to her now, and she imagined that someday, somehow, it would make her beloved, too.

AT THE WEDDING, Rachel took Sadie's bouquet as the bride held out her hand for the modest gold band Saul pushed down her finger. Then the glass was smashed underfoot and shouts of mazel tov mixed with clapping. After the ceremony, the assembled Jews of Leadville lingered in the synagogue, offering the new couple kisses and handshakes and slipping them folded dollar bills. Max had told Rachel there used to be so many, the synagogue could barely contain them all; now they were lucky to have enough men for a minyan. Goldie and Nathan invited everyone to share in the wedding cake. As long as a bottle had been opened by the rabbi for religious purposes, they all enjoyed small glasses of wine.

Max sidled up to Rachel and took her elbow. "I'm wanting to ask you something. Would you come over here?" He led her to the far corner of the room, where two chairs had been pulled close together. When they sat, Max's knees bumped into Rachel's. He pulled out his shirttail to wipe his glasses.

"What is it, Uncle?" Rachel asked, her eyes following the circle of his silver hair from mustache to sideburn and around to the other side.

"I talked it over with the rabbi yesterday, and he advised me to talk to you plain and simple." He cleared his throat. "So, here it is, Rachel. Could you ever think of me as something more than your uncle?"

She wasn't sure what he was asking. Did he want to take the place of her father, to adopt her? Her expression prodded Max to explain himself.

"Sadie and Saul, they're moving away today. My son, he's going to start his own family now. And what am I left with, alone in my shop? Your brother, he's a restless one. What if he leaves, tries his luck somewhere else?"

"Can't he work for you, making deliveries, like Saul said?"

"I hardly got enough business to keep my own head above water. But you, Rachel. Since you came, it's been good, working with you. How we talk when you take the inventory. That I need, someone in the shop, to help with the stock. And the lady customers, they like having a woman to deal with. But what will they say, a young woman and a grown man living together like that? You can't sleep on a cot in the kitchen all winter. But if we were married, we could stay together, upstairs. I'd take care of you, Rachel, if I was your husband."

Rachel's heart cowered behind her ribs. She had to swallow, hard, before she could speak. "But you're my uncle. You're older than my father."

"I'm not too old to be a husband, and a father." He tilted his chin up. The sun, slanting through the synagogue windows, bounced off his glasses. "There's lots of older men who get themselves a young wife. Rabbi says an older man is more understanding and patient. As for me being your uncle, it's true, it's not so usual here. But back in the old country this is what happened sometimes, to keep a family together. And the rabbi says he'll bless the marriage."

Rachel remained silent. Max had one more argument to make.

"Maybe soon we'd start a family together. Wouldn't you like that, Rachel, to have a baby all your own?"

Rachel's stomach was curdling, but her mind ticked like a clockworks. It was revolting to contemplate marrying her uncle, but the prospect of refusing him made her realize how dependent she was on this man. She considered and rejected every option she could imagine. To buy herself time, she said simply, "Uncle Max, I don't know what to say."

"You think about it, Rachel. Maybe it's a new idea for you, you have to get used to it. I'm also driving out to Colorado Springs this afternoon. I decided to give the bedroom suite from my own wedding to Saul and Sadie, so I'm going to take it in my truck. I thought maybe it'd be nice to get a new bed. For a fresh start?" Max closed his hand over her knee. "I won't make it back tonight, so you don't have to answer me until tomorrow."

Rachel blinked. "Tomorrow?"

"I could wait until you turned sixteen to get married, if you want, so we'd just be engaged for now. But, well, I can't have a young girl living in my shop unless there's an understanding between us." Max took her hand. He pulled her toward him and pressed his mouth against her lips. Beneath the hair of his mustache, Rachel could feel the hardness of his teeth followed by the damp tip of his tongue. A chill shivered through her as someone walked on her grave. Max pulled away. "Besides, where else can you go?"

Nathan's voice carried above the murmur. "Time to go home."

The word rang false in Rachel's ear. Rabinowitz Dry Goods could only be her home if she let her uncle become her husband. Then it occurred to her—Sam would never stand for that. Once she told him, he would take her away. They would leave together, maybe find Papa, make a real family for themselves. A smile pulled at her mouth as she followed Max out of the synagogue. Rachel thought of that scene in the movies where a girl is tied to railroad tracks and the train is coming. She relished the certainty that Sam would save her.

"Maybe it's for the best," Sam said that night when Rachel told him about Max's proposal. Everyone else had gone to Colorado Springs, the newlyweds in the back of Nathan's sedan, Max following with his old bedroom furniture tied down in the truck. Sam was reclining on his cot in the kitchen, a lit cigarette between his lips.

Rachel couldn't believe she heard him right. "He wants to marry me, our own uncle!"

"He said he'd wait till you were sixteen, didn't he?" Sam stood and reached up to the top of the Hoosier cabinet, taking down a small bottle. "Max's medicinal brandy." He pulled the cork with his teeth and took a swig. "Not bad. Not bad at all." He stretched out on the cot again, alternating inhalations with sips of liquor.

Rachel was alarmed. "He'll know you drank some."

"I don't care. You just pretend you don't know anything about it, let him blame everything on me."

Rachel sat beside her brother on the cot. "I'm not going to pretend anything. You've got to take me away from here, Sam."

"You're birthday's what, nine months away? This could work for us, Rachel. You know I've been wanting to get out of here, and I saved up a lot, but not enough for both of us to get anywhere and have anything left once we got there. Besides, I want some adventure, after all those years being told what to do, those damn bells ringing every hour of the day." Sam shook his head as if there were water in his ears. "Drove me crazy, those bells. But where the hell was I gonna go with you to worry about? Now I know he'll take care of you, I can go."

"But, Sam, it's disgusting! You can't leave me here, to that."

"I'm not really gonna let him marry you, Rachel. By the time you're sixteen, I'll be settled somewhere, and I'll send for you. Promise." He gazed at the ceiling, already lost in his imaginary adventures.

Rachel watched the forgotten cigarette in her brother's hand burn out. He was supposed to save her, not leave her behind with nothing more to cling to than the memory of his word.

"You promised you'd get me from the Infant Home, too."

Sam bolted up. "I was just a little kid, Rachel. I couldn't do anything about that. You want to blame someone, blame our damn father, the bastard, for turning us into orphans."

"No, Sam, it wasn't his fault, running away after Mama's accident. He was just scared." Rachel caught her brother's hand. "I don't really blame you, you know that. You can't blame him, either."

"I can't blame him?" Sam pushed her aside and pounded up the stairs. He came back down a minute later with a knapsack. "You want to find our father so bad? Here!" He yanked out a crumpled envelope and threw it at Rachel. While she pulled out a tattered sheet of paper and smoothed it enough to read the writing, Sam aimed a barrage of words at her.

"Max wrote to our beloved Papa when I showed up here. He's living in California if you want to go find him. The address is right there on the envelope. You know what he had to say to me when Max told him I ran away from the orphanage and came out here all on my own?"

Sam tore the letter from Rachel's hands. "'Dear Son,'" he read, his words slurred with anger. "'Glad to hear you're out in Leadville. I heard through Max you ended up in the Orphaned Hebrews Home. I knew they'd take good care of you and your sister, better than what I could have done. But now Max tells me you're working in the mine. Maybe you could spare a few dollars to send my way? I've been sick lately. . . .'" Sam threw the letter on the floor. It drifted under the cot. Rachel got down on her hands and knees to retrieve it.

"Money! That's what he wants from me, after all these years. Max says it's always the same with him. He came out here, after Mama died. Stuck around leeching off Max until he finally ran him off. Max says to me, do what you want, but I'm not throwing good money after bad on my brother no more."

Rachel was reading the words scrawled on the paper. Her own papa's handwriting. "If he's sick, Sam, we should help him. We should go to him." It was as if the lies she told to the Cohens and the Abramses were coming true after all.

Sam lit a fresh cigarette, the flame reflected in his eyes. "Let him die if he's so sick. I'm not sending him a penny from what I earned, chipping away underground. He left us, Rachel. We don't owe him a thing."

Rachel started to object, but Sam cut her off. "Look, you do what you want. You don't trust me to send for you? Fine, then go on back to the Home."

Rachel thought of the curled insole of Naomi's shoe, of Amelia's shorn hair. Shame washed over her. "I can't go back there, Sam. Let me come with you, wherever you're going."

He shook his head. "I tried, Rachel, all those years, I tried to watch out for you. You don't think I would've run away a long time ago if it wasn't for you being in the Home? I can't protect you anymore. I never could. I mean, look at you!" He flung his hand at the cloche hat. He intended only a gesture, but he knocked it from her head.

Rachel inhaled, as if stricken.

"Oh, Rachel, I'm sorry." He stooped to retrieve it. "I didn't mean it like that."

She took the hat from him, held it on her lap. She sensed the glare of electric light on her smooth scalp. She lifted her chin and tried to hold Sam's gaze, but he turned his attention to the floor. She recalled the way Sam's eyes had slid away from her face, that first day in Reception, when she mistook Vic for her brother. All these years, she'd thought it was guilt that turned his head. Now she saw the truth—that he couldn't stand the sight of her.

"You go ahead, Sam. I'll stay here. Maybe I'll go find Papa myself. Or maybe I'll end up marrying Uncle Max after all." To hurt him back, she said, "It couldn't be worse than Marc Grossman."

Blood rose into Sam's cheeks, mottling his skin. "It won't come to that, Rachel. I promise."

The word was such a lie, Rachel switched off the light so she wouldn't have to see her brother's face.

If Rachel ever slept, she didn't know it. She listened to Sam in the night, pilfering supplies from the shelves in the store. Knowing the inventory by heart, she could guess from the location and quality of the sound what he was taking: duffle, blanket, canteen, knife. He'd be gone by morning, of that she was sure. She turned over on her cot, covering her ears with the blanket. She heard a muffled jingle sometime before dawn.

In the morning, Rachel felt strangely numb as she adjusted the inventory ledger to cover her brother's theft. She wandered silently through the building, picking up a piece of ribbon that had fallen from Sadie's dress, peeking into Max's dusty bedroom. For a while, Rachel couldn't account for the novelty of it. Then she realized—she had never before in her life had a place entirely to herself. Sitting at the kitchen table, she read again her father's letter, then spread out what was left of Naomi's stolen money. It might be enough for a coach ticket to Sacramento, but she'd be arriving with nothing in her pockets to find a man she hadn't seen in a dozen years. A man who was sick and needed money himself. A man who had left his children behind.

Rachel looked through to the store. She liked working there, talking with customers and organizing the goods. She even liked Max, just not for a husband. Maybe she would stay on awhile longer. Then she thought of Max's tongue sliding across her teeth, his hands on her waist every time she climbed a ladder. He might say he'd wait until she was sixteen, but alone in the store, she wasn't sure his word could be trusted.

In the quiet kitchen, Rachel realized she was homesick. Not for her brother and the father she could hardly remember, but for the dorms and dining hall and play yard of the Castle. She missed Nurse Dreyer. She missed Naomi. The money on the table, the braid in her case: they were a wall between her and the place that had been her home. She dropped her head onto her arms. Even if she wanted to, she couldn't go back. She would have to choose between her brother's promises, her uncle's proposal, or the uncertain prospect of her father.

She heard the whine of an engine. Wiping her eyes with the back of her hand, she looked out the window and recognized Mr. Lesser's truck. Of course, it was Sunday. Max hadn't left an order, though. Mr. Lesser knocked on the kitchen door. Rachel tucked the money and her father's letter in her pocket, then went to let him in. She could at least offer him lunch until Max returned. He'd come so far.

All the way from Denver.

Chapter Sixteen

NIGHT SHIFT PROVED TO BE AS EASY AS FLO promised—I could see why she preferred it. Just one other night nurse came on Fifth. Lucia and I knew each other from shift changes, and we chatted easily about the patients until she settled herself behind the nurses' station with an elaborate piece of crocheting, a christening dress for her granddaughter, she said. Gloria signed off on all the night's doses and locked up the medication room before clocking out. The doctors were good about prescribing sedatives for those patients whose opiates didn't already guarantee us a quiet night. Aside from dispensing meds and checking beds, we didn't expect to have much to do until dawn.

Just as I finished organizing my cart for eight o'clock rounds, the storm Flo predicted finally broke. The sky flickered like a neon sign advertising thunderclaps. Wind burst through open windows, sweeping rain over sills and slamming doors. Thunder boomed above our heads. Light fixtures rattled. Bulbs dimmed and recovered. Someone screamed.

Lucia and I rushed to close windows in the patients' rooms. We ran into each other in the hallway, trailed by our wet footprints.

"Mr. Bogan fell getting out of bed," Lucia panted. "Will you help me with him?"

"Let me just call down for a janitor first." I did, then together we got Mr. Bogan up. Tangled in his sheets, he'd drifted over the side of the bed, sinking gradually to the floor.

"Thank God you didn't break a hip, Mr. Bogan," Lucia said as we settled him back on the mattress.

"I'm sorry, I had to use the toilet. I duh-duh-didn't mean to cah-cah-cah-cah-cah-cause any trouble."

Lucia saw that he had soiled himself. "You're no trouble, dear. Let's get you cleaned up." She looked over her shoulder at me. "I can manage here if you want to check on the others."

I dashed into the next room. Already the floor was puddled with rain. Working my way down the hall, I closed windows, calmed agitated patients, straightened sheets, promised to return with medications. A Negro janitor arrived, steering his wheeled bucket with the long mop handle. He followed me down the hall, drying the floor in each room as I left it.

In Mildred Solomon's room, the old woman's moans mixed with booms of thunder like the soundtrack of a horror movie. At four o'clock rounds, I'd only administered half the prescribed dose and by now it was wearing off. I noticed the bedsheets had gotten wet from the rain driven through the window. I'd have to change them, and probably the nightgown and diaper, too. The thought made me shudder. But now that all the windows were closed, I'd have to get the meds out first. Coming through the doorway, I nearly collided with the janitor.

"I'll start back down the other end of the hall after this room," he said.

"Thank you so much." He was a young, gentle-seeming man. I wished I knew his name, but I so rarely worked nights, we'd never met.

I think he read my expression because he said, "My name's Horace."

"Thank you, Horace."

"You're welcome, Nurse . . . ?"

"Rabinowitz."

"You're welcome, Nurse Rabinowitz." Horace placed the mop in the bucket and began rolling it through the doorway as I stepped past him. He stopped, his eyes following me.

"Is there something else, Horace?"

"If you don't mind my saying so, Nurse Rabinowitz, and I don't mean anything by it, but I can't help remarking on your hair. I'm in art school, you see, days, and I don't know as I've ever seen that particular shade of red."

Mildred Solomon's moans were seeping into the hallway. "I'm sorry, I have to go get the medications." I turned away from Horace as he entered the room.

The chaos of the storm had unnerved me; I knocked the cart against the nurses' station, jumbling the cups of pills and rolling the syringes. My hands shook as I reorganized the medications. Brushing hair out of my eyes, I surveyed the cart to make sure nothing was missing. I looked up and saw Horace coming down the hall. Having finished mopping out the last of the rooms on Fifth, he was steering his bucket toward the freight elevator. Impulsively, I pulled open a drawer and took out a pair of scissors.

I left the cart and walked quickly, unpinning my hair as I went. A thick lock unrolled down my neck like a lizard's tongue. I lifted the hair away from the nape of my neck, pulling it taut. With the scissor held just above my ear, I placed the hair between its blades and cut. The shearing sound reminded me of the first time I cut this hair, how the scissors chewed through the braid in greedy bites.

I coiled the hair in my palm. "Horace, wait."

He stopped, the rolling bucket stilled so suddenly water sloshed out.

"Here." I held out my hand. He took what I offered. The red strands crackled and curled around his brown fingers.

"I don't quite know what to say, Nurse Rabinowitz."

"It's for your art studies. Don't worry," I said, stepping back, "it's not really mine."

Horace tucked my strange gift into the chest pocket of his coveralls. I retrieved the cart and pushed it into a patient's room. The thunder grew distant as the summer storm rolled out to sea.

THE STORM HAD disturbed the routines of night shift. It was after nine before all of the patients were dry and settled and medicated—all except one.

"I'll take this in for Dr. Solomon," I said to Lucia. "I expect to stay for a while. She's near the end, I think."

"That's kind of you. You know, no one else calls her Doctor. But you knew her, didn't you? Gloria told me she treated you when you were little. Were you sick?"

I suppressed an urge to blurt out the truth. Instead, I simply nodded. "It was a long time ago."

Lucia suggested I go ahead and spend the night sitting beside the dying woman. "Take her midnight dose with you, too. I'll do the rest of that round myself. It's mostly bed checks at that hour, anyway. If you want to be with her, I mean."

"I do, thanks." I picked up another syringe and marked the chart, writing down a time that hadn't happened yet. Lucia settled back with her crocheting as I walked to Dr. Solomon's room. My hand curled around the vial of unused morphine in my pocket. I hoped it wasn't too full for what I'd be holding back, though I supposed I could just rinse the extra down the sink. I wondered why I hadn't done that from the beginning. What did I think I was saving it for?

In Dr. Solomon's room, I closed the door and sat by the bed. I'd neglected her since the storm. Covered with only the wet sheet, she was curled on her side, whimpering. I examined the old woman, trying to gauge the extent of her pain from how her jaw moved as she ground her teeth, the way her eyeballs rolled under the closed lids. She needed a dose badly, but first I had to clean her up and change the linens.

I rolled the sheets toward Dr. Solomon's spine. Leaning over, I slipped my forearms under her neck and knees and hugged the body toward me, exposing the other side of the bed. I removed the damp sheets, tucked in dry ones, then pulled off her nightgown and removed the soiled diaper. Naked, Dr. Solomon looked like a shriveled chick fallen from a nest. Violent thoughts crowded my mind as I cleaned and dressed her, but my hands moved with practiced gentleness.

"That's better," she muttered, making herself comfortable in the clean sheets. "What took you so long?"

It startled me, hearing her speak when she'd just been so limp in my arms. She must have been pretending, waiting until I was done caring for her body to reveal her mind was alert. "The storm kept us busy, but I'm here now. You remember who I am?"

"Why do you keep asking me these silly things? I told you, I'm not senile. It's just that damn morphine. He prescribes too much." She licked her lips. "You have some for me, don't you?"

"I have your dose, but we have to talk first." I was determined to get through to her this time. I would wrench from her the words I deserved to hear: *I was wrong, I'm so sorry, please forgive me.*

"About the X-rays again? That was so long ago. Why don't you ask me about something else?" She squared her shoulders, extended her neck. "I ran my department, did you know that? I was the first woman in the city to be head of radiology. Not at a teaching hospital, no, I didn't publish enough for that. So many surgeons wanted me to read their X-rays I never had enough time to conduct another study. The years, they slip away. One day I looked up and three decades had gone by. I wasn't planning on retirement—can you see me wasting my time around a mahjong table? The cancer is what drove me out. I'm only sixty years old. My career should have lasted ten more years at least. Get me some water."

She was infuriating, complaining about cancer at sixty when here I was, twenty years younger, about to be butchered because of her. I held the glass of water to her lips while she sipped, my fingers so tense I could have broken the glass. I welcomed the anger, counted on it to fuel me through the night, justify whatever I had to do to get my apology. Once I told Mildred Solomon about Dr. Feldman's plans for me, she'd have to think about someone other than herself for once. She'd have to give me what I was owed.

"Did you bring my pudding?"

"What?"

"My chocolate pudding. I told that other nurse to tell you I wanted chocolate pudding. Did she?"

I'd forgotten, and anyway, I wasn't in the business of doing her bidding. "Never mind about the pudding. I want to talk to you."

"Then I'll get my dose, right? Well, I can bargain, too, you know. You can torture me all you want, but I won't talk unless I get my pudding. Even a convict gets a last meal." She crossed her arms, though I could see their weight against her ribs was painful. She set her mouth in a hard line and looked away, all the determination and tenacity she'd used to make her way in a man's world brought to bear on this ridiculous request.

"It's too late now, the kitchens are closed." She turned her head, her chin quivering from the effort. "Oh, for God's sake, I'll go see what I can do."

In the cafeteria, I caught the last kitchen worker as she was setting out a platter of sandwiches wrapped in waxed paper for the night staff. She led me back into the kitchens. In one of the refrigerators, there was a shelf of leftover pudding bowls covered in Saran Wrap. I took the fullest one, intent on depriving Dr. Solomon of any more excuses. She might be dead before I came back to work after three days off, one last shift before my surgery. This needed to happen tonight.

"I've been dreaming of this." She spooned the pudding into her mouth in maddeningly tiny portions, smacking her lips after each taste. My arm grew tired of holding the bowl beneath her chin. Between spoonfuls, I rested the bowl on her lap, my hand cupped beneath it. Through the back of my hand I felt a spasm as pain radiated from her bones.

She hadn't quite finished when the spoon dropped to the blanket. "That's enough," she said, without even a thank-you, as if I were a waitress in a diner. She dropped her head against the pillow and let her eyes drift closed as her tongue circled her lips. "That taste takes me back. My mother used to make me chocolate pudding for breakfast. When I had chicken pox, all I could stand to eat was cold pudding. Even after I got better, I refused anything else in the morning. I remember her standing at the stove after supper, stirring a pot of pudding to leave in the icebox overnight. Is there any smell more wonderful than milk just before it burns?"

"I remember my mother lighting the stove in the morning," I said, then stopped myself. Reminiscing with Mildred Solomon was not on my agenda. "Listen to me now. I had an appointment with an oncologist this morning." She didn't respond. "About my tumor, remember you felt it?"

"I remember. I'm not senile. Did he think it was malignant?"

"He's performing surgery next week. He'll examine the cells while I'm on the table. I won't know until I wake up how much will be left of me." I thought of my child-self strapped to her table, Dr. Solomon dripping chloroform onto the mask. I took her chin in my hand and made her look at me. "It's from the X-rays you gave me. From your experiment. You did this to me. What do you have to say for yourself?"

Her gaze never wavered, though her eyelids twitched and fluttered. "You think everything is my fault. Women have breast cancer all the time. So maybe you have cancer, that's terrible, sure. But what about me? It was probably giving all those X-rays that put this cancer in my bones. I'm not sorry about that, how could

I be? It's a waste of time, regretting the past. Besides, you don't know for sure."

"Even if it's not cancer, I've gone through my whole life damaged." I touched my wig. "Damaged because of you."

"You think being bald ruined your life? So what if you wear a wig. So do the Orthodox, so do a lot of women. Look at you. You're a pretty girl. You have a good job, a profession. Are you married?" She paused, considering. "Were you able to get pregnant, after the X-rays?"

As often as I regretted not having children, I'd always thought it was my own nature that denied me mothering. Now I wondered if Mildred Solomon hadn't robbed me of that, too. "I don't know, I never tried." I hesitated, wavering between the truth that felt like a lie and the lie that felt like the truth. "What if I am married, what's it to you?"

I instantly regretted it. She seized on my words. "Then you have something I never did. I could never get married and keep my career. We can't all be Madame Curie, can we? I know what those other doctors used to say about me behind my back, some of them to my face even. You have no idea what I went through."

I didn't want to see anything from her point of view. It muddied my anger, confused my sense of justification. Still, my mind conjured an image of Dr. Solomon as a young woman with that little tie around her neck, pushing her way through a crowd of white-coated men. I knew all too well what words they would have called her.

I clutched my breast. "But what about me? What will be left of me after this? Don't you feel sorry about that?"

"At least you have someone who'll be with you when you die. Who do I have?"

"You have me." I tried to sound sinister, wanting Dr. Solomon to realize how helpless she was, how completely in my power. Instead, the three words were a simple statement of fact. Of all the people in the world to have at her deathbed, she was down to me.

Mildred Solomon's mouth hung open; she was panting from the pain. "I'm ready for another dose." She spoke like a doctor giving orders. "We can talk more later, Number Eight, but only if you give me some now."

"My name is Rachel, I've told you that. But you don't care, do you? Even now, I'm just a number to you. All the children at the Infant Home were nothing more than numbers to you." I thought of the tattoo on Mr. Mendelsohn's frail arm. "Just numbers, like in the concentration camps."

She gripped the sheets. "How can you say such a thing? You were in an orphanage, not some concentration camp. They took care of you, fed you, clothed you. Jewish charities support the best orphanages, the best hospitals. Even this Home is as good as it gets for old people like me. You have no right to even mention the camps."

Of course the orphanage wasn't a death camp, I knew that, but I wasn't backing down. "You came into a place where we were powerless, you gave us numbers, subjected us to experiments in the name of science. How is that different from what Mengele did?"

Dr. Solomon sat up, the movement agonizing her hipbones. She pointed a wavering finger at me. "Don't you dare call me a Mengele! He was a sadist, not a scientist. And how did you come to be in the Infant Home anyway? Were you rounded up by Nazis and stuffed into a boxcar? Of course not. The agency was just taking care of you, so you didn't end up on the streets. You might as well blame everything on whatever it was that killed your parents. My research was your chance to give something back to society, for all that was given to you." She lay back, her hands cupped around her hips. "I saw those newsreels, just like everyone else. What we did was nothing like the Holocaust. You don't know what you're talking about."

But I did know. "My brother, he was in a unit that liberated one of the camps." I lowered my head, my voice a whisper. "He said all those women with their heads shaved, they reminded him of me."

If Mildred Solomon had chosen that moment to offer me the smallest kindness, a tender touch, I would have dissolved into tears in her withered arms, lavished her with painkillers, served her chocolate pudding for every meal. All I'd ever wanted from this woman, I realized, was the faintest echo of a mother's love. Couldn't she sense it?

"Nonsense. Now you listen to me, Number Eight. Either smother me or give me some morphine, because if you don't I'm going to scream bloody murder."

Defeated, I squeezed just enough morphine into the IV to shut her up. Her eyes sank back into her head, her mouth relaxed into a slack oval. What remained of her dose filled my vial. I sat on the edge of her bed, watched as the pain eased its grip on her tensed muscles. It wouldn't last long. What else could I do, what other words could I deploy, to wrench from this woman even a hint of contrition? How could she deny me this, after everything I'd given her, all she'd taken from me? If it hadn't been for me and the other orphans she used as material, she couldn't have conducted the study that earned her a coveted position. If she didn't regret how she'd used us, she should at least be grateful. After all, her career was built on our bodies.

No one else looking at the frail creature in that bed would have seen her for what she was: obstinate, selfish, cruel. Curled up, she took up such a small corner of the mattress. What time was it anyway? The watch face on my wrist looked blurry. I hadn't realized how very tired I was. I felt myself keeling sideways. My shoulder reached the mattress, then my head. I pulled up my knees, nudging Mildred Solomon over to make room for my legs. I folded my arm under my head and fell asleep at her feet.

Chapter Seventeen

ACHEL STOOD ON THE PORCH OF THE HOUSE ON COLFAX Avenue, hesitant, now, to ring the bell. Coming here had seemed such a good idea when it occurred to her. She'd asked Mr. Lesser to give her a ride in his delivery truck, making up a story about meeting Max in Denver. She'd put a sandwich in front of him while she gathered her things, helping herself to a wool coat and a pair of sturdy shoes from the shop, not even bothering to cover her theft in the ledger. Her uncle could consider it a bride price, she thought. The bride who got away.

When Mrs. Abrams opened the door, it took her a moment to put a name to the young woman with the cloche hat and cardboard suitcase.

"Is that you, Rachel? Come in out of the cold." Mrs. Abrams drew her into the foyer. She placed her palm on Rachel's cheek, concerned. "Is everything all right, dear?"

At the tender touch, Rachel burst into tears. "My parents are gone, Mrs. Abrams. I'm an orphan now. I didn't know where else to go."

Mrs. Abrams wrapped Rachel in her strong arms. "My poor, dear girl. I'm so sorry for your loss."

Soon they were sitting by the fire, hot cups of coffee in their hands. Rachel told Mrs. Abrams a convincingly simple story. "By the time I got to Leadville, Papa was on his deathbed. Mama had worn herself into sickness caring for him, and a month later she passed, too. I was left alone with my father's brother. That's why my parents went to Leadville when Papa got sick, because my uncle was there. After Mama died, I thought I could stay with him and keep house, but yesterday he told me I could only stay if I married him. I don't want to do it, but I hardly have any money, and he says I have nowhere else to go." Rachel looked down. "I didn't know who to talk to about it, until I thought of you."

Mrs. Abrams was indignant. "My God, Rachel, no man should bully you into marrying him, your own uncle least of all. Women have the vote for heaven's sake, have had it in Colorado for decades already. Look at me, dear." Mrs. Abrams took Rachel's face in both her hands. "You're a person, Rachel, your own person. You don't have to go back to Leadville. You'll stay here, with us, in the Ivy Room, until you decide what's next for you."

It was more than Rachel had hoped for. "I promise I'll find work and pay my way."

"Well, we'll figure that out later. Dr. Abrams will be home soon. Come, help me set the table."

Over a dinner of brisket with carrots and kasha, Mrs. Abrams presented Rachel's plight to her husband.

"If Jenny wants you to stay with us, then of course I agree," he said. "I'm glad to hear you intend to find work. You do know the

Hospital for Consumptive Hebrews is a charity? With this stock market crash, I expect we'll be getting more and more patients, especially with winter coming on. Our nurses are going to need all the help they can get. Why don't you come work for us?"

"Oh, thank you, Dr. Abrams, that would be perfect, then I can pay my room and board."

"You don't need to pay us, Rachel," Jenny Abrams said. "Taking you in, that's our mitzvah. Save your money or spend it how you decide. We're expecting Althea to come out in the summer, maybe by then you'll want to travel back east with her family. For now, though, you have a home with us."

"And, if you work hard," her husband said, "a place at the hospital."

Rachel was flooded with gratitude until a doubt cramped her stomach. "Dr. Abrams, I don't know what Mrs. Cohen told you, but I hadn't finished my nursing course when I had to come out here for my father. I was only helping in the orphanage infirmary, for an apprenticeship. I don't have my degree."

Dr. Abrams raised his eyebrows. "Althea may have exaggerated your credentials, but it's no matter. I'll start you off as an aide, and the head nurse will judge your skills from what you can do. Was it in Manhattan or Brooklyn, your apprenticeship?"

"Manhattan."

"Then that would be the Orphaned Hebrews Home, am I right?"

Rachel was surprised he knew it; she had no idea how renowned the Home was in charitable circles. She nodded without considering the consequences. "Thank you both so much." She threatened to cry again, but Mrs. Abrams stopped her.

"That's enough, dear. You're a Coloradan now." As if that explained everything. And somehow, it did.

That night in the Ivy Room, Rachel luxuriated in the warmth of an eiderdown quilt. Again Sam had left her behind, and again she'd managed to make her own way. She gave a cruel thought to where her brother was at that moment—huddled in the corner of a freezing freight car, or maybe warming his hands at some hobo's campfire? Wherever he was, she hoped he was miserable.

Mrs. Abrams accompanied Rachel to the hospital the next morning, taking her on the streetcar that came up Colfax Avenue. Through the fogging windows, Rachel watched the downtown mansions getting shabbier with each passing block. They gave way, finally, to a jumble of shops and bakeries and a synagogue until the city opened up, flat and broad.

"Here we are," Mrs. Abrams announced, pulling the cord. Rachel looked around for a big castle like the Home, but there wasn't one. Instead they started down a dirt street with large tents pitched along its length. At the end of the street was the main hospital building—no turrets or towers, only two stories high, with a wide porch on which beds were lined up. In each bed, a tubercular patient was bundled under a thick quilt, puffs of breath visible in the cold.

Mrs. Abrams noticed Rachel staring. "Didn't your father take heliotherapy?" Rachel shook her head at the unfamiliar word. "No wonder, then. It's the only reliable cure for tuberculosis." Rachel remembered reading in Nurse Dreyer's copy of *Essentials of Medicine* that treatment for the disease consisted of rest, rich food, fresh air, sunlight, and, if possible, freedom from worry. She wondered how someone with tuberculosis could not be worried.

Mrs. Abrams introduced Rachel to the head nurse before excusing herself. "I have a million things to do today. I'll see you home for dinner. You remember the streetcar stop, don't you?" Rachel assured her that she did.

After a brief interview, Rachel was given a uniform and put to work. She was relieved to find the nurse's cap was shaped like a hood that tied behind her neck, covering her head entirely. She spent the morning dealing with bedpans and bleach. At lunch, she was enlisted to bring trays to the patients. The food confused her until she caught on that the Hospital for Consumptive Hebrews, unlike the Home, kept kosher. Meals were rich and ample—that day it was whole milk and soft-boiled eggs for lunch, veal cutlets and roasted potatoes for dinner. The nurses kept coats hanging in the corridors for when they went out onto the porches to care for the patients, whose ruddy faces were turned to the November sun. The tents along the street, Rachel learned, also housed patients, the cold, dry air deployed like a weapon against the bacteria burrowed in their lungs.

Rachel happily followed the directions of the nurses throughout the day, doing the tasks she was assigned, taking breaks when she was told to, eating the sandwiches and drinking the coffee set out in the staff kitchen. Though children brought up in the Orphaned Hebrews Home complained about the regimentation of institutional life, for the rest of their lives most were never so happy as when they had a routine to follow. Rachel was helping wheel in patients' beds when she was told Dr. Abrams wanted to see her in his office.

"Ah, Rachel, yes. The head nurse tells me you've been working hard today."

"Yes, I like the work very much. Thank you again, Dr. Abrams."

"I'm glad to hear it. Also, I telephoned the Orphaned Hebrews Home today and asked for the Infirmary."

Rachel froze, anxiety bubbling up from her gut. The Home seemed such a world away, it had not occurred to her a simple phone call could link them. She braced herself for the look of betrayal on Dr. Abrams's face. She was nothing but a runaway orphan who had insinuated herself into their home with her lies. Of course they would cast her out. She was already plotting how far from Denver the little money she had could take her.

"I spoke with a Miss Gladys Dreyer. We had a frank discussion about your situation out here." Dr. Abrams paused; Rachel was light-headed from being unable to breathe. "She gave you a wonderful recommendation, said you were a good nursing student and that we were lucky to have you." Rachel, stunned, stammered something. Dr. Abrams checked his pocket watch. "You go on home now. Please tell Mrs. Abrams I'll be along by seven."

As Rachel closed the door to his office, her relief was so acute she collapsed into a chair in the hallway, cradling her head until she regained her composure. She had never expected Nurse Dreyer to cover her lies. It could only mean Gladys didn't know it was Rachel who had stolen Naomi's money and cut Amelia's hair, though she must have realized who had stolen her hat. Had Rachel been forgiven? Relieved as she was not to have been exposed, the kindness made her ashamed of herself. She swore she'd make Nurse Dreyer's falsehoods as true as possible by learning everything she could about nursing.

When Mrs. Abrams opened the door and ushered Rachel into the warm house, she felt guilty all over again. She helped set the table, and soon enough Dr. Abrams arrived, accompanied by two interns in need of a home-cooked meal. Mrs. Abrams chided him for giving her no warning, but the amount of food she'd prepared told Rachel she was used to unexpected guests. Rachel was quiet through dinner—the men talking medicine, Mrs. Abrams joining in when the conversation turned to politics. After helping clean up, Rachel asked Dr. Abrams's permission to bring an anatomy book from his study upstairs with her. "Take the one by Henry Gray," he said. "Leave me the new edition, but there's an older one you can keep if you like." In the Ivy Room, Rachel pored over the illustrations, so superior to the sketches in Emerson's *Essentials*, and set herself a plan of study.

Before the month was over, Rachel had fitted herself into all the patterns of the hospital. The work was more satisfying than assisting in the Infirmary, more important than taking inventory. At home, Rachel had proved hopeless at even the simplest cooking tasks, so it became her job to set and clear the table, Mrs. Abrams sitting with her husband by the fire while Rachel washed the dishes.

On the last day of the month, Rachel was called into the hospital office. "Sign here," the accountant said, pointing to a ledger, then handing over an envelope.

"Is everything all right?" Rachel asked, unsure what the transaction signified.

The accountant pushed up her glasses and checked the ledger. "I assure you, it's all there. You started November fourth, correct? Check if you want to." Realizing she was being paid, Rachel stammered no, she was sure it was fine. She could hardly wait to get back to the Ivy Room and open the envelope. It wasn't much—she was a girl, after all, working as a nurse's aide for a charity—but it was the most money Rachel had ever come by honestly. It made her feel like she was a person making her own way.

Keeping only enough to pay her fare on the streetcar, Rachel stashed the money in her case, next to Amelia's braid. She decided then and there no matter how long it took, she would save up enough to pay back Naomi. She imagined going down to the Western Union office with the cash, bills freshly ironed. How surprised Naomi would be to get the cable. How Rachel, forgiven, would be able to go home.

A NEW PATIENT arrived who soon became Rachel's favorite. Mary wasn't like the poor immigrants out from New York to recover on the charity of the hospital. She was from Philadelphia, young and wealthy. "I was, at any rate," she whispered, her voice husky from coughing. Rachel had wheeled her bed out onto the porch for the day. Shivering, Mary pulled her mink stole around her neck. "Even before the crash, my father was living on credit, running up bills, lying to his clients. We didn't know. I was in a private sanatorium in the Catskills, very posh. Last week, my mother showed up. Needed me home for the weekend, she told them, grandmother's funeral, we'd be back Monday, no need to settle the bill, which was suspiciously overdue. I was crying over my grandmother all the way down the drive until my mother told me to shut up." Mary paused to catch her breath while the cold air brought blood into her pale cheeks.

Rachel set out Mary's lunch of creamy milk, hardboiled eggs, and buttered bread, but she had no appetite. "I know how they are in places like this—help me eat it or they'll badger me no end.

Just take what I haven't touched." Rachel ate one of the eggs and a piece of bread while Mary talked. "Mother put me on a train for Denver with my steamer trunk like I was off to Europe. Handed me a bottle of codeine syrup, told me to cover my mouth and not to cough or I'd be kicked off. Spent her last dollars on the ticket." Mary pushed away her half-empty glass of milk. "Seems Father had locked himself in his study, hadn't come out for days. He finally confessed to my mother he was ruined. So, she shipped me off here, another charity case for the Hospital for Consumptive Hebrews." Rachel cleared the meal and left Mary to doze, fur pulled around her face, eyelashes catching the occasional snowflake.

On days Mary was too weak to talk, she implored Rachel to tell her own story. There wasn't enough time while working for extended conversation, so Rachel took to visiting Mary on her days off. It was a relief for her to have someone with whom she could speak the truth about herself. Mary encouraged her, pledging complete and utter secrecy. "I swear, I'll take it to my grave, Rachel."

"That's not funny, Mary. You'll see, you'll be well by spring." Sitting on Mary's bed, Rachel whispered to keep the words between the two of them. She told Mary about her parents and the Home, about Sam running away and how she met the Cohens in Chicago, about Leadville and Max, about Dr. and Mrs. Abrams taking her in. Mary sympathized with Rachel over Sam, was appalled to hear about her uncle's proposal, and agreed that she shouldn't go looking for her father. One day Rachel even went so far as to talk about the Purim Dance.

"Men are animals," Mary said, the flush in her cheeks for once not from the cold. "Always stayed as far away from them as I could. Wasn't easy, with my mother throwing parties and parading me around like a debutante, dragging the revolting sons of the nouveau riche over to fill in my dance card. I was almost grateful when the doctors diagnosed me. At least it kept the boys away. Now, tell me more about Naomi."

Rachel did: how Naomi defended her plate at dinner, stood up for her in the dorm, visited her in the Infirmary, smacked anyone who tried calling her a name worse than Egg.

"Why'd they call you that?"

Rachel was surprised at the question. With her head hidden by the nurse's cap or the cloche hat, Rachel had forgotten how few people realized she was bald. Dr. and Mrs. Abrams must have noticed, but they were nonchalant about it, knowing there were any number of medical reasons why someone could develop alopecia. Reluctantly she let Mary see what she looked like with her cap off. "It happened at the Infant Home, from X-rays is what they told me. I don't really remember."

"Explains your eyebrows. I guess I had wondered about that." Mary tilted her head, appraisingly. "It's strange, but kind of pretty in a way."

"That's what Naomi always said." An unexpected blush overtook Rachel. Mary noticed.

"I had a friend, too, at finishing school. My particular friend. She wasn't allowed to see me anymore after I contracted tuberculosis. She used to write, but her mother read one of my letters and put a stop to it. Said our friendship was unnatural."

Rachel was astonished. It seemed impossible for the same accusation that had been leveled at Naomi to fit Mary as well. She must have meant something else, Rachel decided. With shaking hands, she put her nurse's cap back on and changed the subject. Searching for something Mary would like to talk about, she asked about the clothes in her steamer trunk.

"The only thing I liked about those dances were the dresses, Rachel. I had one from a shop on Park Avenue, satin so soft it was like melted butter. The trunk is in my room. Wheel me inside and show me my things. It'll make me feel better."

Rachel got permission from the head nurse, and the girls spent the rest of the afternoon rummaging through the trunk. As Rachel held up dresses that were of a finer quality and more modern than anything she could imagine affording or choosing, Mary recounted where they were purchased and when she had worn them.

"Choose something for yourself, Rachel," Mary whispered. All the talking was irritating her lungs. She waved away Rachel's objections with a limp hand. "Do it for me, to make me happy."

Rachel picked the plainest dress, a drop waist in green wool. Mary insisted she try it on, declaring the result a success. "You practically look like a flapper," she said before giving in to a fit of coughing. Over the next few weeks, Rachel accepted three dresses and a pair of hand-stitched shoes.

The evening after Christmas, Dr. and Mrs. Abrams invited Rachel to light menorah candles with them and were amazed to find she couldn't recite the simple prayer. Dr. Abrams lamented the assimilationists back east who were so eager to be American they forgot how to be Jewish. Mrs. Abrams told her husband not to get started. "We'll just teach her," she said, and soon enough Rachel was speaking the Hebrew words and lighting the shammes.

"The doctor and I have a gift for you," Mrs. Abrams said, handing Rachel a package. Rachel didn't seem to know what to do with it. "Is something the matter, dear?"

"I don't think I've ever unwrapped a gift before." She pulled away the paper to reveal a brand-new printing of *Essentials of Medicine*.

"When I spoke with Miss Dreyer, she said you were using this in school. I thought you'd like to have your own copy," Dr. Abrams said.

Rachel thanked them both, promising herself to memorize every word. Sitting with the kindly couple by the fire, the menorah candles burning down, wearing Mary's dress and shoes, her gift by her side, a cup of coffee in her hand and a plate of cake on her lap, Rachel could almost believe there really was a monarch of the universe capable of performing miracles.

ONE MORNING OVER breakfast, Mrs. Abrams said, "Simon's birthday is in February and I want to find something special to send him. It's your day off, why not come with me? We'll make it an adventure." Rachel had promised Mary she'd visit that afternoon, but her morning was free, so she accepted Mrs. Abrams's invitation.

Rachel took a dollar from her savings, wanting to get Simon a present herself. Bundled up against the cold, they took the streetcar up Sixteenth and went in and out of the shops along Market. Mrs. Abrams purchased an illustrated edition of Webster's dictionary for her grandson, but Rachel wanted her gift to be more whimsical. Remembering how fascinated Simon had been by the story the porter told them on the train, she asked Mrs. Abrams where she could buy a model or a carving of a horse.

"If you don't tell Dr. Abrams, I'll take you down Hop Alley. There's a shop that sells carvings, everything you can imagine. I bought a chess set there, years ago." She led Rachel farther up Market then turned down the alley that ran behind Twentieth Street. It was narrow, just enough space for the backs of the brick buildings to face off against each other. The doors and windows along the alley were filled with signs printed in Chinese characters and posters decorated with dragons and flowers. Two white men wearing last night's top hats stumbled out of a door and scurried down the alley, hiding their faces. Mrs. Abrams pulled Rachel closer. "Here it is."

They entered a cramped little shop, the teetering shelves stacked floor to ceiling with carvings in jade and quartz and onyx. Rachel scanned the shelves until her eyes settled on a rearing horse, his mane cut so thin the light shone through the stone. She brought it to the shopkeeper. He named a price and Rachel dipped her hand into her pocket for her dollar, but Mrs. Abrams stopped her. Despite the apparent language barrier, the shopkeeper and the doctor's wife bartered with gusto, and in the end Rachel paid less than half the original sum.

The women retraced their steps, but just before they turned the corner Rachel spotted, in a window, a series of drawings of women with flowing hair: blond, auburn, brown, jet. One looked so much like the wig she'd tried on at the Tabor Opera House, Rachel paused. She saw an arrow pointing up the fire escape stairs and, painted on a door, English lettering above Chinese characters: MRS. HONG'S HOUSE OF HAIR. In a second-story window, Rachel thought she saw a bald head. As she looked, a small woman came into view and placed a wig on the form.

"Come along, Rachel, we don't want to linger here," Mrs. Abrams said, eyeing another jittery young man scuttling up the alley. Rachel followed reluctantly, her heart drumming against her ribs.

At the house on Colfax, Rachel ran up to the Ivy Room. She pulled her cardboard case out from under the bed and opened it. Taking up the thick braid of Amelia's hair, she stroked it like a pet. She draped the braid over her scalp and imagined it already a wig to rival Madame Hildebrand's. After carefully wrapping Amelia's hair in newspaper, she took the carved horse out of her pocket and replaced it with what was left of Naomi's money, as well as all she'd been saving to repay her, nearly every cent of three month's pay.

"Give my best to that dear girl Mary," Mrs. Abrams called as Rachel went out the door.

"I will," Rachel lied.

It was past noon by now, but Hop Alley still seemed half asleep. Rachel had heard the rumors and imagined what businesses lay behind the shuttered windows—opium parlors, gambling halls, brothels that catered to unfaithful husbands and wifeless Chinese men. Rachel mounted the fire escape steps, her shoes slipping on the slick metal. At the second-story landing, she pulled at the door handle. It stuck, then popped open, flinging Rachel against the railing. For a second she thought she'd fall, imagined Mrs. Abrams reading a notice in the *Denver Post* about a bald white girl found dead in Hop Alley.

But she didn't fall. Regaining her balance, she entered Mrs. Hong's House of Hair. It wasn't a showroom. Rachel understood why Mrs. Hong always went to Madame Hildebrand's dressing room. Stage actresses and wealthy socialites wouldn't come themselves to this barren space. Paint flaked from the plank floor and plaster had fallen away from the masonry walls, exposing ragged patches of brick. Bare bulbs dangled from wires like descending spiders, augmenting the weak light filtering in through filmy windows. A worktable occupied the center of the room. Along the walls were shelves of wig forms labeled in Chinese characters. Rachel wished she could decipher the names of the women whose heads they represented.

A curtain of bamboo beads skittered open and a little girl stopped at the sight of Rachel. She called back in excited syllables, and in a moment Mrs. Hong herself appeared. Rachel had expected a more imposing figure, but the woman was petite, her braided hair pinned around her head like the route on a treasure map. She wore a square black jacket and shapeless trousers, which Rachel assumed were confined to the workroom—she'd never seen a woman walking around Denver in such attire. Rachel thought if she had passed her on the street in a skirt and blouse, she might have taken Mrs. Hong for Cherokee instead of Chinese.

Mrs. Hong sent the little girl back through the beaded curtain. An expert at summing up a woman from her clothes and bearing, Mrs. Hong assessed Rachel. She noted the hem of a fashionable dress and the expensive hand-stitched shoes but couldn't figure the old-fashioned wool coat. Something about the girl didn't quite add up. The hat, however—Mrs. Hong understood instantly what the cloche hat was hiding.

"Welcome to Mrs. Hong's House of Hair, but please, this is where we make the wigs. It is not a place for a lady to come. We could make an appointment for later today if you would allow me to visit your home." Mrs. Hong gestured toward the door.

"No, wait. Madame Hildebrand told me about you. I met her in Leadville, at the Tabor Opera House. She let me try one of your wigs."

Mrs. Hong's dark eyebrows arched into narrow bridges. "But Madame Hildebrand has never been here."

"No, I know, but I passed by this morning and I saw your sign."

Mrs. Hong relaxed her outstretched arm. "Madame Hildebrand is a very discerning customer. Are you also a singer?"

"No, I was just in the audience. I met her backstage." Rachel was too nervous to explain properly. She tried again. "I brought this." Rachel stepped up to the table and placed her package on it, folding back the newspaper. In the dreary workroom, Amelia's hair glowed and flickered. "Madame Hildebrand said your wigs were expensive, but you see, I already have the hair. How much would it cost to make it into a wig?"

Mrs. Hong touched the braid. The hair was gorgeous. She could see from Rachel's coloring it had never been her own, but how she had acquired it was none of Mrs. Hong's business. What she did know was that it would be a pleasure to work with this hair. Still, it would need to be washed and combed, divided and sewn. It would keep her girls busy for weeks, not to mention making the custom form and the cap. She knew what price she'd give to Madame Hildebrand in similar circumstances. She doubted this Leadville girl had the means, but she named that price anyway, as any businesswoman would.

What little color there was in Rachel's cheeks drained away. The price Mrs. Hong gave was double what she could earn in an entire year. Madame had been right; Rachel could never afford to have something so beautiful. Struck dumb by disappointment, she began wrapping the braid with shaking hands.

Mrs. Hong read the authenticity in Rachel's reaction. Accustomed to dramatic bouts of bargaining for everything from bolts of silk to baskets of onions, Mrs. Hong had expected her first price to be countered, but now she saw she'd aimed too high and frightened the girl. "Wait," she said, placing her hand on the braid. The hair came alive under her palm, curling around her fingers. She made another guess about Rachel. "Doesn't your father want to pay for the wig, as a gift for his lovely young daughter?"

Rachel shook her head. "I'm an orphan. I work as a nurse's aide at the Hospital for Consumptive Hebrews. I've saved most of three month's pay, but . . ." Rachel's voice faded as she considered the pittance in her pocket.

Mrs. Hong, however, asked, "How much do you have?"

Rachel realized she wasn't being refused—Mrs. Hong was negotiating. She berated herself for not bargaining the way Mrs. Abrams had over the horse carving. Rachel took the bills out of her pocket and placed them on Mrs. Hong's worktable. It was all the money she had in the world.

"And this is what you earned in three months?"

"More than that. That's my earnings." Rachel divided the pile; the money she'd taken from Naomi was still creased where it had been folded to fit into her shoe. "And this is my savings."

Mrs. Hong calculated. Because the girl was providing the hair, the sum on the table would cover her initial expenses for materials, but it was labor and skill that made her wigs so precious. She longed now to transform the crackling braid on her table into a head of hair, imagining the business she could drum up by show-ing it off, but she needed to make some profit. "This isn't half what it will cost me, out of my own pocket, to make the wig. I have a business here, mouths to feed, rent to pay. I'm not running a charity."

Rachel tried to regain her bargaining position. "I can pay you most of what I earn for the next"—she did some math—"the next seven months, but I need the wig by September. I'm going back east for nursing school, so it has to be finished by the end of summer." Rachel was surprised by the words that came out of her mouth. She'd only meant to set a limit for the price of the wig, but as soon as she'd expressed the idea, she was taken by the possibility.

Mrs. Hong tallied the total and considered the girl's offer. She wouldn't lose money, but she would barely profit. She needed something to sweeten the deal. Since the stock market crash, people everywhere were losing jobs. Mrs. Hong wondered if this girl could keep hers through the spring and into the summer. Maybe. Maybe not. It was a bet Mrs. Hong was willing to make.

"I'll tell you what, Leadville Orphan Girl. You give me all you have now, as a deposit, and I will begin making the wig. You keep up the payments every month. With your final payment on Sep-tember first, the wig will be finished, and it will be yours."

Joy spread over Rachel's face. Mrs. Hong wondered if the girl knew how beautiful she was. "Yes, of course, I will, Mrs. Hong, I'll come next month and every month."

"There is one more thing. This is a very special price. If Madame Hildebrand or any of my other customers ever hear what I let you pay, they'd be furious. I am taking food out of my own mouth to make you this offer. And I will be doing all the work before you finish paying. What if you don't pay me after all? I need some protection." Mrs. Hong paused. "If you miss a payment, or don't pay in full by September, I keep the hair and the wig and everything you've paid so far. Agreed?"

Rachel did, eagerly. What was money to her if she could anticipate having Amelia's hair for her own? The little girl was called out from behind the beaded curtain and sent running into the alley. She returned in minutes with a wrinkled man who carried a roll of paper and a box containing ink and pen. In Cantonese, he wrote out two copies of the terms of Mrs. Hong's agreement with Leadville Orphan Girl. Mrs. Hong took up the calligraphy pen to create the character of her name, and Rachel signed as well.

"Now then, let's get to work."

Hours later, Rachel left Hop Alley in the last light of the winter day. All of her money and Amelia's hair were with Mrs. Hong. In her pocket, a folded piece of inscrutable paper was all the promise she had that she would get everything she bargained for.

The next day, Mary asked Rachel why she hadn't visited her. Too full of excitement to keep it to herself, Rachel told Mary all about the Opera House and Madame Hildebrand and Mrs. Hong's House of Hair. Without mentioning the theft of Amelia's braid, she told Mary that yesterday she'd gone to the shop and bargained hard with the wig maker, settling on a price she could afford for a lovely wig made from dark red hair.

"Why red?" Mary asked. "You'd look more natural as a brunette."

"She had these braids of hair for me to choose from, and that one just seemed so alive."

Lingering with Mary's lunch tray, Rachel recounted the rest of the afternoon she'd spent at Mrs. Hong's. "She had me sit in a chair, and one of the little girls—"

"Eat this, will you? I haven't touched it. What are the girls' names?"

"I don't know, Mrs. Hong always talks to them in Chinese. I'll ask her next month. Anyway, she sat me in a chair. You know that ointment, Vaseline? Well, Mrs. Hong rubbed that all over my scalp. Then one of the girls handed her strips of gauze dipped in plaster, and she wrapped them around my head like a mummy. I had to sit there for a long time while the plaster dried, then she cut it off my head with a scissors."

"Weren't you scared?"

"I was, but the little girl held my hand, and Mrs. Hong said, 'Don't worry, Orphan Girl, nothing's going to hurt you.' Then after she took off the plaster cast, the other little girl washed my head. They're both so adorable. I started to sing the alphabet song just to entertain her, and she sang along! I didn't know she could speak English. But then Mrs. Hong sent her into the back room. She's very strict with the girls."

"Are they her daughters?" Mary blotted her mouth with the napkin. It came away spotted with blood. She hid it under her pillow.

Rachel had wondered this herself. Mrs. Hong ordered the girls around like servants, but it was no worse than the monitors at the Home. What did Rachel know, anyway, of how mothers treated daughters? "I don't know. I'll see if I can find that out, too."

For the rest of the month, Rachel's workdays flew by. Her afternoons off were spent visiting Mary, and each Friday evening, she helped with the Shabbat dinner, the table filled out by interns from the hospital invited into the warm circle of the house on Colfax. The day after collecting her next wage envelope, Rachel made her way back to Hop Alley to make her payment to Mrs. Hong. She lingered at the workshop, her curiosity emboldening her to ask about the girls.

"This one, I call her Sparrow, because she chatters all the time, and that one I call Jade, to make her strong. Now go, do your work!" The girls darted into the back room. Mrs. Hong lowered her voice. "They call me 'auntie,' but they're nothing to me. Their mother pays me to keep them, teach them a trade. Their fathers were customers, Chinese men, but she doesn't know which ones."

Rachel parted the beaded curtain to watch the girls at work. Sparrow was combing out long strands of hair, and Jade, the older of the two, was operating a sewing machine, stitching layers of hair to strips of linen. The way they worked made Rachel think of girls in a garment factory, though where that impression came from she wasn't sure.

In April, Mrs. Hong asked Rachel to stay in the workshop. "I need you for a fitting." She lifted a tightly knit cap off a plaster form and settled it on Rachel's scalp. With a long needle and silk thread, Mrs. Hong plucked at the cap, snugging it to cup the back of Rachel's head and hug her temples. As Mrs. Hong worked, Rachel asked her how she came to have the wig shop. Instead of answering directly, Mrs. Hong launched into an oblique story.

"When the Chinese men came to America to build the railroad, they weren't allowed to bring their wives and children. After the railroad was finished, some of them went home, some stayed here. The railroad crossed Indian country, and some of the Chinese men set up trading posts on the frontier. Sometimes an Indian woman would stay with the Chinese man, to work in the trading post. If the Chinese man decided to come into Denver to open a laundry, the woman might leave her people and follow him, wash the clothes, have his children. The white people write the laws so the Chinese man can't bring his own wife here, but they don't mind if he lives with an Indian woman he will never marry." A hardness came into Mrs. Hong's voice and she seemed to speak more to herself than to Rachel. "The white people, they think Indians and Chinese are both dirty, no matter how clean we make their shirts."

After a minute of silence, Rachel asked, "What happened to Mr. Hong?"

Mrs. Hong straightened her back. "What makes you think I ever got married? Married women work themselves to death, all their money goes to husbands who gamble it away. Why would I ever do that to myself? I call myself 'Mrs.' because my clients like to think I'm a respectable widow. Ladies are always suspicious of a woman who isn't some man's wife."

Before Rachel left, she stopped in the back room to wave goodbye to the girls. She thought it sad that they didn't go to school, and cruel when Jade whispered how their auntie kept them locked in the shop when she went out on a delivery or to take an order. There was no one to rescue the girls if Mrs. Hong exploited them, no recourse if they were treated harshly. Maybe she should mention it to Mrs. Abrams? Then Rachel reconsidered Sparrow and Jade, their features too Oriental to pass for white, their skin too light to conceal their mixed parentage. Rachel thought of their mother's profession and knew there was a worse kind of life Mrs. Hong was saving them from.

As she rode the streetcar back to the comfortable house on Colfax, Rachel imagined where, if not for the agency, she and Sam might have ended up: in back alleys or boxcars, on soup lines near Hoovervilles. Rachel had often wondered how it would have been if the agency lady had found her and Sam a foster home. They might have gotten lucky—a cozy apartment with a nice family, a foster mother kind as Mrs. Berger, a foster father generous as Dr. Abrams. Or maybe not. Who would she have turned to if, in that cozy apartment, lived a boy like Marc Grossman? For the first time, Rachel began to appreciate what she herself had been saved from by the Home.

Chapter Eighteen

MILDRED SOLOMON'S CHEST WAS PRESSED AGAINST my back; the back of my head rested on her clavicle. She wrapped her arms around me. Our gentle breathing rose and fell in unison. I felt a tug. Was she plucking at my fingers, wanting more morphine? Looking down, I saw a needle threaded with yarn as rough as horsehair poking through the tendons of my hands.

I woke with a gasp, the dream worse than ever. I could actually feel the burn of seawater in the back of my throat. Wiping drool from my mouth, I sat up on the bed and adjusted my wig. Focusing on my watch, I saw it was past midnight. Mildred Solomon moaned and shifted in a fitful sleep. What dreams, I wondered, haunted her? I doubted I was in them.

The room was suffocating, the window closed since the storm. I got up and opened it, wishing I had one of Flo's cigarettes to pass the time until Dr. Solomon woke again. It wouldn't be long now.

That talk about concentration camps put me in mind of Sam and the story he told me after returning from the war. I remembered him calling from the pay phone on Amsterdam Avenue, his voice on the line instantly familiar, collapsing the years since he'd gone to war. I told him I would have met him at the dock if I'd known when his ship was coming in. "It was a madhouse at the harbor," he said. "I didn't want you messed up in all that." Was he worried I'd be grabbed and kissed by a returning soldier, or that my wig would be knocked off in the jostling crowd?

"Did you know they'd turned the Home into a barracks?" he was saying. "I couldn't believe it when the truck stopped here to let us off. We're in F3, can you imagine? I never even saw the inside of a girls' dorm the whole time I lived here. Why don't you come up and see me?"

I did, running from that old apartment in the Village to the closest subway stop, the Broadway line seeming to crawl uptown as I counted the seconds until I saw my brother again.

I told the guard at the entrance who I was there to meet. Soon enough, Sam emerged from the Castle. It was strange to see him come through those oak doors a grown man instead of a little boy. He walked with purpose, almost a swagger. I'd been so afraid during the war that he'd be wounded or killed, as Simon Cohen had been. But there Sam was, whole and handsome. The rainbow patch of his division was bright on his shoulder, but the washed-out green of the uniform made his eyes glint like steel. Sam lifted me up in a hug that lasted so long, a few other soldiers started to whistle. Embarrassed, we crossed the street and sat on a bench beneath a gingko tree, facing our former Home.

"Can you beat that, Rachel? I run away from this place out to Leadville, hobo up and down the West Coast, end up on an apple farm in Washington State, come back to New York to enlist, get shipped off to Europe, and after all that where do I end up? Right back where I started." He shaded his eyes to look up at the clock tower. "Makes sense, in a way. Military barrack's hardly different from being in the Home. Except back then, I was just a kid. At least in the military, I'm a man. I can stand up for myself." His jaw tightened, and I saw, beneath his swagger, the wounded orphan who snuck out of the Castle all those years ago.

We didn't know how to start talking about what we'd seen and done since last we were together. It's no wonder we struggled to re-connect. It wasn't just the war—my brother and I had been living separate lives since that agency lady pulled us apart. Other grown siblings had a home to go back to, parents to visit on holidays, grandparents to host the seder. Between us, Sam and I didn't know how to make a family. Our conversation turned to the pictures from Japan that had come out in *Life* magazine: clothes melted onto naked bodies, skin dissolving into bubbling sores, babies being born deformed. When I read that people who'd escaped the atomic blast were getting sick from the radiation, their hair falling out, I couldn't help but feel a strange kinship. At the time, all I knew was that the X-rays I'd gotten as a child had made me bald. That night in Mildred Solomon's room, I wondered if the cancer had been growing in me even then.

To Sam, I said, "Sometimes I ask myself if there's any limit to the harm people can do to each other."

"No," he said. "There's no limit." He stared across the street, his eyes distant, as if he were watching a movie projected on the side of the building. "When our division liberated Dachau, it was like we had walked into hell. You've seen the newsreels?" I nodded, picturing the skeletal survivors herded into relocation camps, held there until the world could figure out what to do with Europe's remaining Jews. "Believe me, they don't show all of it, not by a long shot. We had to call in a construction battalion to move the bodies, they were piled so high. Imagine that, then add in the smell of rot and shit and smoke." Sam's grip on his knees was turning his knuckles white. "No, don't. Don't imagine it. I'll have it in my head long enough for both of us."

I thought I'd seen the worst of it in the hospital. Soldiers with missing limbs or blown-out eyes. Scars that meandered the length of a man's body like a map of the Mississippi. But the things Sam was saying made me feel sick in a part of my stomach so deep I hadn't known it was there. I covered his hand with mine. He turned his palm up to accept the gesture. We sat for a long time like that, not caring anymore if we looked like sweethearts.

"What are you going to do after you're decommissioned?" I meant for a job; I assumed he'd be staying in New York. I was already planning to invite him over for Friday-night dinners, memories of Shabbat with the Abramses shaping my imagination. Not that I'd attempt to cook—if we wanted anything edible, I'd have to take out a roasted chicken from the deli on the corner—but no matter. We'd manage, this time, to be a real family.

"I wanted to talk to you about that," he said. "You know, the more I think about it, the more it seems my whole life has been preparing me for just one thing. I mean, after roaming around all those years, when the war broke out I was glad to have a reason to sign up. Good thing I came back here to enlist, though. I heard from my one buddy out west he spent the whole war guarding a Japanese internment camp in Wyoming. What a waste of time that would've been. Fighting gave me a purpose, and I was good at it. Kept most of my guys alive, killed a lot of theirs. It's pretty simple." Sam paused, let go of my hand to knock a cigarette out of the pack he pulled from his pocket. He held one out for me, but I shook my head. Still, when he lit it, I inhaled deeply, wanting to remember everything about this moment.

"I'm going to Palestine, Rachel. I'm going to get past those damn British detention camps to join the Haganah. I'm going to fight until we have a country of our own."

I hung my head, stunned. Sam was leaving me behind, again. My idea of us being a family was a childish fantasy I'd clung to because my brother was the only person in all the world who really, truly, belonged to me. I may have been living like a married woman, but not a single piece of paper existed to attest that she and I were family. No matter how often we swore our allegiance to one another, she could never be more than my friend, my room-mate.

Sam was leaving, but at least this time he was telling me where he was going, and why. He talked about the United Nations and the politics of partition with such passion, I knew there was no use arguing with him. Instead I tried to memorize the way his eye-lashes fluttered in the sunlight and how his ears wiggled slightly as he talked. I knew it would be a very long time until I saw him again. Thinking back on it that night, as I looked down at the dark city street below Mildred Solomon's window, it occurred to me I might not live long enough to ever visit my brother, to ever meet my sister-in-law, to ever see my only nephew.

"How about you?" Sam asked, taking my hand. "What's next for you?"

I took a deep breath. I'd regretted the things I left unsaid when he went to war, had promised myself if I had another chance I'd tell my brother the truth about myself. He flinched when I used the word *lesbian*, but I didn't want there to be any misunderstanding. My heart was pounding so hard I felt dizzy. I was afraid he'd be ashamed of what I was, the way he was ashamed of how I looked. I was afraid he'd think this, too, was somehow his fault, the result of his failure to protect me. It took him awhile to meet my eyes, but when he did, he said, "Who am I to judge, as long as you're happy."

I hadn't realized how heavy the unspoken words had been until they were lifted from me. "I am happy, Sam, I promise."

"There's something I should have said to you a long time ago, too. I'm sorry, Rachel, about Uncle Max. I shouldn't have left you with him. I just didn't know how else to take care of you."

"Don't blame yourself, Sam. I don't. Well, I did at first, but not anymore. We were supposed to have parents to take care of us, but we didn't. It wasn't our fault. Anyway, I managed to take care of myself, didn't I? Just promise me you'll do the same and try to stay safe."

"I'm not going to Palestine to be safe, Rachel. I'm going to fight." Sam squeezed my hand before letting it go to light another cigarette. "I'll be fighting for both of us, for all of us. No Jew will ever be truly safe until we have a homeland." It seemed to me Sam was right about that. Without a state, our people were as vulnerable as orphans without a home.

"Liberating that camp changed me, Rachel. We weren't prepared for what it was like, no one could've been. I remember thinking they never would have gotten me in there without a fight."

"That's just it, though, isn't it? Everyone who fought back had already been killed." I've heard people say they can't understand how the Nazis managed it, the murder of millions, but it didn't start with cattle cars and gas chambers. They began it all by reviving the medieval idea of sorting and separating Jews. We were demonized, dehumanized, ghettoized, all before being transported to the camps, the crematoriums out of sight until the last stretch of track. At every step along the way, the ones like Sam who stepped out of line were cut down, an example made of their resistance.

"I guess you're right." Sam took a deep drag of his cigarette, smoke seeping out of his nose. "The other guys, they were all wondering, what was it about the Jews that the Germans would do this to them? The further we got into that camp, the more we saw, the Jewish soldiers in our division started looking to me, you know, because I was older, like they were waiting to see what I was going to do about all this. You know what I did? I grabbed one of those Nazis out of the pen where we'd rounded them up. I dragged him out into the mud and put him on his knees. And I said—I wanted to scream, but I said it real quiet, almost a whisper, so he actually tilted his head up to hear me—I said, *Ich bin Jude.* And then I shot him." Sam dropped the cigarette butt and ground it out under the toe of his boot. "After that, the guys went crazy, started executing Nazis all over the place until some officer showed up and put a stop to it."

What I feared, while Sam was at war, was that he would be killed, not that he would become a killer. I wasn't troubled by the thought of him shooting an enemy in battle. That was something he had to do to save himself or his men, to win the war. But what he'd just described was murder, wasn't it? Yet I wasn't appalled by his confession. To Sam, that killing was justified by the horrors surrounding him. I was thinking, though, of Sam's Nazi prisoner, on his knees in the mud. If he had looked around at the piles of rotting bodies and become conscious of the monstrous magnitude of his deeds, wouldn't he have welcomed the quick sting of a bullet over a lifetime of guilt and shame? To me, Sam's shot sounded not like an assassination, but a mercy.

"Smells like rust, all that blood," Sam said. "That's what you can't wash off. Not the blood itself, but the smell of it."

"I know what it smells like. I'm a nurse, remember?" I looked down at my fingers, folded in my lap. "You're not the only one who's ever gotten blood on their hands."

Sam pulled one knee up on the bench and turned to face me. "Since I saw those camps, all I keep thinking is, that could have been me, you know? Me and you. If we'd been living in Germany or Poland or wherever the hell our people came from, that would have been us. It made me feel like more of a Jew than the Home ever did. Back then, it was all Hebrew this and Hebrew that, marching bands and baseball teams, but that's not what it's about. It's not about God, either, or the Torah. It's about survival." There was a defiance in Sam's eyes I recognized from the night he refused to apologize to the superintendent, a brightness that made the steel glint. If we had been in Europe, me and Sam, he'd have fought to the death before allowing himself to be herded onto one of those trains. That left the people like me. Was it possible the rest of us, like orphans in an institution, were so used to doing as we were told we made it easier than it should have been to round us up?

We said our good-byes, pretending they weren't forever. I watched Sam disappear through the old oak doors as the Castle swallowed him up. For what he was planning, an official discharge made no difference. He soon shed his American uniform and boarded a ship bound for the Mediterranean. Since that day, all I had of him fit in the glove drawer of an old steamer trunk: the postcards I'd saved, the letters he'd sent, that one roll of film.

In the dark behind me, Mildred Solomon groaned in her sleep. She had said there was no comparison between her work at the Infant Home and those terrible experiments in the camps, and she was right, of course she was. But did the children on Dr. Mengele's table feel any differently than I did on hers? No matter her motives, the way she used us was the same. No wonder she couldn't apologize. It would destroy a person, wouldn't it, to admit to doing that kind of harm?

I should have gone ahead and given her a full dose. I had no reason to allow Mildred Solomon to rise again to consciousness. I knew now she'd never give me what I wanted. There would be no apology, no remorse. I should have emptied the syringe and left her sleeping while I walked out of this room and into the bright hallway, shutting the past behind me.

Except it was impossible for me to leave the past behind. It was multiplying inside me, the tumor generating new cells by the minute. After my operation, if I woke up to find my breasts lopped off, black thread knotted across my chest, it would be as if Dr. Solomon herself had wielded the knife.

I kept my back to her, looked out the window at streetlamps, lit windows, occasional headlights. Above, the city's glow turned the black sky gray. The lights made me realize it was indifference, not darkness, that made the night dangerous. Deeds committed in the city's small hours were not so much hidden from view as ignored, as if the few of us awake in the dead of night had all agreed to turn away our eyes. It was like the people in those villages downwind of the death camps. It wasn't as if they couldn't smell the smoke; they just pretended not to know what was happening. It occurred to me there was nothing I couldn't get away with between midnight and dawn.

If I couldn't get the contrition I yearned for, why not exact justice instead, like my brother had done? Mildred Solomon would be dead soon enough, no matter what I did or didn't do. Why not transform the inevitable into something intentional? Why should I leave her to die, alone and ignored, a few days or weeks from now, when her death tonight, witnessed, could mean so much more? For once, I could stand up for myself, an adult now instead of a child, my weapon a needle of morphine instead of a pistol. I could do it now, before the old woman awoke. In the middle of this indifferent night, no one would notice if I took a woman's life.

Suddenly dizzy, I clutched at the windowsill to keep myself from falling backward into the room. The idea pulsed through my arteries, throbbing in my neck. I saw now that withholding Mildred Solomon's morphine could be elevated from a selfish act to a noble endeavor. What a perfect opera it would make! The curtain rises on a child strapped down and chloroformed like an animal, then falls on an old woman put down like a dog past petting.

Somewhere in my sleep-deprived brain were all the reasons why killing Mildred Solomon would never bring me peace, but I was too exhausted to know them. I took the vial of morphine from my pocket and weighed it in my hand. It would be so simple to fill the syringe and press the plunger. There was nothing to stop me. Down the hall, Lucia was surely asleep over her lap of yarn. In the morning, the day nurse who found a terminal patient passed away during the night would think nothing of pulling up the sheet to cover the body. There would be no questions, no inquiry, no autopsy. No one would know.

Not even Mildred Solomon.

I backed away from the window. It wouldn't be worth doing if Dr. Solomon didn't know. I wanted to see the realization in her eyes, wanted the doctor to know what her good little girl, her bravest patient, was about to do. I had been her material to do with as she pleased. Now I was the one in control. If she couldn't feel remorse for what she'd done to me, then at least she'd know, before she died, how it felt to have your life in someone else's hands.

Groping along the wall, I found the switch and turned on the light. I blinked against the sudden brightness. Rinsing a cloth in the sink, I touched it to the old woman's face.

"Time to wake up, Dr. Solomon."

Chapter Nineteen

RACHEL WENT IN TO THE RELIEF SOCIETY DRIPPING WET from a thunderstorm that slowed the streetcars and made her late. She was excited to tell Mary what she had learned from Mrs. Hong, to talk over her thoughts about Sparrow and Jade. Because of the rain, the patients were all inside instead of out on the porches. Their ragged breathing and harsh coughs echoed through the hallways.

Rachel went into Mary's room. The bed was empty, the mattress rolled up, twisted wires exposed. At first she thought Mary must have been moved. Then the truth became apparent. She sat on the iron rail of the bed, too stunned to cry. The head nurse saw her there. "I'm sorry, Rachel, I didn't mean for you to find out like this. Mary's fever spiked yesterday. Her heart just couldn't take it. I know you cared about her, but we have another patient waiting to come in from the tents. Would you disinfect the bed for me?" Silently, Rachel nodded. The nurse placed a warm hand on her shoulder. "It comes with the job. We never get used to it, but we do learn to bear it."

Rachel washed down the bed with bleach, puzzling out the mystery of how a person could be alive one minute and gone the next. She'd seen it happen, when her mother died. That was a moment she could still recall, the shift in her mother's eyes from seeing to not-seeing. She would have hated to witness that change in Mary, but still she wished she'd been with her at the end. It broke Rachel's heart that Mary had died alone, so far from her family and friends. The Hospital for Consumptive Hebrews would notify Mary's parents, she supposed. There was a graveyard nearby, burial expenses covered by the charity, but it was up to the families to send money for a headstone. From what Mary had told her, Rachel doubted the grave would ever bear her name. With the help of another nurse, she put a fresh mattress on the frame. Before Rachel's shift was over, a woman who spoke no English was tucked up in Mary's bed. Agitated and breathless, she called out in Yiddish, the guttural sounds spattering her lips with sputum.

In the darkness of evening, Rachel let the streetcar carry her down Colfax Avenue. She was so lost in her thoughts she missed the Abramses' house and had to walk back from the next stop. Opening the door, she found the dining room lit with candles and full of voices—she'd forgotten it was Shabbat. "Come, sit with us, Rachel," they beckoned, but she shook her head and slunk upstairs to the Ivy Room. When Mrs. Abrams came to check on her, she found Rachel staring out the rain-streaked window.

"I heard about Mary. I'm so sorry, dear. Did you know she wanted you to have all of her lovely things? Usually they would have been donated back to the hospital, but Dr. Abrams had the interns bring her steamer trunk home for you. I'll ask them to carry it up before they leave." She paused. "You know, I invite the interns as much for you as for them. I thought you might take a liking to one of them. Such fine young men. It's how Althea met

David, after all. And they're not old like your uncle! Has there been anyone you liked?"

Rachel shrugged. It hadn't occurred to her to notice them.

Mrs. Abrams recommended a hot bath. Rachel took the suggestion, sinking under the water to muffle the sounds of conversation drifting upstairs. Afterward Rachel returned to her room to find the trunk standing on end in the middle of the floor. Nearly her height, it looked larger here than it had in the hospital. She undid the clasps and pulled the handles. It opened like a book on its spine. On one side was a neat stack of shut drawers, each with a tiny glass knob; on the other, a curtain behind which the dresses hung. Rachel parted the curtain, as she had done before at Mary's instruction, and slid her hands through the familiar inventory. She felt fine wool and stiff linen, satin and silk. Beneath the dresses were the shoes, four pairs all in their places. Rachel leaned in and inhaled a smell from before the tuberculosis and the hospital: scented powder and polished leather.

Rachel pulled off her orphanage nightgown, intending to try on the dresses and shoes, one after another, as she knew Mary would have wanted her to. Then she realized such dresses weren't meant to be dropped over a naked torso, that the shoes would scratch her bare feet. She sat down on the floor and began pulling open drawers, looking for a camisole and stockings. The smallest drawer on top held hairpins and combs, a few rings, a string of false pearls. Next were gloves and handkerchiefs, then underwear. She found camisoles with the slips and silk scarves. The stockings were below that. Rachel wondered what was left for the bottom drawer. Pinching the glass knob, she pulled it open.

Letters, photographs, ribbon. A diary closed with a locked

hasp. A china doll with a broken arm. An unfinished embroidery still on its hoop, threaded needle poked into the stretched fabric. A seashell.

Rachel handled Mary's things like found treasure, respecting the locked diary, listening to the shell, cradling the broken doll. She shuffled through the photographs, recognizing Mary as a child astride a spotted pony; as a girl posed with her mother in a circle of flowers; as a debutante, escorted by her father, his tuxedo a dark contrast to her shimmering gown. There was a photograph of Mary and another girl, arm in arm on a path beneath trees. There they were again at the shore, their tangled legs dissolved in the surf. And again, hand in hand on a porch swing, feet lifted, heads tossed back with laughter.

This must have been the friend Mary mentioned. Her particular friend. The girl was pretty enough, though not nearly as lovely as Mary. Rachel held the photograph closer. Whereas the camera brought out the shape of Mary's features, the other girl seemed indistinct, her jawline and hairline and nose blurring together. But her eyes, they were what kept her from being plain. Expressive and wide, the eyes were always fixed on Mary's face. The way she looked at Mary was something Rachel recognized. It was the way Naomi had looked at her, that last night at the Home.

Rachel rarely allowed herself to think of that night, the way Naomi had touched her, how they had kissed. Remembering made her heart twitchy, her stomach queasy with guilt. To distract herself, Rachel replaced the photographs in the drawer, took out the bundle of letters, untied the ribbon.

They were all written to Mary, the varying addresses charting her movements: at home from boarding school for holidays, care of the White Star Line during a trip abroad, and finally to the sanitarium in the Catskills. The return addresses changed, too, but the name was always the same. Sheila Wharton. There were none of Mary's letters to Sheila—the letters Sheila's mother found and burned before forbidding her to see Mary again.

Rachel shivered. She pulled the eiderdown quilt from the bed and wrapped it around her naked body. Kneeling in front of the gaping trunk, she drew a letter from its envelope. Mary had said Sheila's mother thought their friendship was *unnatural*. It was the same word the monitor had used to warn her about Naomi, but Rachel couldn't quite believe that Mary and her friend had done the things she and Naomi had done. If they had, Rachel was sure they would never have written about it. She didn't even know what words they might have used.

Rachel unfolded the first letter. The paper smelled like flowers. She glanced over the page of perfect script, searching for a phrase a mother might object to. *When I lick my lips, I can still taste you.* The words swam before Rachel's eyes. She had to blink, hard, to bring the swooping lines back into focus. She pinned the paper to the floor and began again from the beginning.

It was midnight before Rachel carefully folded away all the letters, tied them back up, shut them in the drawer. She closed the trunk and did the clasps then shoved it into a corner of the room, scratching the floor. Crawling into bed, she switched off the light. Sheila had written to Mary about love and kisses, about the kinds of things Rachel and Naomi had done and more, things Rachel had never even thought of. These thoughts now monopolized her mind's eye, like a movie projected on the inside of her eyelids.

Of the hundreds of girls at the Home, some of them had friendships so passionate they might have been unnatural, but Naomi was the only one Rachel had known. Now she knew for sure of another girl—no, two girls—who were the same way. But for Mary and Sheila, it was more than kissing in secret. They had plans to travel to Europe together: to sketch in Venice, hike the Alps, visit Paris, explore London. Sheila mentioned other girls in her letters, too, though Rachel suspected some of them were characters in stories and not real girls she knew. But still. There was a new sort of life revealed in those letters, a life Rachel had never known enough to imagine, a life where two best friends could have, between them, all that mattered in the world.

Rachel allowed herself now to remember how strange it was, that night with Naomi, that it hadn't felt strange at all. Naomi's hands and mouth on her skin had seemed the most natural thing in the world. Beyond the confines of a narrow orphanage bed, what kind of life might she and Naomi have dreamed of? Not Europe, of course, but being together, sharing an apartment, going to movies. The picture of Mary and Sheila at the ocean reminded Rachel of the day Naomi took her to Coney Island. That must have been the day they found the seashell; Rachel imagined Sheila presenting it to Mary, Mary promising to keep it always. But what had Rachel done to Naomi? Stolen the tuition money her uncle and aunt had given her and run away in the middle of the night. It was unforgivable.

Naomi must hate her. Sam had abandoned her. And now Mary was dead. Under her quilt, the enormity of her losses swooped down on Rachel like crows to carrion.

Rachel was loath to get out of bed the next morning. Mrs. Abrams brought her a cup of tea and some toast, telling her that

Dr. Abrams would let the head nurse know she wasn't feeling well. "It's hit you hard, Mary's death, hasn't it? Dr. Abrams tries not to get attached, but I see it affects him, too, the loss of a patient. Would you like me to help you sort through her things?"

Rachel panicked at the idea of Mrs. Abrams seeing Mary's letters, imagined her recoiling in disgust. "No, thank you, Mrs. Abrams. I already looked through the trunk. It's just her clothes, nothing else. I'll get ready for work."

"All right, dear. You'll come down when you're ready." She gave Rachel a kiss on the forehead, which left her wondering if Mrs. Abrams would have treated her so kindly if she had known the truth—that Rachel was a thief and a liar; that she, too, was unnatural.

When Rachel finally rose to get dressed, she stared at herself in the mirror, remembering the names she had been called at the Home: Martian, lizard, boiled egg. Only Naomi had ever thought her pretty. *So smooth and beautiful.* Rachel understood, for the first time, what Naomi must have felt for her. It wasn't paid protection. It was more than friendship. It could have been love, if Rachel hadn't ruined everything.

She should have sent Naomi fifty dollars as soon as she'd earned enough to make up the difference, returned the money with a letter in which she explained how sorry she was. Instead she'd squandered it all on the wig. Rachel realized now that every hurt she visited on Amelia only rebounded, worse, on herself. What tragedy would she bring down on her own head once she started wearing Amelia's hair? But if she stopped making payments now, she'd lose everything she'd invested. Rachel had banked on being beautiful once she had the wig, but wondered what good that would do her now. So what if the interns around Mrs. Abrams's table began to notice her, started conversing with her about the topics she was memorizing from her *Essentials of Medicine*. What if one of them did propose, like Dr. Cohen had done to Althea? Althea and her mother would never understand why Rachel would decline to become a doctor's wife, to keep his house, have his children.

That night after work, Rachel ignored the trunk, tried not to think about Naomi or Sheila's letters to Mary, but she found it hard to concentrate on her reading. *In cross-section, the tubercular lung, because of its combination of white, gray, and green colors, resembles some beautiful glass marbles.* She considered, again, the interns. Mary had said all men were animals, but Rachel knew that wasn't true. It was because Mary never had a brother, Rachel decided. Sam had let her down, yes, but between them was a connection that could never be broken. And Vic had always been good to her. She thought of Sunday afternoons in the Reception House, his asking her to dance, how he'd kissed her cheek that last day they spoke. Rachel thought, too, of the admiration and affection Dr. Abrams showed his wife, the respect with which he treated all the nurses. But even if one of the interns had been as protective as Sam, as gentle as Vic, as appreciative as Dr. Abrams, she knew there would always be a lonely place inside her that could only be reached by a girl like Mary or Sheila. A girl like Naomi.

How it must have hurt Naomi, after what they had shared that night, to think Rachel had only been in her room to steal from her. Rachel feared Naomi would think she'd used her affection as a distraction, knowing Naomi could never complain without implicating herself. It was partly true, Rachel had to admit, but not really, not deep down. When she finally switched off the light, Rachel's imagination overlaid the images evoked by Sheila's letters on her memories of Naomi. Her hands explored her own body as she pictured the things she and Naomi could have done. Could still do, one day, if Naomi ever forgave her. If Rachel ever went home.

The next morning Rachel decided it was cowardly to hole up in Colorado, allowing the Abramses to shower her with unwarranted kindness, leaving Naomi to think the worst. As she dressed for work, Rachel promised herself that after the wig was finished, she would go back to New York, find work in one of the city's charity hospitals. She optimistically calculated how far her meager earnings might be stretched, how soon she'd be able to repay her friend. As for the trip, she'd heard the railroads were coupling the old immigrant cars onto the back of the Limiteds, offering plain seats on hard benches for Depression prices. After her last payment to Mrs. Hong, she'd have to work another couple of months before she could afford even the cheapest fare—or hadn't Mrs. Abrams said Althea and the children would be coming in the summer? Perhaps she could travel east with them. If she accompanied them to Chicago, Dr. Cohen might even buy her a ticket on to New York.

DAYS AND WEEKS rolled by as Rachel pushed beds in and out of the sun, changed bedpans, served meals, wiped blood and spit from chins. In April, Rachel was surprised at the seder dinner to realize she was the youngest at the table. Self-consciously reading the questions in front of the Abramses and the interns, she couldn't help but compare this sincere and somewhat tedious occasion to the hectic Passovers at the Home, the ritual meal rushed to keep pace with the ringing of the bells.

As spring turned the corner toward summer, the Hospital for Consumptive Hebrews became ever more crowded. Back east, impoverished immigrants, facing hard times, were working or worrying themselves sick. Covering their coughs and brightening their cheeks with pinches, tubercular patients spent their last coins on a ticket for the city they hoped would cure them.

Althea, insulated from the rabble in her Pullman compartment, arrived with the children in time for Independence Day, again without her au pair. Rachel gathered, from tearful conversations accidentally overhead, that Dr. Cohen had kept the au pair home last year for reasons other than illness, that Althea had recently found out, that the au pair had been dismissed, and Althea had gone home to her mother. Though sorry for Althea's distress, Rachel welcomed the distraction of a house full of children. At dinner, the table was too crowded now for interns; after the dishes were cleared, the family spent evenings doing puzzles and listening to the radio. On her days off, Rachel filled the hours she once spent with Mary taking Henry and Simon and little Mae, who was running now with headlong confidence, to Sloan's Lake. Between the busy hospital and the hectic house on Colfax, long summer days quickly passed.

In August, Rachel again took her earnings to Hop Alley. Mrs. Hong, measuring progress on the wig to match Rachel's payments, assured her it would be complete on September first, when the contract would be fulfilled. Before leaving the wig shop, Rachel trailed her hand through Amelia's hair. The strands seemed to reach for her fingers. Though she knew now she should have repaid Naomi instead of investing in the wig, she couldn't help but be entranced by its beauty, excited by the prospect of becoming beautiful herself. Naomi might think she was pretty the way she was, but Rachel knew the rest of the world didn't see her that way. She told herself Naomi wouldn't begrudge her this slice of stolen beauty.

Mrs. Hong watched from the fire escape as Rachel walked away. She wished now she had held out for more money so she could keep the wig on display a few months longer. Her orders had gone up since she had been bringing it as a sample to show customers, one of whom offered her three times what Rachel had managed to pay. But the girl had kept up her end of their agreement, and Mrs. Hong was nothing if not true to her word.

Rachel mentioned her sixteenth birthday to Mrs. Abrams, who insisted on serving a cake with candles, Rachel's first, to the delight of the boys, who helped her blow them out. Over bites of cake and sips of coffee, Rachel was glad to hear plans for the end of summer being discussed. She had worried that Althea would never forgive Dr. Cohen, ruining her idea of traveling with them. But the previous week Althea had received a contrite letter from her husband, followed yesterday by an apologetic telegram, and finally, that morning, by a pleading long-distance telephone call. Dr. Abrams, deeply betrayed by the infidelity of his former intern, offered again for Althea to move back home with the children. But Mrs. Abrams, despite her commitment to rights for women, knew what was best for her daughter. Althea needed to be someone's wife, needed to have a man's arm to hold on to. If she waited much longer, Dr. Cohen's contrition might turn to resentment.

"You should go home, dear," Jenny Abrams told her daughter, "but if you want my advice, you and David will go away together, just the two of you, for a while. He needs to remember why he married you, and you need to remind him you're more than the mother of his children."

"But you are our mother!" Simon protested.

"Who'll take care of us?" Henry asked.

Althea met her mother's gaze. The trouble had all started with the au pair. Rachel looked up from her cake to find their eyes on her.

"I'd love to help with the children," she said, eliciting cheers from Simon and Mae; even Henry smiled. "What I mean is, I'd be glad to help when you travel to Chicago, Mrs. Cohen." She tried to explain that she would be going on to New York, but Mrs. Abrams interrupted.

"Why, that's perfect! Then Rachel can stay with the children while you and David take a nice trip." Rachel swallowed awkwardly and had a coughing fit that kept her from objecting while Simon babbled about all the things he would show her in Chicago.

"Why not just make Rachel our new au pair?" Henry asked.

"What a clever boy you are, Henry," Althea said, turning to Rachel. "Dr. Cohen would pay you twice what you're earning at the Consumptive Hebrews. You won't get a better offer than that."

"I'm afraid I couldn't work for you in Chicago." Rachel knew how selfish and ungrateful she would sound for refusing, and on what grounds? Althea would never believe she preferred emptying bedpans in a charity hospital to being an au pair to a successful Hyde Park physician's family. Rachel couldn't very well say she was eager to return to the girl she hoped would love her. She reached for the excuse she'd used with Mrs. Hong. "I've decided to go back to New York to finish nursing school. I'm sorry to tell you like this, Dr. Abrams, but I'll be leaving the hospital."

"That's a fine plan, Rachel, I'm glad to hear it," Dr. Abrams said, then caught his wife's glare from across the table. "My daughter would be lucky to have you as au pair to her children, but you've become a skilled nurse's aide, and I applaud you for wanting to complete your education."

Mrs. Abrams was clearly disappointed. "You could take night classes in Chicago, couldn't you?"

"The girl is from New York, Jenny," Dr. Abrams said. "Don't pressure her if she wants to go home."

"But you will travel with us in the Pullman?" Althea asked.

"Yes, of course, though I was hoping—"

"That's settled, at least. We'll leave on the thirtieth. Henry's starting his new school this year, and he needs to be home before Labor Day."

As much as Rachel liked the idea of going back to New York, she needed to earn back Naomi's money before she could think of paying tuition for nursing school. After the table was cleared, Rachel peeked into Dr. Abrams's study. "May I have a word with you?"

"Come in, Rachel. Have a seat." She sank into the leather arm-chair across from his. "What is it?"

"I was wondering, is nursing school very expensive?"

"It depends. Have you decided where you'll apply? I'd suggest Mount Sinai Hospital School of Nursing. My recommendation would be influential there—I've trained a number of their interns over the years—and they have housing for the nursing students."

"Do you think if I worked, like I do now, that I could pay the tuition?"

"There are some jobs at the hospital for students, but you'll be too busy studying to work many hours."

"In that case, I'll need to get a job for a couple of years before I can afford nursing school. Maybe you could give me a reference for that?"

"I'm confused. If you need to work, then why not work for Althea? Are you afraid you haven't saved up enough?"

"I haven't saved anything, Dr. Abrams. As it is, I won't even have train fare from Chicago to New York."

He frowned. "I don't understand, Rachel. I know you haven't been frivolous with your money. You've hardly spent a cent that I can see. I assumed you were saving it all. Where has it gone?"

Rachel hesitated, but there was no getting around the truth. "I'm putting it all toward a wig. I bargained hard with Mrs. Hong— she's the wigmaker—for a good deal but it's still terribly expensive because it's custom. I give Mrs. Hong practically all of my pay every month, and I still have one more payment left."

Dr. Abrams looked incredulous. "You've spent all of your money on a wig?"

Rachel hated for him to think she was a vain and foolish girl. She wondered if he couldn't fathom what it meant to her because he'd never really seen her without her head covered. At first she'd assumed he was disinterested, but she had come to believe he was too polite to ask about her baldness. She reached up and took off the cloche hat. He tried to hide it, but Rachel saw him recoil.

"Now do you see why I need it, Dr. Abrams?"

"I'm sorry, Rachel, I assumed you were accustomed to it, but you're a young woman, of course you want to look normal." He gestured for her to put the hat back on. "Do you mind telling me how long you've had your condition?"

"My condition?"

"The alopecia. When did it start?"

"I've always been this way. It's from the X-rays treatments I had at the Infant Home."

"The Infant Home? Why were you in a Home?"

Rachel had forgotten, for a moment, the lie she was living with the Abramses. As she realized what she'd just revealed, dread clenched her stomach and a flush rose up her neck that engulfed her face. Her brain was too slow to invent another story. Accepting the inevitable, she confessed that she'd been an orphan long before she showed up on their doorstep. Hanging her head, she braced herself for Dr. Abrams's anger.

"Tell me, your story about this uncle of yours wanting to marry you, was that the truth?"

In this, at least, Rachel was guileless. "Yes, it really was. He owns a store, in Leadville, Rabinowitz Dry Goods. When I first got there, I thought he was my father who ran away when my mother died. After my brother left, he said I could only stay with him if we were engaged."

Dr. Abrams nodded. "I'm glad you were finally honest with me, Rachel. The nurse I spoke with when I checked your reference explained about you and your brother running away from the Orphaned Hebrews Home. She was very glad to know you were safe. Mrs. Abrams and I have been hoping you'd come to trust us enough to tell us the truth."

Rachel had no idea how to respond. She resisted the urge to

throw her arms around his neck. All she could say, tears on her face, was, "Thank you, Dr. Abrams."

"As for the rest of it, let me think things over for a while. We'll talk again in a few days."

Disoriented, Rachel retreated to the Ivy Room. He hadn't accused her, hadn't yelled, hadn't slapped. Rachel thought of Superintendent Grossman, his face red and sweating as he raised his hand against Sam. She thought of her father, that knife in his hand as he grappled with her mother. She thought of her uncle, the tip of his tongue pushed between her lips. Rachel could only imagine the way Dr. Abrams was treating her was what other people meant when they used words like *father* and *family*.

DR. ABRAMS WAS in his office at the Hospital for Consumptive Hebrews, a stethoscope casually slung around his neck, peering through his wire-rimmed glasses. He was reading again about Dr. Solomon's tonsil experiment. He had asked one of his interns, the day after his talk with Rachel, to go to the university library to see if there was anything about the Hebrew Infant Home and X-rays, and here was the distressing article on his desk. To use healthy children in such a dangerous experiment struck him as a violation of trust. He understood now, as Rachel didn't, how unnecessary the excessive radiation exposure was that had caused her alopecia. He'd thought her profligate to pour all of her earnings into an expensive custom-made wig, but now he felt a debt was owed to her. Without her knowledge or consent she'd given so much already, and for what? It was a grandiose notion to propose that tonsillectomies might be replaced by X-rays. When Dr. Abrams refused to treat his tubercular patients with chest X-rays, there were some who'd thought him backward, but he'd been proven right—where they had been used, X-rays had only further weakened the lungs. Dr. Abrams understood that medical advances required experimentation, but to recklessly use such young children galled him. The intern said this was Dr. Solomon's only published article; Dr. Abrams could only hope this M. Solomon, whoever he was, no longer worked with children.

When, a few days later, he called Rachel into his study, he decided to keep his knowledge to himself. It would only wound the girl more, he thought, if she knew how needlessly she'd been disfigured. Let her continue to believe her baldness was the unfortunate consequence of some life-saving treatment, while he took it on himself to make it up to her, as far as he was able. Telephone calls had been placed, letters written on her behalf, money withdrawn from his own account. Dr. Abrams had only to present the fait accompli.

Rachel began to say, once more, how sorry she was for having lied to him and Mrs. Abrams. He stopped her, placing his hand on her knee, the touch brief and comforting. "Don't apologize, Rachel. I believe in judging people by their actions more than their words. You have proven yourself to be helpful and hardworking. The nurses at the hospital all speak well of you, you've been of great assistance to Jenny, and my grandchildren adore you. So, you want to return to New York and go to nursing school, correct?"

Once again, Rachel had boxed herself into a corner by not telling the truth. She'd realized he was right—if her goal was to earn back Naomi's money, working for Althea for a year would be the best choice. It made sense to earn the tuition money that way, too, though her urge to return to New York was as insistent as a ringing bell. She intended to tell Dr. Abrams that she'd decided on Chicago, knowing it would please him, but he interrupted her.

"Did you know the Hospital for Consumptive Hebrews funds a nursing scholarship at Mount Sinai? The condition is that, after completing the course, the recipient will work here, but you've already done that, haven't you? So, I put you up for the scholarship, and I'm pleased to tell you I was notified this morning that you have been selected. The scholarship will cover your tuition and housing, with a small stipend for books and expenses. When you arrive, the dean will test you to see how much you've learned on your own and place you in the appropriate classes. I wouldn't be surprised if you finished in a year. You'd be welcome to return, but as I said, that won't be a condition."

Rachel couldn't quite believe what he was saying. "But why?"

"Why what, Rachel?"

"Why are you and Mrs. Abrams so good to me? What did I do to deserve it?"

He looked amused. "If good only came to those who deserved it, the world would be a bleak place. In your case, though, our kindness has been amply rewarded, and at such little effort on our part. It's our pleasure to know you'll be a productive citizen, caring for others, able to take care of yourself. You know the Hebrew phrase *tikkun olam*?" Rachel shook her head. "I'm sure it's the principle behind the orphanage that cared for you. It's the belief behind the Hospital for Consumptive Hebrews as well. It means it is everyone's responsibility to help someone else, for the good of us all. You've made it easy for us to live up to that belief, Rachel."

Rachel expressed every iteration of gratitude she could think of until Dr. Abrams made her stop. They spoke a few minutes longer about nursing school and the courses she would be taking. Rachel finally got up to say good night, thinking Dr. Abrams must have other things to do. As she was leaving his study, she turned in the doorway. "I'm sorry, but I was wondering about my last pay. Since Mrs. Cohen plans to travel on the thirtieth, would it be possible, do you know, for me to collect my wages before then?"

"Of course, Rachel, just let the accounting office know the twenty-ninth will be your last day."

"Would you mind very much if my last day was the twenty-eighth?"

Dr. Abrams waved her off. "Just tell the accounting office. Oh, and I'll make sure Dr. Cohen pays your train fare on to New York."

Rachel left his study and went up to the Ivy Room, her mind jumping with plans. She'd make her final payment to Mrs. Hong the day after collecting her last pay, then depart for Chicago with Mrs. Cohen and the children. She'd arrive in New York practically penniless, but it would just be one night before school started—maybe she could spend it on a bench in the lobby of Penn Station. Tuition and housing with a stipend—she could hardly believe it. It was even better than if Nurse Dreyer had gone in front of the Scholarship Committee. She was grateful, truly, though more con-founded than ever about how she could earn back Naomi's money. Rachel wondered how long it would be, if she was very frugal with her stipend, before she could afford Naomi's forgiveness.

August galloped to a close, spurred on by Althea's preparations for departure. Before she knew it, Rachel was being handed her pay for the month. The next day, their last in Denver, she exasper-ated Althea, who already took Rachel's time with the children for granted, when she told the family she could not help with their packing. "I have something I need to do before we leave," she said, excitement and anticipation showing in her face. After Rachel rushed out of the house, Mrs. Abrams said to her daughter, "If I didn't know better, I'd think she was running off to say good-bye to some young man."

When Rachel arrived in Hop Alley earlier than expected, Mrs. Hong held back her frustration. She had been planning to show the wig that evening to a new client, a final opportunity to use the remarkable hair as an advertisement of her skill. Still, she didn't begrudge the girl the successful fulfillment of their contract. Mrs. Hong called in the calligrapher as a witness and made a show of setting fire to the scroll with their signatures on it, the three of them crowded on the fire escape, the burning paper fluttering down to the narrow lane of bricks.

To mark the occasion, Rachel had worn one of Mary's prettiest summer dresses, linen that felt cool against the backs of her thighs. Mrs. Hong sat Rachel in front of a mirror and snugged the wig over her scalp. It framed her pale face, bringing out touches of pink in her cheeks and gold flecks in her dark eyes. Amelia's hair seemed glad to have been liberated from the arrogant girl's head and delivered to this more appreciative recipient.

"Miss Rachel is so beautiful," Jade whispered. Sparrow clapped her hands.

"One more thing," Mrs. Hong said, lifting Rachel's chin. She sketched in eyebrows with an auburn wax pencil. "There."

Rachel turned back to her reflection. For the first time in her life, she saw beauty. Mrs. Hong's hand rested on her shoulder. Rachel turned and dropped a kiss on the fingers. In return, she felt a secret squeeze, then Mrs. Hong stepped back.

"Why aren't you girls working?" she snapped. Sparrow and Jade jumped.

"Wait." Rachel stopped them. "For you," she said, placing in each little hand, fingertips already calloused, a shimmering length of satin ribbon. The girls closed their fists over the simple treasures, then glanced at Mrs. Hong.

"Fine, fine, just get back to work," she said. The girls skittered away, the bamboo rustling from their passing.

"I'll wear it home." Rachel stood. As Mrs. Hong placed the form into a cylindrical box and topped it with a round lid, she instructed Rachel to always put the wig away properly, to brush and care for it. Lifting the box's braided handles, Rachel said good-bye and clattered down the fire escape. The cloche hat lay forgotten on the worktable.

Mrs. Abrams and Althea were amazed to see Rachel come up the walk wearing the wig. Without admitting she'd cut the hair herself, she finally explained how she'd spent so many of her days off, as well as all her earnings. Little Mae tried to touch it, but for once Althea stepped in and pulled back her daughter's sticky hand.

"You look like a real lady," Simon said, though Rachel couldn't tell if this was a compliment or a complaint.

"You look lovely, dear," Mrs. Abrams said. "But then, you always did."

That night in the Ivy Room, Rachel placed the wig on its form inside the box and draped Mary's dress over the trunk to keep it from wrinkling. Various labels glued to the trunk's lid made it seem as if Rachel had taken a steamship across the Atlantic and trains around Europe. At least she could add her own tag from

Denver to New York. It was a long time before she slept. Her head bare on the pillow, she felt her scalp wanting the wig.

In the morning, Rachel hovered as Henry helped Dr. Abrams muscle the steamer trunk downstairs. She was unreasonably nervous of it falling open, the drawers tipping forward, certain letters spilling out. But the straps and catches held, and the trunk was sent off to the station with the rest of Althea's luggage. Rachel left her old cardboard suitcase under the bed and emerged from the Ivy Room carrying the hatbox instead. From head to toe, not a stitch or a strand was original to her.

"You are your own person now, Rachel," Mrs. Abrams reminded her as she left the house on Colfax, her strong arms pulling Rachel close for an embrace. Rachel thought she understood what that meant and nodded. Dr. Abrams saw the family off at the station. Simon had outgrown the little boy who just last year had put his hand in Rachel's. He walked ahead while little Mae hung from her arm and Althea struggled with her wriggling little boy, a baby no longer.

At Chicago's Union Station, Dr. Cohen approached his wife and children, hat in one hand and flowers in the other. Althea tried to hold herself stiff, but the way she sank into his arms showed how much she needed him to love her. As promised, Dr. Cohen presented Rachel with a train ticket. Simon warned her about traveling alone. "Don't trust anyone, Rachel, especially men with black masks."

"You've been listening to too much radio, Simon." Knowing he wanted a kiss but considered himself too old for one, Rachel extended her hand. They parted friends with a vigorous shake and promises to keep up their correspondence.

On the train to New York, Rachel practiced being her new

self. For the first time, people saw her without guessing at the smooth nothingness hidden under her wig. She noticed people's eyes finding her face and hair, saw their faces soften, their mouths lift into smiles. She smiled back, pleased to be perceived as pretty. A strange excitement sparked in her, keeping her from sleep. Though she had a year of school and then who knows how many months of work to get through before she might be able to repay Naomi, she felt with each passing mile that she was getting closer to where she belonged.

Chapter Twenty

"TIME TO WAKE UP, DR. SOLOMON."

In the harsh illumination of the overhead light, Mildred Solomon's withered skin looked gray. She blinked and twisted, pain pricking at her bones. On the nightstand, I placed the syringe for her midnight dose beside the full vial. She was a doctor—seeing the amount of morphine I'd collected, she'd understand its lethal potential. That's what I wanted to see—the look Sam had seen in that Nazi's eyes: fear, recognition, surrender. I remembered how Dr. Solomon used to bend over my crib, the way she'd look down at me as she plotted her experiments. How I'd gaze up at her, hungry for attention, pleased and proud she'd chosen me. I placed my hand on my breast, recalling Dr. Feldman's yellowed fingers, knowing it was Mildred Solomon who had reached across time to plant this cancer in me. She'd set the clock on my whole life, ticking down the years, months, minutes. How many did I have left? Too few, because of her. She'd robbed me of my portion, decades lopped off that should have been mine. What life she had left could be measured in hours. Small recompense though they were, they belonged to me now. I had only to claim them.

"Water," she croaked, the point of her tongue circling her cracked lips. "I'm thirsty."

I propped her up, held a cup to her mouth, tilted it so she could drink. "Better?"

She shrugged. It was wearing on her, I could see, this uneven cycle of morphine—too much, enough, too little. The pulse in her neck vibrated, her bony chest fluttered. Her eyes lolled around the room, confused, questioning.

"Do you know where you are, Dr. Solomon?"

"Of course I do. I'm not senile. It's that damn doctor, he prescribes too much." She focused on me. "You're Number Eight, aren't you? I remember you. Did you get my pudding?"

"I did. That's over now. Look at me, Dr. Solomon. Do you remember what I showed you?" I lifted her hand to my breast, pressed the fingers against its swell.

"Your tumor, yes. I remember. I'm not senile. You think it's my fault, for those X-rays, but you're wrong. My cancer, that's from the X-rays I gave. Are you sorry for me? No, you're not. You might have gotten cancer anyway. You could be hit by a bus on your way home. Would that be my fault, too?" She shivered, clutched at the blanket. "When I was little, I had chicken pox. The only thing I'd eat was chocolate pudding. My mother made it for me every night, put it in the icebox for my breakfast."

Her eyes drifted, aimless. For a moment, time folded in on itself and she was a girl, small as I had been at the Infant Home, a little girl sick in bed. I imagined myself, for a second, a mother, taking care of my own child. Of its own accord, my hand reached out and stroked her hair. She turned her plaintive gaze on me.

"Can I have my pudding now?"

Just like that, the spell was broken. She was no monster, merely a pathetic, dying woman, shrunk down to the simple desires of a child. I was equally pathetic, also dying, reduced by self-pity to the petulant impulses of a toddler. Smacking down what few days she had remaining would gain me nothing but shame.

A great, gulping sob erupted from my throat. I staggered to the window as every emotion of the last few days converged in sadness. I had never been more lonely than in that moment. If only I could have sent my spirit floating above the stars to Miami, I would have gladly left my body an empty sack on the floor.

Instead I was alone with Mildred Solomon. I felt her eyes on my heaving back. I hadn't wanted her to witness the pain she'd caused me, had wanted only to visit that pain on her. A week ago, I would have argued that the world was divided between those capable of inflicting pain and those whose fate it was to be hurt, that Mildred Solomon and I were on opposite rims of that canyon. I knew now any one of us could cross over. It wasn't innate—only the choices we made determined which side we lived on. From whichever point one started, stepping out on that rickety bridge was a risk, planks threaded together with twine, the sway in the middle fearsome. Exhilarating as it had been to be suspended above that chasm, rules of time and space and right and wrong all falling away, one look down had been enough to sober me. I had scurried back to my starting place, unable to finish the crossing.

As I calmed down, I heard Mildred panting. I looked behind me, saw tears distorting her eyes. For a second, still, I imagined she cried for me, but no. From Dr. Solomon would come no soft words tossed across the room.

"The pain, it's too much. I need the morphine now."

I came away from the window and picked up Mildred Solomon's midnight dose, long past due. I stared at the syringe in my hand. It was the full amount the doctor prescribed—more than enough to push back her pain. More than she wanted. I picked up the glass vial, intending to slightly adjust her dose, forgetting it was full.

It was the first time Dr. Solomon had seen it. Her eyes widened. "Why do you have so much?"

"It's meant for you." My voice was flat. "Every time I held some back—making you talk, making you suffer—I saved the extra, until I had enough."

"Enough for what?"

"Enough to kill you," I whispered. The words sounded like a line delivered by an actress who'd lost her motivation. I doubted she even heard me. Not that I was worried she'd tell anyone. Kept to her prescribed dose, she was unlikely to ever speak coherently again.

I took a breath. I was done meddling. I would follow the doctor's orders. After this injection, I would leave Mildred Solomon to her painless sleep. I'd go sit by the nurses' station until my shift ended, then change out of my uniform and walk out of the Old Hebrews Home. I had no desire to see any further into the future than this.

"How much?" Her voice quivered with excitement.

"What?" I didn't understand her question.

"How much morphine?"

I glanced down, though I already knew the answer. "The vial is for blood draws, it holds two hundred milligrams."

"And there's more in the syringe?"

I showed it to her, liquid up to the line marked fifty. She smiled, her dry lips stretched so wide they cracked.

"What did you say your name was again, Number Eight?"

"Rachel Rabinowitz. You don't think you're going to report me, do you?"

"Report you? No, Rachel, no, I don't want to report you. I want you to give it to me. All of it. I want this to be over. I want it more than anything. Now, while I can still talk to you and tell you what I want. Now, while you can be with me, so I won't be alone."

I frowned, tilting my head. Could I be hearing this right?

"Don't say no, Number Eight. Please. You know I don't have much longer. I want to decide it for myself. That doctor will never let me decide anything. But you, you're a good girl, you'll help me, won't you?" Mildred Solomon's words tumbled over each other. "Please, it's going to happen so soon, you can't imagine the pain."

"Why should I care about your pain? Did you care about mine?" I said the words, but they were just hollow sounds.

"We've been over that. Never mind. Consider it your revenge if it makes you happy. Just please, give it to me, give it all to me now."

"Not for revenge, no. I won't do that. I wanted to, do you know that? I could have. But I didn't."

Frustrated tears wet her cheeks. "Then do it to prove you're a better person than I am. So what if I met Marie Curie, if she shook my hand? I was wrong, is that what you want to hear? I'm sorry. There, I said it. I'll say anything you want me to, Number Eight, but please, just do this for me." Her words were coming too fast for me to process their shifting meaning. "If you won't, then let me. I'll do it to myself."

Dr. Solomon grabbed at the vial and the syringe. My hands went slack. I didn't even have to be involved. I could let it happen without being responsible. But she was fumbling with the syringe, her hands too shaky to maneuver the needle. Even if she managed to draw up more morphine, she wouldn't be able to reach the valve on the IV. I wondered what she would do in her desperation. Plunge the needle through her thin skin? I imagined the puncture deflating her.

I took back the syringe and the vial. She didn't have the strength to resist. Hands empty again, the old woman wept like a baby.

"No one listens to me. No one does what I say."

"Are you certain this is what you want?"

She quieted herself. "Yes, yes it is."

I knew in my bones she was speaking the truth. This was her choice now, not mine. What a mockery was being made of my intentions. Without another word, I pushed the needle through the rubber stopper of the vial, filling the syringe completely, and squeezed the morphine into her IV.

"All of it, Number Eight. All of it."

I refilled the syringe, pushed the plunger. I watched my hands inject the fatal dose as if someone else controlled their actions, then I sat on the edge of the bed. Mildred Solomon grabbed my hand.

"You'll stay with me, won't you?"

"I will."

"Good girl," she said, patting my knuckles. "Good girl." Her words seemed to come from far away.

I observed her breathing become shallow and ragged. Soon the diaphragm would be too numb to pull in breath, the heart too starved for oxygen to keep up its rhythm. The end would be quiet. I didn't have to stay to know what would happen.

But I did stay. Until the carotid artery stopped pulsing. Until the face became slack, eyes sinking into the skull. Until dawn lifted the darkness.

Only then did I leave Mildred Solomon's body, closing the door behind me. I told Lucia that the patient had gotten her medication and was resting quietly. As I heard myself say the words, I was surprised at how true they sounded. I marked the chart and put the syringes in the autoclave. Later, when I went into the nurses' lounge to change, I placed the empty vial, wrapped in my handkerchief, on the floor. Like the groom at a wedding, with a stomp of my foot I shattered the glass.

THE BRIGHT MORNING outside the Old Hebrews Home blinded me. I waited on the building's steps for the sunspots to fade from my vision. Walking to the subway, my legs felt liquid. I thought I would look different to the people I passed, branded by what I'd done. But no one fixed me with an accusing stare. The streets carried the same traffic, the sidewalks the same pedestrians as they had yesterday and would tomorrow. I looked around at the crowd waiting on the platform, wondering if anyone else among us had taken a life. Apparently, it didn't show.

Underground I didn't have long to wait for a train. I tried resting my eyes as it rocked along, but I was afraid of giving in too soon to sleep. At the Times Square transfer, I was glad to be distracted by a family that sat across from me. The husband was struggling with a clumsy assortment of wicker baskets and beach bags. The mother's straw hat was knocked off by the squirming toddler she lifted onto her lap. The hat rolled toward me as the train lurched forward. I picked it up and handed it to the son, a little boy with a ball cap on. It looked like his mother had stitched the Yankees insignia on it for him.

"What do you say to the nice lady?" his father said.

"Thank you, ma'am," the boy said in a pretty voice. Tufts of kinky hair escaped the confines of his cap. He seemed to be four or five years old. The same age I was at the Infant Home. The same age my nephew was by now.

"You're welcome," I said, resisting the urge to wrap him up in my arms.

They settled in, the family with their baskets and bags packed around their feet, toddler wedged between parents, boy beside them. He twisted to look out the window, even though there was nothing to see but streaking darkness as we moved under the city. His neck was so slender its fragility alarmed me. Below his little legs with their dimpled knees, an untied shoelace dangled. I wanted with all my heart to kneel before him and tie it in a bow.

As the subway rocked along its tracks, I couldn't keep the drowsiness at bay any longer. When the train emerged to cross the river, the brightness forced my eyes closed. I turned my face to catch some breeze from the open window, my head resting against the vibrating glass.

"Lady." I felt a nudge. "Lady, wake up, it's the end of the line."

I pulled my sticky eyelids apart. The boy was tugging at my sleeve.

"Everyone has to get off now, lady."

"All right, thank you, I'm awake." My head was throbbing, my vision blurry. Through the open doors of the train car, I saw his father with the beach bags, his mother holding the toddler's hand. They beckoned to the boy.

"Gotta go now, lady."

"Okay, have fun," I said, because that's why people came out to Coney Island on a summer morning. I stood unsteadily and made my way onto the platform, squinting against the sun. I practically sleepwalked down Mermaid Avenue, bumping into people as I shuffled along, heading away from the boardwalk and the crowded beach. The modern apartment blocks that had replaced the old warehouses and workshops rose up ahead of me, our building among them.

I checked for a letter or postcard, but our box was empty. If it wasn't for her name on the card I might have begun to believe I'd invented her. I'd call, I promised myself, and this time she'd answer. I'd call as soon as I got some rest. I was afraid I would have a breakdown if I heard her voice now in my raw exhaustion.

I pushed the button for the elevator and let my eyes shut for just a moment. Listening for the elevator bell, I heard the lobby door open, footsteps across the terrazzo floor. I looked and saw Molly Lippman carrying a grocery bag. Stepping back, I feigned impatience, readying a comment about deciding to take the stairs. But it was too late to avoid her. The elevator arrived as Molly came up beside me. We entered together. I hoped she'd see how tired I was and not talk to me today.

"Rachel, darling, you look asleep on your feet. Did you do a double shift? The elderly must be so demanding."

I muttered something, watching the elevator light blink past each floor. I willed it to move faster.

"My mother, blessed woman, was so good it was like a sickness, but in her last days, oh, what a handful she was. So, what's new with you?"

The elevator jerked to a stop and the door slid open, but the ordeal wasn't over yet. I mumbled some words about work and the weather as we walked side by side to our adjacent apartment doors. I fished my key out of my pocketbook and held it ready.

"Tell me," she said, putting her hand on my arm, "have you had that dream again? I haven't stopped thinking about it, it was so interesting." Molly set her bag on the floor, making herself comfortable for an extended conversation. I pushed my key into the lock. The notched metal clicked into the tumbler, the sound of my escape.

"I have to run, Molly," I said, turning the handle. "Take care."

"But, Rachel, dear, I meant to tell you who I saw at the grocer's. . . ."

I shut the door, snuffing out my neighbor's words. I was relieved to have escaped Molly but reluctant to face the empty apartment. When I last went through this door, I'd been on my way to see Dr. Feldman and hope was still a straw I could clutch. I could hardly believe it was only yesterday morning. Where did all the hours go? My last birthday and this one would soon match up like the corners of a folded sheet, the months in between ironed away. I wanted them back now, those unnoticed days.

As for the future, I couldn't see any further into it than the couch across the room. In the steps it took me to reach it, I pulled off my dress, stepped out of my sandals, rolled down my stockings. In my slip, I stretched across the upholstery, the nubby fabric rubbing at my skin. It should have been uncomfortable, but somehow it wasn't, like scratching an itch. I watched the sunlight slanting into the room, chopped into slices by the window blinds. In each lit slice, specks and threads swirled.

I closed my eyes, observing the pink latticework inside my lids. I wanted nothing more than the oblivion of sleep. Instead I pictured the woman on Dr. Feldman's wall, her face impassive to the dashed lines that crossed her chest. He'd said I was lucky that my tumor was still operable, but I didn't feel at all grateful. My mind reviewed a lifetime of ways I was unlucky. I might as well have been counting sheep.

I was nearly asleep when the sound of a key in the lock startled me into alertness. It had to be Molly using the extra key we'd once exchanged with her. I cursed myself for never having gotten it back.

Chapter Twenty-one

PENNSYLVANIA STATION WAS A HOTHOUSE, THE SUN BEATing down on the glass ceiling of the train shed. Rachel felt perspiration beading on her scalp and worried for the wig. She left the trunk and her hatbox at the luggage check and walked out to the street unencumbered. There was the thrill of emerging onto Eighth Avenue, the noise and energy of New York made new again by her time out west. Rachel had the day to kill and a night to get through before she could report to nursing school. She'd decided the station was the safest place to spend the night but didn't want to draw attention to herself by settling on a bench too early. With no particular destination in mind, she began walking uptown. In Mary's clothes and Amelia's hair, she sought out her reflection in shop windows, surprised each time that the pretty girl she saw was really her.

The squealing trumpets and rat-a-tat drums of a marching band drew Rachel toward Times Square. Crowds lined the sidewalks, blocking her view. Shouldering through, she saw the Labor Day parade coming down Broadway. Leaning against a light pole, she decided that watching the parade would be a fine way to pass the time. Her stomach protested as a food cart rolled by. She spent the last pennies in her pocket on a pretzel, the hard squares of salt crunching between her teeth, and an Italian ice, the frozen sweetness a relief for her thirst as labor unions and school groups and politicians paraded past.

It was when she saw the color guard carrying a banner ahead of the Orphaned Hebrews Home marching band that Rachel stood up straight and swiveled her head, looking for a place to hide—the impulse of a runaway. Then she relaxed, reminding herself no one from the Home was looking for her anymore. As she watched the marching band approach, nostalgia overwhelmed her. After a year away, the injustices and rigors of the Home were temporarily forgotten as Rachel remembered the familiar companionship of a thousand siblings, the reassuring knowledge that a bell would always ring to tell her what to do. What a comfort it had been—never having to worry where her next meal would come from or where she would sleep that night.

The parade halted for a performance. The Orphaned Hebrews Home band was arrayed in front of her, the leader who'd presided over the Purim Dance stepping in front of the children to lift his baton. The spectators around her cooed at the adorable orphans in their humble outfits and remarked on the precision of their playing. Rachel thought of the long hours of practice in the yard, dust kicked up as they marched across the gravel. They had no choice but to be perfect.

Across the street, standing apart from the crowd, she saw Vic, arms folded across his chest, watching over the band as they played. Of course, Rachel thought, he was a counselor now. It was his job to march alongside and keep an eye on the children, then shepherd them back up Broadway at the conclusion of the parade.

Rachel's eyes darted around, seeking out Naomi. But no. The band was only boys, and the F1 girls were too young for the color guard. Naomi's girls would have watched the parade farther up Broadway and then retreated to the Castle. Relief was quickly followed by yearning as Rachel felt how keen she was to spot her friend.

For the thousandth time, Rachel ran it through in her mind, hoping somehow, this time, she'd figure a faster way to save up enough to repair their friendship. Again, the calculation yielded a span of a year at least, more likely two, before Rachel could accumulate the price of forgiveness. She feared Naomi would have found by then, among the young women at the Teachers College, a new friend, a particular friend, Rachel demoted in Naomi's memory to an adolescent crush that had ended in betrayal.

The Orphaned Hebrews Home band sounded its final flourish. For a moment, the parade was quiet, waiting for the momentum of the marchers ahead to start its movement up again. Rachel noticed a few people taking advantage of the stillness to dart across the street. Impulsively she, too, stepped off the curb and crossed the wide pavement, ducking behind the band director and skirting the color guard's banner. Just as the band stood at attention, ready to resume marching, Rachel came up to Vic. He was the one person in New York who felt like family, and his familiarity suggested to Rachel a possibility. She could explain to him about taking Naomi's money, that it was only to follow Sam, tell him how sorry she was, that she intended to pay it back. She could ask him if Naomi hated her. Maybe he could mediate between them, convince Naomi to accept Rachel's apology. They could be friends again, Rachel working to repay her even as they spent their days together. Rachel knew, now, the kind of friendship they were ca-

pable of. With a thrill of hope, she approached Vic, blocking his
path as he walked the parade route, his blue eyes scanning ahead.

"Excuse me, miss," he said, stepping around her.

"Wait." She grabbed his sleeve, turning him back.

Vic looked directly at Rachel. She remembered their first meeting, how she'd assumed from his friendly smile that he was her
brother, not the scowling boy beside him. So few people in the
world had known her as long as Vic had. His gaze felt like coming
home. She smiled up at him.

"You shouldn't be out in the street, miss." He pulled his arm
away, turned his face downtown, hurried to catch up with the
band. Rachel, shocked, stood apart from the curb until a mounted
policeman clopped up, the horse's tossing head chasing her back
into the crowd.

HE HADN'T RECOGNIZED her. Of course, Rachel told herself. It
was because of the wig and her new clothes. She should have said
something before it was too late. Still, his blank stare had shaken
her, as if she'd become a ghost. Even if he had known her, what
chance was there that Vic could heal the rift between herself and
Naomi? Whether or not she ever paid Naomi back, it was a fantasy
for Rachel to think she could reverse the damage she'd done.

She felt the crowds pressing in on her. Someone bumped her
shoulder, spinning her around. Rachel heard a mumbled apology
but couldn't see clearly enough to distinguish the speaker. The
pressure of people, the heat of the sun, the noise of the parade,
all became too much. Rachel sensed the emptiness of a subway
entrance and descended. Underground, she stood by the turnstile, intending only to regain her composure, when she spotted

a dropped token on the filthy floor. Bending to pick it up, she thought she might as well spend the coming hours moving back and forth under the city. At least there would be the illusion of progress. When a train whooshed up to the platform, she trudged through its open doors without looking to see if it was going uptown or down. Inside the carriage, she was held up through the sway and jerk by the people packed tightly around her. By the time the passengers thinned enough for someone to offer her a seat, she sank into it, the sleepless night from Chicago catching up with her. When the train emerged from underground, sunlight flickered over Rachel's closed eyes. She watched the liquid spots floating across her corneas. If she had any desire left, it was that the train would never stop moving.

"End of the line, miss, all passengers exit at Surf Avenue."

A hand on Rachel's shoulder shook her awake. A uniformed conductor was leaning over her, the brim of his hat casting his face in shadow. She stood and swayed for a moment, catching at a hanging strap. Cautiously, she wobbled onto the platform. As she was herded through the turnstile, she realized her mistake. She should have switched trains at a free transfer station, kept her pointless journey going, stretching the value of her found token across as many empty hours as possible until finally making her way back to Penn Station. Her bleary eyes searched the ground, but there were no more tokens to be found.

Emerging from the station, Rachel had no idea where she was until she saw the distinctive circle of the Wonder Wheel, the undulating tracks of the Cyclone. Coney Island, of all places. She must have slept longer than she realized to have reached the end of the Beach line. A fresh pang of regret stabbed her. The happiness promised in that picture of Mary and Sheila by the sea would never be hers. She seemed destined to remain alone in the world, always an orphan.

A light turned green and she crossed the street, carried by the momentum of the people around her toward the boardwalk. Music spilled from the open doors of ramshackle establishments. Hawkers shouted their wares as parents yelled at their children. The burned-sugar smell of cotton candy mixed with the meaty scent of hot dogs and the vinegar sting of sauerkraut, taunting Rachel's stomach and reminding her of her poverty. She kept her eyes cast down, scanning the wooden planks for the gleam of a dropped coin, but she spotted nothing.

Rachel decided to go down to the beach. There she could shed her shoes, spend a melancholy afternoon staring at the waves or dozing on the sand, sheltered from scrutiny by the holiday crowds. On her way, she passed the carousel. She recognized the carved horses from the workshop of Naomi's Uncle Jacob, the bright painted colors as Estelle's handiwork. Everything she saw seemed designed to prick her with regret, display for her again the happiness she might have had. The operator saw her standing there and opened the gate, his hand held out, but Rachel pulled at her pockets and showed her empty hands, indicating she couldn't afford the ride. She watched his eyes take in her dress, her face, her beautiful hair. With a jerk of his chin, he drew her in. Apparently pretty girls rode for free, an economy of beauty to which Rachel had never been privy. It occurred to her that this was how she'd get back to Penn Station: a pretty girl by the turnstile with a story about dropping her coin purse on the sand would inspire someone to press a token into her hand. Her mood lightened for a moment as Rachel grabbed a pole and was swept up onto the rotating platform. She hoisted herself onto a horse's saddle, lifting and sinking, turning and turning.

Carnival music jingled in her ears. She felt the ocean breeze on her face, the vague taste of salt on her tongue. Each time the horse rose, her head felt lighter. Each time it sank, her stomach compressed. Dizzily, she watched the world around her swing past in a blur. In the blur, a figure stood out. On the next circle of the carousel, she craned her neck, looking. There. Short hair tucked behind ears. A belt cinched around a dress. Rachel sat up, impatient now with the moving platform that pulled her away from what she thought she saw.

As she rounded again, Rachel trained her eyes on the spot, but no one was there. A rush of disappointment constricted her throat. She must have imagined it. But she hadn't. There, walking toward her against the turning of the carousel, a hand settling momentarily on each passing mane, was Naomi, her upturned collar flapping white among the painted horses.

Rachel watched Naomi approach, bracing herself for the anger she was sure would come. But there was Naomi, close enough now to touch, looking puzzled, surprised, happy—anything but angry. Rachel couldn't understand it. Then it occurred to her that Naomi, like Vic, might not recognize her. The thought was terrifying. As ashamed as she was of herself, the notion of Naomi not knowing her was devastating. She tugged the wig off her head, exposing the smooth curve of her skull.

"It's me, it's Rachel."

Naomi placed a hand on Rachel's cheek, her arm moving with the rise and fall of the horse. She smiled. "Of course it's you. It's always been you. Don't you know that?"

Rachel slid from the horse's saddle, swaying as her feet met the moving platform. Naomi threaded a steadying arm around her waist and guided her through the laughing children to one of the carved benches that hugged the inner circle of the carousel. They sat together, the wig spilling its strands across Rachel's lap. Naomi reached for it. Rachel expected Naomi to take the wig of stolen hair and toss it into the carousel's greasy gears. It was as much as she deserved.

"So that's what happened to Amelia's hair." Naomi laughed a little. "You should have heard her screams when she woke up that morning. You hadn't slept in the dorm for so long, no one ever thought it was you. There was always someone jealous of that hair. Monitors gave them all standing lessons for a week, but no one confessed. But you know what? I think Amelia was glad, after all, to be rid of it. She got a short bob, which looked gorgeous of course." Naomi settled the wig back on Rachel's head. "Where'd you get it made into a wig?"

"At Mrs. Hong's House of Hair, in Denver." Rachel wondered how so many months could fit into so few words.

"Colorado? So Vic was right. He figured you'd gone after Sam. Did you find him?"

Rachel nodded. How was Naomi so calm and conversational, after what Rachel had done to her? "He was in Leadville, with our uncle. But nothing was what I thought it would be."

She must not know, Rachel thought. But how could Naomi not know it was Rachel who stole her money? She hadn't known who cut Amelia's hair, and children were always stealing from each other—the disappearance of coins or ribbons or sweets was epidemic at the Home. When Naomi checked her shoe and found the money gone, she must not have suspected Rachel. It was the only explanation. How else could Naomi be sitting beside her, a hand on Rachel's hand, their hips pressed together by the turning of the carousel? All the reasons she thought Naomi was lost to her disappeared. Naomi didn't know the truth. Rachel, relieved, finally smiled.

"So tell me. Was fifty dollars enough to get you all the way to Colorado?"

Rachel's cheeks flushed hot with shame. Naomi did know everything. Now she would turn Rachel away, return her betrayal. Rachel's face went from red to white. She braced herself for the blow.

"You could have told me," Naomi said. "I know you were just protecting me, though, not telling me your whole plan. When they asked if I had given you the money, helped you run away, I never had to lie. I was so broken up at first, they could see I was telling the truth. Then Nurse Dreyer convinced Mr. Grossman to pay me back from your account, and that's when I realized you'd had it worked out all along."

Rachel told herself to nod her head, to smile like she knew what Naomi was talking about, hoping her confusion didn't show. She managed to say, "Was there enough?"

Naomi nodded. "I don't know how much you had from your mother's insurance, but I think there's still some left. The Home gets to keep it, though, Nurse Dreyer told me. Whatever's in a kid's account, if they run off, the Home keeps it. Too bad Sam couldn't have figured a way to get his share of the insurance like you did." Naomi seemed to be expecting a reply. Rachel's brain froze between trying to figure out what just happened and simply being amazed. It was like witnessing a magic trick.

"I didn't tell you because I thought you'd try to talk me out of running away," Rachel said. Would that be enough? She hoped so. If Naomi never knew the truth, they could be friends again. More than friends. They could be the way Mary had been with Sheila. Sentences from their letters scrolled across Rachel's mind. Thinking of them with Naomi beside her made it hard for Rachel to breathe.

"I guess you were right then, because I would've tried talking you out of it. After what we did that night, the last thing in the world I wanted was to let you go. I can't tell you how much I missed you and worried about you. Seems like I thought about you every single day."

"I thought about you, too," Rachel said, reading the hurt in Naomi's eyes.

"Oh well, you're here now, come back to me after all." Naomi put her hands on either side of Rachel's face. "You have come back to me, haven't you?"

It was that easy. All Rachel had to do was let Naomi believe the lie, and it would be true. She didn't care anymore about being unnatural. Now all she wanted was to have a life with Naomi like Mary and Sheila never got to have. She leaned forward and kissed her lips, their faces hidden by the carved sides of the bench.

"I'm here, aren't I?"

Naomi's smile was like the sun breaking through clouds. "Then I'll just have to forgive you."

It was more than a magic trick, Rachel thought. It was a miracle.

"I got another counselor to cover for me today. I'm on my way to my aunt and uncle's. How did you know where to find me?"

What could Rachel say, that it was an accident without intention? "I saw Vic at the parade."

Naomi nodded, as if that explained it. She pulled Rachel to her feet and led her across the platform of the carousel. Standing at the edge, she grabbed Rachel's hand and counted to three. Laughing, they jumped together, holding each other up as the ground stopped spinning.

Chapter Twenty-two

THE DOOR SWUNG OPEN. THERE SHE WAS, STRUGGLING to extract the key, a shopping bag weighing down her arm. I thought I was dreaming. I sat up. She saw me, dropped the bag, kicked the door shut, ran to me.

"Where have you been all night? I was worried sick. I almost called the police."

Her fingers circled my arms. I felt the crescents of her nails bite into my skin. She wasn't a dream—she was real, and she was back.

Something loosed inside me that had been holding tight all day, all night, all week, all summer. I sighed so deeply I got dizzy. I dropped my head against her shoulder. "Are you really home, Naomi?"

"I'm here, aren't I? Where have you been, that's what I want to know." She held me at arm's length, looked me up and down. "You look like you haven't slept in days. And is that Amelia's hair you've got on? When did you start wearing that old wig again?"

I pulled it off and dropped it on the floor. My scalp felt liberated. She bent to pick it up. "Leave it," I said. "I'm done with it now."

"Just let me put it away."

I swatted at her hand. "I said leave it!"

"Rachel, what's the matter with you?"

It wasn't how I'd envisioned welcoming her home. She couldn't tell from the way I was acting, but seeing her put me over the moon. Her skin was dry from the Florida sun, little wrinkles reached out from the corners of her eyes, and her dark hair was streaked with gray, but I could still see in her face the girl she used to be. She was even more beautiful than she was at eighteen, all those years ago. I wanted to tell her all this, but just the thought of it threatened tears.

"Nothing. Everything." I cleared my throat. "When did you get back?"

"Yesterday. Uncle Jacob was feeling so much better, I changed my ticket and came back early."

"Yesterday?" I couldn't believe it. At any time during my long and terrible night, I could have walked away from Mildred Solomon, hailed a taxi, and been in bed beside her. I could hardly wrap my mind around it. "Why didn't you let me know you were coming home, Naomi?" My voice was heavy with regret. "I called and called but no one answered."

"I wanted to surprise you is all. Is that such a crime? Anyway, the last couple of days were pretty hectic. Uncle Jacob's neighbor had us over for a farewell dinner, and he wanted me to go with him to his lawyer's office before I left. Listen to this—he gave us the apartment, Rachel."

She expected excitement, but my mood was too dark. "Gave it to you, you mean."

"Well, technically, sure, he signed it over to me. But isn't that great? It's not just a free sublet anymore. You know he made plenty when he sold his old workshop to the developer, that's why he never charged us for taking over the apartment when he moved down to Miami. I guess being so sick got him thinking, though. He always meant to leave it to me, but he didn't want me to have to pay an inheritance tax, so he decided to give me the apartment now."

"So we don't have to live here, then? We could sell it, move back to the Village?"

She smiled at me, like a teacher whose pupil has finally figured the solution to a problem. "That's what I'm trying to tell you. Now you tell me, where have you been all night? I thought you were working, so I called the Old Hebrews Home, just to ask when you'd be getting off, but the receptionist said you weren't on shift yesterday."

I was trying to understand. "What time was that, when you called?"

"As soon as I got home, around one o'clock. And later, when you still weren't home, I called back to ask for Flo, to see if she knew where you were, but she wasn't scheduled last night."

I tucked a gray-streaked strand behind her ear. "We switched shifts is all. Flo worked yesterday and I worked last night. It was kind of last-minute, I guess the receptionist didn't know."

She rolled her eyes. "How could I not have thought of that? I knew I was being silly, worried you were hurt or something. I thought you must have stayed in Manhattan. I was about to start calling around to our friends to see if they'd heard from you."

"You should have asked the switchboard to put you through to Fifth if you wanted to talk to me. I've told you a hundred times not to worry about Gloria."

"Oh well, you're here now. Let's start over, okay? Rachel, surprise, I'm back!"

I had to laugh. "Oh, Naomi, I'm so happy to see you!" We kissed then, and held each other. I felt myself fit into the contours of her body. The soft pressure where our breasts met reminded me what was in store and I pulled away.

"Something's wrong, isn't it? What's the matter, Rachel?"

Where to start—back at the Infant Home, with everything I now knew had happened to me there? I was too tired to go back to that beginning. I could buy some time, simply say I was upset because a patient died on my shift, but she'd know I wasn't telling the whole truth. I recoiled from confessing what I had done in the night. Rules of right and wrong didn't seem to apply as I helped Mildred Solomon die, but in the light of day, what if mercy sounded like murder?

I drew a breath. I'd start at Dr. Feldman's office. It was only yesterday morning. Mildred Solomon could come into the story later. I needed only to begin with the ache I felt, the lump I found. I parted my lips but couldn't make myself say the word. *Cancer*—it sounded like a curse. The tumor would have to speak for itself, I decided. I pulled the straps of my slip off my shoulders, reached behind my back to unclasp my bra. I pulled her hand close to the diseased breast, preparing myself for her reaction.

Her hand shaped itself to the familiar roundness. "Oh, Rachel, I know, it's been so long." She leaned me back against the couch. Her lips found my temple, my cheek, my chin, then traveled down my neck and shoulder, settling on the lifted nipple with a moan.

I intended to push her away, to tell her no, that wasn't what I meant. But in the moment it took my hands to find her shoulders, the sensation spreading from my nipple had shivered into knees and fingertips, sparked between my legs. A moment ago, I was so exhausted my body seemed made more of water than bone. Now it was reanimated by desire, with an agenda of its own.

I realized how much I wanted this, one last time without her knowing. Giving myself over to my body, I pulled her closer. Her left hand gathered in the small of my back, arching my chest. The right followed the line of my leg until her fingers found their favorite place. I closed my eyes and watched the colored lights swim across my vision.

Her kisses traveled from my knee to my navel and back down again, cheek and teeth nuzzling the curves of my thigh. Then she draped my leg over the back of the couch and dipped her head. Her tongue and fingers explored my inner landscape, navigating its furrows, cresting its ridges, circling its outcroppings. There is a place where the roof of a cave becomes the floor of a sea, yielding yet rough. She found it. I imagined myself a mounted butterfly, wings flapping open and closed, pushing against the pin that fixed me. My ears were filled with the roar of surf. I came in waves that shuddered my muscles.

She pulled herself on top of me, kissed me. I licked her lips, greedy for the ocean taste on her mouth. She rocked against me until she came, her cry muffled in my shoulder. Shifting her weight, she settled her head into the crook of my arm. Our feet twisted together. I felt myself lifted from my body on a rising tide of sleep. As oblivion welcomed me, I wondered if this was what dying would feel like.

I WOKE ALONE in darkness, a sheet tucked around me on the couch. I was amazed at the number of hours I'd slept—she must have tiptoed around the apartment all day. I didn't blame her for finally going to bed. The couch was no place for a good night's sleep, as the ache in my hip and the stiffness in my neck were telling me. Back when I was working shifts, Naomi would arrive home from teaching at exactly four o'clock every day, never sure if I'd be awake and eager to talk or sound asleep from working all night. I taught her to leave me as she found me, to follow her own routine whatever schedule I was on.

I was glad for the time to myself. Wrapped in the sheet, I got to my feet and padded to the bathroom. I paused by her bedroom door to reassure myself she really was there. I discerned her warm shape in the bed, heard the silly sound of her snore. I resisted the urge to curl myself around her like a puppy. Now that my rested mind was alert and calm, I needed to gather my thoughts before we spoke again. I closed the door so my wanderings wouldn't wake her.

I showered in cool water, rinsing off the sweat and worry of the past two days. I avoided touching my breast, didn't lift my arm too high—the gestures that had allowed me to hide the truth from myself for who knows how many months. I was so much happier then, not knowing. But my ignorance hadn't slowed the renegade cells, mindlessly dividing and multiplying whether I was aware of them or not. If Mildred Solomon had stayed downstairs, how long would my ignorance have lasted—until the metastasized cells ulcerated my breast?

I still blamed Mildred Solomon's selfish ambition for my cancer, still cursed the X-rays for causing this tumor, but I had to acknowledge it was her arrival on Fifth that had prodded me to discover what had been done to me. If I hadn't found Dr. Feldman's article, how large would my tumor have grown before I felt it? Past the point of surgery, I had to concede. It made my head ache to balance both thoughts at once: that I had Mildred Solomon to thank for revealing the cancer she herself had given me.

The bathroom mirror reflected my body back to me. I let my hands follow its curves and hollows, cupping and scooping out, the sheen of my smooth skin showing every dimple and imperfection, every swell and touch of pink. I imagined my scars after the surgery, bandoliers of stitches crossing my chest. I'd look like Frankenstein's monster. Then Naomi's voice popped into my head, as if she were standing behind me and speaking over my shoulder, saying no, not a monster—an Amazonian warrior. Ridiculous, yet the idea did make me straighten my spine. Why not let her name it? The reality would be the same either way. My body had already sacrificed so much in the name of science, and for no good reason. This time, there would be a reward for the flesh it gave up to the surgeon's knife: Rachel Rabinowitz, alive awhile longer.

My stomach growled and I had to laugh at my digestion, ignorant of its fate, concerned only with the now. Tying a robe around myself, I went into the kitchen. I put up the percolator and looked to see if Naomi had gotten milk at the grocer's. She had, and more: the open refrigerator revealed a treasure of pastrami and coleslaw; a paper bag on the counter yielded hard rolls seeded with poppy. I ate at the table, my eyes following the swirls in the Formica as I reveled in the taste and texture of food in my mouth.

I took the coffee onto the balcony. The sky was dark enough to show a few stars despite the competing glow of streetlamps. It put me in a philosophical mood, and I gazed for a long time, my mind entertaining half-understood concepts like relativity, distance, and time. That I could see a star meant that its light had journeyed from the far reaches of the universe to land, on this night, at this moment, in my eye. A haphazard coincidence—or had I always been its destination, my upturned face on this Coney Island balcony foretold millennia ago? No, that way of thinking wasn't for me. Like Mr. Mendelsohn, I didn't believe in destiny or fate. Other people found comfort in imagining God pulling the strings on their lives, but it would drive me crazy trying to figure out His inscrutable reasons for everything.

In the coming months, so much would be beyond my power, but there were things I could look forward to. Moving back to the Village for one. There wouldn't be time, before my surgery, for Naomi to sell this place, but she and I could take a day to go apartment hunting around Washington Square, put a deposit down on a place with bright windows and water that wasn't brown. We'd move as soon as I felt up to it. Our old friends would start dropping by again, the two of us free in their presence to be ourselves. We'd go out to our favorite restaurants, the occasional patron off the street clueless as to the true meaning of so many tables occupied by pairs of women. We'd stroll the narrow sidewalks, searching out those couples of men walking slightly too close together, the backs of their hands touching as if by accident. When Naomi's uncle moved to Florida she had convinced me it was a good idea to move out here, and I had to admit the money we'd saved would come in handy now, but she knew what it meant to me—had come to realize what it meant to her, too—to know we weren't alone in the world.

There was something else I'd been putting off for too long. After we moved, once I had my strength back, I would go visit my brother in Israel. I knew Naomi wouldn't like me to be so far away, but she'd have to let me grab my chance to see Sam and Judith and Ayal before it was too late. I wanted to meet this woman who was my sister, to feel the weight of my nephew on my lap. I thought of the wall they had built around their kibbutz, topped with barbed wire and patrolled by soldiers, men and women both. I hoped peace would come soon. I hated to think of Ayal growing up behind walls the way we had. Sam ought to know better than anyone that no child should grow up that way.

I guessed I'd return to work after that, though I knew as soon as the thought crossed my mind that I could never go back to the Old Hebrews Home, not even for one last shift. Not that I feared discovery for what I'd done to Mildred Solomon—knowing their routines and regulations, I was certain I'd never be suspected. I could even imagine facing Gloria and Flo again. After all, wasn't I practiced in telling them falsehoods? No, it was simpler than that. I was done with Homes. Instead I'd look for a position in an office, like Betty had with Dr. Feldman: more paperwork than caretaking, no heavy lifting of patients in and out of bed. I wished I could tell the truth about myself so I wouldn't have to waste my energy on lies, but one false word could ruin me and Naomi both. It was such a little thing to say roommate or friend instead of lover or wife. I'd try not to let it tax me so.

The stars were starting to fade as darkness loosened its grip on the sky. An engine idled in the street below as a stack of morning papers was tossed onto the sidewalk in front of our building. The custodian would come out soon, bring in the stack, cut the twine, walk the halls, drop the news on our doorsteps. I looked out at the emerging shape of the Wonder Wheel and cast my mind into the future. Dr. Feldman said the operation could buy me five years, maybe more. I swore to myself I'd live them well.

I went inside and put up a fresh pot of coffee. It was about time I told Naomi everything, no waiting for morning. I carried two cups into the bedroom, set them on the nightstand, stroked her arm to wake her.

"What time is it?" she mumbled, sitting up.

"It's early. I made coffee."

"I can smell it." She switched on the light and lifted the rim to her lips, blowing at it before sipping. We looked at each other—me clean and smooth, her frowzy from sleep. It still seemed a miracle to have her back again. When our cups were empty, I took a deep breath. There'd be no more avoiding the tears that were in store for us today.

"I have to talk to you about something, Naomi."

My tone must have alerted her. "What is it, is something wrong?"

The word—*cancer*—caught in my throat, that hard C stuck like a swallowed bone. I struggled to push it out, stuttering like Mr. Bogan. I fished around for something to take the place of the word I meant to say, something that would meet the level of concern in her eyes.

"Colorado," I said, avoiding it yet again. "Do you remember back when I ran away from the Home, to Colorado?"

"Sure." She frowned, wondering, no doubt, where this conversation was going.

"There's something I never told you about that." It was so many years ago it couldn't possibly matter anymore, and yet I felt that wave of shame. "When I took your money, I didn't know anything about my account. I had no idea you'd get paid back. The truth is, I stole it. I stole from you."

Naomi considered me for a long moment, as if trying to puzzle out the face in a Picasso portrait. "I never wanted to believe that, but maybe I always knew. I mean, that's what I thought at first, and it made me feel so terrible, like you used me and then tossed me away when you were done with me. It made me feel as bad about myself as I did about you. But when Nurse Dreyer arranged for me to get paid back, it was the only thing that made sense, to think you meant it all along. I mean, it was the only thing that fit with how I felt about you, how I thought you felt about me."

"It did fit, more than what I did. I look back on it now and it's like I was a hypnotized version of myself. I was so desperate to find Sam, to find my family, it blocked out everything else. Even you."

"So when you came back, you must have expected me to be mad at you."

"I didn't think you could ever forgive me. I thought I'd ruined any chance I had to be with you."

"But you came back anyway." She cupped the back of my naked scalp. "That was brave of you."

How much confession did one conversation require? Instead of explaining the haphazard coincidence of how I came to be on the carousel at that moment on that day, I simply nodded.

"I would have forgiven you, you know that, if you had just asked."

"But I never did. I let you believe a lie all these years."

"It's not too late, is it? Ask me now."

"Naomi, I'm so sorry I stole your money. I'm sorry I lied to you. Please forgive me."

She smiled and kissed me. "Done. Now, is there any more coffee? Or was there something else you wanted to talk about?"

I was drawing my breath when I heard a dull thud as the newspaper hit our apartment door. "Just a minute, I want to check something." I ran out for the paper, found the time for sunrise, checked the clock. Less than an hour away. It would be my last reprieve before telling her everything.

I came back into the bedroom and tugged at her arm. "Listen, we'll talk more later, but I want you to get up. I want you to come to the beach with me."

"To the beach? But it's still dark out."

"No, it isn't, it's getting light. I want to see the sunrise. Please?"

"Why don't you just come to bed?" She pulled back the sheets, inviting me in. Any other day I'd have been tempted.

"It'll be my birthday present, this sunrise, okay? It's all I want."

Naomi pouted. "That not fair, you're bribing me."

"I know." I tugged her out of bed, shoved her toward the bathroom. "Just throw something on." I exchanged my robe for shorts and a top, not even bothering with a wig. "We have to hurry."

We could see well enough in the shadowless dawn, the silvery light coming ahead of the sun like a crier. The boardwalk was deserted. Our sandals slapped over the wood planks and down the steps to the beach. Barefoot now, the freshly raked sand sifted through our toes. We sat down near the water, the horizon a distant line. The heat wave had broken and the air off the ocean was fresh. I hadn't thought to grab a sweater.

"Here, share mine," she said. We each thrust an arm through a sleeve, the cotton knit stretched across our two backs.

The planet turned toward the sun as it always does. We lay back on the sand as color claimed the sky: first pink, then lavender, and finally, blue.

Acknowledgments

MY SINCERE THANKS FOR READING AND RESPONDING to drafts of the novel go to Art Berman, Neil Connelly, Catherine Dent, Misun Dokko, Anna Drallios, Margaret Evans, Marie Hathaway, Alex Hovet, Stephanie Jirard, Helen Walker, Karen Walborn, Petra Wirth, and Rita van Alkemade. This story would not have existed without the inspiration of my late grandfather, Victor Berger, who grew up in the Hebrew Orphan Asylum of New York, and his mother, Fannie Berger, who worked there as Reception House counselor. I am also indebted to my grandmother, Florence Berger, keeper of our family's history; to Leona Ferrer, Disclosure Coordinator of the Jewish Child Care Association; to Susan Breen and Paula Munier of the Algonkian Pitch Conference; to Jeff Wood of Whistlestop Bookshop; and to Shippensburg University of Pennsylvania. I am deeply grateful to everyone at William Morrow, especially Tessa Woodward, without whose guidance this novel would not be what it is today.

References

Here are some of the sources—books, museums, archives—that inspired and informed *Orphan #8*.

Abrams, Jeanne E. *Jewish Denver 1859–1940*. Chicago: Arcadia Publishing, 2007.

Beloff, Zoe, Ed. *The Coney Island Amateur Psychoanalytic Society and Its Circle*. New York: Christine Burgin, 2009.

Bernard, Jaqueline. *The Children You Gave Us: A History of 150 Years of Service to Children*. New York: Jewish Child Care Association, 1973.

Blair, Edward. *Leadville: Colorado's Magic City*. Boulder, CO: Fred Pruett Books, 1980.

Bogan, Hyman. *The Luckiest Orphans: A History of the Hebrew Orphan Asylum*. Chicago: University of Illinois Press, 1992.

Caprio, Frank S., M.D. *Female Homosexuality: A Psychodynamic Study of Lesbianism*. New York: Citadel Press, 1954.

Donizetti, Pino. *Shadow and Substance: The Story of Medical Radiography*. New York: Pergamon Press, 1967.

Emerson, Charles Phillips, M.D. *Essentials of Medicine: A Text-book of Medicine for Students Beginning a Medical Course, for Nurses, and for All Others Interested in the Care of the Sick.* Philadelphia: J. B. Lippincott Company, 1925.

Friedman, Reena Sigman. *These Are Our Children: Jewish Orphanages in the United States, 1880–1925.* Hanover: Brandeis University Press, 1994.

"Gilded Lions and Jeweled Horses: The Synagogue to the Carousel." American Folk Art Museum, 45 West Fifty-third Street, New York, NY. February 2, 2008.

Grodin, Michael A., and Leonard H. Glantz. *Children as Research Subjects: Science, Ethics, and the Law.* New York: Oxford University Press, 1994.

Hales, Carol. *Wind Woman.* New York: Woodford Press, 1953.

Hebrew Orphan Asylum Collection, American Jewish Historical Society Archives, Center for Jewish History, 15 West Sixteenth Street, New York, NY.

Hess, Alfred F., M.D. *Scurvy Past and Present.* Philadelphia: J. B. Lippincott, 1920. Available online through *HathiTrust Digital Library.*

Howe, Irving. *World of Our Fathers: The Journey of the East European Jews to America and the Life They Found and Made.* New York: Harcourt Brace Jovanovich, 1976.

Jessiman, Andrew G., M.D., and Francis D. Moore, M.D. *Carcinoma of the Breast: The Study and Treatment of the Patient.* Boston: Little, Brown and Company, 1956.

Jewish Consumptives Relief Society Collection, Beck Archives, University Libraries, University of Denver, Denver, CO.

Lesbian Herstory Archives, 484 Fourteenth Street in Brooklyn, NY.

Lower East Side Tenement Museum, 103 Orchard Street, New York, NY.

Mould, Richard F. *A Century of X-rays and Radioactivity in Medicine: With Emphasis on Photographic Records of the Early Years.* Philadelphia: Institute of Physics Publishing, 1993.

Museum of the City of New York, 1220 Fifth Avenue, New York, NY.

New York Academy of Medicine Library, 1216 Fifth Avenue at 103rd Street, New York, NY.

Nyiszli, Dr. Miklos. *Auschwitz: A Doctor's Eyewitness Account.* 1960. Foreword by Bruno Bettelheim 1960. Trans. Richard Seaver 1993. New York: Arcade Publishing, 2011.

The Unicorn Book of 1954. New York: Unicorn Books, 1955.

Wesley, J. H., M.D. "The X-Ray Treatment of Tonsils and Adenoids." *The Canadian Medical Association Journal* 15.6 (June 1925): 625–627. Available online through *PubMed Central.*

Yezierska, Anzia. *Bread Givers.* 1925. New York: Persea Books, 1999.

About the author

About the book

Insights,
Interviews
& More...

Meet Kim van Alkemade

Margaret Evans

KIM VAN ALKEMADE was born in New York City and spent her childhood in suburban New Jersey. Her late father, an immigrant from the Netherlands, met her mother, a descendant of Eastern European Jewish immigrants, in the Empire State Building. Kim attended college in Wisconsin, earning a doctorate in English from UW-Milwaukee. She is a professor at Shippensburg University and lives in Carlisle, Pennsylvania. Her creative nonfiction essays have been published in literary journals including *Alaska Quarterly Review*, *So To Speak*, and *CutBank*. *Orphan #8* is her first novel. ❧

The True Stories That Inspired *Orphan #8*

Motion to Purchase Wigs Approved

In July 2007, I was doing family research at the Center for Jewish History in New York City, sifting through some materials I'd requested from the American Jewish Historical Society archives. The idea of writing a historical novel was the furthest thing from my mind when I opened Box 54 of the Hebrew Orphan Asylum collection and began leafing through the meeting minutes of the Executive Committee.

The minutes gave intimate glimpses into the day-to-day operations of an orphanage that, in the 1920s, was one of the largest child care institutions in the country, housing over 1,200 children in its massive building on Amsterdam Avenue. On October 9, 1921, the Committee authorized $200 ▶

The Orphaned Hebrews Home was inspired by the real Hebrew Orphan Asylum in Manhattan. Dedicated in 1884, it occupied two city blocks until it was demolished in the 1950s. It is now the site of the Jacob Schiff Playground. Photograph from author's collection.

(over $2,000 in today's dollars) to costume children for the "Pageant on Americanization." The question of band instruments demanded much of the Executive Committee's attention: in October 1922, the decision to change from high- to low-pitched instruments was deferred; in April 1923, $3,500 was approved to equip the band with low-pitched instruments; in January 1926, the theft of the new band instruments was reported to the Board. Syphilis was a concern, too, with the Committee instructing the superintendent in January 1923 to work with the physician regarding syphilitic cases; by October 1926, nineteen cases of syphilis were diagnosed in the orphanage, fourteen of them in girls.

But it was a motion made on May 16, 1920, that caught my eye and became the inspiration for *Orphan #8*. On that day, the Committee approved the purchase of wigs for eight children who

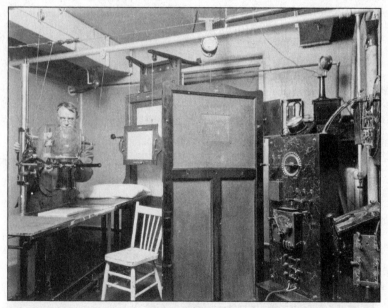

My description of the X-ray room at the Hebrew Infant Home was inspired by this 1919 photograph of the X-ray room at Vancouver General Hospital—where no medical research involving children was conducted. Courtesy of Vancouver Coastal Health.

had developed alopecia as a result of X-ray treatments given to them at the Home for Hebrew Infants by a Dr. Elsie Fox, a graduate of Cornell Medical School. Questions cascaded through my mind. Who was this woman administering X-rays? Why did the orphanage have an X-ray machine, and what were the children being treated for? What might have happened to one of these bald children after she had grown up in the orphanage? How would this have influenced the course of her life?

I remembered then a story my great-grandmother, Fannie Berger, used to tell about her time working as Reception House counselor in the Hebrew Orphan Asylum. She'd been hired by the superintendent in January 1918 when she went to the orphanage to commit her sons to the institution after her husband had absconded. One of Fannie's jobs was to shave the heads of newly admitted children as a precaution against lice. It was a task she disliked, but refused only once. ▶

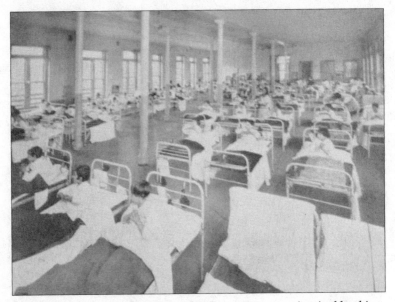

Rachel's dormitory in the Orphaned Hebrews Home was inspired by this photograph of a dormitory in the Hebrew Orphan Asylum. Courtesy of The New York Academy of Medicine Library.

The True Stories That Inspired *Orphan #8* (continued)

We used to drive out to Brooklyn when I was little, my mom and dad and brother and I, to visit my Grandma Fannie. We'd often find her on a bench outside her building, chatting with other old ladies. Up in her tiny apartment we'd perch uncomfortably on the day bed while we visited—I can't imagine, now, a child with the patience for such an afternoon. I remember Fannie telling a story about the time a girl with beautiful hair was committed to the orphanage. It may be my imagination rather than my memory that makes this particular head of hair so remarkably red. Fannie was so taken with this girl's hair that she refused to shave it off, took her request all the way up to the superintendent, who finally gave permission. In my Grandma Fannie's telling, it was a singular moment of bravery, her refusal to shave this one girl's head of hair.

At the Center for Jewish History, reading about the children who had been given X-ray treatments at the Hebrew Infant Asylum, I

The Hebrew Orphan Asylum baseball team, circa 1920. My grandfather, Victor, is seated in front of his brother Seymour, the team's "pillar of strength." Photograph from author's collection.

wondered what if these bald children were in my great-grandmother's care when this other girl came into Reception, the girl with hair so magnificent Fannie would challenge authority to preserve it? I imagined the contrast between these two girls escalating into a rivalry, the hair itself becoming their battleground. That was the moment Rachel and Amelia were created, and with their inception the idea for a novel began to emerge.

Contractor of Waists

There is some mystery to the disappearance of my great-grandfather, Harry Berger, a contractor in the shirtwaist industry who'd been born in Russia in 1884 and arrived in New York in 1890. On the admission form to the orphanage, it is remarked that "Father is tubercular and is at present in Colorado with his brother," which gives the impression that illness and the inability to work were behind Harry's decision to leave his wife and three young sons. But the story I remember hearing is that Harry had gotten a young Italian woman who worked for him pregnant; when her family threatened to kick her out, Harry asked his wife ▶

I imagined Rabinowitz Dry Goods to look much like Isaacs Hardware Store in Leadville, Colorado. Courtesy of the Beck Archives, Special Collections, University Libraries, University of Denver.

if the girl could live with them. Fannie refused, but she hadn't been prepared for Harry to up and leave. Decades later, suffering from dementia, Fannie relived the day he left, pleading from her nursing home bed to the ghost of her husband: "Don't leave, Harry. Think of the boys. Put back the suitcase, we'll get through this."

They didn't get through it. Harry ran off to Leadville, Colorado. Fannie couldn't go home to her parents because she'd defied her father in marrying Harry—unlike Fannie's obedient sister, who'd been married off by their father to a rich uncle. After Harry left, Fannie sold her household effects for a total of $60. She might have turned, in desperation, to prostitution—many abandoned mothers occasionally did—or tried to eke out an existence on charity. Instead, she went to the Hebrew Orphan Asylum, like thousands of parents before her, who, for reasons of death or desertion or illness, were unable to care for their children.

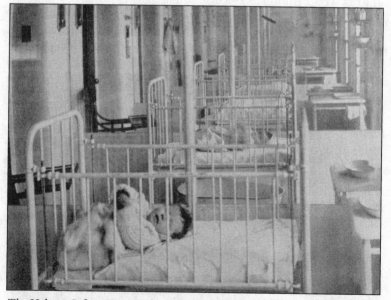

The Hebrew Infant Home, where Dr. Solomon conducted her research, was inspired by the real Hebrew Infant Asylum. This picture shows the glassed-in babies in the isolation ward. Courtesy of The New York Academy of Medicine Library.

Like many inmates of the Hebrew Orphan Asylum, my grandfather Victor and his brothers, Charles and Seymour, were not really orphans, and certainly not up for adoption. What was unusual was that their mother ended up living at the institution to which she had committed them. In 1918, the orphanage was experiencing a serious shortage of help. With so many men in the military, women had greater employment opportunities, making jobs at the orphanage—with its low wages, long hours, and residence requirements—a hard sell. While Fannie always said it was a miracle that the superintendent offered her a position on the very day her sons were admitted to the institution, it's also true that her poverty and desperation to be near her children made her an ideal candidate.

When Fannie started working at the orphanage as a domestic in the Reception House, Charles was only three years old—too young for the Hebrew Orphan Asylum. He was sent to the Hebrew Infant Asylum, where he soon contracted measles. When Fannie went to visit him, she wasn't allowed into the ward and could only stand in the hallway listening to his cries. When Charles recovered, Fannie threatened to quit unless her son was allowed to live with her in the Reception House. After Charles was old enough to join his brothers in the main building, Fannie was promoted to counselor and her duties included helping to process new admissions. Every child committed to the orphanage spent weeks quarantined in Reception. Besides having their heads shaved, they were evaluated by a doctor for physical and mental condition, tested for diphtheria, vaccinated and given an eye test, a dental exam, and surgery to remove their tonsils and adenoids. My great-grandmother Fannie often let the traumatized children cry themselves to sleep at night in her arms.

Ever Efficient Boy of the Home

Even before my discoveries at the Center for Jewish History, I'd wanted to learn all I could about the institution where my grandfather Victor had grown up—an institution so large it was its own census district. I'd read *The Luckiest Orphans*, the most complete history of the Hebrew Orphan Asylum ever written, and was so appreciative of the insight it gave me into my ▶

Fannie and Victor at the Hebrew Orphan Asylum. Photograph from author's collection.

grandfather's childhood that I wrote the author, Hyman Bogan, a letter of thanks. Apparently, he wasn't used to getting fan mail. I was amazed when I answered my phone one evening in 2001 to hear a strange man's voice say, "Is this Kim? You wrote to me about my buh-buh-buh-book." Hy later told me his stutter had begun after being slapped on his first day in the orphanage.

I asked if I might meet him in New York for an interview and he was delighted at the prospect. Together we toured Jacob Schiff Playground, the public park on Amsterdam Avenue where the massive orphanage once stood. Much of my fictional depiction of life in the Orphaned Hebrews Home was inspired by Hy's words and memories. Thanks to him, I was able to imagine Rachel's life in the orphanage, from clubs and dances to loneliness and bullying.

My research suggests that my grandfather Victor flourished at the Hebrew Orphan Asylum. By the time he was a high school senior, he was a salaried captain—a position just below counselor—as well as vice-president of the Boys' Council, a member of the Masquerade Committee, secretary of the Blue Serpent Society, and a member of the varsity basketball team. He was "the hustling young business manager" for *The Rising Bell*, the orphanage's monthly magazine. Upon his graduation from DeWitt Clinton School, Vic was praised for his "stick-to-it-iveness" and "pleasant personality." A "brilliant future in the outside world" was predicted for this "ever-efficient boy of the Home." Though he rarely spoke of his childhood in the orphanage, he did express his gratitude for the institution in which he lived from age 6 to 17.

But I knew there was another side to Victor's childhood memories. In 1987, my dad had gone missing; for two months, we'd had no inkling of his whereabouts. When Victor said, "I want to talk to you about your father," I was expecting the same optimistic platitudes I'd been hearing for weeks: that everything would turn out fine, how brave I was, how strong. I couldn't have been more mistaken. "Your father left you. You just forget about him from now on." I knew Victor's attitude was misplaced—if we were sure of anything, it was that my dad hadn't run away to start a new life somewhere else—but my grandfather had gotten my attention. "My father left us, too, when me and my brothers, your uncles Seymour and Charles, were just little boys." I understood now. Victor was offering me advice, one orphan to another, on how a child gets through life without a father: just forget about him.

"We got a letter from my father once, did you know that?" This was news to me. I'd always assumed my great-grandfather had ▶

The dining room in the Orphaned Hebrews Home, where the Purim Dance was held, was inspired by this photograph of Thanksgiving dinner at the Hebrew Orphan Asylum. Courtesy of The New York Academy of Medicine Library.

11

vanished, whereabouts unknown. Until I started researching my family history, I didn't even know his name. "When your Grandma Fannie worked at the Reception House in the orphanage, we used to visit her on Sundays, me and my brothers. One time, she read us this letter she'd gotten from California, that our father was sick and would we send money for his treatment. She asked us boys what should she do. We told her not to send him a dime. A few months later she got another letter saying that he died, and would we send money for a headstone. Me and my brothers, we said no. He left us, like your dad left you. We didn't owe him a thing, and neither do you. Remember that."

What amazed me more than the revelation of the letters was Victor's anger. It radiated off him, like heat rising over asphalt. Seventy years had elapsed and still he was mad at his father for making him an orphan. In April, the melting snows would expose my father's body, revealing that I was the daughter of a suicide, the outcome I'd suspected all along. Surely, that was different from

This picture shows patients suffering from tuberculosis being treated with heliotherapy at the Jewish Consumptives' Relief Society, my inspiration for the Hospital for Consumptive Hebrews. Courtesy of the Beck Archives, Special Collections, CJS and University Libraries, University of Denver.

the way Harry Berger had left his family? But however they left us, Victor and I were both children abandoned by their fathers.

Instead of following my grandfather's advice to forget, however, I became intensely curious to know more. I began researching my family history, learning all I could about Harry Berger, the man who left his wife, forcing her to commit their sons to the Hebrew Orphan Asylum. Eventually, that research led to the discoveries that inspired me to write *Orphan #8*.

Conditions among Animals

The question that remained was about the woman who had conducted the X-ray treatments that left the children bald. Dr. Mildred Solomon is a completely imaginary character, unlike her counterpart in the novel, Dr. Hess. He was inspired by the real Dr. Alfred Fabian Hess, who was an attending physician at the Hebrew Infant Asylum during the years in which my novel is set, and where he conducted research into childhood nutritional diseases, including rickets and scurvy. His infant isolation ward ▶

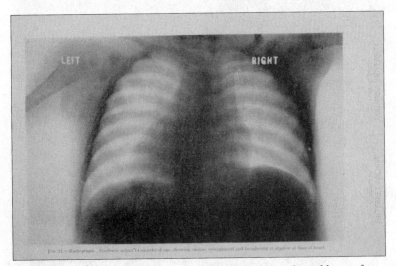

An X-ray of a 14-month-old baby with scurvy and an enlarged heart, from Scurvy: Past and Present *by Dr. Alfred Hess (Philadelphia: Lippincott, 1920).*

was lauded in a 1914 article in the *New York Times*, which stated that "the great advantage of the glass walls" was that "neither nurse nor doctor need pay many visits to the children under their care."

In the novel, my character's dialogue is inspired by the real Dr. Hess's own writing; in fact, the long passage Rachel reads in the medical library is a direct quote. And yes, he was married to the daughter of Isidor and Ida Strauss, who went down on the Titanic.

The real Dr. Hess was often assisted by Miss Mildred Fish, coauthor on some of his nutrition studies and my inspiration, along with Dr. Elsie Fox, for Dr. Solomon. My research took me to the New York Academy of Medicine, where I began to understand my character of Mildred Solomon more fully—the struggles she would have gone through, the pressures she was under, the goals to which she aspired. Dr. Solomon's confrontation with Rachel gives the elderly woman a chance to defend her life's work and her actions.

In the early twentieth century, the medical field was becoming

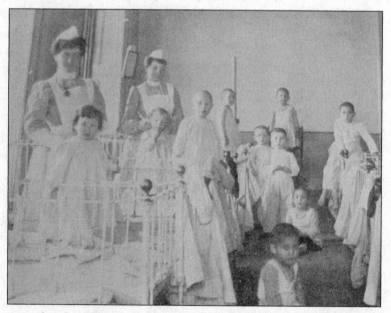

A ward at the Hebrew Infant Asylum, circa 1908. Courtesy of The New York Academy of Medicine Library.

more scientific, and research became increasingly privileged. Amazing discoveries seemed to justify whatever methods were necessary to achieve the miraculous vaccinations and treatments that conquered disease and relegated conditions, such as rickets and scurvy, to the pages of American history. Today, the ethics of many such experiments have been condemned: the testing of the polio vaccine on children in an orphanage; the study of untreated syphilis in prisoners; the sterilization of people who are impoverished or intellectually disabled. Sadly, disenfranchised people have often been "material" for medical experimentation.

It seems impossible now, however, to look back on experiments like those conducted by Dr. Fox and Dr. Hess and not see them through the distorting lens of the Holocaust. When telling people what *Orphan #8* is about, I have learned that saying the words "Jewish children" and "medical experiments" in the same sentence is almost guaranteed to elicit a remark about Nazis. It seemed inevitable that Rachel herself, looking back on her childhood, would draw the same comparison, and only fair to allow Dr. Solomon to defend herself from these charges.

A Wall They Cannot See

Joan Nestle, cofounder of the Lesbian Herstory Archives, came to Milwaukee to give a lecture while I was in graduate school there. She read to us from a letter given to the archives by a woman who had endured the humiliation and fear of a police raid on a lesbian club in the 1950s. When I imagined Rachel and Naomi's relationship, at first I thought no further than their romantic reunion at the carousel. But as I developed the novel, I realized how important it was to explore the ways in which the characters would have responded to the repressive era in which they lived. As a lesbian writing at the time explained, "Between you and other women friends is a wall which they cannot see, but which is terribly apparent to you. The inability to present an honest face to those you know eventually develops a certain deviousness which is injurious to whatever basic character you may possess. Always pretending to be something you are not, moral laws lose their significance."

In the 1950s, psychiatry in America purported that ▶

Postcard by Photobelle W.I. Courtesy of the Lesbian Herstory Archives Photo collection, found images folder.

homosexuality was a psychological disorder that could be cured through analysis and therapy. The prevailing scientific view, as expressed by Dr. Frank Caprio in *Female Homosexuality: A Psychodynamic Study of Lesbianism* (New York: Citadel Press, 1954), was that homosexuality resulted from "a deep-seated and unresolved neurosis." Caprio explained, "Many lesbians claim that they are happy and experience no conflict about their homosexuality, simply because they have accepted the fact that they are lesbians and will continue to live a lesbian type of existence. But this is only a surface or pseudohappiness. Basically, they are lonely and unhappy and are afraid to admit it, deluding themselves into believing that they are free of all mental conflicts and are well adjusted to their homosexuality."

As adults, Rachel and Naomi would have lived with the dual experience of their relationship being both invisible (as female spinster roommates) and dangerous. Lesbian teachers and nurses, in particular, were fearful of losing their jobs and reputations. Living in the Village would have helped to ease their sense of isolation. As Caprio helpfully notes, "The Greenwich Village section of New York City has for many years been known as a center where lesbians and male homosexuals tend to congregate, particularly those with artistic talent." But when Naomi's Uncle Jacob offers them his apartment rent-free, the move out to Coney Island exacerbates their sense of isolation.

The Coney Island Amateur Psychoanalytic Society would have been one group where homosexuality was not condemned. Sigmund Freud's 1909 visit to Dreamland, Luna Park, and Steeplechase Park led him to confide to his diary that the "lower classes on Coney Island are not as sexually repressed as the cultural classes." Freud's visit to Coney Island was the inspiration for the 1926 formation of the Amateur Psychoanalytic Society, which met monthly and hosted an annual Dream Film award night—home movies which dramatized significant dreams and presented the dreamer's accompanying analysis. One of them, "My Dream of Dental Irritation" by Robert Troutman, openly explores a gay theme. According to Zoe Beloff, editor of *The Coney Island Amateur Psychoanalytic Society and Its Circle* (New York: Christine Burgin, 2009), "Troutman says he was drawn to the Coney Island Amateur Psychoanalytic Society as a teenager struggling to come to terms with his homosexuality."

As adults, Rachel and Naomi would have lived and worked in a society that denigrated and maligned their sexuality. In the orphanage, however, the atmosphere may have been more permissive. One man, recalling his years at the Hebrew Orphan Asylum in response to a survey, matter-of-factly observed, "As far as homosexuality was concerned, I think there was plenty of it going around. In my own case, I jerked off quite a few fellows, and they did likewise to me." For girls, intense crushes—including love notes, jealous intrigues, and displays of affection—were common, though these relationships were widely understood as immature substitutes for the heterosexual attractions that were expected to eventually replace them. Unless, of course, the girls bravely chose to live "a lesbian type of existence."

—Kim van Alkemade ❧

The carousel at Coney Island amusement park in the 1950s. Jewish woodcarvers from Eastern Europe crafted many such horses. Close-up from photograph in author's collection.

Reading Group Guide for *Orphan #8*

1. Was Harry Rabinowitz wrong to run away? What might have been different had he stayed?

2. What might have been different if Rachel could have told her friend Flo the truth about her relationship with Naomi?

3. Was Dr. Solomon wrong to use Rachel in her experimental study of the X-ray tonsillectomy?

4. In what ways did the Orphaned Hebrews Home benefit the children who grew up there? How were the children affected by that experience?

5. Was it selfish of Sam to leave Rachel in Leadville with their Uncle Max? Why do you think Sam keeps leaving his sister behind?

6. If Dr. and Mrs. Abrams had known that Rachel was "unnatural," do you think they would have still been kind to her?

7. What do you think of the way Mrs. Hong treats Sparrow and Jade?

8. Is Dr. Solomon to blame for causing Rachel's tumor, or should she be thanked for spurring Rachel's discovery of it in time for treatment?

9. How have the medical attitudes about treating women with breast

cancer changed since Dr. Feldman's time?

10. Would Rachel have been justified in giving Dr. Solomon an overdose of morphine in revenge?

11. How do you think Naomi will react when Rachel tells her about the cancer and her upcoming surgery?

12. What other walls have the characters built around one another, or themselves, in the novel? ⟳